ALSO BY JENNY COLGAN

The Loveliest Chocolate Shop in Paris
Amanda's Wedding
Talking to Addison
Looking for Andrew McCarthy
Working Wonders
Do You Remember the First Time?
Where Have All the Boys Gone?
West End Girls
Operation Sunshine
Diamonds Are a Girl's Best Friend
The Good, the Bad and the Dumped
Welcome to Rosie Hopkins' Sweetshop of Dreams

PRAISE FOR JENNY COLGAN

"She is very, very funny."

—*Express*

"A delicious comedy."

—*Red*

"A Jenny Colgan novel is as essential for a week in the sun as Alka Seltzer, aftersun, and far too many pairs of sandals."

—*Heat*

"Fast-paced, funny, poignant, and well observed."

—*Daily Mail*

"Hugely entertaining and very funny."

—*Cosmopolitan*

"A funny, clever page-turner."

—*Closer*

"Chick-lit with an ethical kick."

—*Mirror*

"A quirky tale of love, work, and the meaning of life."

—*Company*

"A smart, witty love story."

—*Observer*

"Full of laugh-out-loud observations…utterly unputdownable."

—*Woman*

MEET ME AT THE
cupcake café

A NOVEL IN RECIPES

JENNY COLGAN

sourcebooks
landmark

Published by Sourcebooks Landmark, an imprint of Sourcebooks
P.O. Box 4410, Naperville, Illinois 60567-4410
(630) 961-3900
sourcebooks.com

Originally published in 2011 in Great Britain by Sphere. This edition issued based on the paperback edition published in 2013 by Sourcebooks Landmark, an imprint of Sourcebooks.

Library of Congress Cataloging-in-Publication Data

Colgan, Jenny.
  Meet me at the Cupcake Café : a novel with recipes / Jenny Colgan.
    pages cm
  (paperback : alk. paper) 1. Life change events—Fiction. 2. Women in the food industry—Fiction. 3. Confectioners—Fiction. 4. Conduct of life—Fiction. I. Title.
  PR6053.O4225M44 2013
  823'.914—dc23
                                        2013010789

Printed and bound in Canada.
MBP 10 9 8 7 6 5 4 3 2 1

To anyone who's ever licked the spoon.

a word from jenny

I left home just before my seventeenth birthday and the idea of learning to cook or bake before I left would have been greeted with a typically teenage shrug. I had been a miserably fussy eater as a child—I wouldn't even eat cheesecake—and I spent my student years living off the traditional diet of crisps, beans, chili, and cider.

When I was twenty-one, I had a boyfriend who was aghast that I couldn't actually cook *at all* and who taught me how to make my first white sauce out of sheer exasperation. After that, it was one step forward, two steps back: the onion soup where I didn't realize you had to do anything to the onions before you stuck them in some boiling water; the lemon cake where too much bicarbonate of soda reacted with the acid of the lemons to make something akin to the chemical composition of chalk; and—an ongoing problem—I now have about nine thousand discarded recipes for scones because no matter whether I use tonic water, or whisked milk, or room temperature this and that, some round, hard, tasteless discs always end up sitting at the bottom of the tray. My mum, a fantastic baker and scone-maker who used to plonk me on the kitchen cabinets and let me lick the mixer arms while she made fairy cakes, says I should give up on the scones and just use the shop-bought mix, even she does these days. But I refuse to let it go.

Anyway. Then I had children, and in a desperate desire to make sure they didn't have to suffer the miserable indignities of being the child who doesn't eat anything, I wanted to give them the broadest repertoire of tastes possible. Which also, of course, meant learning to cook.

To some people, cooking is an innate gift. My sister-in-law is an extraordinary cook. Give her ten minutes in a kitchen, and she will conjure up something heavenly out of thin air, tasting and testing and altering as she goes along. I will never be like that. I still get upset when my husband serves beetroot.*

But I can, finally, just about make good, wholesome food for my family (we'll just ignore that whole fish guts incident for now), and seeing as I was in the kitchen anyway, I found that if you've got a mixer, it actually doesn't take terribly long to rustle up a chocolate sponge or some peanut butter cookies. I'm a staunch believer in Jamie Oliver's mantra of "it doesn't matter what you eat; just make sure it has as few ingredients as possible," and I realize that even when I think my life is hectic, half an hour is enough to grab some flour, sugar, butter, and an egg and to make up a batch of the most flexible recipe of all—the cupcake—and look like a proper chef while I'm at it. Of course, the children take it totally for granted and loudly ask what they are having today and argue over whose turn it is to use the mixer, just like we did, but that's all right. I'm doing it because I enjoy it.

And suddenly it seemed like I wasn't alone. Suddenly, cupcake cafés started springing up everywhere, and I was absolutely gripped by *The Great British Bake-Off* on telly. There's even an annual cupcake festival: www.cupcakecamplondon.co.uk. And Issy's story here was inspired by all of that and, in the end, by the simple desire to make something sweet for the people you love.

---

*Oh, come on. I am right about this. Beetroot is total horse food. One of the worst sentences I've ever heard was after arriving back tired from a trip away, only to be greeted by my other half keenly announcing, "You know how you don't like beetroot? Well, I reckon you're going to like it my new way." I swear, I nearly cried.

I hope you like it too—whether you bake already, or if you think one day that you'd like to (see the Caked Crusader's fantastic beginner's guide at the back of the book), or if you think, "totally, no way, would I ever get sucked into that," as I did, once upon a time, or are just a contented consumer. Come, pull up a chair...

Very warmest wishes,
Jenny

author's note

I have successfully tested all the recipes in this book (N.B., for cooking times, please be aware that I don't use a convection oven), and they're all yummy. Except for Caroline's Bran and Carrot Cupcake Surprise. There, you're on your own.

JC x x

drop scones

• • • •

* 1 cup self-rising flour
* 2 tbsp superfine sugar. Can be licked off spoon.
* 1 egg. Budget for four eggs if working with children under seven.
* 2¼ cups whole milk. 1¼ cup for recipe, plus one glass to be taken with results.
* Pinch of salt. This is a small amount of salt, Issy. Tinier than your little finger. Not too much! Not! Oh. That's too much. Never mind.

Put the dry ingredients into a bowl and stir well.

Make a well in the center—a well, that's like a place you get water. Like Jack and Jill. Yes. Drop in the egg. Whee! Yes, and milk.

Whisk everything together thoroughly. The batter should have a creamy consistency. Add a little more milk if necessary.

Preheat and butter a grill pan. Grampa will pick up the pan. Do not try to lift the pan. Good. Now let the mix drip off a spoon. Don't rush it. A few splatters on the side of the pan is fine. Now let Grampa flip them, but you can hold the handle...yup, that's it. Hurrah!

Serve with the remainder of the milk, butter, jam, cream, and whatever else is in the fridge, and a large kiss on the top of the head for being a clever girl.

I ssy Randall refolded the piece of paper and smiled.
"Are you absolutely sure about this?" she said to the figure in the easy chair. "This is the recipe?" The old man nodded vehemently. He held up one finger, which Issy recognized immediately as his cue for a lecture.

"Well, the thing is," Grampa Joe began, "baking is…"

"Life," filled in Issy patiently. She'd heard the speech many times before. Her grandfather had started sweeping up in the family bakery at the age of twelve; eventually he had taken over the business and run three large bakeries in Manchester. Baking was all he knew.

"It is life. Bread is the staff of life, our most basic food."

"And very un-Atkins," said Issy, smoothing her cord skirt down over her hips and sighing. It was one thing for her grandfather to say that. He had spent his whole life skinny as a rake, thanks to a full-time diet of extremely hard physical work that started with lighting the furnace at 5:00 a.m. It was quite another when baking was your hobby, your passion—but to pay the bills you were sitting down in an office all day. It was hard to show restraint when trying out… She drifted off, thinking about the new pineapple cream recipe she'd tried that morning. The trick was to leave enough of the pith in to give the flavor bite, but not so much that it turned into a smoothie. She needed to give it another shot. Issy ran her hands over her cloudy black hair. It went well with her green eyes but created absolute bloody havoc if it rained.

"So when you describe what you're making, you must describe life. Do you see? It's not just recipes…next thing you'll tell me you're measuring in metric."

Issy bit her lip and made a mental note to hide her metric scales the next time Grampa visited the flat. He'd only get himself worked up.

"Are you listening to me?"

"Yes, Gramps!"

They both turned to look out of the window of the assisted living facility in north London. Issy had installed Joe there when it became clear he was getting too absentminded to live on his own. Issy had hated moving him down south after he'd spent his life in the north, but she needed him close enough to visit. Joe had grumbled of course but he was going to grumble anyway, moving out of his home to anywhere that wouldn't let him rise at 5:00 a.m. and start pounding bread dough. So he might as well be grumpy close by, where she could keep an eye on him. After all, it wasn't as if anyone else was around to do it. And the three bakeries, with their proud, shiny brass handles and old signs proclaiming them to be "electric bakers," were gone now; fallen prey to the supermarkets and chains that favored cheap white pulp over handcrafted but slightly more expensive loaves.

As he so often did, Grampa Joe watched the January raindrops fall across the window and read her mind.

"Have you heard from…your mother recently?" he said. Issy nodded, noting as ever how hard he found it to say his own daughter's name. Marian had never felt at home as a baker's daughter. And Issy's grandmother had died so young, she hadn't had long enough to provide a steadying influence. With Gramps working all the time, Marian had rebelled before she could even spell the word, hanging out with older boys and bad crowds from her teens, getting pregnant early to a traveling man who had given Issy her black hair and strong eyebrows and absolutely nothing else. Too much of a questing spirit to be tied down, Marian had often left her only child behind while she went off in search of herself.

Issy had spent most of her childhood in the bakery, watching Gramps as he manfully beat the dough or delicately shaped the lightest, most mouth-melting filigree cakes and pies. Although he trained bakers for each of his shops, he still liked to get his own hands white with flour, one of the reasons Randalls were once the most popular bakers in Manchester. Issy had spent countless hours doing her homework under the great Cable Street ovens, absorbing through her pores the time and skill and care of a great baker; much more conventional than her mother, she adored her gramps and felt safe and cozy in the kitchens, even though she knew, of course, that she was different from her classmates, who went home to little houses with mums and dads who worked for the council, and dogs and siblings, and ate potato waffles with ketchup in front of *Neighbors* and didn't wake up before the sun, the smell of warm bread already rising from far below.

Now, at thirty-one, Issy had just about forgiven her troubled, untethered mother, even though she of all people should have known what it was like growing up without your mum. She didn't care about the sports days and school outings—everyone knew her grandfather, who never missed one—and she was popular enough, rarely without a cast-off box of scones or French cakes to bring to school occasions, while her birthday party spreads were the stuff of local legend. She did wish someone in her life had cared a little more for fashion—her grandfather bought her two cotton and one woolen dress every Christmas, regardless of age, style, or size, even when everyone else she knew was in legwarmers and Pineapple T-shirts, and her mother would swoop back at regular intervals with strange hippy-style garments that she was selling at festivals, made of hemp or itchy llama wool or something else equally impractical. But Issy never felt short of love in the cozy flat above the bakery where she and Gramps would eat apple pie and watch *Dad's Army*. Even Marian—who on her flying visits would strictly admonish Issy not to trust men, to stay off the cider, and always follow her rainbow—was a loving parent. Nevertheless, sometimes, when she saw happy families larking in the park or parents cradling their newborns, Issy felt a desire at the pit of her stomach so strong, it felt like a physical gnawing for the traditional, the safe.

It was no surprise to anyone who knew the family that Issy Randall grew up to be the straightest, most conventional girl imaginable. Good A-levels, good college, and now a good job with a thrusting commercial property company in the City. By the time she was ready to start work, Gramps's bakeries were all sold: victims of his getting older and the changing times. And she had an education, he had pointed out (sadly, she sometimes thought); she didn't want to be getting up at sparrow's fart and doing hard manual labor for the rest of her life. She was set for better things.

But deep down she had a passion for kitchen comforts—for cream horns, balanced with the perfect weight of caterer's cream and light, flaky pastry, set off by the crunchiest diamond crystals of clear sugar; for hot cross buns, baked at Randall's strictly during Lent and Lent only, their cinnamon and raisins and orange peel spreading an exciting, sticky smell to half the road; for a perfectly piped butter icing on top of the highest, lightest, floatiest lemon cupcake. Issy loved all of those things. Hence her project with Gramps: to get as many of his recipes down on paper as possible, before—although neither of them ever referred to it—but before, or in case, he started to forget them.

● ● ● ●

"I got an email from Mum," said Issy. "She's in Florida. She's met a man called Brick. Really. Brick. That's his name."

"At least it's a man this time," sniffed her grandfather.

Issy gave him a look. "Shhh. She said she might be home for my birthday. In the summer. Of course she said she'd be home for Christmas, but she wasn't."

Issy had spent Christmas in the home with Gramps. The staff did their best, but it wasn't all that great.

"Anyway." Issy attempted a smile. "She sounds happy. Says she loves it over there. Said I should send you over for some sun."

Issy and Gramps looked at each other and burst out laughing. Joe got tired out crossing the room.

"Yes," said Gramps, "I'll just go catch the next plane to Florida. Taxi! Take me to London Airport!"

Issy tucked the sheet of paper away in her handbag and stood up.
· "I have to go," she said. "Um, keep doing the recipes. But you can keep them quite, you know, normal if you like."

"Normal."

She kissed him on the forehead.

"See you next week."

• • • •

Issy got off the bus. It was freezing, with dirty ice on the ground left over from a short day's snowfall just after New Year. At first it had looked pretty, but now it was getting a little ropy around the edges, especially poking through the wrought-iron fencing of the Stoke Newington Municipal Offices, the rather grand edifice at the end of her street. Still, as ever, Issy felt pleased to be stepping down. Home, Stoke Newington, the bohemian district she'd stumbled upon when she moved south.

The smell of hookahs from the little Turkish cafés on Stamford Road mingled with the incense sticks from the Everything for a Pound shops, jostling next to expensive baby boutiques that sold children's designer Wellingtons and one-off wooden toys, perused by shoppers with Hasidic ringlets, or headscarves; crop tops and patois; young mothers with buggies; older mothers with double buggies. Despite her friend Tobes once joking that it was like living in the bar in *Star Wars*, Issy loved it all. She adored the sweet Jamaican bread; the honey baklava sitting out by the cash registers in the grocers; little Indian sweets of dried milk and sugar, or dusty slabs of Turkish delight. She liked the strange cooking smells in the air as she came home from work, and the jumble of buildings; from a handsome square of pretty flat-fronted houses to blocks of flats and red-brick conversions. Albion Road was lined with odd shops, fried chicken joints, cab firms and large gray houses. It was neither commercial nor residential but lay somewhere in between, one of the great winding thoroughfares of London that once upon a time had led to its outlying villages, and now connected its suburbs.

The gray houses were stately, Victorian, and potentially expensive. Some of them remained grotty subdivided flats with bicycles and damp wheelie bins cluttering up the front gardens. These boasted several doorbells with names crudely taped to them, and recycling boxes piled high on the curb. Some of them, though, had been reconverted into houses and gentrified, with reclaimed oak front doors, topiary trees on the steps and expensive curtains leading to polished hardwood flooring and stripped-back fireplaces and big mirrors. She loved the area's mix of shabby and new, traditional, rough and ready and smart and alternative, with the towers of the City on the horizon, and the tumbledown churchyard and crowded pavements…All types of people lived in Stokey; it felt like a microcosm of London; a village that reflected the city's true heart. And it was more affordable than Islington.

Issy had lived here for four years, since she moved out of south London and onto the property ladder. The only downside had been moving out of range of the tube. She'd told herself that didn't matter, but sometimes, on an evening like this with the wind cutting between the houses and turning noses into red dripping taps, she thought perhaps it did. Just a bit. It was all right for the posh yummy mummies in the big gray houses; they all had 4×4s. She did wonder sometimes, when she saw them out with their huge, expensive buggies and tiny, expensive bodies…she did wonder how old they were. Younger than her? Thirty-one wasn't old, not these days. But with their toddlers and their highlights and their houses with one wall covered in smart wallpaper…she did wonder. Sometimes.

Just behind the bus stop was a little close. It was lined with tiny shops, older places that had been left behind by the Victorian development. Once upon a time, they would have been stables or produce stores; they were quirky and oddly shaped. There was an ironmonger's with ancient brushes around the door, old-fashioned toasters for sale at inflated prices, and a sad-looking washing machine that had been sitting in the front window for as long as Issy had been coming to the bus stop; a telephone/Wi-Fi/Internet office that stayed open at strange hours and invited you to send money to places; and a newsagent that faced onto the road and was where Issy picked up magazines and Reese's peanut butter cups.

Right at the very end of the row, tucked into the corner, was a building that looked like an afterthought, somewhere to use up the spare stones. It was pointed at one end, where a triangular corner of glass stuck out toward the road, widening into a bench, with a door coming out onto a small cobbled courtyard with a tree in ·it. It looked quite out of place, a tiny haven in the middle of a village square, something absolutely out of time—like, Issy had once reflected, an illustration by Beatrix Potter. All it needed were bottle-glass windows.

Wind blew up the main road once more, and Issy turned off toward the flat. Home.

• • • •

Issy had bought her flat at the very height of the property boom. For someone who worked in the property business, it hadn't been very astute. She suspected prices had started to decline about thirty minutes after she'd picked up her keys. This was before she began dating her boyfriend, Graeme, whom she'd met at work (although she had already noticed him around, as had all the other girls in the office); otherwise, as he had said several times, he would certainly have advised her against it.

Even then, she wasn't sure she'd have listened to him. After hunting through every property in her price range and hating all of them, she'd been on the point of giving up when she got to Carmelite Avenue, and she'd loved it straightaway. It was the top two stories of one of the pretty gray houses, with its own side entrance up a flight of stairs, so really it felt more like a little house than an apartment. One floor was almost entirely an open-plan kitchen/dining room/sitting room. Issy had made it as cozy as possible, with huge faded gray velvet sofas, a long wooden table with benches, and her beloved kitchen. The units were going cheap in the sales, almost certainly because they were a very strong shade of pink. "Nobody wants a pink kitchen," the salesman had said, slightly sadly. "They just want stainless steel. Or country cottage. There's nothing in between."

"I've never seen a pink washing machine before," Issy had said encouragingly. She hated a sad salesman.

"I know. Apparently it makes some people feel a bit queasy, watching their washing go around in one of those."

"That would be a drawback."

"Jordan nearly bought one," he said, momentarily perking up. "Then she decided it was too pink."

"Jordan decided it was too pink?" said Issy, who had never thought of herself as a particularly pink and girly type of person. This, however, was such an endearingly full-on Schiaparelli pink. It was a kitchen that just wanted to be loved.

"And it's really seventy percent off?" she asked again. "Fitted and everything?"

The salesman looked at the pretty girl with the green eyes and the cloud of dark hair. He liked rounded girls. They looked like they would actually cook in his kitchens. He didn't like those sharp ladies who wanted sharp-edged kitchens to keep their gin and face cream in. He thought kitchens should be used to make delicious food and pour lovely wine. He sometimes hated his job, but his wife loved their annually updated discount kitchens and cooked him wonderful meals in them, so he soldiered on. They were both getting terribly fat.

"Yup, seventy percent off. They'll probably just throw it out," he said. "On the scrapheap. Can you imagine?"

Issy could imagine. That would be very sad.

"I would hate for that to happen," she said solemnly.

The salesman nodded, mentally locating his order pad for a sale.

"Seventy-five percent off?" she said. "After all, I'm practically donating to charity. Save the Kitchen."

And that was how the pink kitchen had arrived. She had added black-and-white-checkered lino and implements, and after guests had first screwed up their eyes and rubbed them to get the spots away, then tentatively opened them again, some were surprised to find that they actually quite liked the pink kitchen, and they certainly liked what came out of it.

Even Grampa Joe had liked it, on one of his carefully choreographed visits, and had nodded approvingly at the gas hob (for caramelizing) and the electric oven (for even heat distribution). And these days, Issy and the sugar-sweet pink kitchen seemed made for one another.

In it she felt properly at home. She would turn the radio up and bustle around, gathering her vanilla sugar, her finest French pâtissiers flour that she bought from the tiny alimentaire in Smithfield and her narrow silver sieve, and selecting which of her trusty wooden spoons she would use to whip her lighter-than-air sponge into shape. She cracked eggs perfectly two at a time into her large blue-and-white-striped ceramic mixing bowl without even glancing, and used her eye to measure out the exact amount of creamy, snowy Guernsey butter that never went in the fridge. She got through a lot of butter.

Issy bit her lip sharply to stop herself beating the cake mix too hard. If it got too much air in it the mix would collapse in the oven, so she slowed her arm right down and tested to see if it would peak. It would. She had squeezed in fresh Seville orange juice and was planning to attempt a marmalade icing, which would either be delicious or quite peculiar.

The cupcakes were in the oven and she was on her third batch of icing when her flatmate, Helena, pushed open the door. The trick was to balance out the flavor so it wasn't too tart or too sweet, just perfect...She noted down the exact combination of ingredients that would give just a delicate edge in the mouth.

Helena never arrived subtly anywhere. She simply wasn't capable. She entered every room bosoms first—she couldn't help it. She wasn't fat, just tall, and extremely generously proportioned in true fifties style, with large creamy breasts, a tiny waist, and a wide bottom and thighs, crowned by a towering mass of Pre-Raphaelite hair. She would have been considered a beauty in any period of history other than the early twenty-first century, when the only acceptable shape for a beautiful woman was that of a hungry six-year-old who had inexplicably grown solid apple-shaped tits out of her shoulder blades. As it was, she was constantly trying to lose weight, as if her broad, alabaster shoulders and luscious curved thighs were ever going anywhere.

"I have had a *terrible day*," she announced dramatically. She glanced up at the cooling racks.

"I'm on it," said Issy hurriedly, putting down her icing sugar nozzle. The oven dinged. Issy had dreamed of an Aga—a big pink Aga—even though it couldn't get up the stairs, or in any of the windows...and even if it did there wasn't room to plumb one in...and even if there had been, the floor wouldn't have been able to take the weight...and even if it had, she couldn't have stored the oil...and even if she had, Agas were no use for making cakes; they were too unpredictable. Plus she couldn't afford one. Nonetheless, she still kept the catalog hidden away in her bookcase. Instead she had a highly efficient German Bosch, which always was at the temperature it said it was going to be and always timed everything perfectly to the second, but it didn't inspire devotion.

Helena looked at the two dozen perfect cakes emerging from the oven.

11

"Who are you cooking for, the Red Army? Give me one."

"They're too hot."

"Give me one!"

Issy rolled her eyes and started squeezing on the icing with an expert flick of the wrist. Really, of course, she should wait till the cakes had cooled enough not to melt the buttercream, but she could tell Helena wasn't capable of waiting that long.

"So what happened?" she asked when Helena was comfortably ensconced on the chaise longue (she'd brought her own chaise longue when she moved in; it suited her. Helena never liked to expend more energy than was absolutely necessary) with a vast vat of tea and two cupcakes on her favorite polka-dot plate. Issy was pleased with the cakes; they were as light and fluffy as air, with a delicate sense of oranges and cream, delicious, and they wouldn't spoil your dinner. She realized she'd forgotten to get in anything for dinner. Well, they were dinner then.

"I got punched," sniffed Helena.

Issy sat up. "Again?"

"He thought I was a fire engine. Apparently."

"What would a fire engine be doing inside an Accident and Emergency department?" wondered Issy.

"That's a good question," said Helena. "Well, we get all sorts."

Helena had known she wanted to be a nurse when she was eight years old, which was when she'd taken all the pillowcases in the house and arranged all her stuffed animals in hospital beds. At ten, she'd insisted that her family start calling her Florence (her three younger brothers, all of whom were terrified of her, still did). At sixteen, she left school and went straight into training the old-fashioned way—on the wards under a matron—and despite much government meddling in the system, now she was a Grade B ward manager ("Call me Matron," she'd said to the crusty old consultants, who happily complied) and practically ran the busy A&E department at Hemel

Park, still treating her trainees as if it were 1955. She had almost been in the newspapers when one had informed on her for carrying out a fingernail inspection. Most of her girls, however, adored her, as did the many junior doctors she had prodded and guided through their first anxious months, as did her patients. When they weren't off their heads and throwing punches, naturally.

Even though she made more money, got to sit down all day, and didn't have to work ridiculous shifts, Issy, in her safe corporate job, sometimes envied Helena. How lovely to work at something you loved and knew you were great at, even if it was for a pittance and you occasionally got punched.

"How's Mr. Randall?" asked Helena. She adored Issy's granddad, who admired Helena as a damn fine woman, accused her of continuing to grow taller, and opined that she wouldn't be out of place on the front of a ship. She had also cast her formidable professional eye over every care home in the district, an act for which Issy felt she would be forever in her debt.

"He's good!" said Issy. "Except when he's good he wants to get up and go baking, so he gets cross and starts cheeking that fat nurse again."

Helena nodded.

"Have you taken Graeme in to see him yet?"

Issy bit her lip. Helena knew full well she hadn't.

"Not yet," she said. "I will, though; he's just been so busy with stuff."

The thing was, Issy thought, that Helena tended to attract men who worshipped the ground she walked on. Unfortunately, she found this incredibly annoying and spent most of her time crushing on hot alpha males who were only interested in women with the BMI of a small shaky dog. Nonetheless, anyone looking for a normal—or normal*ish*—relationship couldn't hope to compete with Helena's admirers, who wrote screeds of poetry and sent roomfuls of flowers.

"Mmm," said Helena, in the exact same tone she used to teenage skate punks who came in with broken collarbones. She popped another cake in her mouth. "You know, these are divine. You really could be a professional. Are you sure they don't contain one of my five a day?"

"Definite."

Helena sighed. "Oh well. We all need something to aspire to. Quick! Telly on! It's a Simon Cowell day. I want to see him be cruel to someone."

"You need a *nice* man," said Issy, picking up the remote control.

So do you, thought Helena, but she kept it to herself.

orange cupcakes with marmalade icing for a grumpy day

• • • •

Multiply all ingredients by four to get too many cupcakes.

* 2 whole oranges, divided. Try not to buy bitter oranges. Blood oranges may be useful to squeeze out frustration.
* 16 tbsp butter, melted. Use the fire of your righteous anger to melt the butter if a pot isn't handy.
* 3 whole eggs. Plus an additional three to break therapeutically by throwing at the wall.
* 1 cup sugar. Add more sugar if life needs a little sweetening.
* 1 cup self-esteem-raising flour
* 3 tbsp marmalade
* 3 tbsp orange zest

Preheat oven to 350°F/gas mark 4. Butter cake tins.

Chop one orange—yes, skin and all—into chunks and place in your mixer with the melted butter, eggs, and sugar. Mix on high until well combined and the satisfying noise of the mixer makes you feel a bit better. Pour the mix into a bowl with the flour and whack repeatedly with a wooden spoon until subdued.

Bake in the oven for 50 minutes. Allow to cool for five minutes in the tin, then turn out onto a wire rack to cool completely. Spread marmalade on the top. Attempt to rediscover zest.

I ssy folded up the letter and put it back in her bag, shaking her head. She hadn't meant for Gramps to have a bad day. It must have been discussing her mother again. She wished...She'd tried to bring it up with Marian, that Gramps would appreciate a letter every now and again. Obviously it wasn't working. Well, there wasn't much she could do about that. It was such a plus to know, anyway, that he was somewhere where they'd stamp and send his letters. The last few months, when he was turning on the oven in the flat at 5:00 a.m. prompt every morning but then forgetting why, had been difficult for everyone. Besides, she had problems of her own, she thought, glancing at her watch. There are pretty horrid days to go back to work, and then there's today, Issy thought, peering out along the length of the queue to see if the bendy bus was starting to trundle around the corner of Stoke Newington Road. An ungainly thing, it always took a few attempts to make the sharp bend, all the while being honked at by vans and yelled at by cyclists. They were taking them out of commission soon. Issy couldn't help feeling sorry for them, poor, silly buses.

Yep, the first Monday after Christmas had to be right up there with rotten blooming days really. The wind was raw against her face and tugging at her new Christmas hat, which she'd bought in the sales thinking its knitted stripes might be quirky and young and cute. Now she suspected it made her look more like Haggis McBaggis, the lady with all the bags she pushed along in a shopping trolley, who sometimes hung around the bus stop but never got on a bus. Issy usually gave her a half smile but tried not to stand downwind, hugging her large tin of cupcakes.

No Haggis today, she noted, as she glanced at the faces next to her—the same faces she stood next to in rain, snow, wind, and the occasional sunny spell. Not even an old lady who pushed a trolley about wanted to get up this morning. Some of the familiar faces she nodded to; some, like the angry young man who fiddled relentlessly with his phone with one hand and his ear with the other, or the older chap who surreptitiously plucked at his flaky scalp, as if having dandruff somehow rendered him invisible, she didn't acknowledge at all. But here they all were, every day, standing in the same places, waiting for their bendy bus and wondering how crammed full of people it would be when it finally arrived to bear them off to shops, offices, the City, and the West End of London, scattering them down the arteries of Islington and Oxford Street, then scooping them up again at night, in the dark and the cold, when condensation from tired bodies would steam up the windows and children, late from school, would draw faces and teenagers would draw penises.

"Hi there," she said to Linda, the middle-aged lady who worked in John Lewis, with whom she occasionally shared a greeting. "Happy New Year."

"Happy New Year!" said Linda. "Made any resolutions?"

Issy sighed and felt her fingers drift to her slightly uncomfortable waistband. There was something about the miserable weather, the dark, short days, that made her feel like staying in and baking, rather than going out and taking some exercise and eating salad. She'd baked an awful lot for the hospital at Christmas too.

"Oh, the usual," said Issy. "Lose a bit of weight…"

"Oh, you don't need to do that," said Linda. "There's nothing wrong with your weight!" Linda was a middle-aged shape, with one bosom, generous hips, and the most comfortable shoes she could find for standing up in all day in haberdashery. "You look lovely. Take a picture now and look back on it in ten years if you don't believe me. You won't believe how good you looked." She couldn't resist glancing briefly at the tin Issy was carrying. Issy sighed.

"These are for the office," she said.

"Of course they are," said Linda. The other people in the bus queue were coming forward now, making inquiring faces and asking Issy how her holiday had gone. She groaned.

"OK, you gannets." She opened the tin. Wind-chilled faces cracked into smiles showing winter teeth; iPod buds were removed from ears as the bus stop cheerfully descended on the marmalade cakes. Issy had, as usual, made twice as many as she thought she might need so she could feed the office and the bus queue too.

"These are amazing," said the man through a mouthful of crumbs. "You know, you could do this for a living."

"With you lot, I feel like I do sometimes," said Issy, but blushing with pleasure nonetheless as everyone clustered around. "Happy New Year, everybody."

The entire bus queue started to chat and perk up. Linda of course was doing nothing but worry about her daughter Leanne's wedding. Leanne was a podiatrist and the first person in Linda's family to go to college, and she was marrying an industrial chemist. Linda, proud as punch, was organizing the entire thing. She had no idea how difficult it was for Issy, having to listen to a mother who wanted nothing more than to put in corsetry eyelets for her twenty-six-year-old's wedding to a wonderful man.

Linda thought Issy had a young man but didn't like to pry. They did take their time these days, didn't they, these career women? She ought to get a move on, pretty girl like that who could cook; you'd think she'd get snapped up. But here she was, still catching the bus on her own. She hoped her Leanne got pregnant quickly. She was looking forward to giving her discount card a bit of a workout in the baby department too.

Issy, closing her tin and still seeing no sign of a bus, glanced behind her into Pear Tree Court. The oddly shaped shop with the grilles tightly down looked like a grumpy sleeping man in the drear gray light of a January London morning, bin bags set outside still waiting for collection.

Over the last four years, various people had tried to turn it into a business of one kind or another, but they had all failed. Perhaps the area wasn't up and coming enough, perhaps it was the proximity of the ironmonger's, but the little children's clothes shop with its exquisite Tartine et Chocolat French designs—at eye-watering prices—had not lasted long; nor had the gift shop, with its foreign editions of Monopoly and Penguin Classics mugs; nor the yoga shop, which had painted the entire frontage a supposedly soothing pink, put a tinkling Buddha fountain outside by the tree, and sold incredibly expensive yoga mats and Gwyneth Paltrow–style soft bendy trousers. Issy, while far too intimidated ever to set foot inside, had thought it might do rather well, considering the high numbers of local trendies and yummy mummies, but it had turned out not to be, and once again there was a *For rent/inquiries* board in yellow and black, clashing horribly with the pink, showing in the window. Of the little tinkling Buddha there was no sign.

"That's a shame," said Linda, seeing her looking at the closed-down shop. Issy hmmm'd in response. Seeing the yoga shop every day—and the lithe, ponytail-swinging honey-colored girls who worked there—had just reminded her that now she was over thirty, it wasn't quite as easy to stay a size eight as it used to be, especially when you had Issy's grand passion. It wasn't as if she could ever have been a skinny minny, not in her grandfather's house. When she came home from school, Gramps, although he must have been tired from a full day's work already, would beckon her into the big kitchens. The other bakers would stand out of her way and smile at the little girl, while barking at each other in their rough voices. She would feel embarrassed just to be in there, especially when Gramps announced, "Now, your education truly begins." She had nodded, a round-eyed quiet child, prone to blushing and self-consciousness; feeling out of place at a primary school whose rules seemed to change on a weekly basis, understood by everyone but her.

"We shall start," he said, "with drop scones. Even a child of five could make a drop scone!"

"But Grampa, I'm *six*!"

"You're not *six*!"

"I am! I'm *six*!"

"You're two."

"I'm *six*!"

"You're four."

"*Six!*"

"Now here is the secret to the drop scone," he said seriously, after he had made Issy wash her hands and patiently scooped up the four eggshells that had fallen on the floor. "It's in the burner. Not too hot. A hot burner kills pancakes. Gently now."

He held on to her, up on the brown kitchen stool that wobbled slightly because of the hole in the linoleum, her small face poised in concentration as she let the mixture drip gently off the wooden spoon and into the pan.

"And patiently now," he said. "You can't rush these things. A burnt drop scone is no life. And this cooker..."

Joe had poured all his energies into his beloved granddaughter, teaching her the techniques and tricks of baking. It was his fault, thought Issy. She would definitely bake less this year, lose a couple of pounds. She realized she was thinking this while absentmindedly licking orange buttercream off her fingers. Soon!

● ● ● ●

Still no sign of the bus. As Issy looked around the corner, glancing quickly at her watch, she felt a heavy raindrop hit her cheek. Then another. The sky had been gray for so long now, it seemed, you could never tell when rain was coming in. But this was going to be a bad one; the clouds were nearly black. There was no shelter at the bus stop at all, unless you counted three centimeters of guttering from the newsagent's behind them, but the proprietor didn't like them leaning against his windows and often said so when Issy went in to get her morning newspaper (and occasionally a snack). The only thing to do was hunker down, cram your hat over your head, and wonder, as Issy sometimes did, why she wasn't living in Tuscany, California, or Sydney.

Suddenly a car—a black BMW 23i—squealed up to an illegal stop on the yellow lines, splashing most of the queue, some of whom groaned while some swore prodigiously. Issy's heart lifted—and simultaneously sank. This would not make her popular with her number 73 posse. But still. The door opened opposite her.

"Wanna ride?" came the voice.

• • • •

Graeme wished Issy wouldn't do this. He knew this was where she had to get the bus, but it made her look such a martyr. She was a lovely girl and all that, and there was no doubt he quite liked having her about and everything, but he needed his own space, and it just wasn't the done thing, sleeping with someone—someone your junior—from the office. So, anyway, he was glad she understood about not staying over—that was lucky, he was busy and couldn't have handled someone right now who would give him a lot of aggro—but then when he was heading into work, feeling pretty good in his X-series, thinking about corporate strategy, the last thing he needed to see was Issy standing soaking bloody wet at the bus stop, her scarf up around her neck. It made him feel uncomfortable, like she was not doing her part somehow by being so…so wet.

• • • •

21

Graeme was the best-looking person at Issy's firm. By far. He was tall, honed from the gym, with piercing blue eyes and black hair. Issy had already been working there for three years, and his arrival had caused a stir with everyone. He was definitely cut out for property development; he had an authoritative, fast-moving style, and a manner that always said if you didn't snap up what he was selling, you were going to miss out.

At first Issy had regarded him as one might a pop star or a television actor: nice to look at, but stratospherically out of her league. She'd had plenty of nice, kind boyfriends, and one or two total arseholes, but for one reason or another, nothing had ever worked out; they weren't quite the right man, or it wasn't quite the right time. Issy didn't feel she was in the last chance saloon just yet, but she also knew, in the back of her mind, that she would like to find someone nice and settle down. She didn't want her mother's life, hopping from one man to the next, never happy. She wanted a home and a family. She knew that made her hopelessly square, but that was how it was. And Graeme clearly wasn't the settling-down type; she'd seen him pull away from the office in his little sports car with gorgeous-looking skinny girls with long blond hair—never the same one, although they all looked the same. So she put him out of her mind, even as he cut a swathe through the office's younger girls.

That was what made it such a surprise to both of them, when they were sent on a training day to the company's head offices in Rotterdam one week. Trapped indoors by the howling rain, their Dutch hosts having retired to bed earlier than expected, they had found themselves together in the hotel bar, getting on far better than they'd have expected. Graeme, for his part, was intrigued by the cloudy-haired, pretty, curvy girl who sat in the corner and never flirted or pouted her lips or giggled when he walked by; she turned out to be funny and sweet. Issy, slightly giddy on two Jägermeisters, couldn't deny the absolute attractiveness of his strong arms and stubbled jaw. She tried to tell herself that it meant nothing, that it was just a one-off, nothing to worry about, a bit of fun, easily explained away by the alcohol and kept a secret, but he was terribly attractive.

Graeme had set about seducing her partly for something to do but had been surprised to find in her a softness and a sweetness he hadn't been expecting, and that he really rather liked. She wasn't pushy and sharp-angled like those other girls, and she didn't spend her entire time complaining about the calories in food and retouching her makeup. He had rather surprised himself by going against one of his golden rules and calling her after they got back. Issy had been both surprised and flattered and had gone around to his off-plan minimalist flat in Notting Hill and made him an outstanding bruschetta. They had both enjoyed the experience very much.

So it had been exciting. Eight months ago. And gradually Issy had started—naturally, she couldn't help it—she had started to wonder if maybe, just maybe, he was the man for her. That someone so handsome and ambitious could have a gentler side too. He liked to talk to her about work—she always knew who he was talking about—and she liked the novelty factor of making dinner for him, and them sharing a meal, and a bed.

Practical Helena of course had not failed to point out that, in the months since they'd got together, not only had he never stayed over at the flat, but he often asked Issy to leave before morning so he could get a proper night's sleep, that they went to restaurants but she had never met his friends or his mother, that he had never come with her to see Gramps, that he'd never even called her his girlfriend. And that while it might be nice for Graeme to play housie on a casual basis with some girl from the office, Issy, at thirty-one, might be looking for a little bit more.

Issy tended to stick her fingers in her ears at this point and sing la la la. The thing was, well, yes, she could break it off—although there was hardly a line of eligible suitors, and certainly none as hot as Graeme in view. Or, perhaps, she could make his life so pleasant and lovely that he would see how awful things would be without her and propose. Helena thought this plan very over-optimistic and did not keep this thought to herself.

Graeme grimaced to himself in his BMW and turned down Jay-Z to pick up Issy. Of course he'd stop on a rainy day. He wasn't some kind of bastard.

• • • •

Issy folded herself into the low-seated car as gracefully as she could, which wasn't very. She was conscious that she'd just exposed her gusset to the bus queue. Next to her, Graeme, before she'd had a chance to arrange herself or put her seat belt on, was already nudging into the traffic, without bothering to signal.

"Come on, you arseholes," he growled. "Let me in."

"Do I wanna ride?" asked Issy. "Have you gone American?"

Graeme glanced at her and raised an eyebrow. "I can let you out if you like."

The rain pounded hard on the windscreen as if answering the question for her.

"No, no thank you. Thanks for picking me up."

Graeme grunted. Sometimes, she thought, he really hated being caught out in a good turn.

• • • •

"Well, we can't really go public, because of the office," Issy had said to Helena.

"What, even after all this time? And you think they don't already know?" Helena had countered. "Are they all idiots?"

"It's a property developer's," Issy said.

"OK," said Helena, "they're all idiots. But I still don't see why you can't stay over at his house once in a while."

"Because he doesn't want us walking into the office together," Issy had said, as if it was the most natural thing in the world. And it was, wasn't it? It wasn't as if eight months was terribly long. There was plenty of time for them to formalize things, decide when to take it to the next level. It just wasn't the right time at the moment, that was all.

Helena had sniffed in a characteristically Helena way.

The traffic getting into town was terrible, and Graeme growled and swore a bit under his breath, but Issy didn't care—it was just so nice to be in the car, cozy and warm, with Kiss FM blaring out on the radio.

"What are you up to today?" she asked conversationally. Normally he liked dumping the stresses and strains of the office onto her shoulders; he could trust her to be discreet. Today, though, he glanced at her.

"Nothing," he said. "Nothing much."

Issy raised her eyebrows. Graeme's days were never nothing much; they were full of jockeying for position and being the Billy Big Bollocks. Property development was a profession that encouraged that sort of behavior. That was why, she sometimes had to explain to her friends, Graeme could appear a little…aggressive. It was a facade he had to keep up at work. Underneath it all she knew, from their many late-night chats, from his moods and occasional outbursts, that he was a vulnerable man; sensitive to the aggression in the workplace; worried, deep down, about his status, just like everybody else. That was why Issy was so much more confident of her relationship with Graeme than her friends were. She saw the soft side of him. He confided to her his worries, his hopes and dreams and fears. And that was why it was serious, no matter where she woke up in the morning.

She put her hand on his on the gear stick.

"It'll be all right," she said softly. Graeme shrugged it off, almost rudely.

"I know," he said.

• • • •

The rain got heavier, if anything, as they turned into the street near Farringdon Road that housed the offices of Kalinga Deniki Property Management, or KD as it was known. It was a sharp chunk of modern glass, six stories high, that looked out of place among the lower-set red-brick flats and offices. Graeme slowed the car.

"Would you mind…?"

"You're not serious, Graeme."

"Come on! How would it look to the partners, me driving in in the morning with some office clerk?"

He saw Issy's face.

"Sorry. Office manager, I mean. I know it's you. But they won't know what to think, will they?" He caressed her cheek briefly. "I'm sorry, Issy. But I'm the boss, and if I start condoning workplace romances…all hell will break loose."

For a moment, Issy felt triumphant. It was a romance! Officially! She knew it. Even if Helena did occasionally imply she was an idiot, that it was just a convenient thing for Graeme to have a spare ear around.

As if reading her thoughts, Graeme smiled at her, almost guiltily.

"It won't be forever," he said. But he couldn't deny the slight relief he felt when she stepped out of the car.

• • • •

Issy stumbled through the puddles. It was hosing it down so hard that only a few minutes' walking up Britton Street were enough to render her as completely soaked as if she'd never had a lift at all. She ducked into the ladies' loos on the ground floor, which were cutting-edge (so guests could never figure out how to turn on the taps or flush the loos) and usually empty. A few blasts of the hand dryer were all she could muster for her hair. Oh great, it was going to look like a complete frizzathon.

When Issy took the time and properly blow-dried her hair and used lots of expensive products, it made beautiful shiny ringlets that fell in tinkly twists around her neck. When she didn't, which was most days, she ran a huge risk of frizz, especially in the wet. She looked at herself and sighed. Her hair looked like she'd knitted it. The cold wind had put some color in her cheeks—Issy hated her propensity for blushing at everything but this wasn't too bad—and her green eyes, fringed with lots of black mascara, were fine, but the hair was undoubtedly a disaster. She scrabbled around in her bag for a clip or hairband but came up empty-handed except for a red elastic band dropped by the postman. That would have to do. It didn't quite go with her floral print dress and tight black cardigan, worn with thick black tights and black boots, but it would have to do.

Slightly late, she said good morning to Jim, the doorman, and hopped the lift up to the second floor, which was accounts and admin. The salesmen and the developers had the floor above, but the atrium was made of solid glass, which meant it was always easy to see who was around and about. Up at her desk she nodded to her workmates, then realized with a start that she was late for the 9:30 meeting she was meant to be minuting, the meeting where Graeme would talk about the results of the board meeting to staff lower down the chain. She cursed under her breath. Why couldn't Graeme at least have mentioned it to remind her? Crossly, she grabbed her laptop and ran for the stairs.

• • • •

In the meeting room, the senior sales team was already seated around the glass table, trading banter with one another. They glanced up uninterestedly when she walked in, muttering apologies. Graeme looked furious. Well, it was his fault, thought Issy mutinously. If he hadn't left her to wade through a flood, she'd have made it on time.

"Late night?" snickered Billy Fanshawe, one of the youngest, cockiest salesmen, who thought he was irresistible to women. It was annoying how often his sheer persuasive belief in this proved it to be true.

Issy smiled without showing her teeth at him and sat down without grabbing a coffee, even though she desperately wanted one. She sat next to Callie Mehta, the only senior woman at Kalinga Deniki. She was director of Human Resources and looked, as ever, immaculately groomed and unperturbed.

"Right," said Graeme, clearing his throat. "Now we're all finally here, I think we can start."

Issy felt her face beam red. She didn't expect Graeme to give her any special favors at work, of course she didn't, but she didn't want him thinking he could pick on her either. Fortunately nobody else noticed.

"I spoke to the partners yesterday," said Graeme. KD was a Dutch international conglomerate with branches in most major cities in the world. Some partners were London-based but spent most of their time on airplanes, scoping out properties. They were elusive and very powerful. Everyone sat up and listened attentively.

"As you know, it's been a bad year here…"

"Not for me," said Billy with the self-satisfied look of a man who'd just bought his first Porsche. Issy decided not to minute that.

"And we've been hit hard in the U.S. and the Middle East. The rest of Europe is holding up, as is the Far East, but even so…"

Graeme had everyone's attention now.

"It doesn't look like we can continue as we are. There are going to have to be…cutbacks."

Beside Issy, Callie Mehta nodded. She must have known already, thought Issy, with a sudden beat of alarm inside her. And if she knew, that meant "cutbacks" would be staff cutbacks. And staff cutbacks meant…redundancies.

She felt a coldness grip at her heart. It wouldn't be her, would it? But then, it certainly wouldn't be the Billys of the operation; they were too important. And accounts, well, you couldn't do without accounts, and…

Issy found her mind racing ahead of her.

"Now this will be strictly confidential. I don't want these minutes circulated," said Graeme, looking at her pointedly. "But I think it's fair to say they're looking for a staff reduction of about five percent."

Panicking, Issy did the figures in her head. If they had two hundred staff, that was ten redundancies. It didn't sound like a lot, but where did you trim the fat? The new press assistant could go, probably, but would the salesmen have to get rid of their PAs? Or would there be fewer salesmen? No, that didn't make sense; fewer salesmen and the same amount of admin support was a stupid business model. She realized Graeme was still talking.

"…but I think we can show them we can do better than that, aim for seven, even eight percent. Show Rotterdam that KD is a twenty-first-century lean, mean business machine."

"Yeah," said Billy.

"All right," said somebody else.

But if it was her…how would she pay the mortgage? How would she live? She was thirty-one years old, but she didn't really have any savings; it had taken her years to pay off her student loan, and then she'd wanted to enjoy London…She thought with regret of all the meals out, all the nights in cocktail bars and splurge trips to Forever 21. Why didn't she have more put by? Why? She couldn't go to Florida to live with her mum, she couldn't. Where would she go? What would she do? Issy suddenly thought she was going to cry.

"Are you getting this down, Issy?" Graeme snapped at her, as Callie started discussing packages and exit strategies. She looked up at him, almost unaware of where she was. Suddenly she realized he was looking back at her like she was a total stranger.

3

I ssy hadn't had enough cakes left over from the bus queue for the office the day before, and anyway she would have felt hypocritical handing them out in a jaunty fashion after what she'd overheard in the meeting. However, the entire team had gathered around, demanding a treat after the break and were horrified.

"You are why Ah come to work," François, the young ad designer, had said. "You bake like aha, the pâtissiers of Toulon. *C'est vrai.*"

Issy had blushed bright red at the compliment and searched among the recipes her grandfather posted to her for something new to try. And although she felt slightly sneaky doing it, she wore her smartest, most businesslike navy dress with the swingy hem and a neat jacket. Just to look like a professional.

It wasn't raining quite so hard today, but a chill wind still cut through the bus queue. Linda, concerned about Issy's anxious expression—she was developing a little furrow between her eyebrows, Linda had noticed—wanted to suggest a cream but didn't dare. Instead she found herself babbling about how haberdashery had never been so busy—something to do with everyone taking on a huge dose of austerity and starting to knit their own jumpers—but she could tell Issy was barely listening. She was staring at a very sleek blond woman being shown the outside of the little shop by a man she vaguely recognized as one of the many local estate agents she'd met when she bought her flat.

The woman was talking loudly, and Issy edged a little closer to hear what she was saying. Her professional curiosity was piqued.

"This area doesn't know what it needs!" the woman was saying. She had a loud, carrying voice. "There's too much fried chicken and not enough organic produce. Do you know," she said earnestly to the estate agent, who was nodding happily and agreeing with everything she said, "that Britain eats more sugar per head than any country in the world except America and Tonga?"

"Tonga, huh?" said the estate agent. Issy clasped the large Tupperware carton of cupcakes closer to her chest, in case the woman turned her laser gaze on her.

"I don't consider myself to be a mere foodie," said the woman. "I consider myself to be more of a prophet, yah? Spreading the message. That wholegrain, raw cooking is the only way forward."

Raw cooking? thought Issy.

"Now, I thought we'd put the cooker over here." The woman was pointing bossily through the window into the far corner. "We'll hardly be using it."

"Oh yes, that would be perfect," said the estate agent.

No, it wouldn't, thought Issy instantly. You'd want to be near the window for good venting, so people could get a look at what you were doing and you could keep an eye on the shop. That far corner was a terrible place for the oven; you'd have your back to everything the entire time. No, if you wanted to cook for people, you needed to do it somewhere you could be seen, to welcome people in cheerfully with a smile, and…

Lost in her reverie, she barely noticed the bus arriving, just as the lady said, "Now, talking about money, Desmond…"

How much money? wondered Issy idly, climbing in the back door of the bus, as Linda wittered on about cross-stitch.

• • • •

The mirrored glass of the office exterior walls looked blue-gray and cold in the chilly morning light. Issy remembered that her new year's resolution had been to walk up the two flights of stairs every day but groaned as she decided that actually if you were carrying large items (like twenty-nine cupcakes in a big Tupperware) then you were allowed to take the lift.

As she entered the administration floor, clicking her entry pass (with the wildly unflattering photograph laminated onto it forevermore) to go through the wide glass doors, she sensed a strange quietness in the air. Tess, the receptionist, had said a quick hello but hadn't engaged her beyond that—normally she was full of gossip about office antics. Ever since she'd started seeing Graeme, Issy had stayed away from office nights out, just in case she had a couple glasses of wine too many and accidentally spilled the beans. She didn't think anyone suspected anything. Sometimes she wasn't sure they'd actually believe it. Graeme was so handsome and such a go-getter. Issy was pretty, but she wasn't a patch on Tess, for instance, who wore tiny miniskirts but still managed to look beautiful and sweet rather than tarty, probably because she was twenty-two; or Ophy, who was six feet tall and stalked the hallways like a princess rather than a junior payroll clerk. Still, that didn't matter, Issy told herself. Graeme had picked her, and that was all there was to it. She still remembered them stumbling outside the Rotterdam hotel to get away from the others—they'd both pretended they smoked, even though neither of them did—and giggling their heads off. The sweet anticipation before that first kiss; the way the black sweep of his long eyelashes made a shadow on top of his high cheekbones; his sharp, tangy Hugo Boss aftershave. She'd lived a long time on the romance of that first evening.

And nobody would ever believe it, but it was true: they were definitely dating. He was definitely her boyfriend. And there he was, standing at the far end of the open-plan office, just in front of the conference room, with a serious look on his face, clearly the cause of the silence over the twenty-eight desks.

Issy put the cupcakes down with a thud. Her heart thudded likewise.

• • • •

"I'm sorry about this," Graeme said, when everyone was in. He had thought about his approach for a long time. He didn't want to be one of those weasel bosses who don't tell anyone what's going on and let people find out from rumors and gossip. He wanted to show his bosses he could make the tough choices, and he wanted his staff to see that he could be straight with them. They still wouldn't be happy, but at least he could be straight.

"You don't need me to tell you what things are like," said Graeme, trying to sound reasonable. "You're seeing it yourselves; in accounts, in sales, in turnover. You guys deal with the bread and butter, the nuts and bolts, the figures and projections. You know the harsh realities of business life. Which means that although what I have to say is difficult, I know you'll understand it, and I know you won't think it's unfair."

You could have heard a pin drop in the office. Issy swallowed loudly. In one sense, it was good that Graeme was coming right out and telling everyone. There was nothing worse than being in an office where senior staff wouldn't tell anyone anything and everyone lived in a climate of suspicion and fear. For a bunch of estate agents, they were being remarkably honest and upfront.

But still, she'd thought they might wait. Just a little. Mull it over, see if things picked up in the next month or so, or wait till spring. Or take a partners' vote or…With a sinking heart, Issy realized these decisions had probably been made, at some level, months ago; in Rotterdam, or Hamburg, or Seoul. This was just the implementation. The little people stage.

"There isn't a nice way to do this," said Graeme. "You'll all get an email in the next half hour to let you know if you're staying or going. And then we're going to be as generous to you and as reasonable as we possibly can. I'll see those of you who aren't going to be staying with us in the boardroom at eleven." He glanced at his Montblanc watch.

Issy had a sudden image of Callie, the head of Human Resources, poised with her finger over the Send button on her computer like a runner at the starting line.

"Again," said Graeme, "I'm sorry."

He retreated into the boardroom. Through the slatted Venetian blinds, Issy could see him, his handsome head bent toward his laptop.

Instantly there was a flurry of panicky noise. Everyone charged up their computers as quickly as they could, pressing the refresh button on their email programs once a second, all muttering to themselves. This wasn't the nineties, or the zeros, when you could bounce from one job to another in two days: a friend of Issy's had once picked up two redundancy checks in eighteen months. The number of jobs out there, the number of businesses out there—it all seemed to be shrinking and shrinking. For every vacancy there were more and more applicants, and that was if you could even find a vacancy, not to mention the millions of school leavers and graduates joining the market every month…Issy told herself not to panic, but it was too late. She was already halfway through one of her cupcakes, crumbs carelessly scattering the keyboard. She must breathe. Breathe. Two nights ago, she and Graeme had been under his navy blue Ralph Lauren duvet, safe and comfortable in a world of their own. Nothing was going to happen. Nothing. Next to her, François was typing furiously.

"What are you doing?" she asked.

"Updating my CV," he said. "This place is feeneeshed."

Issy swallowed and picked up another cake. Just as she did so, she heard a ping.

Dear Miss *Issy Randall,*

We are sorry to inform you that due to a downturn in economic

34

progress and with no improvement in our forecasts for the growth of commercial property uptake in the City of London this year, the directors of Kalinga Deniki CP are making redundant the post of *Office Manager Grade 4 London Office*, with immediate effect. Please go to *Conference Room C* at *11:00 a.m.* to discuss your ongoing options with your line manager, *Graeme Denton.*

Yours sincerely,
Jaap Van de Bier
Human Resources, Kalinga Deniki

"It was," as Issy said later, "the way they had obviously created some kind of macro to drop all the details in. Nobody could even be bothered to write a personal message. Everyone got the same note, all over the world. So you were like losing your job and your whole life, but they put less thought into it than that thing you get to remind you to go for a dental check-up." She thought about it. "And I need a dental check-up."

"Well, it's free now you're unemployed," Helena had said kindly.

• • • •

The open-plan office was the cruelest way of working ever invented, thought Issy suddenly. Because clearly everyone was on show all the time and had been making a point of looking happy and jolly and fine, when obviously the company wasn't happy and jolly and fine and maybe if a few more people had been in offices with doors they could have broken down and wept and then maybe done something about fixing it rather than pretending everything was absolutely fine until twenty-five percent of the staff had to be let go. All around the office came gasps or cheers; someone punched the air and shouted, "Yes!" before glancing around in a panic and whispering, "Sorry, sorry…it's just my mother's in a care home and…" before trailing off awkwardly. Someone burst into tears.

"Well, fick me," said François and stopped updating his CV. Issy was frozen. She just stared at the screen, resisting the temptation to refresh it one last time, as if that could possibly bring a different result. It wasn't just the job—well it was, of course, the job; to lose your job was the most upsetting, depressing thing ever. But to know that Graeme…to realize that he had had sex with her, let her cook him dinner, all the time knowing…knowing that this was going to happen. What…what was he thinking? What was he *thinking*?

Without pausing to think—if she had, she'd almost certainly have let her natural timidity stop her—Issy jumped out of her seat and approached the boardroom. Fuck waiting till eleven o'clock. She wanted to know about this *now*. She almost knocked on the door but instead boldly walked straight in. Graeme glanced up at her, not entirely surprised. But she'd understand his position, surely.

Issy was furious.

"Issy. I'm so sorry."

She gritted her teeth.

"*You're* sorry? You're blooming sorry! Why didn't you tell me?"

He looked surprised.

"Well, of course I couldn't tell you. Company confidentiality. They could have sued me."

"I wouldn't have told them it was you!" Issy was stricken that he didn't even trust her that much. "But I could have had some warning; sometime to prepare myself, get myself together a bit."

"But it wouldn't have been fair for you to have that advantage," said Graeme. "Everyone else would have liked the same."

"But it's *not* the same," shouted Issy. "For them it's just a job. For me it's a job and it's not getting to hear it from you."

She became aware of a large group of people behind her, listening in through the open door. She turned around furiously.

"Yes. That's right. Me and Graeme have been having a secret affair. That we've been keeping from the office."

There were some murmurs but not, Issy noticed in her heightened emotional state, the surprised gasps she'd been expecting.

"Well, yes, everyone knew that," said François.

Issy stared at him. "What do you mean, everyone?"

The rest of the office looked slightly sheepish.

"*Everyone* knew?" She turned back to Graeme. "Did you know that everyone knew?"

To her horror, Graeme was also looking sheepish.

"Well, you know, I still don't think it's good for morale to have people flaunting personal relationships at work."

"You knew?!"

"It's my job to know what my staff is talking about," said Graeme primly. "I wouldn't be doing my job if I didn't."

Issy gazed at him, speechless. If everyone knew, why all the creeping around and the secrecy?

"But…,but…"

"Issy, would you like to sit down so we can start the meeting?"

Issy became aware of five other devastated-looking people inching their way into the boardroom. François was not among them, but Bob from Marketing was. He was scratching what looked like a new patch of psoriasis on the side of his head, and suddenly Issy hated the firm…Graeme, her colleagues, property management, and the whole damn capitalist system. She turned on her heel and stormed straight out of the office, catching her box of cakes with her hip as she went and scattering them everywhere.

● ● ● ●

Issy needed a friendly ear, and pronto. And Helena was only ten minutes away. She wouldn't mind.

Helena was stitching up a young man's head, none too gently.

"Oww," he was saying.

"I thought you did stitches with glue nowadays," said Issy, once she'd stopped sniveling.

"We do," said Helena grimly, pulling the needle tight, "except when some people *sniff* glue, then think they can fly over barbed-wire fences. Then they don't get any glue."

"It wasn't glue; it was lighter fluid," said the pasty-looking young man.

"That's not going to make me give you any glue," said Helena.

"No," said the man sadly.

"I just can't believe it, Len," said Issy. "I can't believe that bastard would let me walk into work in the rain knowing all the time that one, he was going to fire me, and two, everyone knew we were going out together. They must all think he's a nobber too."

"Mmm," said Helena noncommittally. She had learned over the years not to diss any of Issy's men; she often dragged them back in again, and that was uncomfortable for everyone.

"He sounds like a bell end," said the young man.

"Yeah!" said Issy. "You sniff glue and even you know he's a bell end."

"It's lighter fluid actually."

"Well, you're better off out of it all," said Helena. "You know you're always saying you don't like…being a medical student," she added quickly for the patient's benefit.

"You can only be better off out of it," said Issy, "if you have somewhere to be better off in. Whereas I'm looking at the most depressed job market for twenty years, no jobs in my sector even if the rest of the market was fine and…" She dissolved into tears again. "I'm single again, Len! At thirty-one!"

"Thirty-one is *not old*," asserted Helena firmly.

"Come on. If you were eighteen, you'd think it was old."

"It's really old," said the young man. "And I'm twenty."

"And you won't live to see thirty-one if you don't stop your ridiculous habits," said Helena firmly. "So you keep out of it."

"I'd do you both though," he said. "So you don't look that over the hill yet."

Helena and Issy looked at each other.

"See?" said Helena. "Things could be worse."

"Well, it's nice to know I've still got something to fall back on."

"And as for you," said Helena, finishing up his wound with an expertly applied pad and bandage, "if you don't give up that stuff, you won't be able to get it up for anyone. Not me, not her, not Megan Fox, do you understand?"

For the first time, the young man looked frightened.

"Really?"

"Really. You might as well lop your bollocks off for all the good they'll do you."

The young man swallowed. "It's time for me to get off the stuff anyway."

"I'd think so, wouldn't you?" Helena handed him the card of the local cessation project. "On your way. Next!"

A worried young woman ushered in a toddler with his head crammed in a saucepan.

"That really happens?" said Issy.

"Oh yes," said Helena. "Now, Mrs. Chakrabati, this is Issy. She's a medical student; do you mind her sitting in?"

Mrs. Chakrabati shook her head. Helena leaned down.

"Ravi, I cannot *believe* you are in here again. You are not a pirate, understand?"

"*I-is-pirate!*"

"Still, this is better than the cheese grater, remember?"

Mrs. Chakrabati nodded fervently as Helena went searching for the castor oil.

"Len, I'd better go."

Helena looked up sympathetically. "You sure?"

Issy nodded. "I know I stormed out, but I need to go and…well, at least find out about my redundancy payment and stuff."

Helena gave her a hug.

"It's going to be fine, you know. Fine."

"People say that," said Issy. "What if, sometimes, it doesn't turn out fine?"

"I will fight them with my *pirate things*!" shouted Ravi.

Issy crouched down and spoke to the saucepan.

"Thank you, sweetheart," she said. "It might come to that."

• • • •

Walking back into the office again was nearly unbearable. Issy felt so nervous and ashamed.

"Hey," she said sadly to Jim on reception.

"I heard," said Jim. "I'm really sorry."

"Me too," said Issy. "Oh well."

"Come on, love," he said. "You'll find something. Better than this place, I'm sure."

"Hmmm."

"I'll miss your cakes."

"Well, thank you."

Issy bypassed the second floor and went on up to the top, straight to Human Resources. She didn't think she could face talking to Graeme again. She checked her phone for the ninth time. No texts. No messages. Nothing. How could this be happening to her? She felt like she was walking in a dream.

"Hello, Issy," said Callie Mehta softly, looking immaculate as ever in a soft fawn suit. "I'm sorry. This is the worst part of my job."

"Yeah, and mine," said Issy stiffly.

Callie lifted out a file. "We've worked out a package that's as generous as we can be…Also, as it's the beginning of the year, we thought rather than working out your notice, if you like you can take your full holiday entitlement and we'll continue paying for that."

Issy had to admit that seemed quite generous. Then she cursed herself for falling for it. Callie probably trained for this kind of thing all the time.

"And here…if you like, and it's completely up to you, we're funding resettlement courses."

"Resettlement courses? That sounds a bit sinister."

"It's like a training and guidance course, to help you figure out…where next."

"To the dole queue in this climate," said Issy tightly.

"Issy," said Callie, kindly but quite firmly. "Can I just tell you…in my career I've been made redundant three times. It is upsetting but, I promise, it's not the end of the world. Something always comes up for the good people. And you're one of the good people."

"That's why I'm out of a job," said Issy.

Callie frowned slightly and put her finger on her forehead.

"Issy, I'm going to tell you this, from what I've observed…it may not be welcome, but I hope you don't mind, just in case it helps."

Issy sat back. This was like being told off by the headmistress. While simultaneously losing the ability to buy food.

"I've noticed you around. You're obviously bright, you've got a degree, you're pleasant to the people you work with…"

Issy wondered where this was going.

"Why are you just an office administrator? I mean, look at the salesmen; they're younger than you, but they're driven and committed… You have talents and skills, but I just don't see where they've been used with you running around chasing up expenses and timesheets. It's like you just wanted to hide away doing something safe and a little dull, hoping nobody would notice you."

Issy shrugged uncomfortably. She bet Callie Mehta didn't have a mother who rushed about and wanted people to notice her all the time.

"It's not too late in life to change direction, you know. I'm sure you think it is but," Callie checked the paper in front of her, "thirty-one is nothing. Nothing at all. And I will say that if you end up doing the same job for someone else…I think you'll probably be as dissatisfied there as you have been here. And don't tell me that's not true, please. I've worked in HR a long time and I'm telling you, redundancy is the right choice for you now. Because you're still young enough to do what you want. But it may be your last chance. Do you understand what I'm saying?"

Issy felt her face burn up. All she could do was nod, at the risk of breaking down completely. Callie twisted her wedding ring.

"And…and Issy, I'm so, so sorry if you feel I'm speaking out of turn here, I know it's very unprofessional of me and I shouldn't lay myself open to accusations of listening to office gossip…but I really, really want to say something and I'm sorry if it's hard to hear. But I would say it's also high risk to think some man is going to come along and look after you and take care of everything for you. It may well happen, and if it's what you want then I hope it does. But if you can find something you love to do, that you really enjoy on your own terms…well, that's a nice thing to have in your life."

Issy swallowed hard. Even her ears felt hot.

"Do you love what you do?" she found herself asking.

"Sometimes it's difficult," said Callie. "But it's always challenging. And it's never, ever boring. Could you say the same?"

Callie pushed the piece of paper across the desk. Issy picked it up and looked at it. Nearly twenty thousand pounds. A lot. That was a lot of money. That was life-changing money. Surely.

"Please don't spend it all on lipstick and shoes," said Callie, obviously trying to lighten the mood.

"Can I spend a little bit?" said Issy, appreciating the gesture, and Callie's frankness. Well, actually at the moment it burned in the pit of her stomach. But she felt there was kindness in it.

"A little bit," said Callie. "Yes."
And they shook hands.

• • • •

It was less of a going-away party down at the Coins, more of a wake. The other eight in total who were scheduled to leave had also been offered their holidays, so there was no point in anyone hanging around beyond the end of the week. It shortened the torture considerably, which was a small mercy, thought Issy.

The pub had always been warm and cozy, a nice haven away from shards-of-glass office blocks and cutting-edge rental space. With its yellowed walls from the days before the smoking ban, its unpretentious draught beer and crisp packets, its patterned carpet and the landlord's fat dog always on the lookout for treats, it looked like a thousand other pubs in London, although it was, reflected Issy, one of a dying breed—a bit like her. Then she tried to shake herself out of her melancholy mood—so many people from the office had turned up, it was rather touching. No Graeme of course. In a way she was pleased about that. She didn't know how she'd react if she ever had to make polite conversation with him again. Which was just as well, seeing as he hadn't even bothered to ring her to see how she was doing.

Bob from Marketing was roaring drunk by 7:00 p.m., so she propped him up on the corner of the banquette and let him go to sleep.

"To Issy," said François when toasts were being raised. "And now that she is leaving us, let the only plus side be that we will all finally stop putting weight on."

"Hear, hear!" shouted the others. Issy looked at them in consternation. "What do you mean?"

"If your cakes weren't so bloody delicious," said Karen, a heavy-set bookings clerk who rarely chatted to her, "I wouldn't be so bloody fat. Oh, OK, I would, but I wouldn't enjoy getting fat quite so much."

"Do you mean my silly cakes?" said Issy. She'd had about four glasses of rosé, and things were getting blurry around the edges.

"They are not *silly cakes*," said François. "Never say that. They are as good as Hortense Beusy, the best pâtissière in Toulon. *C'est la vérité*," he said seriously. He'd had a lot of rosé too.

"Oh, nonsense," said Issy, coloring. "You're all just saying that because I bring in free cakes. They could taste like monkey poo and everyone would still scoff them because it's better than working. At that…hellhole," she added daringly.

Everyone shook their heads.

"It's true," said Bob, temporarily lifting his head from the bar. "You're much better at baking than you are at admin."

There was some nodding around the bar.

"You mean to say you were just tolerating me because of my delicious cakes?" said Issy, stung.

"No," said François. "Also because you were shagging the boss."

• • • •

Issy had sobered up quite quickly after that. One last look around, one last kiss for everyone, even the people she hadn't really liked—she felt herself getting melancholy suddenly, as if Kalinga Deniki had been a family rather than a cutthroat bunch of property specialists out to make a fast buck. And for the Coins; it would be far too tragic to ever stop by there again, as if she was deliberately trying to run into all her old workmates. So with a slight croak to her voice she petted the old dog and scratched behind his ears, which he liked almost as much as salt and vinegar crisps, and bade farewell to the company.

"Pop in and see us," said Karen.

"With cakes!" added somebody.

Issy promised faithfully that she would. She knew she wouldn't, couldn't. That chapter of her life was over. But what came next?

4

not going to work
nutella cookies

• • • •

* 1 cup self-rising flour
* 2 tsp baking powder
* 7 tbsp soft butter
* 1 cup white superfine sugar
* ½ tsp bicarbonate of soda dissolved in hot water
* 2 tbsp warm golden syrup
* 6 tsp Nutella
* 1 gossip magazine
* 1 pair pajamas

Preheat the oven to 390°F/gas mark 6.

Sift flour and baking powder in a bowl. Rub in butter; add sugar, bicarb, syrup, and two tsp Nutella. Roll into walnut-sized balls and place on a greased baking tray, pressing down the center of each ball with your thumb. Bake for about ten minutes.

While baking, eat four remaining tsp Nutella. Eat entire tray of cookies while reading gossip magazine and wearing pajamas.

Optional garnish: tears.

T hank goodness Helena worked shifts, which meant she was often at home in the mornings. Issy wasn't sure afterward how she'd have coped if she'd had to face those first couple of weeks alone. To begin with, there was some sort of novelty value in not having to set an alarm, but it soon wore off and she would lie awake, fretting, into the night. Of course she could pay off some of her mortgage with the redundancy money, that would keep the wolves at bay for a while, but it didn't solve the fundamental problem of what the hell she was going to do with her life now. And the Situations Vacant looked absolutely hopeless: full of fields she knew nothing about or entry-level jobs that she was too old for and frankly wouldn't keep her in Starbucks. Nobody in property seemed to be hiring, and Issy knew that when they did, they would have a huge pool of redundant specialists to choose from. Good people too.

Helena and Gramps were encouraging, telling her to keep her head up, that something would turn up, but it didn't feel like that to Issy. She felt untethered, rootless, liable to spin off at any moment (not entirely helped by people saying things like "Why don't you take a year off and travel the world?" as if her presence was entirely unnecessary). It took her all day to get to the newsagent's to buy a paper and some Smarties (little buttons of candy-covered chocolate) to make a Smartie cake. She found herself sculpting sad people out of icing, little sugar flowers with spots of rot appearing. It wasn't good. She didn't want to do anything: leave the house, play Scrabble with Gramps. And no Graeme, of course. That stung too, horribly. Issy was realizing she had had more invested in this relationship than she'd ever let herself think.

• • • •

Helena felt bad too. Obviously she hated to see her friend sad—apart from anything else, it meant she didn't have her best mate to go out and have a laugh with—but she was fundamentally a generous soul and understood Issy had to grieve for what she had lost. It was tough in the flat though; all through the miserable days of January and February, it was horrible coming home to a dark, unheated house, with Issy cloistered in her bedroom, refusing to change out of her pajamas. The flat had always been such a haven, mostly because Issy made it so, made it comforting and warm and always with something to nibble or taste. After some harrowing days at work, all Helena wanted was to curl up on the sofa with a cup of tea and a slice of one of Issy's experiments so they could have a good gossip. She missed it. So it was with selfish motives in mind too that she decided it couldn't go on and that Issy needed a stern dose of tough love.

Tough love she could do, thought Helena, dabbing on moisturizer one morning. Real love, that wasn't exactly falling into her lap right now, but, she told herself firmly, she didn't have time to worry about it. Dressed in a plum velvet top that made her look, she felt, pleasingly gothic, she marched into the sitting room. Issy was sitting in the gloomy light, eating dry Crunchy Nut Cornflakes out of a bowl in her pig pajamas.

"Darling. You have to get out of the flat."

"This is my flat though."

"I mean it. You have to do something; otherwise, you'll turn into one of those shut-ins who sit in their bedrooms in their pajamas weeping and eating beef curry."

Issy stuck out her bottom lip. "I don't see why."

"Because you've put on two pounds in a week?"

"Oh, thanks."

"I mean, why don't you volunteer for a charity or something?"

Issy gave her a hard stare.

"How is this meant to make me feel better exactly?"

"It's not about making you feel better. It's about being a friend to you right now, the kind of friend you need."

"A nasty one."

"The best you're going to get, I'm afraid."

Helena glanced at the pink-striped see-through plastic bag beside Issy, filled with Smarties.

"Have you been *out*? Did you go to the corner shop?"

Issy shrugged, embarrassed.

"You went to the corner shop in your pajamas?"

"Hmmm."

"But what if you'd bumped into John Cusack, hmmm? What if John Cusack had been standing right there, thinking, I'm sick of all these Hollywood actresses, why can't I find a real girl with real home values? Who can bake? Someone like her, only not wearing her pajamas, because obviously that makes her a *crazy person*."

Issy swallowed. Behave like you might meet John Cusack at any minute was a prevailing mantra of Helena's and had been since 1986, which was why she never went out without her hair and makeup done absolutely perfectly, dressed in her best. Issy knew better than to dispute it.

Helena looked at her. "Graeme hasn't called, I take it?"

Of course, they both knew he hadn't. It wasn't just about the job. But for Issy, it hurt so much to own up to the truth. That actually what she had thought was love and real and something special might just, when all was said and done…might just have been a stupid office romance after all. It was awful, unbearable to think about. She was getting no sleep, next to no sleep. How could she have been so stupid? All that time, when she thought she was so professional, coming into work every day in her little dresses and cardigans and smart shoes, thinking she was keeping her private life so separate, thinking she was being so clever. When in fact everyone was sniggering because she was shagging the boss—and worse, it obviously wasn't even a serious relationship. That thought made her bite her own fist in anguish. And that nobody even thought she was any good at her job, she was just some cheery idiot who could make cakes. Oh God, that was almost worse. Or just as bad. It was all bad. It was awful. There didn't seem to be the least point in getting out of her pajamas. Everything was shit, and that was the end of it.

Helena reckoned there was patience, then there was submission.

"Well, fuck 'im," she heard herself saying. "So what, your life is over now because your boss no longer requires personal services?"

"It wasn't like that," said Issy quietly. It hadn't been, had it? She tried to think of some moments of tenderness, some sweetness or kindness he'd done for her. Some flowers maybe, or a trip away. Annoyingly, in eight months, all that came to mind was him telling her not to come over one night, he was tired from work, or getting her to help him file his management reports. (She'd been so pleased, she recalled, to be able to take some of the strain off him; exactly, she thought, why she'd make him a perfect wife. Oh God, what an idiot!)

"Well, whatever it was like," said Helena, "it's been weeks, and frankly, you've done enough wallowing in your pit. It's time to get out and claim the world again."

"I'm not sure the world wants me," said Issy.

"Well, that is total bullshit, and you know it," said Helena. "Do you want me to start again on my Poor Souls list?"

Helena's Poor Souls list was a record of terrible cases she saw in A&E—the genuinely neglected, the genuinely abandoned: the children who had never been loved, the youngsters who had never heard a kind word in their lives, leaving the National Health Service to pick up the pieces. It was unbearable to hear, and Helena only ever used it as an argument winner in really desperate cases. It was a cruel trick to play now.

"No!" said Issy. "No. Please. Anything but that. I can't hear about the orphan with leukemia one more time. Please don't."

"I'm warning you," said Helena. "You count your blessings or else. And while you're doing that, move your fat arse and go and do that redundancy course they promised to send you on. At least it'll get you out of bed before noon."

"One, my arse is half the size of yours."

"Yes, but I'm in proportion," Helena explained patiently.

"And two, I only sleep late because I can't sleep at night."

"Because you sleep all day."

"No. Because I'm depressed."

"You're not depressed. You're slightly sad. Depressed is when you're a new arrival in this country and someone confiscated your passport and forced you into prostitution, and—"

"*La la la la!*" sang Issy. "Stop it, please. I'll go, OK? I'll go! I'll go!"

● ● ● ●

Four days, a haircut, and some ironing later, Issy stood back at her regular bus stop, feeling like an imposter. Linda was interested to see her; Issy hadn't seen her before she left, and Linda had grown worried over the weeks, then thought maybe she'd got a nice car or moved in with that sulky-looking man who picked her up from time to time. Something good anyway.

"Did you go on a nice long holiday? Ooh, how lovely to get away in the winter; it is dreadful."

"No," said Issy sadly. "I got made redundant."

"Oh," said Linda. "Oh dear. I am very sorry to hear that, dear, very sorry. Still, you young folk; you'll find something else in five minutes, won't you?"

Linda was proud of her podiatrist daughter. No chance of Leanne being out of work, as she often said, "as long as people have feet." It took a lot to make Issy wish she'd been a podiatrist, but this was turning into one of those days.

"I hope so," said Issy. "I hope so."

Her attention was distracted by someone behind her. She glanced around. It was the tall blond lady again, at the deserted pink shop. She was trailing along behind the same slightly defeated-looking estate agent.

"I'm just not sure the feng shui is going to work, Des," she was saying. "And when you're trying to give people a holistic body experience, it's really, really important, do you understand?"

No it's not, thought Issy mutinously. It's important that you put your oven in the right damn place so you can run the rest of the shop. She thought of Grampa Joe. She must get up to visit him, she really must. It was unforgivable having this time off and not making the effort.

"Get the smell right, give 'em a smile, be where you can see them," he would say. "And give them the best damn cakes in Manchester, that's important too."

She inched over yet again so she could hear what the woman was saying.

"And twelve hundred a month," Issy heard. "It's far too much. I'm going to be using the best quality vegetables in town. People need raw vegetables, and they're going to learn it from me."

The woman was wearing tight leather trousers. Her stomach was so flat it looked like she lived on thin air. Her face was a peculiar mix of very smooth skin and wrinkly bits, presumably where the Botox was wearing off.

"Everything organic!" she trilled. "People don't want nasty chemicals in their bodies!"

Apart from their foreheads, thought Issy. She wondered why she had taken such a dislike to this woman. Why should she care that the woman was going to have a silly raw juice café in her little shop? She meant, Issy corrected herself, the little shop. The little hidden shop, in the little secret square that never seemed as loved and cared for as it should be. Of course, she knew, knew completely that having a shop that was hard to find and tucked away was far from ideal. Very.

Something struck her. She was used to working in commercial property where space went for fifty or sixty pounds a square foot. She eyed up the shop. Plus there was a basement, the sign said, which doubled the space straightaway. Issy did some quick calculations in her head. That made it about fourteen pounds a square foot. OK, obviously this was in a London suburb, and not entirely a posh one at that. But still, twelve hundred a month—say eleven hundred if the woman was right and could negotiate a discount, which in this market she should be able to. If she could take out a six-month lease on that to do…well, to do something. To bake, maybe. Now she didn't have an office to offload her experiments on; her freezer was filling up, and she was running out of storage. Just last night, a particularly fine peanut butter and Nutella cookie recipe she'd invented had overflowed her very last Cath Kidston cookie tin. She'd had to eat her way out.

Issy closed her eyes as the bus came around the corner. That was ridiculous. There were millions of things involved in working with food, not just taking on a rent. There was health and safety, and food hygiene, and inspections and hairnets and rubber gloves and standards and employment law, and it was completely impossible, and stupid, and she didn't even want to work in a café.

Linda nodded over to the woman standing outside the shop, who was pontificating loudly on the benefits of beetroot.

"I don't know what she's going on about," she said as they boarded the 73 together. "All I ever want in the morning is a nice cup of coffee."

"Hmmm," said Issy.

• • • •

The redundancy course, although it wasn't called that anymore than it was called the "spat-out old losers club," was held in a long conference room in a nondescript building off Oxford Street in full view of the Forever 21 flagship store at Oxford Circus. Issy thought this was very unfair in the scheme of things, a tantalizing glimpse of a life now out of reach.

There were about a dozen people in the room, from the bullish and sulky-looking, who gave the impression they'd been sent on this course as a kind of detention, to the utterly terrified, to one man who was digging in his briefcase and smoothing down his tie in a manner that made Issy suspect that he hadn't told his family he'd been made redundant and was still pretending to go to work every day. She half grimaced around at everyone. Nobody made a friendly face back. Life was always easier, reflected Issy, when you were carrying a large Tupperware full of cakes. Everyone was happy to see you then.

A woman in her fifties with a tired, impatient face arrived on the button of 9:30, launching into her spiel so briskly that it rapidly became clear that the only people overworked in the current climate were redundancy resettlement trainers.

"Now, starting your positive *new life*," she announced, "the first thing you must do is treat job hunting as a job in itself."

"Even shittier than the one you've just been ousted from," said one of the young men with a belligerent sneer. The trainer ignored him.

"Firstly, you have to make your CV stand out from the two million CVs circulating at any one time."

The trainer spread her lips in what Issy supposed was meant to be a smile.

"And that's not an exaggeration. That is the approximate number of CVs being submitted for available vacancies at any given time."

"Well, I'm feeling empowered already," muttered the girl sitting next to Issy. Issy glanced at her. She was glamorous and perhaps slightly overdressed—with jet-black ringlets, bright red lipstick, and a fuchsia mohair jumper that totally failed to conceal massive bosoms underneath. Issy wondered if she'd get on with Helena.

"So how do you make yours stand out? Anyone?"

One of the older men raised his hand.

"Is it acceptable to lie about your age?"

The trainer shook her head severely.

"It is *never*, under *any* circumstances, permitted to lie on your CV."

The girl next to Issy put her hand up immediately.

"But that's just stupid. Everyone lies on their CV. And everyone assumes that everyone else lies on their CV. So if you don't lie on your CV, they'll assume you have so that you're in fact even worse than you've just said you are, plus if they find out you haven't told a single lie on your CV, they'll assume you're a bit stupid. So it's a bad idea."

There was a lot of nodding from around the table. The trainer ploughed on regardless.

"So, you need to stand out. Some people like to use raised fonts or even write their CVs in rhyme to give them that extra edge."

Issy raised her hand.

"Can I just say that I've been hiring staff for years, and I hated gimmicky CVs; I always threw them in the bin. Whereas if I got one with no spelling mistakes, I'd interview them immediately. Hardly ever happened though."

"Did you assume they were lying on them?" asked the girl.

"Well, I'd mentally downgrade all their A-level results and their degree class, and I wouldn't press them too much on their love of independent film," said Issy. "So, yes, I suppose so."

"There you go," said the girl. The trainer had gone pink and tight-lipped.

"Well, you can talk all you like," said the trainer. "But it's still all of you who are sitting here."

• • • •

At lunchtime Issy and the ringleted girl fled. "That was the most hideous thing *ever*," said the girl, whose name was Pearl. "It was actually worse than getting the boot."

Issy smiled gratefully. "I know." She looked around. "Where are you going for lunch? I was thinking Patisserie Valerie."

Patisserie Valerie was a long-established fancy-cakes-and-tea chain in London, which was always crowded and always a delight. They had a new vanilla icing she'd heard about that she was anxious to try. The girl looked a bit uncomfortable, and Issy immediately remembered how pricey it was.

"Uh, my treat," she added quickly. "My redundancy payment is not bad, thank goodness."

Pearl smiled and wondered if she could make the sandwiches in her bag last till later. "OK!" she said. She had always wanted to try the shop, with its fantastical-looking wedding cakes with icing spun out of impossibly small sugar roses and dramatically iced risers in the window, but it always seemed crowded and busy and hard to squeeze into, which made it the kind of place she normally avoided.

Ensconced in a tiny wooden booth, with black-clad French waitresses maneuvering tarte au citron and millefeuille expertly over their heads, they swapped horror stories. Pearl had been the receptionist at a building firm where things had gotten gradually worse and worse. She hadn't even been paid for the last two months and, seeing as she was raising a baby single-handed, things were getting slightly desperate.

"I thought this might help," she said. "My Restart sent me here. But it's just rubbish, isn't it?"

Issy nodded. "I think so."

Nonetheless, Pearl stood up boldly and squeezed her way over to the manager of the shop.

"Excuse me, do you have any vacancies?"

"I'm very sorry," said the man charmingly. "No. Plus, you see, we are a small shop."

He indicated the tiny tables, all pressed very close together. The lithe waitresses were hopping in among them. Pearl, frankly, wouldn't have a chance.

"You know, I am very sorry."

"Oh God," she said. "You're absolutely right. I am too fat to work in a cake shop. *And* I'd make them feel so guilty they'd order the salad."

Completely unbowed, she returned to Issy, who had spent the previous three minutes blushing hideously on Pearl's behalf.

"That's exactly what the budget airline said. I'm not allowed to be wider than the aisle."

"You're not wider than an aircraft aisle!"

"I will be on the new planes they're bringing in. Everyone has to stand up in them, packed in like cattle. They put a belt around your neck and attach you to the wall."

"I'm sure that's not true," said Issy.

"It's true," said Pearl. "Trust me. As soon as the belts stop decapitating the crash test dummies, you'll be standing all the way to Malaga. On one leg if you forget to print out your boarding pass before you get to the airport."

"Well, I'm never having a holiday ever again, so that scarcely matters," said Issy. Then she realized she was using a ludicrously self-pitying tone in front of someone who rented a flat that she shared with her baby and, it seemed, her mother, and changed the subject.

"Shall we get back?"

Pearl sighed. "Well, it's either that or a shopping spree down Bond Street and a quick stop into Tiffany's."

Issy smiled wanly. "Well, at least we got cake."

"We did," said Pearl.

5

peppermint creams

• • • •

For you, as sweet as you are.

* 1 egg white
* 2 cups icing sugar
* peppermint essence

Beat the egg white until frothy—do not overbeat. No, that is just enough. Perfect. Stop now.

Sieve in the icing sugar and now the mixture should be stiff. Yes, there is a lot of icing sugar on the floor. Don't worry about that now. Don't stand in it. Don't…OK, your mother is going to have a fit.

Right, just a couple of drops of peppermint essence…just a couple, otherwise it'll taste like toothpaste.

OK, are your hands clean? Now, make it into paste—yes, like play dough. No, you can't eat play dough. Now, we're going to roll it out and you can cut out circles. Well, yes, or I suppose you can have animal shapes…a peppermint cream horsy, that's fine. Oh, a dinosaur? Well, yes, I don't see why not…There we are. Now we have to put them in the fridge for 24 hours.

Well, no, I suppose we could test just one.

> Well, I suppose they don't all have to go in the fridge. Or, no,
> any of them.
>
> Love, Gramps

I f Issy shut her eyes, she could smell the sweet peppermint creams,
melting on her tongue.

"Come on," Helena was berating her.

"I am a brave person," Issy was trying to say in the mirror, brushing
her teeth.

"That's right," said Helena. "Do it again."

"Oh *God*," said Issy. She was about to spend the day marching cold
into estate agencies and asking for work. She thought she was about
to throw up.

"I am a brave person."

"You are."

"I can do this."

"You can."

"I can handle inevitable repeated rejection."

"That's going to be useful."

Issy turned around. "It's all right for you, Len. The world is always
crying out for nurses. They're hardly going to start closing all the hospitals."

"Yeah, yeah, yeah," said Helena. "Shut up."

"You'll see," said Issy. "One day they'll get robots to do it all and
then you'll be out of a job and sorry you weren't more sympathetic to
me, your best friend."

"This is better than sympathetic!" retorted Helena, stung. "This
is *useful*!"

Issy was starting near the flat. If she could find a job within walking
distance, so much the better. No more wet bloody mornings standing
outside Pear Tree Court and forcing her way onto the 73—well, at
least that was a nice thought.

The door to Joe Golden Estates pinged as Issy went in, her heart in her mouth. She reminded herself she was a calm professional, with experience in the property trade. There was only one man in the office, the same distracted-looking balding chap who had been showing that woman around the shop.

"Hello!" said Issy, too surprised to remember why she was there. "Aren't you renting Pear Tree Court?"

The man peered up at her with a wary look in his eyes.

"Trying to," he said gruffly. "Bit of a bloody nightmare."

"Why?"

"Doesn't matter," he said, suddenly remembering where he was and switching into salesman mode. "It's a fabulous property, so much character and loads of potential."

"Hasn't every business that's gone in there failed miserably?"

"Well, that's because…that's because they're not approaching it the right way."

I will make friends with him, *then* ask him for a job, Issy told herself. I will ask him for a job…shortly. Soon. In a bit. Yes.

But what actually came out of Issy's mouth was, "I couldn't take a look at it, could I?"

●　●　●　●

Des, of Joe Golden Estates, was sick of his job. He was sick of his life, if he was being honest. He was tired of the market, tired of being on his own in an empty office, tired of endless to-ing and fro-ing with this stupid Pear Tree Court property as one person after another thought they could make a go of it, when, pretty as it was, it remained a commercial property that didn't actually face a road. People got dreams in their heads that were nothing to do with business. This looked like another one.

Then he had to go home and sympathize with his wife. It wasn't that he didn't adore their baby, it wasn't that at all; it was just he did need a night's sleep now and again, and he was sure that everyone else's baby wasn't still waking up four times a night at five months. Maybe Jamie was sensitive. It still didn't explain why Ems hadn't gotten out of her pajamas since the birth. It had been a while now. But if he ever mentioned anything, she started screaming at him that he didn't understand what it was like to have a baby, then Jamie would start screaming, plus her mother was usually over, sitting in his spot on the sofa, badmouthing him, he suspected. Then it would all get so noisy he'd wish himself back at work again for five minutes' peace and quiet. He hadn't the faintest idea what to do.

For the first time in what felt like weeks, Issy sensed a tiny flame of curiosity spark inside her. As Des somewhat reluctantly opened up the heavy door with three different keys, she glanced around, just in case the scary blond lady was behind her somewhere, and would scream at her to get the hell out of her shop.

Because she could see at once that while there were all sorts of problems with it (no road frontage being only the most glaringly obvious), 4 Pear Tree Court had a lot of plus points too.

The large glass window faced west, which would let plenty of sunlight into the shop in the afternoon, making it a nice place to come and sit and linger over coffee and a cake when business typically was quieter. Issy tried not to let her imagination run away with itself. Although the alley had rubbish and a stray bicycle skeleton in it, it also had cobbles and, although it was as unhealthy, stunted, and metropolitan a specimen as one could hope to find anywhere, there was a real live tree next to the ironmonger's. A real live tree. That was something too. Once you were inside the court, the noise from the traffic seemed to fade away; it was as if you were stepping back to a quieter, gentler time. The little row of shops was higgledy-piggledy and jammed together and looked a little like something out of Hogwarts, and number 4, with its low wooden doorway, odd angles, and ancient fireplace, was the sweetest of them all.

The frontage had been left dusty and uncared for, with pieces of old shelving strewn everywhere, along with mail for previous owners from yoga retreats, fair trade children's clothing manufacturers, homeopathic societies, and the local council. Issy waded through them.

"Oh yes, I should probably have moved those," murmured Des, looking slightly embarrassed. You should have, thought Issy. If one of KD's agents showed a property like that…Mind you, he did seem very tired.

"Things busy in your line of work these days?" she asked nonchalantly. Des looked down, stifling a yawn.

"Hmmm," he said. "They just repossessed our snazzy little cars."

"The little Minis with the rock bands stenciled on them?" asked Issy in horror. They were a staple of bad London parking.

Des nodded. His wife had been furious.

"But apart from that, amazing," he said, trying to pull it back together. "In fact, I've just taken an offer on this place, so if you wanted it you'd have to be quick."

Issy narrowed her eyes.

"Why are you showing it to me if someone else has already offered on it?"

Des cringed. "Well, you know. Want to keep the market buoyant. And I'm not sure if it'll go through."

Issy thought about the blond woman. She'd seemed very sure.

"The client is, ahem, just going through some 'personal issues,'" said Des. "And we do often find that an initial burst of enthusiasm for new ventures can…ahem, tail off when the settlement comes through. One way or the other."

Issy raised her eyebrows.

"And what were you thinking of doing with it?" asked Des. "It has B/C/D permission."

She looked around. She could visualize the whole thing—little mismatched tables and chairs, a bookshelf where people could bring books to exchange, the lovely low-slung glass catering desk where she could array her cupcakes in different flavors and pretty pastels, making sure there were cake stands in the windows to tempt people in off the road. Making up little gift presentation boxes for parties, maybe even weddings…could she cater on such a level, though? That was huge. Mind you, if she took someone on…

Issy realized through her reverie that Des was waiting for an answer.

"Oh, I was thinking a little café," she said, feeling her ever-present blush rising to the surface. "Just something small."

"Oh, that's a great idea!" said Des enthusiastically.

Issy felt her heart leap. It couldn't…she couldn't really be serious about this, could she? Although, here she was…

"Sausage sandwich and a cup of tea for a pound fifty. Perfect for around here. All the builders and commuters and council workers and nannies and that. Scone and jam a pound."

His face had become quite animated.

"Actually, I was thinking more…a kind of bakery place," she said. Des's face fell.

"Oh," he said. "One of those poncey joints where they charge two fifty for a cup of coffee."

"Well, there'd be delicious cakes," said Issy.

"Yeah, whatever," said Des. "Actually the other bidder wants to open a café too, just like that."

Issy thought back to the blond woman. Hers would be nothing like that! she thought indignantly. Hers would be warm, and inviting, and cozy and indulgent and somewhere to come and enjoy yourself, not somewhere to come and feel like you were atoning for bad behavior. Hers would be a lovely focal point for the community, not for people to neck raw carrots while typing on their BlackBerries. Yeah. Exactly!

"I'll take it!" she said suddenly. The agent looked at her in surprise.

"Don't you want to know how much it is?" he asked.

"Oh yes, of course," said Issy, suddenly totally flustered. What on earth was she thinking? She wasn't qualified to run a business! How could she manage? All she could do was bake cakes, and that would never be enough, surely. Although how, a little voice inside her said, how will you ever know unless you try? And wouldn't you like to be your own boss? And have your lovely cleaned-up, gorgeous local café in this perfect spot? And have people come from far and wide to taste your cupcakes and sit and relax for half an hour, read the paper, buy a gift, enjoy a little bit of peace and quiet? Wouldn't that be a nice thing to do every day: sweeten people's lives, give them a smile, feed them? Wasn't that what she did in her life anyway; didn't it make sense to take it to the next level? Didn't it? Now she had this once-in-a-lifetime cash, this once-in-a-lifetime opportunity?

"Sorry, sorry," she said, confused. "I'm jumping way ahead of the gun. Can I just have a brochure?"

"Hmmm," said Des. "Have you just got divorced by any chance?"

"I wish," said Issy.

• • • •

She studied the brochure for hours and hours. She downloaded forms from the Internet, tried working out some rough costings on the backs of envelopes. She spoke to a small business adviser and wondered about a cash-and-carry card. Issy felt so excited she couldn't contain it. She hadn't felt this alive in years. At the back of her mind, all she could hear was one thing: I could do this. I could really do this. What was stopping her?

• • • •

The following Saturday, Issy made good use of the slow bus up to Gramps's home; she worked on some calculations and schedules in her newly purchased notebook and felt a little rising bubble of excitement. No. She mustn't. It was a daft idea. Although, after all, when else was she going to have the chance to do something like this? On the other hand, would it be a total disaster? What would make her different from everyone else who had gone into that space and failed miserably?

The Oaks was an austere ex-stately home. The organization had done its best to keep some kind of a homey feel—the baronial hall remained intact. There had been money left over when Gramps had sold his bakeries and Helena had recommended the Oaks as the best of its kind. But still. There were handrails; the industrial cleaning scent; the wing-backed chairs. It was what it was.

Taking Issy up, the plump young nurse called Keavie was as kind as usual, but seemed a little distracted. "What's up?" asked Issy.

Keavie fidgeted. "You should know," she said, "he's not having one of his better days."

Issy's heart sank. Since he'd arrived at the home, although it had taken him a couple of weeks to settle in, he'd seemed to adjust pretty well. The old ladies fussed around him nicely—there were hardly any men there—and he'd even enjoyed the art therapies. In fact, it was a young intense-looking therapist who'd convinced him to start writing down his recipes for Issy. And Issy was so happy to know he was warm and safe and comfortable and well fed. So to hear those words was chilling. Steeling herself, she popped her head around the door.

Joe was propped up in bed, a cold cup of tea by his side. Never a fat man, his weight, she noticed, had fallen away even further; his skin was beginning to sink and drop off his bones, as if it had somewhere better to be. He had kept his hair, though it looked now like fine white fluff on top of his head, oddly like a baby's. He was a baby now, Issy thought sadly. Without the joy, the anticipation, the wonder of a baby: just the feeding, the changing, the carrying around. But she loved him still. She kissed him fondly.

"Hi, Gramps," she said, "thanks for the recipes." She perched at the end of the bed. "I love getting them."

She did. Apart from Christmas cards, no one else had sent her a handwritten letter for about ten years. Email was great, but she did miss being excited by the post. That was probably why people did so much Internet shopping, she reckoned. So they had a parcel to look forward to.

Issy looked at her grampa. He'd had a funny turn before, just after he'd moved, and they'd put him on some new medication. He'd seemed to zone out a lot, but the staff had assured her that he could hear her talking and that it probably helped. At first she'd felt a complete idiot. Then she'd actually found it quite restful—a bit like therapy, she thought, probably. The kind where the therapist doesn't actually say anything, just nods their head and writes things down.

"*Anyway*," she found herself saying now—almost as if trying it out on her tongue, just to see what it sounded like—"I'm thinking of…I'm thinking of doing something new. Of opening a little café. People like little cafés these days. They're getting sick of the same old chains. Well, that's what I read in a Sunday magazine.

"My friends aren't actually being very helpful. Helena keeps telling me to think about VAT, even though she has absolutely no idea what VAT is. I think she's trying to be those scary guys off the telly that make fun of your business ideas, because she always says it in a really growly voice, then snorts like this"—she snorted—"when I say I hadn't thought about VAT, like she's a total millionaire mogul and I'm just some idiot, not fit to run a business.

"But all sorts of people run businesses, don't they, Gramps? Look at you, you did it for years."

She sighed.

"So obviously I remembered to ask you all the intelligent questions about it while you were still in a fit position to answer them. Gramps, *why* didn't I ask you about running a business? I'm such an idiot. Please help me."

Nothing. Issy sighed again.

"I mean, our local dry cleaner has the IQ of a balloon, and he runs his own business. It can't be that hard, can it? Helena reckons he can't look at himself in the mirror without seeing someone else who wants to pick a fight with him."

She smiled. "He is a terrible dry cleaner though.

"But when will I have the chance to do this again? What if I put all the money into my mortgage then don't find a job for eight months? I may as well…I mean, it will be like nothing ever happened. Or I could go around the world but, you know, I'd still be me when I got back. Except a bit older, with sun damage.

"Whereas this…I mean, there's tax and red tape and health and safety and food standards and hygiene practice and fire regulations. It's doing it the way you want it, subject to an incredibly narrow pre-scribed range of things that are actually allowed…It's probably the stupidest thing I've ever thought of, totally doomed to fail, bankrupt me, all of that."

Issy looked out of the window. It was a cold, clear day; the grounds of the home were beautiful. She saw an old lady, bent over, gardening in a tiny flower bed. She was completely engrossed in what she was doing. A nurse came past, checked she was all right, and then went on her way again.

Issy remembered coming home from school—her horrible modern comprehensive full of horrible girls who made fun of her frizzy hair— and making a strawberry tart from scratch, pastry as light as air, and the glaze as fine and sweet as fairies' breath. Gramps had sat down in silence with a fork and not uttered a word as he savored every bite, slowly, and she stood at the end of their terraced kitchen, at the tiny back door, hands clasped over the front of her now far too small apron. When he had finished, he had put down his fork carefully, reverently. Then he had looked at her.

"You, love," he had said deliberately. "You are a born baker."

"Don't talk crap," her mother had said, who was home that autumn, doing a course to become a yoga teacher that she never finished. "Issy's got brains! She's going to go to college, get a proper job, not one where she has to get up in the middle of the night for the rest of her life. I want her in a nice office, keeping warm and clean. Not covered head to toe in flour, passed out from exhaustion in a chair every night at six p.m."

Issy barely listened to her mother. But her heart was aflame with her grandfather's praise, rarely bestowed. In her darker moments, she did wonder sometimes if any man would ever love her as much as her gramps did.

"I mean, I've done so much admin in my life, I'm sure I'll figure it out...but when I saw Pear Tree Court, I just realized...I could have a shot. I could. I know I could. A chance to bake for people, to make them happy, to give them somewhere lovely to come—I know I could do it. You know how I can never get people to go home after parties?"

It was true, Issy was famously welcoming and a too-good host.

"I'm going to see if I can get a six-month lease. Not pump all my money into it. Just give it a shot to see if it can take off. Not risk everything."

Issy felt as if she was trying to talk herself out of it. Suddenly, startling her, her grampa sat up. Issy flinched as his watery blue eyes struggled to focus. She crossed her fingers that he would recognize her.

"Marian?" he said at first. Then his face cleared like the sun coming out. "Issy? Is that my Issy?"

Issy's heart lifted with relief.

"Yes!" she said. "Yes, it's me."

"Did you bring me some cake?" He leaned over confidentially. "This hotel is all right, but it has no cake."

Issy peered into her bag. "Of course! Look, I made Battenberg."

Joe smiled. "It's soft for when I don't have my teeth."

"It is."

"So what's with you, my darling?" He looked around. "I'm here on holiday, but it hasn't been terribly warm. It's not very warm."

"No," said Issy. It was boiling in the room. "I know. And you're not on holiday. You live here now."

Gramps looked around for a long time. Finally, she realized it was sinking in, and his face seemed to fall. She reached over and patted his hand, and he took it and changed the subject briskly.

"Well? What have you been doing? I would like a great-granddaughter, please."

"Nothing like that," said Issy. She decided to try her idea out loud again. "But...but...I've been thinking about opening a bakery."

Her grandfather's face broke open into a wide grin. He was delighted.

"Of *course* you are, Isabel!" he said, wheezing slightly. "I just can't believe it took you all this time!"

Issy smiled. "Well, I've been very busy."

"I suppose," said her grampa. "Well. I am pleased. I am very pleased. And I can help you. I should send you some recipes."

"You do that already," said Issy. "I'm using them."

"Good," said her grandfather. "That's good. Make sure you follow them properly."

"I'll do my best."

"I'll come down and help out. Oh yes. I'm fine. Totally fine. Don't worry about me."

Issy wished she could say the same about herself. She kissed her gramps good-bye.

"You always perk him up," said Keavie, walking her out of the door.

"I'll try and get up more often," said Issy.

Keavie sniffed. "Compared to most of the old folks in here," she said, "he's doing pretty bloody well by you."

"He's a nice chap," she added as Issy left. "We've got fond of him in here. When we can keep him out of the kitchen."

Issy smiled. "Thank you," she said. "Thank you for looking after him."

"That's our job," said Keavie, with the simplicity of someone who knew her vocation in life. Issy envied her.

• • • •

Emboldened, Issy marched back into her flat. It was a wet Saturday night and obviously she didn't have a date and Graeme hadn't called, that scuzz, and anyway he often didn't see her on Saturday nights because he'd be out with the lads or up early for squash, so it hardly mattered, she told herself, nevertheless conscious of how much she missed him. Well, she wasn't going to call him, that was for sure. He'd tossed her out on the street like garbage. Swallowing heavily, she went into the cozy sitting room to find Helena, who was another dateless wonder but never seemed to mind about it quite so much.

Helena did mind, of course, but didn't think it was particularly helpful to add to Issy's woes at this particular point in time. She didn't like being single at thirty-one any more than Issy did, but she didn't want to lard on the misery. Issy's face was tense enough already.

"I've made a decision," Issy announced. Helena raised her eyebrows.

"Go on then."

"I think I should go for it. For the café. My gramps thinks it's a great idea."

Helena smiled. "Well, I could have told you that."

Helena did think it was a good idea—she had no doubt about Issy's ability to bake the most delicious cakes, or the skills she'd bring to working with members of the public. She worried a little more about Issy handling the responsibility of her own business, and the paperwork, seeing as she'd rather watch *World's Goriest Operations* than open her own Visa bill. This bothered her a little. Still, anything at the moment was better than moping.

"Just for six months," said Issy, taking off her coat and going into the kitchen to make some chocolate-covered popcorn. "If it fails, I won't be bankrupt."

"Well, that's the spirit," said Helena. "Of course you won't fail! You'll be brill!"

Issy looked over at her. "But…"

"What?"

"It sounds like you want to put a 'but' in there."

"Then I shan't," said Helena. "Let's open some wine."

"Can we call someone?" said Issy. She had seen so little of her friends recently and had an inkling she was about to see a lot less. Helena raised her eyebrows.

"Well," she said. "There's Tobes and Trinida, moved to Brighton. Tom and Carla, thinking of moving. Janey, pregnant. Brian and Lana, got the children keeping them in."

"Oh yes," said Issy, sighing. She remembered when she and Helena and the gang had all met, back at college. Then they were all in and out of each other's houses, breakfast, lunch, dinners that lasted all night, weekends away. Now everyone was settling down, talking about IKEA and house prices and school fees and having "family time." There wasn't much popping in anymore. She didn't really like the sense that since they'd all turned thirty, there seemed to be two tracks opening up, like a railway line out of a junction; lines that had been parallel were now drawing inexorably farther apart.

"I shall open the wine anyway," said Helena firmly, "and we can make fun of the TV. What are you going to call it, by the way?"

"I don't know. I thought maybe Grampa Joe's."

"That makes it sound like a hot dog stand."

"Do you think?"

"Yes."

"Hmmm. The Stoke Newington Bakery?"

"There is one of those. It's that little place on Church Street that sells dusty Empire biscuits and jumbo sausage rolls."

"Oh."

"You're selling cupcakes, aren't you?"

"Definitely," said Issy, her eyes shining as the corn started popping in the pot. "Large and small. Because, you know, sometimes people don't want a great big cake; they want something tiny and delicious and delicate that tastes of rose petals, or a little lavender one that just explodes, or a tiny cupcake that tastes like a blueberry muffin and has a huge blueberry inside that bursts, and—"

"OK, OK," said Helena, laughing. "I get the picture. Well, why don't you just call it the Cupcake Café? Then people can say, 'Oh, you know, that place with all the cupcakes,' and they'll say, 'I can't remember what it's called,' and you can say, 'It's the Cupcake Café,' and everyone will say, 'Oh, yes, let's meet there.'"

Issy thought about it. It was simple and a bit obvious, but still, it felt right.

"I suppose," she said. "But lots of people don't even like cupcakes. How about the Cupcake and Other Things, Some Savory, Café?"

"Are you sure you're cut out for this?" said Helena, in a teasing voice.

"I have a head for business and a body for sin," said Issy. Then she glanced down at the popcorn on her lap. "Unfortunately, the sin appears to be gluttony."

• • • •

Des was trying to cope with what was supposedly colic but mostly meant Jamie arching his back and screaming to get away from him. His wife and his mother-in-law had gone to the spa for some "me" time when Issy rang, and at first he found it a little hard to concentrate. Oh yes, the impulsive one who was just wandering past. He hadn't really expected to hear from her again; he'd thought she was just killing time. Anyway, that other lady had called him too…Damn it! His train of thought was interrupted as Jamie gummed him hard on the thumb.

God, he knew babies weren't capable of being vindictive, but this baby in particular didn't seem to have gotten the memo.

"Oh right. Only that other woman's come back and made me a firm offer."

Issy felt an instant letdown. Oh no, surely not. She had a vision of her dream being dashed before it had even begun.

"I've got a few other places I can show you…"

"No!" said Issy. "It has to be that one! It has to be there!"

It was true, she had fallen in love.

"Well," said Des, sensing a win. "She did offer less than what the landlord was asking for."

"I'll make an offer too," pleaded Issy. "And I'll be a very good tenant."

Des jiggled Jamie up and down in front of the window. At last, the baby was giggling. He wasn't, thought Des, such a bad little chap really.

"Yes, that's what the last four people said," he replied. "And they all shut down within three months."

"Well, I'm different," said Issy. The baby laughed and warmed Des's mood.

"OK," he said. "Let me talk to Mr. Barstow."

Issy hung up, feeling slightly mollified. Helena went into her bedroom and brought out a bag.

"I was going to save this to give you as a proper gift-wrapped present," she said. "But I think you might need it now."

Issy opened it. It was a copy of *Running a Small Business for Dummies*.

"Thank you," she said.

Helena smiled. "You need all the help you can get."

"I know," said Issy. "But I've already got you."

6

lemon getting what you want cake

•　•　•　•

* ½ cup self-rising flour, sifted
* 1 tsp baking powder
* 8 tbsp softened butter
* ½ cup superfine sugar
* 2 large eggs
* grated zest of 1 lemon
* juice of 1 lemon

Icing
* ¼ cup icing sugar
* 2 tsp water
* 1 tsp lemon juice

Preheat oven to 325°F/gas mark 3. Grease loaf tin. Sift flour and baking powder, then add all the other ingredients and beat well, or use a handheld mixer. Spoon into loaf tin.

This is the important bit: Cook for twenty minutes. This is not quite long enough. The cake should be yellow, not brown, but not damp inside. Salmonella poisoning is rarely useful for getting what you want.

While the cake is still warm, apply icing. The icing should

react to the warm cake and separate slightly, oozing into the pores of the cake itself. It should appear almost translucent.

Now, for all intents and purposes, your cake will look like an ugly disaster. When people see your lemon cake they will feel sorry for you. They will sneer at your poor baking skills and take a piece because they feel sorry for you. Then they will taste the soft moist spongy flesh of your cake imbued with lemon icing. Their eyes will pop open with delight. And then, they will do anything you want.

Issy shook her head. Gramps seemed back on form. And actually, this wasn't such a bad idea. Lull everyone into a false sense of security then hit them with it. Just to show what she was capable of. She'd put some pretty spun-sugar things in as well, of course. She stared at her face in the mirror, trying to convince herself that she was shop management, run-your-own-business material. She could. Surely she could. Helena had to rap on the door.

"Are you doing pouty face?" she hollered.

"No," said Issy, remembering Helena's teasing when it used to take her two hours to get ready for dates out of nerves. "Kind of. No. This is worse than a date."

"Well, it is a date," said Helena. "You never know, the landlord might turn out to be cute."

Issy stuck her head around the door and made a frowny face.

"Stop it."

"What?"

"Let me get one disastrous area of my life sorted out at a time, OK?"

Helena shrugged. "Well, if you don't like him, pass him over to me."

• • • •

In the event, this was clearly not going to be necessary. By the time she headed out to meet Mr. Barstow, the landlord of Pear Tree Court, Helena had given her a quick pep talk. She would convince him with her level of organization and research. Or fell him with her secret-weapon Grampa cakes. They should have met near the property, but of course, Issy thought smugly, there were no coffee shops to sit down in, so they met in Des's office. Des had had a shocking night with Jamie. His wife was refusing to get up anymore, so he'd sat with the wee blighter as he howled his guts up, his face a furious red and his little chunky legs contracted up to his chest. Des stroked his hot brow, gave him Calpol and eventually, holding him close, soothed the little lad off to a wriggling, uncomfortable sleep. But he'd had two hours, max. He felt like death in a cup.

The blond woman was there, looking incredibly sleek and expensive in two-hundred-quid jeans, spiky heels and a ludicrously soft-looking leather jacket. Issy narrowed her eyes.

This woman didn't need to earn a living, surely. She probably spent more than Issy's old salary on highlights alone.

"Caroline Hanford," she said without smiling, extending a hand. "I don't know why we're having this meeting; I put my offer in first."

"And we've had a counteroffer," said Des, pouring repulsive sticky black coffee from a push-button machine into three cups, the first of which he gulped down like medicine. "And Mr. Barstow wanted us all to meet to discuss the offers in more detail."

"Didn't you used to have cafetières in here?" Caroline said briskly. She could do with a proper coffee; she hadn't been sleeping properly. Those homeopathic sleeping pills she'd bought at enormous expense didn't seem to be working as well as she'd been assured they would. She'd have to go and see Dr. Milton again soon. He was expensive too. She grimaced to think of it.

"Cutbacks," muttered Des.

"Well, anyway, I'll match the counteroffer," said Caroline, hardly bothering to look at Issy. "Whatever it is. I'm starting this business off on the right foot."

A short, bald man marched into the room and grunted at Des.

"This is Mr. Barstow," said Des unnecessarily.

Caroline let forth a very toothy grin, impatient for this to be over. "Hello," she said. "Can I call you Max?"

Mr. Barstow grunted, which didn't seem to indicate an answer one way or the other. Issy didn't think he looked like a Max at all.

"I'm here to offer you the best deal I can," said Caroline. "Thanks so much for agreeing to see me."

Hang on, Issy wanted to say. Don't you mean to say "see *us*"? Issy knew if Helena were there she would make some remark about this being business and tell her to get tough. Instead she just said, "Hello," then felt cross with herself for not being more assertive. She clasped her favorite cake tin—decorated with a Union Jack—to her side.

Mr. Barstow looked at both of them.

"I've got thirty-five properties in this city," he said in a strong London accent. "Bloody none of them have given me as much trouble as this one. It's been one damn lady thing after another."

Issy was taken aback by his bluntness, but Caroline looked totally unfazed. "Thirty-five?" she cooed. "Wow, you are successful."

"So I don't just care about the money," said Mr. Barstow. "I care about bloody not having someone move out without warning, leaving the back rent unpaid every bloody five minutes, do you understand?"

Both women nodded. Issy fingered her notes. She'd done research into what made a nice café and how a good bakery could add value to surrounding houses and hopefully how many cakes they'd sell every day. (Admittedly, she'd plucked this figure out of thin air, but pasted into a spreadsheet it looked quite good. This way of working had been reasonably successful in property management so she couldn't imagine things were much different in baking.) But before she could speak, Caroline opened up a tiny silver laptop she'd brought with her that Issy hadn't even noticed.

• • • •

Before Caroline had gotten married—to that shit—she'd been a senior marketing executive at a market research firm. She'd been great at her job. Then when the children had come along, it made much more sense to be the perfect corporate wife. She'd poured her energies into her children's extracurricular activities, volunteering for the school board and running the house like a military operation. Had it stopped him fannying about with that floozy in his press office? No, it bloody had not, she thought grimly, waiting for PowerPoint to load. She'd kept working out, eating healthily, rushed to get her figure back after Achilles and Hermia were born. Had he even noticed? He'd worked all hours, come home too exhausted to do much more than eat and fall asleep in front of *Newsnight*, and now appeared to be banging some twenty-five-year-old who didn't have fifteen cat costumes to make for the school play. Not that bitterness was attractive. Caroline bit her lip. She was good at her job. And this was going to be her new job, to get her out of the house a bit.

"I've prepared this presentation," she began. "Now. Extensive market research undertaken by me has shown that seventy-four percent of people say they find it hard to get their five a day, with a further sixty percent saying that if fresh fruit and vegetables were more readily and temptingly available, they'd be fifty-five percent more likely to up their vegetable intake..."

It was relentless. There were screeds of it. Caroline had gone in, out and around the houses. She had categorized the postcodes, designed the website, and sourced organic carrots being grown on an allotment on Hackney Marshes. Nobody was going to beat her on this.

"We'll source locally as much as possible, of course," she simpered. Mr. Barstow watched the entire presentation in silence.

"Now, have you any questions?" she said after twenty minutes, her look defiant. She knew she'd done well. She was going to show him. Start a hugely successful business and then he'd be sorry.

• • • •

Issy's insides had begun to shrink. A few days' Googling was definitely not up to scratch here. In fact, she couldn't give a presentation after that one, so immaculately researched and explained. She would look like a total idiot. Mr. Barstow looked Caroline up and down. She really was extremely impressive, thought Issy. She'd give it to her.

"So what you're saying...." he began. He still hadn't removed the sunglasses he'd been wearing when he came in, even though it was only February. "What you're saying is you're going to stand there all day, in an alleyway off the Albion Road, three hundred meters from Stoke Newington High Street, and try and push beetroot juice."

Caroline was unperturbed.

"I believe my extensive in-depth customer-based statistical analysis, commissioned from a leading marketing agency..."

"What about you?" said Mr. Barstow, pointing at Issy.

"Uh..." Suddenly all Issy's hastily gleaned knowledge seemed to fall straight out of her head. She knew nothing about retail, nothing about business, not really. This was sooo stupid. There was a long pause in the room as Issy searched her brain. Her mind had gone completely blank. This was a nightmare. Des raised his eyebrows. Caroline smirked nastily. She didn't know, though, thought Issy suddenly. They didn't know about her secret weapon.

"Um," said Issy. "I make cakes."

Mr. Barstow grunted.

"Oh yeah? Got any?"

Issy had been hoping for this. She opened the tin. As well as the lemon getting-what-you-want cake, which few could resist trying, she'd gone for a selection of cupcakes to show her range: white chocolate and fresh cloudberry (the acid of the cloudberry neutralized the overweening sweetness of the white chocolate if you got the balance right, which, after extensive experimentation last winter, Issy had, but it was very much a seasonal cupcake); cinnamon and orange peel, which tasted more Christmassy than Christmas cake; and a sweet, fresh, irresistible spring vanilla, decorated with tiny roses. She'd brought four of each.

She could see Caroline raising her eyebrows at the lemon cake, which looked cracked and messy. As she'd known he would, Mr. Barstow stuck a fat hairy hand in the box and took a piece, as well as a vanilla cupcake.

Before anyone else dared move, he took a bite out of each of them. Issy held her breath as he chewed, slowly and deliberately, his eyes closed as if he were a top wine taster at work. Finally he swallowed.

"All right," he said, pointing straight at her. "You. Don't muck it up, love."

Then he picked up his briefcase, turned around, and left the office.

• • • •

For Caroline, it felt like the final straw. Issy went from disliking her to feeling very sorry, particularly as Caroline would never even know that it was she who'd given Issy the idea in the first place.

"It's just, the kids are going to nursery and school now, and that shit's messing me about, and I just…I just don't know what to do with myself," she sobbed. "And I've got one of those big houses just behind the shop, and it would be perfect, and I thought I would show him. All my girlfriends said it would be great."

"That's brilliant," said Issy. "My friends keep telling me it's a terrible idea."

Caroline stared at her as if just realizing something. A thought struck her.

"Of course my friends lie all the time," she said. "They didn't even tell me the Bastard was having an affair, even though they all knew about it." Caroline swallowed painfully. "Do you know he takes her to lap dancing classes? With his own colleagues? On company expenses?" She let out a strangulated giggle. "Sorry. I'm so sorry. I'm not sure why I'm telling you this. Obviously I'm boring."

This was directed at Des, who'd just let out a huge yawn.

"No, no, not at all; colicky baby," stuttered Des. "I'm...I'm really sorry, Mrs. Hanford, I don't know what to say."

Caroline sighed. "Try saying, 'I'm a weasel estate agent who double-let the property.'"

"Uh, for legal reasons, I can't..."

"Would you like a cake?" said Issy, not sure what else to say.

Caroline snorted. "I don't eat cake! I haven't eaten cake in fourteen years."

"OK," said Issy. "Don't worry. Des, I'll leave a couple for you and take the rest home."

Caroline looked longingly at the tin.

"But the children might like them."

"When they get home from school," said Issy, agreeing. "But they have white sugar in them."

"He can pay the dental bills," snarled Caroline.

"OK," said Issy. "How many would they like?"

Caroline licked her lips. "They're...they're very greedy children."

Slightly discomfited, Issy passed over the whole tin.

"Thanks," said Caroline. "I'll...I'll bring the tin back to the shop, shall I?"

"Yes please," said Issy. "And...good luck with finding a venue."

"'Get a little job,' he said, 'to distract yourself.' Can you believe that's what he said to me? Can you believe it? The Bastard."

Issy patted her hand. "I'm sorry."

"Get a little bloody job. Bye, Desmond."

And Caroline banged the door on her way out.

Des and Issy looked at one another.

"Do you think she's scoffing them all in her Range Rover right now?" said Des.

"I'm worried about her," said Issy. "I think I need to make sure she's OK."

"I'm not sure she'd appreciate it," said Des. "I'll give it a couple of days and ring her."

"Will you?"

"Yes," Des said stoically. "And now, you and I have quite a lot of paperwork to go over."

Issy obediently followed him through to the back of the office.

"Did she really take that entire tin of cakes?" said Des sadly. He hadn't liked the look of the lemon cake, but the rest of it had seemed delicious.

"I'm sure I have a spare in tinfoil in my handbag," said Issy, who'd been saving it for a celebratory or commiserative treat, whichever was needed. "Would you like it?"

He did.

•   •   •   •

Issy arrived home with a bottle of champagne. Helena, who got back after her shift weary after stitching up a bottle-throwing incident that had gotten well out of control, suddenly perked up. "Oh my God!" she said. "You got it!"

"It was Gramps's cakes," said Issy with feeling. "I can't believe he's repaying me like this for putting him in a home."

"You didn't put him in a home," said Helena, exasperated to be having this conversation yet again. "You moved him somewhere safe and comfortable. What, you want him here, messing about with your Bosch oven?"

"No," said Issy, reluctantly, "but…"

Helena made an "enough" gesture with her hands. Sometimes it was very reassuring, Issy thought, that she was so bossy and knew her own mind.

"To Gramps," said Helena, raising her glass. "And to you! And the success of the Cupcake Café! Full of hot men. Do hot men go to cake shops?"

"Yes," said Issy. "With their husbands."

The two friends clinked glasses and hugged. Suddenly, Issy's phone rang. She moved to pick it up.

"Maybe it's your first customer," said Helena. "Or that scary-sounding landlord, calling to threaten to whack your kneecaps as a warning."

It was neither. Issy stared at the number on the phone, then pulled out a strand of her hair and wrapped it around her index finger, thinking. Watching the phone, almost, to see what it would do. Naturally, it rang again, startling her once more. Frozen, she slowly—so slowly, and yet the idea of a message being left was more than she could bear—reached out her hand. Helena caught her expression—half terror, half longing—just in time and wanted to reach out, stop her from answering the phone. With that odd sixth sense of close friends, she had known immediately who it would be. But it was too late.

"Graeme?" said Issy huskily.

• • • •

Mind you, reflected Helena, Issy had given her loads of good advice about Imran. And how long had it taken her to stop seeing him? Eighteen months. When he got married. She sighed.

"Babes, where have you been?" said Graeme, as if they'd last chatted about two hours ago and he'd been looking for her in a shopping center.

It had taken more from Graeme to make this phone call than Issy could know. At first he'd told himself that things would have come to an end anyway; he wasn't ready to settle down, it wasn't like they were serious or anything. And he had a lot of work to do.

But then, gradually, as the weeks had gone on and he hadn't heard from her, he'd felt an unfamiliar emotion. He missed her. Missed her gentleness, and her genuine interest in him and what he was doing; missed her cooking, obviously. He'd gone out with the lads, pulled a couple of really fit-looking birds, but when it came down to it...there was something about being with Issy that was just so easygoing. She didn't give him hassle, didn't nag his ear off or want to spend his money. He liked her. It was that simple. Although normally he didn't like to look back in his life, he decided to give her a call. Just to see her. Sometimes after a long day she'd run him a bath and give him a massage. He'd like a bit of that too. And what had happened at the office...It was just business, wasn't it? She had to be let go, that was just how things were at the moment. She'd probably have another job by now anyway. He'd written her an amazing reference, a bit more than her admin skills deserved, and Cal Mehta had too. She'd be over it by now. By the time he picked up the phone, Graeme had managed to convince himself that it would all be cool.

Issy, deliberately not looking at her flatmate, got up and left the room, still carrying the phone. It took her a long time to speak— so long, in fact, that Graeme had to say, "Hello? Hello? Are you still there?"

Over the last few weeks she had lain tossing and turning in bed; the shame and the pain of losing her job would then be overtaken by the misery and frustration of losing Graeme. It was unbearable. Awful. She hated him. She hated him. He had used her like some kind of stupid office perk.

But he hadn't, she heard herself say on one level. There had been something there. There had. Something real. He had told her things...

But had he just been saying those things to any willing ear? Was she a trustworthy place to dump stuff? Was it useful having a professional confidante who would also cook for you and sleep with you? Just handy for him on his way up the career ladder—after all, he was only thirty-five. He had years yet before he even had to think about settling down. And really, why would someone so handsome and successful be interested in her? Those were the 4:00 a.m. thoughts, when she felt so worthless and inadequate that it was almost funny. Not funny, but almost.

And now the café coming along—that had seemed providential; perfect really. Something good and concrete she could pour her energies into; a new door into a new life. A way to leave all her old worries behind her. Start afresh.

"You still there?"

She panicked. Should she play it cool, pretend she'd hardly been thinking about him—when she had, compulsively? She remembered storming out of the office in that huge fit of pique. She remembered some of the more, ahem, inappropriate toasts she'd made about him at her leaving bash. How for the first few days she was sure he'd ring, sure of it, say he'd made a terrible mistake and that he loved her and please could she come back, life was crap without her. Then those days had turned into weeks and over a month and she had a new course now, finally, and there was no going back...

"Hello?" she said finally, her voice coming out like a strangled whisper.

"Can you talk?" said Graeme. This riled her for some reason. What on earth did he think she was doing?

"Not really," she said. "I'm in bed with George Clooney, and he's just gone off to open a fresh bottle of champagne to top up the Jacuzzi."

Graeme laughed. "Oh, Issy, I have missed you."

Issy felt, out of nowhere, a sob hit her throat and desperately tried to gulp it back down. He hadn't missed her! He hadn't bloody missed her! Because if he'd thought about her at all, for one tiny second, he'd have realized the one single solitary time she needed him more than anything or anyone in the world had been after she'd lost her job; her boyfriend; her entire life. After he had decided that she should lose her job. And he hadn't given a shit.

"No you haven't," she managed finally. "Course you bloody haven't. Now you've got rid of me and everything."

Graeme sighed. "I didn't think you'd be like this."

Issy bit down on her lip. "As opposed to what—grateful?"

"Yes, well, you know. Maybe a bit. Grateful to be given the opportunity to go out and do a bit more with your life. You know you're capable, Issy. And anyway, how could I have contacted you before? It would have been completely inappropriate; you must understand that."

Issy didn't say anything. She didn't want him to think he was sounding reasonable.

"Look," he said honestly. "I've been thinking about you a lot."

"Have you really? When you just dumped my job and then dumped me?"

"I didn't dump you!" said Graeme, sounding exasperated. "Your job disappeared. Everyone's job was at risk! And I was trying to protect you from the fact that you and I had a personal relationship, then you went and shouted about it all over the office! That was really embarrassing to me, Issy."

"They all knew about it anyway," said Issy sulkily.

"Well, that's not the point. You yelled about it in front of everyone and made some pretty off-color remarks down the pub, from what I heard."

There is *no* loyalty in offices, thought Issy crossly.

"So why are you calling me now then?" she asked.

Graeme's voice went soft.

"Well, I just wanted to see how you were. What, you think I'm a complete bastard?"

Was it possible? Issy wondered. Was it possible that she had gotten it wrong? After all, she had stormed out of his office, shouting. Maybe she wasn't the only injured party here. Maybe he'd been as shocked and upset as she was. Maybe it had taken quite a lot of guts for him to make this phone call. Maybe he wasn't the arse; maybe he was still— you know—the one.

"Well…" she said. Just at that moment, Helena marched into her room without knocking. She was carrying a hastily erected sign, scrawled on the back of a council tax reminder. In big black letters was written "*NO!*"

Helena punched her fists in the air like they were at a demonstration, mouthing *No! No! No!* very ferociously in her direction. Issy tried to wave her away, but she just advanced even more. Helena was reaching out a hand to grab the phone.

"Shoo!" said Issy. "Shoo!"

"What's that?" said Graeme.

"Oh, it's just my flatmate," said Issy. "Sorry."

"What, the large one?"

Unfortunately Graeme's carrying voice came right over the phone.

"*Right!*" said Helena and made a lunge for the telephone.

"No!" shrieked Issy. "It's fine. I'm fine. I don't need saving, OK. But we do need to talk. So would you mind pissing off for five minutes and giving us some privacy?"

She stared hard at Helena until she retreated back to the sitting room.

"Sorry about that," Issy said finally to Graeme. But he sounded much perkier.

"Are we fine? We're fine," he said, sounding relieved. "Oh good. That's great." There was a pause. "Want to come over?"

"*No!*" said Issy.

• • • •

"You're not going," said Helena, standing in the doorway with her arms folded, and giving Issy the look she gave drunks who turned up bleeding from the head at 1:30 a.m. on a Saturday. "You're not."

"It was a misunderstanding," said Issy. "He's been feeling terrible too."

"So terrible he lost his phone for weeks and weeks," said Helena. "Issy, please. You're making a clean break."

"But Helena," said Issy, fired up. She had necked the glass of champagne as soon as she'd come off the phone and felt a warm glow through her whole body. He had called! He had called!

"He's…I mean…I mean, I really think Graeme might be the one."

"No. He's the boss you had a crush on and you're nearly thirty-two and in a panic."

"That…that's not it," said Issy, trying to get her point over. "It's not. You're not there, Helena."

"No, I'm not," said Helena. "I'm back here, nursing you through tearful nights or mopping you up when he's let you walk home in the rain again, or accompanying you to parties as your plus one because he doesn't want to be seen out and about with you."

"Well, that was because of the office," said Issy.

"Let's see, shall we?"

"I'm sure it'll be different now."

Helena gave her one of her looks.

"Well," said Issy defiantly, "I'm at least going to find out."

"I'm so glad he didn't even have to leave the comfort of his own living room," said Helena to the empty space after Issy had gone. Then she sighed. No one ever listened to good advice.

• • • •

Graeme had a bottle of champagne open too. His flat was, as ever, spotless and minimalist, a huge contrast to Issy's colorful, overloaded home. It was quiet and calm. Robin Thicke was playing on the expensive sound system, which Issy thought might be overdoing it a bit. On the other hand, she was wearing her best soft woolen gray dress and heels. And her Agent Provocateur perfume.

"Hey," he said as he opened the door—he lived in a rather smart newbuild, with carpeted corridors and flowers in the lobby. He was wearing a fresh white shirt, unbuttoned at the collar, with very dark stubble on his fine jaw. He looked tired, a little stressed—and utterly, utterly handsome and gorgeous. Issy couldn't help it. Her insides leaped for joy.

"Hey," she said.

"Thanks…thanks so much for coming over."

She looked nice, Graeme was thinking. Not hot, like those nightclub girls, with their skirts up to their bums and their great manes of long blond hair. They looked sexy, really hot…but sometimes, if he was to be totally honest with himself…sometimes they could look a bit terrifying. Issy on the other hand—she just looked nice. Comfortable. Pleasant to be with.

Issy knew she should have played it cool, planned for a lunch a few days away, given herself breathing space.

But she wasn't cool. She knew that. He knew that. There was no point beating about the bush any longer. Either he was in or he wasn't, and she didn't have months of pussyfooting about to figure out which.

He kissed her lightly on the cheek, and she smelled Fahrenheit, her favorite aftershave. He knew it was her favorite; he was wearing it for her.

She accepted a glass and sat down, perching on his imitation Le Corbusier black leather chair. It was like the first time she'd ever been back here, the mixture of fear and excitement, of being alone in this sleek apartment with this sensual, attractive man she fancied so much she could barely think straight.

"Here we are," he said. "It's funny not to be looking at you from over a desk."

"Yes. Losing the frisson?" said Issy, then wished she hadn't. This wasn't the time for flippant remarks.

"I have missed you, you know," said Graeme, looking directly at her from under his straight black brows. "I know…I think…maybe I took you for granted."

They both knew this was an understatement.

"You took me for granted," said Issy. "No maybe about it."

"OK, OK," said Graeme. He put his hand on her arm. "I'm sorry, OK?"

Issy shrugged. "Whatever."

"Issy, don't say 'whatever'; you're not twelve. If you're cross with me and want to say something, just come out with it."

Issy pouted a little. "I'm cross with you."

"And I'm sorry. It's this fucking job, you know that."

He tailed off. Issy realized suddenly that this was it, this was her moment to say, to ask: What am I to you? Truly? Where are we going? Because if this is back on, it needs to be serious. It really does. Because I am running out of time and I want to be with you.

It was the time to say it. She knew she was very unlikely to see Graeme in such a vulnerable state ever again. This was the time now, to put down the new ground rules of their relationship, to make him say it.

They sat in silence.

She didn't. She couldn't. Issy felt the old familiar blush steal over her face. Why was she such a coward? Why was she so scared? She would ask him. She would.

Graeme crossed the living room. Before Issy got the chance to open her mouth, he was right there in front of her, his eyes, his beautiful blue eyes focused right on her.

"Look at you," he said gruffly. "You're blushing. It's adorable."

As usual, having her blushing pointed out only made it worse. Issy opened her mouth to say something, but as she did so Graeme made a shushing motion, then moved forward very, very slowly and kissed her full and hard on the lips, the way she remembered; the way that had been haunting her dreams for weeks.

First reluctantly, then fully, Issy surrendered to the kiss. She realized how much her body had missed the contact; how much she had missed the feeling of skin on skin; that no one had touched her for two months. She'd forgotten just how good it felt; how good he felt; how good he smelled. Unable to help herself, she let out a sigh.

"I have missed you," breathed Graeme. And for the moment, Issy realized, leaning into him once more, that was going to have to be enough.

•　•　•　•

It wasn't until the next morning, after an extraordinary night, when Graeme was rushing around getting ready that he thought to ask her what she was doing.

At first, Issy was oddly reluctant to tell him, to let light flood into their bubble. She didn't want him to laugh at her. She was enjoying feeling happily tired, her muscles liquid and relaxed, luxuriating in his big bed. She was doing something she rarely got to do: staying all night. It was bliss. She would get up and saunter down to Notting Hill High Street, have coffee, read the papers in Starbucks maybe… Suddenly she could see the positives of being out and about on a weekday; it made her feel like she was bunking off.

But then she remembered with a start: she couldn't bunk off. Not anymore. She had stuff to do. Lots and lots of stuff to do. She'd signed the lease and with the lease came a shop, and responsibility, and work and…She sat bolt upright in a fit of panic. She had an appointment with a small business adviser; she had to examine the property—her café! She had to figure out what work was absolutely essential and what could wait till they were up and running, buy an oven, think about staffing. Last night, starting with the champagne and ending with the most incredible sex with the man currently gelling his hair in the en suite mirror—that had been celebration. Today, she was self-employed. It was starting.

"Ooh," she said. "I have to rush. I have to go."

Graeme looked perturbed but amused.

"Why? Urgent pedicure appointment?"

"No, actually."

And she told him.

Graeme couldn't have looked more surprised if she'd said she was opening a zoo.

"You're what?"

He was halfway through knotting a natty blue tie Issy had bought him, thinking it would appeal to his peacock tendencies and bring out his eyes, both of which it did.

"Yes," said Issy, insouciant, as if this was exactly what she should do and completely unsurprising. "Sure."

"You're opening a small business. We're five minutes out of recession, and you're opening a business."

"Well, it's obviously the best time," said Issy. "Rents are cheap, opportunities are out there."

"Hang on, hang on," said Graeme. Issy was half-pleased at surprising him and half-cross at his evident skepticism. "What type of business?"

Issy stared at him. "Cupcakes, of course."

"Cupcakes?"

"Yes, cupcakes."

"You're going to make an entire business out of cakes?"

"People do."

"Those sugary things?"

"People like them."

Graeme frowned. "But you don't know anything about running a business."

"Well, who does when they start?"

"Almost everyone in catering, for starters. They've all worked in other bakeries for years or grown up in the trade. Otherwise you're sunk. Why didn't you go and work in a bakery if you wanted to bake? At least you'd have seen if it suited you."

Issy pouted. This was exactly what a little niggling voice at the back of her mind told her. But the shop had come up! Her shop! She knew it was right!

"Well, a shop came up that I think is just right, and—"

"In Stoke Newington?" snorted Graeme. "They saw you coming."

"Fine," said Issy. "Be like that. I have an appointment anyway with a small business adviser."

"Well, I hope he's cleared his schedule," said Graeme.

Issy stared at him.

"What?"

"I can't believe you're being like this."

"I can't believe you're throwing away Kalinga Deniki's incredibly generous redundancy package on something so ridiculous. So stupid. Why didn't you ask me?"

"Because you didn't bother to ring me, remember?"

"Oh, for Christ's sake, Issy. Come on. I'll ask around. I'm sure there's a secretarial job going at Foxtons commercial. I'm sure we can find something for you."

"I don't want 'something,'" said Issy mutinously, biting her lip. "I want this."

Graeme threw up his hands.

"But it's ridiculous."

"So you think."

"You don't know anything about business."

"You don't know anything about me," said Issy, which she realized made her sound dramatic and stupid, but she didn't care. She glanced around for her other shoe. "I have to go."

Graeme looked at her, shaking his head.

"Fine."

"Fine."

"You'll ruin everything," he said.

Issy picked up the shoe. She wanted very badly to throw it at him.

"Thanks for the vote of confidence," she muttered as she jammed it on and tottered out the door, berating herself, once again, for being such an idiot.

• • • •

Issy rushed home, shaking. All she wanted to do was get out of these stupid clothes. The flat was silent, but not empty. She could sense Helena around somewhere, feel her disapproval (and Shalimar perfume) wafting in her direction. Well, she didn't have time for that now. She had a meeting at the bank, had to sound clever and professional and get a business plan, even though she'd been up half the night with the biggest wanker in bloody London. She was getting the keys later on that day, giving her a few weeks to spruce up and get ready for business so they could open for the "spring trade." Which sounded optimistic, she thought. Bugger it, bugger it.

Now, what to wear? She pulled open her wardrobe, looking at the array of nonattention-grabbing work suits she'd accumulated. The gray pinstripe? Graeme had always liked it; he thought it looked like sexy secretary. Issy had always wanted to be one of those fashion-y looking girls with the lovely slim top halves, who could wear vests without bras and drop waists. She was never going to be one of those girls, she realized. But she didn't like to dress to emphasize her figure. Helena, on the other hand, had turned it into an art.

She pulled a white shirt closer. Shirts never seemed to fit properly. Sensing someone behind her, she turned around. It was Helena, holding two cups of tea.

"Don't knock," said Issy. "It's only my flat."

"Do you want tea?" said Helena, ignoring her.

"No," said Issy. "I want you to stop wandering into my room uninvited."

"Well, sounds like last night was romantic."

Issy sighed. "Shut up."

"Oh God, that bad. I'm sorry, love."

It was hard to stay angry at Helena for long.

"It was fine," said Issy, taking the tea. "Fine. I don't want to see him again anyway."

"OK."

"I know I've said that before."

"OK."

"But this time I mean it."

"Fine."

"I am fine."

"Good."

"Good."

Helena looked at her.

"Are you going to wear that for your meeting?"

"I have a business now. I have to look the part."

"But that's not your part. You're a baker now, a professional, not someone who carries a folder about while checking Facebook every five minutes."

"That's not what my old job was, actually."

"Yeah, well, whatever."

Helena reached into her cupboard and pulled out a lightly sprigged dress and a pastel cardigan.

"Here, try these on."

Issy looked down. Her head felt too full to concentrate.

"You don't think it's a bit…cutesy?"

"Darling, you're running a cupcake bakery. I think you have to make your peace with twee. And anyway, no I don't. I think it looks pretty and approachable and it suits you, which is more than you can say for porno-secretary."

"This suit isn't…"

Actually, thought Issy, glancing in the mirror, perhaps it was time to get rid of this suit. Dump that stupid office once and for all. And that stupid man…She tried to keep her thoughts away from that particular track, and got changed.

In the new outfit, she did look nicer—younger and fresher. It made her smile.

"There you go," said Helena. "Now you look the part."

Issy glanced at Helena, who was wearing a deep green square-cut-neckline ruched top.

"What part are you dressing for?"

Helena pouted. "Flame-haired Renaissance goddess, of course. As usual. You know that."

• • • •

Issy was nervous going to the bank, extremely so. She'd explained this was just a preliminary chat and they'd said fine, but still it felt a bit like having to go in and explain away her overdraft, just as she had done in college. Graeme liked to check his statements every month and call them up the second he found something he disagreed with. She didn't feel like doing that very often.

"Um, hi," she almost whispered, as she entered the beige-carpeted hush of the bank. It smelled of cleaning products and money. At that moment she would have preferred the armor of her gray pinstripe.

"Can I speak to Mr."—she checked her notes—"Mr. Tyler."

The young girl behind the desk smiled distractedly and leaned forward into her telephone, buzzing her through. Being on the other side of the security barrier was a little disconcerting; open-plan desks were scattered around, with people peering at computer screens. Issy glanced about her, just in case there was any gold visible.

She didn't see anyone who looked like a Mr. Tyler, so she sat down nervously, picking up and replacing a magazine about the bank, too anxious to read anything, letting her fingers fiddle with the pages and hoping she wouldn't have too long to wait.

• • • •

Austin Tyler sat in the head teacher's office, feeling like he was in some kind of déjà vu. It was exactly the same room he used to sit in, kicking his scuffed Start Rite shoes against the chair when he was getting told off for running through the bushes, or fighting with Duncan MacGuire. There was a new headmistress—quite a young woman, who said, "Call me Kirsty," when he'd much rather call her Miss Dubose, and perched on the front of her desk instead of sitting imperiously behind it like Mr. Stroan used to do. Austin, frankly, preferred the old way; at least you knew where you stood. He glanced sideways at Darny and sighed. Darny was staring at the floor crossly, with a glint in his eye that said whatever was coming, he wasn't listening. At ten years old, Darny was smart, determined and absolutely convinced that anyone ever telling him what to do was in severe breach of his human rights.

"What is it this time?" asked Austin. He was going to be late for work again, he knew it. He ran a hand through the thick, unruly reddish-brown hair that was flopping over his forehead. Time for another haircut too, he noticed. As if he could possibly find the time.

"Well," started the headmistress, "obviously we're all aware of Darny's special circumstances."

Austin raised his eyebrows and turned to Darny, whose hair was more auburn than Austin's but stuck up at the front in a very similar fashion and whose eyes were also gray.

"Well, yes, but Darny's special circumstances were six years ago, weren't they, Darny? You can't keep on using it as an excuse forever. Especially not for…"

"Using bows and arrows on the reception class."

"Quite," said Austin, looking disapprovingly at Darny, who stared even more fiercely at the floor. "Do you have anything to say for yourself?" he asked the boy.

"My loyalty is not to you, Sheriff."

Kirsty looked up at the tall, curly-haired man in the slightly disheveled suit and wished she was somewhere else. She wished they were both somewhere else. A bar perhaps. She thought, not for the first time, that this job was totally useless for meeting men. Everyone in primary teaching was female, and it was considered very much "not on" to chat up the dads.

But Austin Tyler of course wasn't exactly a dad…Would that make it OK?

Everyone at the school knew the tragic story. As far as Kirsty was concerned, it only made rangy Austin, with the horn-rimmed specs he kept taking off and putting back on again when he was distracted, even more attractive. Six years ago, when Austin had been a postgraduate student in marine biology at Leeds, his parents and his baby brother (the result of a silver wedding celebration that had given them all the shock of their lives) were involved in a horrible car accident after a lorry tried to do a U-turn on a busy road. The four-year-old in his car seat had been fine, but the front of the car had been completely crushed.

Despite being knocked sideways by grief, Austin had immediately given up his studies—a job where you had to travel the world being patently unmanageable—come home, fought off well-meaning distant aunties and social services, taken a mundane job in a bank, and was raising his baby brother as well as he could (which wasn't always, Kirsty noted privately, as well as he could be doing it if, say, the child had a strong maternal influence in his life…). Now thirty-one, Austin had such a strong bond with Darny that although many women had tried to get in between them, no one had quite managed it. Kirsty did wonder if Darny had scared them off. Or maybe Austin hadn't yet reached the right woman. She just wished the only chance she had to see him was not when she had to talk to him about Darny's behavior.

Still, she made sure she always handled these meetings herself, rather than letting the perfectly competent Mrs. Khan do it, even though it wasn't strictly necessary. It was the best she could do at the moment.

"So would you say," said Kirsty, "that Darny is getting enough of a feminine influence at home?"

Austin ran his hands through his hair again. Why could he never remember to get a haircut? he wondered to himself. I do love longer hair on a man, thought Kirsty.

"Well, he has about nine million well-meaning female relations," he said, biting his lip when he thought of the scorn Darny had for other people coming into the house. (Which, it had to be said, wasn't always at its tidiest. They did have a cleaner, but she refused to pick up after them, which was really what they needed before the true cleaning could begin.) "But no one more permanent, no."

Kirsty raised her eyebrows in what was meant to be a flirtatious manner, but which Austin immediately took to be disapproval. He was always conscious of being scrutinized when he was with Darny and sensitive about it. Darny wasn't an angel, but Austin did the best he could, and was sure that elsewhere the boy would be doing a lot worse.

"We do all right, Darny and I," he insisted. Darny, although still staring at the floor, reached out a hand and squeezed Austin's tightly.

"I didn't mean to…I just meant, Mr. Tyler…Austin. We can't have violence at this school. We really can't."

"But we want to stay at this school," said Austin. "We grew up here! This is our area! We don't want to have to move and go to another school."

Austin tried not to feel a bit panicked as he felt Darny's skinny fingers grip his long ones, but holding on to their parents' home, and his old school, and the area they'd always lived in, around Stoke Newington—well, it hadn't been easy to pay the mortgage, but it had felt so important to give their lives a sense of continuity, not to take Darny's home away as well as everything else he'd ever known. Staying here meant they were within a community of friends and neighbors who made sure they never went without a hot meal if they needed one or a sleepover for Darny if Austin had to work late. He loved the area passionately.

Kirsty moved to calm him.

"No one is saying anything about changing schools. We're just saying…no more bows and arrows."

Darny shook his head violently.

"Are you agreeing with me, Darny? No more bows and arrows?"

"No more bows and arrows," repeated Darny, still refusing to take his eyes off the floor.

"And?" said Austin.

"And, sorry," said Darny, finally looking up. "Do I have to go and say sorry to the reception kids?"

"Yes please," said Austin. Kirsty smiled at him gratefully. She was almost pretty, thought Austin abstractly. For a teacher.

• • • •

Janet, Austin's assistant, met him at the door of the bank.

"You're late," she said, handing him his coffee (white, three sugars—having to grow up very quickly in some areas had left Austin lagging a little behind in others).

"I know, I know, I'm sorry."

"Darny trouble again?"

Austin winced.

"Don't worry," she said, patting him on the shoulder and picking some lint off it at the same time. "They all go through the same phases."

"With bows and arrows?"

Janet rolled her eyes. "Consider yourself lucky. Mine went for firecrackers."

Feeling slightly cheered by this, Austin glanced at his notes: someone looking for a café loan. In this market, very unlikely, and the terms were going to be punishing. Everyone thought the banks made harsh decisions, but actually lending to small businesses was a thankless task. More than half of them would never make it. Trying to spot which half was his job. He turned the corner into a small waiting area.

"Hello," he said, smiling at the nervous-looking woman with the pink cheeks and tied-back, unruly black hair sitting fiddling with a magazine. "Are you my ten o'clock?"

• • • •

Issy jumped up, then inadvertently let her gaze stray to the large clock on the far wall.

"I know," said Austin, wincing again. "I'm so sorry..." He considered telling her he wasn't usually late, but that wouldn't have been strictly true. "Would you like to follow me in here?"

• • • •

Issy followed him through another glass door, which led to a meeting room. It was basically just a glass box set in the middle of the open-plan office. It felt peculiar, as if they were two fish in a tank.

"Sorry. I'm...hi, I'm Austin Tyler."

"Issy Randall." Issy shook his hand, which was large and dry. His hair seemed a little messy for a banker, she noticed. But he had a pleasant, slightly distracted smile and thick-fringed gray eyes—maybe she should put him on her list for Helena. She was swearing off men for good after last night. She felt a growl coming on, but managed to suppress it. Focus! Focus! She wished she'd had more than three hours' sleep.

Austin fumbled about for a pen, noting his client seemed a little stressed. When he'd left Leeds, he hadn't been sure he'd make a natural banker. It was as far from examining coral as he could imagine, but the best thing he could find at short notice; the bank let him take on his parents' mortgage too. However, since joining, he'd worked his way up steadily; it turned out he had excellent instincts about sound prospects and good investments, and as his clients came to know him, they trusted him completely and were very loyal to the bank.

Senior management was reasonably sure big things were going to come to him, although they too wished he would cut his hair.

"Now then," he said, having retrieved a pen from his pocket and blown the tissue fluff off it. "What can we do for you?"

He glanced at the file and realized to his utter horror that this was a different café altogether.

He pulled off his glasses. This was obviously going to be one of those days.

"Uh, why don't you just start from the beginning," he improvised.

Issy gave him a shrewd look. She'd spotted what had happened immediately.

"Don't you have the file?"

"I always like to hear it from the client's own mouth. Paints me a picture."

Issy's lips twitched. "Really?"

"Really," said Austin firmly, leaning forward and clasping his large hands in front of the folder. And while Issy caught the look of a shared joke in his eyes, she felt a spark of excitement at being able to tell her story properly. Either way, she was about to find out if her dream had the faintest possibility of becoming a reality.

"OK," she said. "Well…"

And Issy told him the story—missing out the sleeping-with-her-boss bits and reshaping it more as a lifelong ambition, with lots of hard financial analysis backing it up. The more she told the story, she realized, the more real and plausible it sounded, like a creative visualization. She felt she was making it come true.

"I brought you some cake," she added as she finished. Austin waved it away.

"Sorry, I can't take that. Could be seen as …"

"Me bribing you with cake?" asked Issy in surprise.

"Well, yes, cake, tools, wine, whatever, really."

"Gosh." Issy stared at the tin in her lap. "I really hadn't thought of it like that."

"What, you didn't bring me cakes to bribe me?"

"Well, yes, obviously I did, now you mention it."

They smiled at each other. Austin rubbed his unruly hair. "Pear Tree Court…remind me, but isn't that the tiny tucked-away place off the Albion Road?"

Issy nodded fervently. "You know it!"

"Well, yes…" said Austin, who knew every inch of the area intimately. "But…it's not exactly a commercial area, is it?"

"There are shops there," said Issy. "Anyway, if you build it they will come."

Austin smiled.

"I don't normally take slogans from ghost baseball players as sound business strategies."

Issy nearly forgot herself to remark on how much she loved that film, and didn't he too? But for a banker, he was surprisingly easy to talk to. She'd been dreading this meeting, but now she was here…

"I mean, I'm not sure it's…show me your figures again?"

Austin studied them with some care. The rent was certainly affordable, and when it came to the baking, the raw ingredients weren't expensive. Staff would be easy to find, if Issy was going to do all the cooking. But even so, the profit margins were painful, borderline minimal. For a very long slog.

He squinted at it again and looked back at Issy. It would all be down to her. If she would put the hours in, devote her entire life to cakes and nothing but, then it was just…just about possible. Maybe.

"Here's the thing," he said.

And over the next hour, his second appointment forgotten, he took Issy so thoroughly through every single step of the way to run a business—from national insurance to health and safety, food inspections, banking, marketing, stocking, margins, portion control—that she felt as if she'd spent a year in business school. As he spoke, occasionally taking off his glasses to emphasize a point, Issy could feel her nebulous dreams take real, meaningful shape in his hands; he seemed to be molding the foundations of her castle in the air. Step by step he explained to her exactly what she and she alone would be responsible for; what she'd have to do. And not just for one day or one project; over and over and over again, as long as she wanted to make a living.

After fifty-five minutes, Austin sat back. He had a standard spiel—his "scare 'em straight" speech, they joked in the back office—that he gave to everyone who came in with ideas about setting up a business. If you couldn't face in your mind the workload involved, you were almost doomed to failure before you even started. But with this girl it was a bit different; he'd gone above and beyond to help her and show her the pitfalls and possibilities. He kind of felt he owed it to her after turning up so late—and with the wrong file.

And also, although at first she'd seemed aggressive, almost snarling, once they'd started to talk she'd seemed nice—and she looked so sweet, in her pretty flowered frock—and he wanted her to be very clear about what she would be getting herself into. He was fond of the area she was talking about; he'd grown up near Pear Tree Court and had often hidden there, under the tree, reading a book when that shop was derelict. It was a lovely spot, even though he hadn't imagined anyone else knew about it apart from him.

A little café—being able to sit out with a cup of coffee and a slice of something delicious—didn't seem that bad an idea to him. But in the end it would come down to her.

"So," he said, finishing with a flourish. "What do you think? If the bank was to support you, would you be up to it?"

Normally at this point people said "Sure!" or behaved like they were on *The X Factor* and offered to give it 110 percent. Issy sat back with a thoughtful look in her eye.

This, she knew, was it. A full commitment—if she got the backing from the bank—for life, if everything went well. It would all be on her shoulders. She would never be able to come home from work, forget all about it. She remembered Gramps, eating, sleeping, thinking of nothing but the bakeries. That had been his life. Would it be hers?

But then, if it was a success…maybe she could find other people to help her run it…open another one. All of that was possible too, she knew. She could end up with more freedom. A way to live her life by her own rules, to her own schedule, taking no one's minutes.

A tiny, tiny voice deep down inside her said, "But what about when I want a baby?" She couldn't listen to that voice, she thought angrily. She still didn't have a job at the moment. She didn't have a boyfriend. She could worry about that later.

"Miss Randall?" Austin was pleased she was thinking about it. It meant she'd been listening to him. Too often he had wise guys in here who thought they had all the answers, who didn't listen and tried to talk over the top of him. They rarely lasted.

Issy looked right at him.

"Thanks for giving it to me straight," she said.

"Have I scared the life out of you?" said Austin, apologetically.

"No. No, you haven't. And if the bank will help me out…well, I'd like to bank with you."

Austin raised his eyebrows.

"OK. Well, OK. Good. Obviously I need to talk to a few people…"

He ferreted in his briefcase for the forms she needed to fill out and instead came up with an apple and a catapult.

"You look like Dennis the Menace," said Issy, giggling. She made a mental note to knock him off Helena's list—he wasn't wearing a wedding ring but he clearly had kids.

"Ah yes, we use this on defaulters," he said. He glanced regretfully at the apple as it went back in his bag.

"You look hungry," said Issy.

"I am," said Austin, who had missed breakfast trying to get Darny to eat his.

"Are you *sure* you wouldn't like a cake? I won't tell anyone."

"But I would know," said Austin mock-sternly. He buzzed the intercom on his desk. "Janet, would you mind bringing in a set of business account application forms?"

"But I already—"

Austin took his finger off the intercom.

"I'll let Janet help you with the forms. Then just leave them with reception. I think my eleven o'clock is here."

"Your eleven o'clock has been here for half an hour," said Janet, appearing at the door with a sheaf of forms. She looked at Austin as if he were a naughty schoolboy. "I'll tell him you're just ready." She swept out.

Issy stood up. "Thanks."

"Good luck," said Austin, standing up too, taking off his glasses and holding out his hand. Issy shook it. "If you need anything else, here's my card. And here, would you like a bank pen?"

"You keep it," said Issy. "I wouldn't want anyone to think you were trying to bribe me."

• • • •

Although the weather was still cold and gray, at least it wasn't raining. While Issy knew she had plenty of things to get started on, she also had an awful lot to think about as she crossed the busy Dalston Road—clustered with shoppers unperturbed by the cold, eating sausage rolls from the baker's, or pushing through to the market, or examining laundry baskets outside the bric-a-brac shop. Stoke Newington High Street was a little quieter, with mummies wheeling their buggies to baby yoga and the library; to the vegetarian falafel café, or the churchyard. A toy shop jostled with a posh wallpaper showroom and a thriving independent bookshop.

Then Issy turned again, into Albion Road. The large gray houses stared back at her impassively. Here there were hardly any pedestrians at all, just the long, bendy 73 cutting corners and rendering the road impassable. And there, almost hidden from sight, was the tiny turn-off just on the corner… As she came into Pear Tree Court and saw the sign up in the window—*Rented*—her heart leaped. She sat down, in the cold, on the little bench under the tree. Even in the chill weather, she felt a great sense of peace steal over her. The sun was only just showing its face. It touched a tiny piece of spring onto her winter-pallid face and she closed her eyes in bliss. Winter would come to an end; it would. And here, she would have a little haven in the very epicenter of one of the world's busiest cities. Could she make it her own?

● ● ● ●

When Des arrived to hand over the keys, he found Issy like that, sitting on the bench, looking dreamy and far away. Uh-oh, he thought, worriedly. That wasn't really a good look for the putative owner of a business. That was more the look of someone who had a head full of castles in the air.

"Hey, hello," he said, standing directly in her tiny shaft of sunshine. "Sorry I'm late. My wife was supposed to…Uh, well, never mind."

Issy squinted up at him. "Hi! Sorry, it's just such a relaxing spot. I had a bit of a late night..." She let her voice trail off, remembering. Then she jumped up, trying to recover her professional demeanor. "So let's see what we're dealing with, shall we?"

• • • •

In her years of working with professionally shown buildings, Issy had gained a shrewd eye as to what needed doing in places, and the ability to put a positive spin on it. But as Des ceremoniously handed over the huge set of keys, and she slowly turned them in the three locks on the door to open it, creaking her way tentatively inside, she realized that suggesting to clients what they ought to be doing was very different from planning on doing it yourself. Thick dust lay on an old counter-top; the window was smeared with grime. The last inhabitants might have had spiritual yogic peace, but their housekeeping left a little to be desired. Shelves had been left which would be completely useless to the new enterprise, while more useful things—a sink upstairs, plenty of electrical outlets—were completely missing.

Issy felt her heart beat faster. Was this crazy? The fireplace was lovely, so beautiful, but she couldn't put tables and chairs in front of it if it was lit. She was 100 percent sure the fire officer wouldn't let her light it. That Austin chap had been full and definitive on the subject of whether or not to cross a fire officer. It seemed to be pretty much up there with crossing a U.S. immigration officer.

"There's plenty to do," said Des jovially, hoping he could wrap this up speedily enough to get back before his mother-in-law started to impart to Jamie what she considered to be a few home truths. "But I know it's going to be fine."

"Do you?" said Issy, frantically taking snaps on her digital camera. What had seemed so easy to visualize before—a nice fresh green on the walls; sparkling windows to let the light in; beautiful pastel cakes temptingly set out on cake stands—suddenly was a lot harder to see in this dusty, dingy space.

"And downstairs of course," said Des.

Issy had seen the basement on the plans but hadn't actually been down there yet. She hadn't told anyone this. She didn't want to admit that she'd taken on a business without inspecting every corner of it. Everyone would tut at her.

Tentatively she followed Desmond down the narrow, rickety staircase illuminated by a bare bulb. There was a bathroom halfway down, then at the bottom what she had hoped for—a huge space opening out, with clear venting and plenty of room for the industrial oven she now knew she'd need. There were standpipes for plumbing and a good spot for a desk for paperwork. One poky window at the back looked out onto the basement of the next building along; the light wasn't great, but it would have to do. It would get warm down here too, warm enough to heat the shop. With her perfect, running-to-schedule, high-temperature oven, the kind her grandfather still dreamed of.

"Isn't it wonderful!" she exclaimed, turning to Des with her eyes shining.

Des squinted. It looked like a mucky old cellar to him, but who was he to judge?

"Yeah," he said. "Now, I just have a few things here for you to sign…You must be signing a lot of stuff."

"Yes," said Issy, who had come away with files full from the bank and was waiting for her trading license to come through. The shop already had permission for café usage; it was just getting it to be her café that would be the problem, although Austin had said if her application was successful, he'd be happy to look over the paperwork.

When they stumbled back upstairs, the weak afternoon sun had come around to the front of the building and was sending a watery stream of yellow through smeared glass and motes of dust, and lighting up the fireplace. Yes, it was mucky, Issy thought, revived. Yes, it needed work. But she could work. She could do it. She would show Graeme, who would be so proud of her, and she would bring Gramps down on opening day—she wasn't quite sure how she'd manage that but she'd figure something out—and she'd totally impress Helena and all their friends and bring a whole new clientele to the street and get written up in *Metro* and the *Evening Standard* as a hidden gem, and people would come, and have coffee, and a delicious cake and be perked up by the lovely little courtyard and the beautiful shop and...

Des spotted the woman's face dropping into reverie again.

"OK!" he said, slightly desperately. "Shall we get on? Or I can leave you here if you like; it is yours now."

Issy smiled. "Oh, no, I have lots to do and sort out. I'll leave with you."

He smiled back at her happily.

"How many kilos of coffee are you planning through here anyway?" he asked casually as Issy got to grips with the locks.

"What?" said Issy.

Des grimaced. He'd expected her to at least be au fait with the most basic levels of coffee shop jargon. The brief moment of hopefulness he'd felt at her excitement with the cellar evaporated. He was going to be showing this place again in three months. Oh well, it was all more commission, he supposed, although Mr. Barstow was getting pissed off at him, as if he wasn't the one who selected the tenants in the first place.

"Never mind," said Des, getting out his car keys.

"OK," said Issy. "Well, you'll pop in for a cup when we're open, won't you?"

Des thought of his slashed bonus. "Oh yes," he said. "If I can."

And he shot off to rescue Jamie from the sharp-taloned clutches of his grandmother.

double chocolate cupcakes (commercial)

• • • •

Makes one morning's worth.

* 10 cups double cream
* 10 pounds good quality dark chocolate
* 50 eggs
* 7 cups superfine sugar
* 6½ cups plain flour
* 10 tbsp good quality cocoa powder
* 5 tsp baking powder
* sugar flowers to decorate

Chocolate sauce
* 2¼ pound dark chocolate, broken into pieces
* 3¼ cups single cream

Stir double cream and chocolate in a pan over low heat until smooth. Cool slightly.

Place eggs and sugar in the bowl of your industrial mixer, and beat on high until pale and doubled in volume. Slowly beat in chocolate mixture.

Sift in flour, cocoa, and baking powder, and combine.

Divide the mixture between cases. Bake for 15–20 minutes at 355°F/gas mark 4 until a skewer inserted into the center comes out clean. Cool slightly in pans, then remove cakes from cases. Drink a pint of water.

Meanwhile, for the sauce, place the ingredients in a heatproof bowl over a vat of simmering water (don't let bowl touch water). Stir until the chocolate has melted. Consider calling ex-boyfriend and old boss and crawling on hands and knees, begging till he gives you back your old paperwork job.

Remove from heat and stir until smooth. Wonder how much weight you'll lose doing this. Taste delicious mixture. Decide, probably not that much.

Cool slightly. Serve cakes topped with sauce. Decorate with flowers if using. Collapse in heap, convinced this is never, ever going to work on a daily basis.

O *h God."*
Issy was sitting neck-deep in a pile of paperwork. It had not been as easy to deal with the admin as she had hoped. It was, in fact, a big long chore of filling out the same details over and over again. She had hygiene courses to attend, buying trips to make and all of this before she had sorted out the fixtures and fittings. She had received quotes for the catering oven she wanted and it would have swallowed up her entire budget for everything. So she started looking at second-hand, but even that seemed perilously expensive. And the look she had envisaged for the shop—reclaimed-looking tables and chairs, in pale colors of cream and eau de Nil—was proving pricey too; as if she'd do better actually to reclaim old tables and chairs. And she still hadn't heard from the bank. Why did everything take so long? She couldn't hire anyone till she had a business account, but it felt like they wanted to wait until

she had a business before they would give her an account. It was very frustrating. And that was before you even got to the baking.

Helena paused outside her door. She knew the last week or so had been stressful for Issy. Every day huge forms had arrived in the post: advertising brochures and government forms and official-looking documents in brown envelopes.

Helena had had a hard day herself. A child had come in with suspected meningitis, always a horrible experience. They'd saved her life, but she might still lose a foot. Helena made a mental note to check up on her on the ward the next morning. That was often the problem with A&E; you never found out the end of the story. And now here was Issy huffing and puffing about the place rather than just grabbing every day as it happened and getting stuck in. It could be a bit frustrating.

"Hey," she said, knocking on the door. "How are you doing?"

Issy was ankle-deep in piles of paper.

"Bugger it," she said. "I've discovered the fatal flaw. I haven't worked in a shop before."

"You worked in your grampa's bakery, didn't you?"

"I took twenty-one pence for French cakes. On Saturdays. So the customers could pinch my cheeks and say how bonny I was looking, which, by the way, if you're not from the North, means 'fat.' Oh, why didn't I train to become an accountant?"

She picked up another piece of a paper.

"Or...or a building surveyor."

"I knew I should have stolen some valium," said Helena.

Issy's mouth twitched a little bit. "Oh, Helena. I can't believe I've done this on a whim. I need help." She looked imploringly at her friend.

"Well, don't look at me. I'm just off a twelve-hour shift," said Helena. "And apart from stocking your first aid cupboard and teaching you the Heimlich maneuver again, I'm not sure what I can do for you."

"No," said Issy, sighing. "And my mate Zac said he'd design the menus for me, but that's it."

"Well, that's a start," said Helena comfortingly. "A first aid box, a menu, and some yummy cakes. The rest is just cleaning up."

"I feel so alone," said Issy, who was missing Graeme more than she could admit. The shock of going from seeing him every day to never seeing him at all was one thing. To have a reconciliation, and then to have it all snatched away again…that was hard to process.

Helena sat down.

"But you're going to have to get staff, aren't you? I mean, you're going to have to pay people sooner or later. Maybe if you recruit someone now they could help you with all this stuff as well as the shop when it's open. Do you know anyone?"

Issy thought suddenly of the bright, cheery woman she'd met at the redundancy course.

"You know," she said, scrolling down her phone where she and Pearl had politely swapped numbers, never really expecting to use them, "there might just be something in this networking thing after all. I think she's got catering experience."

She started to push the number as Helena held up her hand.

"Aren't you forgetting something?"

Issy glanced nervously at the piles of forms.

"Shouldn't you wait for the bank to give you the go-ahead—and the overdraft facility?"

Suddenly, Issy felt she couldn't wait until morning. She had been filling in forms and talking to government inspectors for three days; she needed to know. The bank was being horribly slow. She took out the card of Mr. Austin Tyler and dialed the mobile number. OK, so it was after seven, but bankers worked late hours, didn't they?

"There's this chap I thought you might like," she said to Helena. "He's got a kid though. But no wedding ring."

"Oh lovely, married but pretending he isn't," snorted Helena. "Just my type. I'll be in my room, kissing my John Cusack pictures."

• • • •

Austin was bathing Darny, or rather he was attempting the equivalent of holding a squid down in the water while the squid thrashed all of its tentacles to get free. Austin was considering letting the squid go without washing his hair for the ninth night in a row when his phone rang. He retrieved it, granting Darny a temporary victory as he stood up in the bath and started parading up and down it like a soldier, kicking bubbles as he went.

"Stop that," he hissed, which made Darny redouble his efforts.

"Hello?"

Issy heard a strangulated yell from Darny as Austin attempted to make him sit down again.

"Sorry, is this a bad time?"

"Um, just in the bath."

"Oh, sorry…"

"No, not me…Darny!"

"*Soldiers do not sit down to your authority!*" came clearly over the earpiece.

"Ah. You're bathing a soldier," said Issy kindly. She hadn't thought the child would be so old; Austin seemed about her age. Which wasn't, she reminded herself, that young anymore. "Well, that is an important duty."

"Darny, *sit down!*"

"*You're not my superior officer!*"

"Actually, I think you'll find that I am…Sorry about this, but who is it?"

"Oh, sorry," said Issy, embarrassed. "It's Isabel Randall. From the Cupcake Café."

She could hear Austin struggle to remember her. It was excruciating.

"Oh yes," he said finally. "Uh. Yes. How can I help you?"

"This is clearly a bad time, I'm so sorry," said Issy.

Normally Austin would have liked to point out sarcastically that yes, 7:30 on a school night was quite a bad time for all sorts of business inquiries, but there was something in Issy's voice—she was, he could tell, genuinely sorry; she wasn't just being polite but still trying to demand his attention. He groped around for his glasses, which were steamed up.

"OK, soldier, at ease," he said to Darny, handing the boy a camouflage-colored sponge and escaping out of the bathroom.

"Right, what's up?" he said to Issy as cheerfully as he could manage, noticing as he stepped onto the landing that there seemed to be piles of toys and books stacked up all over the house. He wished someone would come and sort it out for him. He knew that it was his responsibility, but he was just so tired all the time. He never seemed to get around to it. And on the weekends, he and Darny liked to hang out downstairs and watch Formula 1. They both felt they'd earned it after a hard week.

"Have you got lots of kids?" said Issy, genuinely curious.

"Oh, no," said Austin. Now he really wished she hadn't called him at home. He had the spiel off pat, but he hated giving it to strangers. "Uh, Darny's my little brother. My...uh, well, we lost our parents, and there's a big age gap, so, um, it's just me looking after him. Boys together, you know! We get along pretty well."

Issy immediately wished she hadn't asked. Austin sounded jaunty enough rolling off his spiel; he'd obviously got it down to just a few words. But of course, she couldn't begin to contemplate the depths of agony beneath the words. There was a silence on the phone.

"Oh," Issy said finally, just as Austin said, "So," to cover the gap. They both gave a little laugh.

"Sorry," said Issy. "I didn't mean to pry."

"Not at all," said Austin. "Perfectly normal question. Sorry the answer is a bit odd. I used just to say yes, he was my little boy..."

Austin didn't know why he was telling her this. It was strange, but there was something warm and friendly about her tone.

"But then I'd get lots of people saying he was so like me, and where was his mum and so on, so it just got more complicated in the end."

"Maybe you should print it on your business cards," said Issy, then bit her tongue in case that was in bad taste.

"Oh, I should," said Austin, smiling. "Definitely. Austin Tyler, dad-stroke-brother. Stroke animal wrangler."

Issy found herself smiling into the phone. "I'm sure the bank would be fine with that."

There was a silence.

"So anyway," she said, getting hold of herself, "I know we have to wait for the official letter and everything, but I've got the keys now and I'm really anxious to start hiring staff and I'm sure it's totally confidential and you're not allowed to tell me so I'll have interrupted your bath time for nothing so…"

"Are you going to apologize again?" said Austin, amused.

"Uh…well, yes I was."

"Come on! What kind of a hardheaded businesswoman are you?"

Issy smiled. For a banker, he was almost flirtatious.

"OK," she said. "Could you possibly give me a heads-up as to whether the bank is going to take my account?"

Of course he knew he wasn't supposed to, and it wasn't officially rubber-stamped yet. But she'd caught him at a vulnerable moment, and he could already hear a lot of noise coming from the other side of the door. And he could never resist a nice-sounding girl.

"Well," he said. "I'm absolutely not supposed to tell you this. But seeing as you asked very nicely, I can say that yes, I have recommended that we open an account for your business with our business."

Issy jumped up and down and clapped her hands.

"The board just has to take my recommendation."

Issy calmed down.

"Oh. Will they do that?"

"Do you doubt me?"

She smiled into the phone.

"No."

"Good. Congratulations, Miss Randall. It appears you're in business."

Issy hung up after thanking Austin a million times, and danced around the room, emboldened once more. Austin hung up and looked slightly quizzically at the phone. Was he imagining things, or had he just quite enjoyed taking a business call? That wasn't like him at all.

"*Austin! Austin!!! My infantry thinks it might need to do a pee in the bath!*"

"*Wait!*"

• • • •

Pearl was sitting under the blankets with Louis. It was freezing outside; freezing. A tiny hint of spring at the end of February had proved to be a cruel chimera. Now a howling gale was blowing, the wind funneling down the tunnels and blowing across the wide open spaces of the estate, making an unsettling amount of noise. Their last combined electricity/gas bill had been absolutely dreadful, so they were huddling together in front of a plug-in fire. Louis had a temperature—he fell sick so easily. She didn't know why. He was mildly asthmatic and seemed prey to absolutely every bug that came along. In cheerier moments she suspected it was because he was so convivial and social; he hugged everyone and caught whatever they had. At other times she wondered, deep down, if he ate enough of the right foods, was outdoors in enough fresh air and greenery to build the proper immunities, or if he just spent too long inside, breathing stale air. She'd told her mum not to smoke indoors, and she did her best, but when it was as cold as today, it felt cruel to make her stand on the stoop, exposed to the passing gangs of teenage boys who would shout and holler at anyone standing alone and looking even remotely vulnerable.

Her phone rang, with a number she didn't recognize. Pulling Louis's sweaty brow to her and giving him a swift kiss, she answered it, turning down the volume on the television.

"Hello?" she said, as cheerily as she could manage.

"Uh, hello," came a timid voice on the other end of the phone. "I don't know if you remember me…"

"Patisserie Valerie!" said Pearl, pleased. "Of course I remember you. And that course was so awful, did you go back?"

"I didn't," said Issy, happy to hear Pearl so glad to hear from her. "In fact, though, the course did work. Because it inspired me to go and do something quite different and actually, you know, network. So, uh, this is me. Networking."

There was a long pause.

"Pearl," said Issy, "this may sound like a stupid question. It's just an on-the-off-chance kind of a thing. But I'm slightly up to my neck in it, and I just wondered if you knew the answer to a question. Do you know how many kilos of coffee a coffee shop should be getting through in a week?"

Not only did Pearl know the answer to this ("One kilo is about a hundred cups, so you'd look to start with about six, move up to eight"), but, having been trained by a major coffee chain as a barista (she'd had to give it up though; she couldn't find childcare to cover the antisocial hours), she knew lots of other coffee-related stuff too. She knew how to tell whether coffee was overripe or burnt, what beans worked best at different times of day, how long you could store coffee and how, *and* she had her food hygiene certificate. The more she talked—and she could certainly talk—the more excited Issy became. They agreed to meet up the next day.

8

Hello, my darling Issy. You know, not every time is right for a big, full-on cake. Sometimes, you want a little essence of sweetness that is more like a kiss, or a friendly word on a sad day. And also, you know what pears are like. Ripe for ten seconds then you've missed it. Whereas this works very well with pears you've just missed, or the hard ones that go all powdery. Cake is a very forgiving mistress to bad pears.

pear upside-down cake

● ● ● ●

* 3 pears, peeled, halved and cored
* 14 tbsp butter
* 15 tbsp superfine sugar
* 3 eggs
* 15 tbsp self-rising flour, sifted
* 3 tbsp milk
* 1 tbsp icing sugar

Arrange the pear halves evenly over the bottom of a buttered dish and set aside. Using a wooden spoon (not the mixer—I know you think the mixer, but I say to you, did I build three bakeries in Manchester with electric mixers? Well, eventually, yes. But at first we did it with the wooden spoon, and so should you), cream the butter and sugar together in a large bowl until the mixture is light and fluffy.

Beat in the eggs, adding them one at a time and mixing well after each addition. Add the flour to the bowl, gently folding it into the mixture, then stir in the milk. Spoon the cake mixture evenly over the pears and smooth the surface.

Cook in a preheated oven at 350°F/gas mark 4 for 45 minutes, until the surface is firm when gently touched and the cake comes slightly away from the sides of the dish.

Remove from the oven, let it cool for five minutes, then turn out onto a serving plate. Dust the top of the cake evenly with icing sugar and serve immediately. Congratulate the pears on a job well done.

Love, Gramps x x

I ssy was getting up just as Helena was coming in from night shift, weary but slightly hysterical from the unit's success in saving all four teenagers from a joyriding smash-up on the A10. "Hey," she said, noticing Issy grinding fresh beans for coffee. "You're perking up!"

"Want one?" said Issy. "I am go-go-go today."

"*No* thank you. I have enough problems sleeping off night shift as it is."

"Well, try and catch up. I think I've found a man for your list."

Helena raised her eyebrows. "Does he have penetrating brown eyes and an offbeat smile?"

"No, Helena. That's John Cusack again."

"Oh yes."

"He's called Austin. He's got reddish-brown hair and works in a bank and—"

"Stop right there," said Helena. "Two gingers? It's a calamity waiting to happen." She smiled at her flatmate. "It's good to see you on form again."

"I got the loan and I'm going to meet a potential member of staff."

"Well, that is just great," said Helena. "Pretend you're always this upbeat."

Issy kissed her and left the flat.

• • • •

Across town, Pearl McGregor turned over in the bed. Something—someone—was kicking her. Hard. It was like being bombarded by a very small elephant.

"*Who* is that elephant in my bed?"

It wasn't really a bed; it was a mattress on the floor. She had a fold-out sofa for their little two-room flat—her mother had the bedroom—but it was just too uncomfortable so they'd got an old mattress and propped it up against the wall during the day. Pearl had tried to smarten it up by sewing a patchwork bedspread and some cushions. Louis was meant to sleep in with her mum, but he always gravitated toward her in the night and woke her up bright and early.

"Coco Pops!" came a tiny voice from deep under the duvet. "Coco Pops, Mummy!"

"Who said that?" Pearl pretended to search the bed. "I thought I heard a voice, but there can't be anyone in my bed."

There were stifled giggles from down by her feet.

"Nope, no one is in *my* bed."

Louis went silent till all she could hear was his excited breathing.

"OK, good, I will go back to sleep and forget about all those elephants."

"*Noooo! Mummy!* Is me!! Wan Coco Pops!"

Louis flung himself into her arms and Pearl buried her face in his neck, sucking in the warm sleepy smell of him. There were a lot of drawbacks to single motherhood, but the alarm clock wasn't one of them.

With the curtains open (also one of Pearl's needlework creations), Louis propped up by the breakfast bar and her mother enjoying a cup of tea in bed, Pearl looked down at her notebook. Today the two of them could maybe go to the drop-in center while she went around the shops. It was absolutely freezing outside but she'd tell her mum that she and Louis should stay as long as they could at the center, so they could turn off the heating in the flat. Tea was fifteen pence there, she could handle that. Then the freezer shop was doing a deal on sausages so she'd buy as many as she could manage. A bit of her felt bad at not budgeting for more fresh fruit for Louis—she watched his adorable baby tummy spill over the top of his cheap pajamas. And nappies. She dreaded buying nappies. She'd tried potty training him but he was barely two, he didn't have a clue what was going on. She just ended up spending more at the laundrette, it didn't make sense. Then she'd go back to Tesco. They must have something coming up soon, they must. And she'd heard that you could work around your childcare… Suddenly, groggily, she remembered. It was today! She was going to see that scatty girl. Something about a coffee shop! She rushed to turn the shower on, just as Louis put his hands up around her neck.

"*Cuggles!*" he shouted joyously, Coco Pops finished, as he launched himself at her again. Pearl hugged him back.

"You are so damn cute," she said.

"TV on," said Louis happily. He knew how to get his mother in a good mood.

"No way," said Pearl. "We have things to do today."

• • • •

It was a bright, frosty Friday morning when Pearl and Issy met outside the Cupcake Café. Their breath showed over the steaming cups of takeaway coffee they'd had to buy four hundred meters up the road. Pearl was dressed in a large pinafore and holding Louis by the hand.

Louis was an exquisite-looking child: roly-poly and caramel-colored, with wide, sparkling eyes and a ready grin. He immediately took the proffered cake from his fond mother and sat down with two racing cars under the spindly tree.

Issy, having left the house in such a positive mood, suddenly felt a bit nervous; this was almost like a blind date. If this worked out, they would be spending eight, nine, ten hours a day together. If it didn't, that could be a disaster. Was it a huge mistake to be planning a business relationship with someone she'd only met once before? Or should she follow her gut instinct?

Her doubts, though, began to fade as she showed Pearl the shop, and took in her obvious excitement. Pearl could see absolutely what Issy saw in it; could envisage it finished. She even insisted on going down into the cellar. Why do you want to go down there? Issy had asked and Pearl had pointed out that before they agreed to do anything they might as well check that she could actually fit into the narrow stairway and Issy said of course she could, she wasn't that big, and Pearl had snorted good-naturedly, but Issy did mentally plan to build out the counter another couple of inches, just for ease of use.

The more Pearl saw, the more she liked it. It had character, this place. And Issy's pear cake had been frankly amazing; lighter than air and lingering. If the venue scrubbed up right—and here in north London, where there were enough people who didn't see anything wrong with paying over two pounds for a cup of coffee, she couldn't see why it wouldn't work—she'd love to work here. Issy seemed nice—a bit naïve in the ways of business, obviously, but everyone had to start somewhere—and a warm, cozy, scented café with friendly hungry people and reasonable hours would be a lot nicer than most of the places she'd worked, that was for sure.

But there was one problem. She loved him to bits but he was, undeniably, a problem.

"What opening hours were you thinking of?" she asked.

"Well, I was thinking eight a.m. That's the time most people are heading for work and might want to grab a coffee," said Issy. "If that works well we could do croissants too, they're not hard to make."

Pearl raised her eyebrows.

"So the hours would be…"

"I was thinking, to begin with, seven thirty till four thirty?" said Issy. "We'll close after lunchtime cakes."

"How many days a week?" said Pearl.

"Uh, I thought see how it goes. If it works well, I'd like it to be only five," said Issy. "But including Saturdays to begin with."

"And how many staff are you going to have?"

Issy blinked. "Uh, well, I was thinking maybe just us to begin with."

"I mean, if one of us is sick or on holiday, or on a break, or…"

Issy felt a bit prickled. Pearl hadn't even started yet and already she was talking about time off.

"Well, yes, I thought we could work that out as we go."

Pearl frowned. She was sad; this was by far the best, the most interesting opportunity that had come along for ages. It would be exciting trying to get a little fledgling business off the ground; she could almost certainly make herself useful here, and there was nothing involved in the job that she hadn't done before. Whereas Issy, she surmised, had done quite a lot of sitting in a nice office checking her Facebook status and might well find all the hard work something of a surprise. Louis was running up to the cellar steps, checking the dark depths with delighted terror, and hopping back to his mother's skirts again.

Issy was looking at her, troubled. When she'd thought of Pearl, it had seemed like the answer to all her problems. But here was the woman now, not jumping at what Issy had assumed would be a fantastic opportunity for her. She swallowed hard. Pearl didn't even have a job. Why was she quibbling about this one?

"I…I'm so sorry, Issy," said Pearl. "I don't think I can."

"Why not?" said Issy, sounding emotional without meaning to. It was her dream after all, nobody else's.

Regretfully, Pearl indicated Louis, who was trying to catch dust motes between his fingers.

"I can't leave him alone with my mother every single morning. She's not that well and it's not fair on her, or me, or Louis. We live in Lewisham; it's a long way away."

Issy was stung, even though she knew it wasn't fair. What a thing to be getting in the way. How did mothers work? she wondered. She'd never really thought about it before. All those nice women who were on the tills at Tesco at 7:00 a.m., or cleaned offices, or worked on the tube lines. What did they do with their children? Did they have children? How was it done? She remembered the mums at KD, always looking harassed, like they'd left something on the bus, trying to sneak out early on end-of-term days, jumping when the phone rang.

"Oh," she said. She glanced at Louis, who was making tracks in the dust with his cars. "Oh, but couldn't you bring him in? He's no trouble. Just a couple of days a week or something?"

Pearl's heart leaped. Around here—playing safely out in the courtyard…warm and safe and not in front of the TV…Well, no. It was stupid.

"I think health and safety might have something to say about that," she said, smiling to show Issy how sorry she was.

"No, but…we wouldn't tell them!" said Issy.

"Do you think that's the way to start a business?" said Pearl. "Lying to health and safety? And don't even get me started on—"

"Fire officers. Yes, so I heard," said Issy. "Terrifying hell fiends."

She glanced at the shop.

"I mean, the ovens will be downstairs…more out of the way. I've decided just to keep the coffee machine up here."

"With superheated steam," said Pearl sweetly.

Issy smiled. "Oh, Pearl, I could really do with you."

At that moment there was a commotion outside the shop. Two men in dirty overalls had wandered up and were finishing off cigarettes and giving them inquiring glances.

"Oh shit, the builders are early," said Issy. She was quite nervous about this; she had no room in her budget to employ an architect or bring in a professional shop fitter so she had to trust that she could explain what she wanted sufficiently clearly. She hadn't been entirely convinced of her ability to do so when she'd called a firm in a whirl of positive activity the day before. Pearl raised her eyebrows.

"Don't go," pleaded Issy. "Let's have another chat anyway, afterward."

● ● ● ●

Pearl folded her arms and stood back as Issy opened the door to the builders. She caught them eyeing her up in a not entirely encouraging way as they introduced themselves as Phil and Andreas. Phil did most of the talking as Issy took them through, trying to explain what she was after—all the old shelving units stripped out; the whole place rewired; the counter moved and opened up; fridges and display cabinets put in, but not to touch the windows or the fireplace; shelving and a storage fridge for downstairs too. As she listed it, it seemed like an awful lot. Now they had their loan, and she had her redundancy payment too of course, but it was a lot of money to put into something before it had even opened.

Phil looked around and sucked his teeth a lot.

"Hmmm," he said. "They're a nightmare, these old buildings. Ain't it listed?"

"No!" said Issy, delighted to be asked a question she could actually answer. "Well, I mean, yes, the outside is, grade II, but the interior is all right as long as we don't pull down any walls or put anything up or brick up the fireplace, as if we would."

"Well, your problem here is we'll have to thread the wiring through the walls, then there'll be a lot of replastering to do, and that's before you even look at the flooring."

"What's wrong with the flooring?"

There were simple wooden boards on the floor, and Issy had been planning just to clean them up and leave them.

"Nah, you can't do that, see," said Phil. Issy didn't see at all. She started to feel embarrassed and uncomfortable. It was awkward being in the presence of people who knew so much more than she did about something that concerned her. She had the sinking sensation that it was a feeling she would get to know well.

Phil was proposing something complicated about lifting the skirting and putting in heating and wiring underneath then basically rebuilding the walls from the bottom up. Issy was looking at him helplessly, feeling out of her depth and nodding slightly, wishing as she did so that her accent wasn't quite so posh. Andreas was groping in his pocket for his cigarettes. Phil took out a camera and a notepad and started to jot down measurements, until Pearl, standing in the shadows, couldn't take it for one more single second.

"Excuse me," she said. Everyone turned to look at her quizzically. "You're a good builder, right?" she said to Phil, who looked slightly wounded.

"I can do anything," he said proudly. "Jack of all trades, me."

"That's great," said Pearl. "We're glad to have you aboard. But I'm afraid we can only pay you for the work that Miss Randall mentioned before. No floorboards, no skirting, no plastering. Just get the units in, get this place squared up—and you know what I mean—and you'll get paid straightaway, no messing. Do one iota more of stuff you aren't asked for, or overcharge us—and you're the fifth quote we've had in—and I'm sorry, but there simply won't be the money to pay you. Do you know what I mean?"

Pearl fixed Phil with a beady eye. He smiled nervously, then cleared his throat. He'd known a few Pearls growing up at school, and he had them to thank for being in a trade now, instead of prison like half of his mates.

"Absolutely. Totally. Not a problem."

He turned back to Issy, who was speechless but happy.

"We'll sort this place out for you, love."

"Great!" said Issy. "Uh, want some upside-down cake? Seeing as you're going to be turning this place upside down?"

•   •   •   •

"You were brilliant," said Issy, as they headed up toward the bus stop, each with one of Louis's hands in theirs. He was swinging as he went, insisting on more with a count of "*Won-doo-free!*"

"Don't be daft," said Pearl. "You've just got to ask for what you want; he wasn't going to bite you. He's in a selling job too."

"I know," said Issy. "The time for being timid really isn't now, is it?"

"Not if you want to make it," said Pearl thoughtfully. Issy looked back at the building. She'd just agreed to put a sizeable chunk of all the money she'd ever had in her entire life, and possibly more money than she'd ever see again, into this thing. Pearl was right. She was beginning to suspect that Pearl might be right about a lot of things.

They reached the bus stop. Issy turned to Pearl.

"OK," she said. "I am going to ask for what I want. I want you. To come and work for me. We'll figure Louis out between us. He'll be going to nursery soon anyway, won't he?"

Pearl nodded.

"Well, couldn't he go to a nursery near the shop? There's loads in Stokey. Come up and sit in the shop while we get opened up and the cakes go in, then pop him up to nursery and come back. He won't be far, and you can spend your lunch hour with him. What do you reckon?"

Pearl thought about it from all the angles. There was no reason Louis couldn't do a state nursery program up here; she felt a bit guilty for even thinking it, but it might not be a bad thing for him to mix with people who weren't all in public housing. Show him a bit of life. It could work. She'd talk to her government-appointed job finder.

"Hmmm," said Pearl.

"Is that a good hmmm or a bad hmmm?" asked Issy excitedly. There was a long pause.

"Well, let's give it a shot," said Pearl. And the two women very formally shook hands.

9

After that, everything moved at double speed. Despite Issy assuming that all the official papers would take months, insurance, licensing, and tax registration were all returned signed and sealed much more promptly than she'd expected. Phil and Andreas, buoyed, she believed, by daily influxes of cake and chivvying from Pearl, were doing a fantastic job; the new units, ordered online, had arrived and fit perfectly; they had painted the walls a soft shade of greige (gray and beige), and she had ordered retro 1950s aprons for Pearl and herself. Pearl sewed on her own extension ties. Issy was adoring her new industrial mixer and couldn't resist trying out more and more esoteric recipes with it. Helena had called a halt at licorice and malt balls.

Over the following weeks, the boys did a lovely job. Several days of hands-and-knees scrubbing by Issy and Pearl, aided occasionally by a grumbling Helena, had sorted out the cellar, while the boys had hammered and drilled and sung along to Cheryl Cole songs on the radio and utterly transformed the place. Whereas before a bare bulb had swung from the ceiling, now there were gently inset halogen lights that made everything gleam softly. Tables and chairs in off-white shades had a gentle patina that made them look old (even though, as they had assured the crusty fire officer, they weren't, and they were painted with flame-retardant paint), the wooden floor was polished to a high shine, and the display cases were of sparkling glass to show off the cakes, with cake stands ready to go on each table. The coffee machine, a second-hand Rancilio Classe 6, which everyone assured them was absolutely the best on the market, fizzed happily away in a corner. (Alas, it was a curious shade of orange, but not everything had to tastefully match.) Issy had lined the mantel over the fireplace with books for people to read (not too many, grumbled Pearl, we don't want tramps staying all day), and smart wooden poles would hold the day's newspapers.

The crockery they had bought in a huge job lot in the IKEA sale; a collection of duck egg, teal, and eau de Nil bowls, espresso cups, and plates that were so cheap they could afford to lose a few here and there to small hands or sticky fingers; and downstairs in the storeroom were industrial bags of flour and huge catering tubs of butter, all ready for the mixer.

But most of all, for Issy, it was the feel of the place: the aroma of cinnamon being liberally sprinkled on delectable, melting soft and yielding brownies that demanded to be scoffed within seconds of coming out of the oven (and Louis often obliged); the heavenly violet scent of the sauce for the blueberry cheesecake. The day they tasted jams for the Victoria sponge, Issy invited all of her friends. Toby and Trinida had come up from Brighton, and Paul and John who'd just gotten married, and even though a few had had to decline, being busy with new babies or house moves or in-laws or any of the million and one crazy things that being in your thirties seemed to entail, lots of people had turned up anyway, and they had all ended up sticky and giggling and slightly sick and decided Bonne Maman raspberry was simply the only way forward, until they could afford to make their own. It had taken a while to get all the stickiness off the wall tiles, but it was so much fun they'd decided to have a proper opening party, to test everything out and say thank you to everyone who'd helped so much so far.

● ● ● ●

Everywhere was spotless, breathlessly spick and span; inspected, ticked off, registered, and ready for action. They were set to open at 7:30 the following morning; Issy hadn't scheduled any marketing or promotion just yet. This was to be a "soft" launch, a quiet week or so for them to find their feet and get into the rhythm of how the café would work. Issy kept repeating this to herself so she wouldn't panic too much if nobody turned up at all.

They would need another member of staff, a part-timer to cover coffee breaks and holidays. Issy was hoping they'd get someone nice and local—a young girl perhaps, or a student needing a few extra quid here and there, who didn't mind working for the minimum wage and (she told herself off severely for even thinking this) was hopefully a bit more flexible and didn't have to look after anyone else.

The local state nursery, Little Teds, had found a place for Louis, which was amazing (Issy had perhaps told a very small lie on the form vis-à-vis Louis's home address—c/o the Cupcake Café—but needs must). But the nursery didn't open till 8:30, so he would have to come and have his breakfast in the café. Issy hoped he'd be happy with a few wooden toys she'd stashed behind the counter to distract customers' children from eating all the sugar sachets, but they'd have to wait and see.

And tonight, she was having a proper little party, a celebration to say thank you to everyone: to Pearl, for teaching her how to make coffee (she was still slightly afraid of the hissing steam pipe, but was learning); to Phil and Andreas, who'd done such a sterling job in the end; Des the estate agent and Mr. Barstow the landlord; Helena, who'd chivvied delivery men and helped her with national insurance forms that had her climbing the wall in frustration; Austin, who'd patiently explained profit margins, portion control, tax accounts and depreciation to her, then explained them again when her eyes had glazed over, then explained them one more time just to check; Mrs. Prescott, a slightly scary-looking local woman who did accounts for small businesses in her spare time and was clearly not someone to be trifled with. She and Austin had looked each other up and down with some understanding.

"What do you think?" Issy had asked Austin nervously afterward.

"Terrified the life out of me," said Austin. "I think she's absolutely perfect. She makes me want to go and file paperwork."

"Good," said Issy. "What about Helena?" She indicated the rather magnificent redhead who was laying into the builders one last time.

"Very…stately," said Austin politely, thinking to himself that actually, with her cheeks all red from the ovens, her soft black hair disheveled and loosening itself from where it had been hastily tied back, her black-fringed eyes, and her apron tied around her shapely form, the one he liked looking at in here was Issy herself. His professional client, he reminded himself sharply.

● ● ● ●

Issy glanced around nervously. Spring had been such a long time in coming this year, till the point where she'd thought it might simply never happen. Then one day it had arrived, like an unexpected gift turning up in the post; suddenly, out of nowhere, and the sun looked down as if surprised to still see people there, and people looked up as if surprised to be looking beyond the ends of their noses for the first time in months. Color was gradually seeping back into the world, and on this late March evening soft light filtered through the plate glass window, illuminating in shafts the gentle colors and restful tones of the Pear Tree Court café. Zac, her old friend, an out-of-work graphic designer, had painstakingly picked out "The Cupcake Café" in white swirly lower-case letters on the gray-brown frontage and it looked beautiful; pretty, but still understated. Sometimes, when she woke too early in the morning, Issy wondered if they weren't being a bit too understated. Then she remembered the look on people's faces when they ate the Bakewell tart her grandfather had taught her to make and bit her lip. Would good ingredients and free-range eggs and good coffee be enough? She and Pearl and Austin, who had happened to pop by that afternoon, had had a coffee-tasting session with all the wholesaler's samples. After four espressos they'd got all wide-eyed and bouncy and a touch hysterical but in the end had settled on two blends, a mellow Kailua Kona, an all-rounder coffee, and a stronger Selva Negra, for those who needed a bit of a pick-me-up in the morning, plus a sweet decaf for pregnant mothers and people who didn't really like coffee, just the smell. Would they cover their rent and the power bills? Would she ever make a living wage? Could she ever stop worrying? She phoned the home again. Were they ready?

• • • •

At his desk at Kalinga Deniki, over in East London, Graeme was puzzled. This wasn't really what he'd expected at all, but he hadn't heard once from Issy. Presumably her business hadn't failed yet. Or maybe it had, and she couldn't bear to break it to him. Well, she would, she would. He idly remembered last Saturday night, when he'd picked up a really fit blond in a nightclub. She had spent the whole night explaining to him the concept of body brushing and why Christina Aguilera was, like, a totally incredible role model. By the morning, when she'd asked him for a carrot smoothie, babe, he was desperate to get her out of the apartment. This wasn't like him at all.

Anyway, he had to concentrate. Work was still down, and he needed something juicy—a really big project—to impress the bosses back in the Netherlands. Something cool and cutting edge and funky, something that would attract high-net-worth buyers just like himself, something with all mod cons. He gazed at his map of London, bristling with pins to mark his current developments. His eye idly traced up from Farringdon to the Old Street roundabout, up through Islington and on to Albion Road, diverting into the tiny, barely legible Pear Tree Court. He could, he supposed, take a look at it.

Issy smoothed down her new dress, which had tiny sprigged flowers on it. What she'd started off feeling was terribly twee, like she was an extra from some American set show about housewives in the fifties, had suddenly come into vogue, and everyone was wearing floral prints with tight waists and little skirts sticking out. She felt slightly better knowing she was on trend, and after all, what was she doing but baking cupcakes? The florals felt right somehow, like their dainty little aprons and the faded Union Jack pillows, Scotchgarded to death of course, that she'd bought to go on the new gray sofa they'd put along the far end of the shop; the sofa was a lovely thing, as hardwearing as they came but as soft and old and homey-looking as a sofa could be.

It was a sofa for curling up on; for children to climb, or couples to perch on. You could watch the shop in motion, or the quiet courtyard outside. Issy was delighted with it.

So that was the back wall, with the sofa underneath a large station clock. On the right was the fireplace, with books above, and then several small tables for two, with mismatched pale gray chairs set at companionable angles. The tables themselves were square; Issy had a hatred of wobbly round tables that hardly held anything. The room opened up as you got closer to the counter—obviously once it had been two rooms, and the outline of the dividing wall remained. Closer to the counter the tables weren't so close together, so you could get a buggy in and people could (hopefully) queue, although it was still quite cramped. Cozy, that's what she meant, cozy. There was one long table near that room's fireplace, for larger groups, with a large, faded pink armchair at its head. At a push you could have a board meeting there.

The counter was lovely, curved, shining, and spotless, with a polished marble top and cake trays stacked high, ready to be filled the following morning. The small-paned windows on this side of the shop were balanced out by the huge floor-to-ceiling windows of the sofa section, which meant that when it got sunny, they'd be flooded with light. The coffee machine behind the counter, next to the door to the cellar, bubbled and hissed rather erratically, and the smell of fresh cakes filled the air.

Issy moved through the shop, saying hello to Mr. Hibbs, the crusty fire officer, who was eyeing the doorway just in case he'd forgotten where it was, and to the salesman from the kitchen shop, whose name was Norrie, who had been delighted when his young client who'd bought the pink kitchen had returned to buy an industrial oven, although she'd driven just as tough a bargain as before. (Issy couldn't believe how much she loved that oven. She'd taken a picture of it and sent it to her grandfather.) Norrie had brought his plump wife, and they were absolutely adoring the little cakes and pies piled around the room for them to sample. Austin's secretary Janet was there too, pink and pleased. "I never get to really see what the bank is doing," she confided to Issy. "It feels like just pushing paper around some-times. It's so lovely to see something real happening." She squeezed Issy's arm and Issy made a mental note not to give her any more of the cheap but tasty sparkling wine Pearl had sourced. "Not just real. Good. Something good."

"Thank you," said Issy, genuinely gratified, and went on filling people's glasses, keeping her eye on the door. And sure enough, at six o'clock, close to his bedtime, as he'd pointed out several times, when the last rays of sun were hitting the narrow passage from the street, a car backed up, completely illegally, into the passageway and a large wheelchair-friendly door pinged open at the back. Keavie jumped down from the front seat to attend to it and out came Grampa Joe.

Issy and Helena rushed to open the door, but Gramps indicated that he didn't want to come in just yet. Instead, he halted the chair in front of the shop. Issy worried about the cold getting to his chest, then watched Keavie tuck him in with a warm tartan blanket that had obviously been ready in the car. He stared at the shop frontage for a long time, his blue eyes turning a little watery in the cold. Well, Issy thought it was the cold.

"What do you think, Gramps?" she said, going out and kneeling down to take his hand. He stared at the delicately painted frontage; in at the softly lit, cozy-looking interior, where you could see the counter with beautiful, ornate cake stands loaded with delicacies and the coffee machine steaming happily; up at the old-fashioned script above the door. He turned his face to his granddaughter.

"It's…it's…I wish your grandmother were here to see it."

Issy grabbed his hand tight. "Come in and have a cake."

"I would love to," he said. "And send some nice ladies to talk to me. Keavie's all right, but she's a bit plump."

"Oi!" shouted Keavie, not in the least bit insulted and already with a cupcake in her hand and a steaming latte.

"Of course, I'm waiting for you, my dear," he said to Helena, who had bestowed a kiss on his cheek as he was wheeled inside. Issy put his chair next to the gas fire that looked real and danced merrily in the original tiled fireplace.

"Well, well, well," said Gramps, gazing around him, "Well, well, well. Issy, this French cake needs a pinch of salt."

Issy stared at him in affectionate irritation.

"*I know!* We forgot to get salt in this morning. Why are you even in that place? There's nothing wrong with you."

Austin glanced around for Darny to make sure he wasn't creating mischief somewhere. Seeing other people's happy families—he knew nothing of Issy's, of course—always made him a little forlorn. To his surprise, he found Darny sitting with a fat little two-year-old, teaching him how to toss stones. The two-year-old, unsurprisingly, was terrible at it, but seemed to be having a great time.

"No gambling!" warned Austin.

There was just one important last piece of the puzzle, hot off the press, that they were still waiting for. Work had picked up, so he was running a little late with it, but any moment now he would—

Zac burst through the door with two large boxes in his hands.

"They're here!"

There was a flurry as everyone bustled around to look. Then they stepped back to let Issy open them.

"Hmmm, let's see," Zac had said. "I do worry about you. But I can get things printed."

Issy tore through the plastic wrappings. Agonized over, endlessly reworked and reworded, tested over and over again, sweated over...and here it was. From out of the fresh, sharp, inky-scented box, slowly, reverently, Issy withdrew her first menu.

It was in the same soft pastels, with eau de Nil and white predominating, as the exterior. Zac had designed an exquisite tracery of pear tree blossom running up the side, like an art deco border. The lettering looked hand-printed and friendly, and was easy to read, and it was made of stiff card—easily replaceable, easily changeable, without having that horrid shiny plastic laminate to wipe off spills.

THE CUPCAKE CAFÉ

MENU
Fresh vanilla and lemon cream cupcakes with candied lemon rind and edible silver garnish

Red velvet cupcakes with a honey and buttermilk icing

English strawberry cupcakes with sugar-spun pansies

Muscadet grape macaroons with parma violet crème

Caramel 70% dark Yves Thuriès chocolate muffins with slow-roasted hazelnuts

SAMPLER PLATE
(one tiny slice of each—you know you want to)

COFFEES OF THE DAY
Kailua Kona slow roast—mild and sweet, from the volcanic slopes
   of Hawaii
Selva Negra—tangy with a medium body, from Nicaragua
Babycino

TEAS OF THE DAY
Rose Petal Black
French Verveine

Issy looked down at Zac, eyes brimming.

"Thank you so much," she said.

Zac looked uncomfortable.

"Don't be stupid," he said. "You've done all this. It's helped me loads, anyway. I've used it as a calling card and got more commissions already."

And then Helen loudly proposed a toast to the Cupcake Café and everyone clinked glasses and Issy made a speech where she said she would try to pay back the bank first (Austin raised his glass at that) before they had a proper celebration, but she thanked everyone for coming now, and everyone fulsomely applauded, even while they had their mouths full of cake and were spraying crumbs everywhere. Gramps was deep in conversation with various people, until Keavie took him back to the home.

Issy glanced outside. There was a shadow at the opening of the passageway. It looked like...no, it couldn't be. Her eyesight was playing tricks under the streetlights. It was just someone passing who looked a little like Graeme, that was all.

•   •   •   •

Graeme had made the excuse to himself that he was checking out another gym to use after work, but he hadn't really been surprised to find his feet heading down Albion Road. What had surprised him, however, was to see the shop full of people—it must be, he realized belatedly, a party and was amazed at how stung he felt that Issy would have a party and not invite him. And he was amazed again at how finished and professional the café looked. It was pretty and inviting, with its warm pools of light projecting out over the cobbles of the courtyard. He glanced around at the other buildings; it was hard to tell if they were occupied or not. But the café looked solid and real, something built and beautiful. Graeme usually saw spaces as square footage, profit and loss, as A, B, or Cs; flipping and auctioning and bidding and transferring invisible amounts of money from here to there and eventually, some of it, to himself. He didn't normally think about what people might do with a space once they had it, whether they would make it beautiful.

Suddenly from inside the café a peal of laughter rang out that he recognized at once as Issy's. He felt his fists tighten in his pockets. Why hadn't she listened to him? This was sure to be a failure. She had no right to sound so happy and carefree. How dare she not come back and ask him what he thought? Biting his lip, he stared up at the bricks of Pear Tree Court. Then he turned on his heel and walked off down the road, back to his sports car.

● ● ● ●

Inside, more fizzy wine was poured and everyone nodded their heads and said that the Cupcake Café was going to be a huge success, and Pearl looked sage and said sure it would be, as long as they remembered to give each of their clients free booze. Issy managed to chat to and individually thank everyone there, which meant she was so caught up in the hurly-burly that she had no chance to speak to anyone for long. Anyway, Pearl was scooping up a snoozing Louis and pointing meaningfully at her watch, which Issy realized with a start meant, "Go home to bed, you're in here at 6:00 a.m.," so she kissed everyone on the cheek, even Austin from the bank, who looked shocked but not entirely displeased, and Helena raised her eyebrows and asked did she think that was a good way of getting her overdraft limit extended. Issy, however, had danced on air all the way home, even after clearing up and locking up after everyone. To see her shop, her café, come alive with people eating and chatting and laughing and having a good time—it was everything she'd ever dreamed of. And after they got home and Helena sent her to bed, she still lay awake, staring at the ceiling, her mind and heart full of plans and dreams and ideas and the future, the future that was…Argh, she looked at her alarm clock. Only four hours away.

10

Won-doo-free!" shouted Louis. And, ceremoniously, Issy turned the quaint *Open/Closed* sign to *Open*. Zac had made that too; he'd thought of everything. She had a stack of his business cards by the till in case anyone asked her who'd done her wonderful graphic design.

Pearl and Issy looked at each other.

"Here goes nothing," said Pearl, and they took their places, expectantly, behind the counter. The entire place was spick and span, the day's produce lined up in the shining display cases, piled high on the stands. The air was scented with coffee and vanilla, with underlying beeswax furniture polish on the wooden tables. The sun was starting a slow spring creep around the huge plate-glass window, where it would illuminate each table in turn, starting with the big sofa on the end.

Issy couldn't keep still. She kept checking her oven, her storage shelves: the huge bags of flour all lined up so neatly, with the boxes of baking soda; baking powder, sugar, then row upon row of flavorings; fresh lemons in a box and the massive fridge filled with cream and big pots of creamy English butter—only the best. Issy had tried to explain the financial element to Austin: that when you chose makeup, some stuff was pretty much the same whatever you bought—an eyeliner pencil, for example, or powder blush—it didn't matter which brand, so you bought the cheapest. But some items—like foundation or lipstick—really, really showed their quality; it was obvious to anyone. So you had to get the best you could afford. And butter for the cakes and the icing had to come from happy cows, in happy fields with lush green grass. And that, she had announced, was that. Austin hadn't understood a word of her analogy, but he'd been quite impressed by her fervor. The baking powder on the other hand, she said, she'd get from a Hungarian lime works if it cut her bottom-line outlay, and they were both happy with that. Issy's store cupboard made her feel secure and orderly, like when she was a little girl and liked to play shop. It gave her a huge sense of satisfaction just to look at everything.

"Are you always like this, or are you making a special effort?" said Pearl. Issy was bouncing on the spot on her toes.

"A bit of both?" said Issy cautiously. Sometimes she wasn't quite sure how to take her member of staff.

"OK, good. Just so we know what we're working with. Would you like me to call you boss?"

"I would *not* like that."

"OK."

Issy smiled. "Maybe if we sell a lot, you could call me Princess Isabel."

Pearl gave her a look, but there was definitely a smile behind it.

At 7:45 a laborer put his head around the door.

"Do you do teas?"

Pearl smiled and nodded. "We certainly do! And our cakes are half-price all week."

The laborer came in cautiously, wiping his feet ostentatiously on the new Union Jack doormat Issy had bought from her friend with a shop, even though it wasn't in the budget and was thus extremely naughty.

"This is a bit posh, innit?" he said. He frowned. "How much is the tea then?"

"One pound forty," said Pearl.

The laborer bit his lip. "Yeah?" he said. "Wow."

"We've got all sorts," added Issy helpfully. "And you can try a few cake samples."

The laborer patted his belly regretfully. "Nah, the missus will kill me. You couldn't make me up a bacon sandwich, could you?"

Pearl made the tea—she had noticed that Issy was overexcited and liable to spill things—and without asking added milk and two sugars and handed it over with a smile, sealing the top of the paper container and adding a holder; it was very hot.

"Ta, love," said the man.

"You sure you don't want to try some cake?" said Issy, a tad overeagerly. The laborer glanced around nervously.

"It's all right, I'm sweet enough, love." He laughed nervously, then paid and retreated. Pearl rang up the till triumphantly.

"Our first customer!" she announced.

Issy smiled. "I think I scared him off though." She looked thoughtful. "What if he's right? What if we are too posh for around here?"

"Well, I'm not," said Pearl, wiping up a tiny drop of spilt milk on the glass countertop. "And nobody wants cake at seven thirty in the morning anyway."

"I do," said Issy. "Everyone will. People eat muffins. Muffins are just an American way of saying, 'I eat cake for breakfast.'"

Pearl looked at her for a second. "God, you're right. Well, that explains a lot."

"Hmmm," said Issy.

For the next hour, curious locals wandered by, wondering who was the latest person to take on the blighted site in Pear Tree Court. Some rudely walked up to the windows, pressed their noses against them, stared hard, then wandered off again.

"Well, that's not very nice," said Issy.

"Iss," said Pearl, who'd had a hard enough morning getting up at a quarter to six, then settling Louis in his new playgroup. "It's not your house. They're not judging you."

"How can you say that?" said Issy, glancing around the empty shop. "It's my heart and soul! They are totally judging me!"

At two minutes to nine, a dark little man with an old-fashioned hat pulled down over his forehead marched past the shop front. Almost completely past, he stopped suddenly and turned forty-five degrees, staring straight in. He looked right at them, regarded them ominously for several moments, then turned and continued on. Seconds later they heard the rattle of metal shutters opening.

"It's the ironmonger!" hissed Issy excitedly. She'd tried to go and meet her new neighbor before, but the rickety little pots and pans shop that adjoined them to the right seemed to keep very odd hours, and she'd never managed to catch anyone in before. "I shall take him a cup of coffee and make friends with him."

"I'd be wary," said Pearl. "You don't even know why those other businesses shut down. We already know he has a peculiar shop. Maybe he has peculiar habits. Maybe he poisoned the mall."

Issy stared at her.

"Well, if he offers me something to drink, I'll just say, 'It's all right, I have a café,'" she said.

Pearl raised an eyebrow but said nothing.

"Well, maybe I'll give it a couple of days," said Issy eventually.

At eleven, a tired, worn-down-looking woman came in with a tired, worn-down-looking child. Although both women fussed over the little girl, she didn't respond, mutely taking the proffered cake sample after shooting a look at her mother, who flapped a hand resignedly.

"Can I have a small black coffee please?" said the woman, who took it but turned down the cake samples (Issy was beginning to get paranoid) and counted out the change. She sat herself and the child on the gray sofa, in between the magazines and the newspapers and not far from the books. But the mother didn't glance at anything. She sipped her coffee slowly as the child sat playing with her fingers, very, very quietly, and the mother stared out of the window. With just the four of them in the space, Pearl and Issy soon found it difficult to talk normally.

"I'm going to put some music on," said Issy. But when she put the new Corinne Bailey Rae disc in her old CD player, now officially donated to the Cupcake Café, and pressed Play and gentle sweet tones filled the space, the woman immediately got up and left, as if the music were an alarm clock or was going to cost her extra. She didn't say good-bye, or thank you, and neither did the little girl. Issy glanced at Pearl.

"This is day one," said Pearl. "And I'm telling you, I do not want to have to nanny you through this, OK? You are a hard-headed business-woman and that is the end of it."

• • • •

But the rain started hammering down, day after day. Pearl's encouragement got more hollow with every quiet day that passed. Feeling horribly weary, and with Pearl having her day off, Issy was in the shop doing accounts (they were tricky and the figures were terrifying, even though Pearl kept telling her not to worry about it; she couldn't help it, and it was keeping her awake). She had two customers, which was better than none, she supposed. First of all the woman had come in again with the small child, which had slightly cheered Issy up; obviously she hadn't been so horrified she'd rushed away, never to darken their doors again. But didn't she have any friends? Couldn't she bring them around, with sticky-fingered children who needed a treat before making their way to Clissold Park? But once again the mother had retrieved her small cup of black coffee and perched herself in the corner of the sofa with her silent child, as if waiting outside the headmaster's office. Issy had smiled nicely and asked her how she was, but the woman's answer, "Fine," with a slightly hunted expression, had put her off asking any further questions.

Issy had leafed through all the Saturday papers—she'd thought she'd be rushed off her feet, but instead she was becoming exceptionally well informed about the world—when the welcome sound of the little bell they'd installed above the door rang out prettily. She looked up and smiled in recognition.

• • • •

Des didn't know what you were supposed to do with a baby. Jamie wouldn't stop crying unless he was being walked up and down. It was still chilly out there, and Jamie was only happy being wheeled about or lifted. The doctor had said it was just a touch of colic and Des had said, "What's colic?" and the doctor had smiled sympathetically and said, "Well, it's the word we use when babies cry for hours every day," and Des had been taken aback as well as disappointed. He had hoped the doctor would say, "Give him this medicine and he'll stop immediately and your wife will cheer up."

Turning back into Albion Road, he hadn't a clue what to do next— the four walls of their little terraced house were driving him crazy until he remembered Issy's café. He might pop in and see how she was doing. Maybe even score a free cup of coffee. Those cakes were quite something too.

• • • •

"Hello, Des!" said Issy eagerly, before registering, one, that Des was probably going to expect a free cup of coffee (which she supposed, grudgingly, he did deserve), and secondly that he was carrying a baby who was screeching his head off. Corinne Bailey Rae frankly could not compete.

"Oh, look at your…"

Issy was never quite sure what to say to babies. She was at that age now where if she made too much fuss over them everyone assumed she was desperately broody and felt sorry for her, whereas if she wasn't interested enough she was considered bitter and jealous and also secretly desperate for a baby but not able to show it. It was a minefield.

"Well, hello, little…" She looked at Des for guidance. The baby screwed up his face and arched his back in preparation for another howl.

"Boy…it's Jamie."

"Oh, little Jamie. How sweet. Welcome!"

Jamie took in a great gulp of breath, filling his lungs. Des spotted the warning signs.

"Uh, can I have a latte please."

He got his wallet out firmly. He had changed his mind about the free coffee thing; the noise pollution was already bad enough.

"And a cake," prompted Issy.

"Uh, no…"

"You're having a cake," said Issy, "and that's the end of it."

At that, the little girl at the end of the sofa raised her sad-looking face. Issy smiled at her.

"Excuse me?" she shouted to the girl's mother, over the noise of Jamie's huge wail. "Would your little girl like a cake? Free of charge, we're newly open."

The woman looked up from her magazine, suspicious immediately.

"Um, no, it's all right, no, thank you," she said, her Eastern European accent suddenly strongly marked; Issy hadn't noticed it before.

"It's OK!" hollered Issy. "Just this once."

The little girl, who was wearing a cheap and slightly grubby pink top that looked too thin for the weather, ran up to the counter, her eyes wide. The mother watched her, her eyes slightly less guarded, then held out her hands in a gesture of reluctant agreement.

"Which would you like?" said Issy, bending close to the little girl on the other side of the counter.

"Pink," came the breathless voice. Issy put it on a plate and took it to her table ceremoniously while Des's coffee brewed.

By the time it was ready, he was marching the baby around the shop, constant movement apparently the only thing that kept him quiet.

"Don't worry about me," he said to Issy's concerned look. "I'll just take a bite every third circuit."

"Fine," said Issy. "How's business?"

Des marched around the room, grimacing.

"Not ideal," he said. "This area has been up and coming for years, but it seems to hit a point beyond which it's just not going to go, do you know what I mean?"

Issy wondered sadly if it would reach all the way to a cupcake café, but she just nodded and smiled.

After about the ninth rotation (Issy was absolutely sure this wasn't ideal for a baby but didn't feel she had the necessary expertise to offer an opinion), the woman at the end of the sofa, who'd dipped her finger tentatively in the icing of her daughter's cupcake, eyed Des with sudden decisiveness.

"Excuse me," she said. Des stopped in his tracks. Jamie immediately started up a yell like a plane taking off.

"Uh, yes?" he said, gulping a mouthful of coffee. "Issy, that really is good," he said out of the side of his mouth.

"Give me your baby," said the woman.

Des glanced at Issy. The woman's face fell.

"I'm not bad lady. Give me your baby. I help him."

"Um, I'm not sure…"

A hideous un-PC silence hit the air until Des realized, with a sense of inevitability, that if he didn't hand over the baby he would look like he was accusing her of something shocking. Like the true Englishman he was, he felt that inadvertently causing offense and embarrassment would, in the end, be simply too painful. Issy smiled encouragingly as he gave the screeching baby to the woman, whose little girl immediately scampered up on tiptoes to have a look.

*"Sa ziza zecob dela dalou'a
Boralea'e borale mi komi oula
Etawuae'o ela'o coralia wu'aila
Ilei pandera zel e' tomu pere no mo mai
Alatawuané icas imani'u"*

the woman sang, immediately enraptured by Jamie, who, surprised to find himself in a stranger's arms, had momentarily fallen silent and was gazing at her with his great blue eyes. The woman gently kissed the top of his head.

"Maybe she's a witch," hissed Des to Issy.

"Shhh!" Issy said, fascinated by what the woman was doing. Jamie opened his mouth to prepare himself for another yell, and calmly and confidently the woman flipped the baby over onto just one arm, until he was lying there on his tummy, his tiny arms and legs flopping toward the floor. He wriggled and squirmed there for a second, Des instinctively moving forward—it looked like he would fall, balanced so precariously on a single limb—and then the impossible happened. Jamie blinked his huge, glass-blue eyes once, twice, then somehow his tiny rosebud mouth found his thumb and he settled. Within seconds, and with all of them watching, as clearly and humorously as in a cartoon, his eyes grew heavy, heavier…and he was fast asleep.

Des shook his head.

"What…what…Have you just slipped him something?"

The woman fortunately didn't understand.

"He is very tired." She looked at Des. "You too are very tired," she said kindly.

Suddenly, and very uncharacteristically, Des thought he was about to burst into tears. He hadn't even cried when Jamie was born; not since his father had died. But somehow…

"I am…a *little* tired," he said suddenly, slumping down next to her on the sofa.

"What did you do?" asked Issy, amazed. It had been like magic.

"Um…" said the woman, clearly searching for the English words. "Hmmm. Let me see. It is like the tiger in the tree."

They both looked at her.

"When little babies have sore tummies…then they like to lie like the tiger in the tree. It helps their tummies."

And sure enough, Jamie did look like a sleepy cat drooping happily over a branch. Expertly, the woman transferred him to his pram on his tummy.

"Uh," said Des, anxious to show that he did, at least, know the first thing about parenting, "you're not meant to put them on their stomachs."

The woman fixed him with a strict look.

"Babies with sore tummies sleep better on tummies. You watch him. He not die."

It had to be said that Jamie looked as utterly blissful as only a tiny baby fast asleep can look. His pale pink pillowing lips were open and only a gentle, tiny lifting of his narrow back could be seen. The woman took the blanket and tucked him in fiercely and tight so he could barely move. Des, used to watching Jamie wrestle and squirm in his sleep like he was fighting an invisible enemy, could only stare.

"I think I'll have another cup of coffee," he said in a disbelieving tone. "And…er…do you think…would you mind passing," he gulped with amazement, "the newspaper?"

• • • •

Issy smiled at the memory. Of course in the end it had netted her about four quid, but Des and the woman, whose name turned out to be Mira, had talked and got along rather well, and for a while at least there was a little hum of conversation in the café; the sound she'd been longing to hear. Then the ironmonger from next door had come up and studied the menu in the window for ages—agonizingly long—before heading off again. Issy had called a hello but he hadn't answered. She was starting to hate the hideously slow beat of the clock. Two teenage girls had come in at lunchtime and carefully counted out enough for one chocolate and ginger cake between them and two glasses of water, but they'd gone by the time the door dinged at half past three. It was Helena.

"That bad, huh?" said Helena.

Issy was amazed to find herself slightly irritated. She was never normally irritated by Helena; they'd been friends for so long. But for her to turn up now, just as she was feeling her most unsuccessful, seemed almost cruel.

"Hey," said Helena. "How's it going?"

"Would you like an unsold cupcake?" said Issy, slightly more sharply than she'd intended.

"Yes," said Helena, and took out her wallet.

"Put your wallet away," said Issy. "I have to throw them out at the end of the day anyway, for health and safety."

Helena raised her eyebrows. "Be quiet. I won't hear of it. I shouldn't really be eating these anyway. Although I did go up another cup size, so there's a bonus."

"A cupcake size!" said Issy. "Ha ha. I am, at least, still hilarious."

"Why don't you close up early; we'll go home and watch *Grosse Pointe Blank* and then phone all our old friends who don't phone us anymore and tell them we're having a lie-in tomorrow when they have to get up at five a.m. and heat bottles?"

"That is tempting," said Issy regretfully. "But I can't. We're open till four thirty today."

"So what about the 'I am master of my own destiny and can do what I like' thing? I thought that was the point of running your own business."

"And," said Issy, "I have to cash up and go through my weekly accounts."

"Well, that's not going to take long, is it?"

"Helena?"

"Too harsh?"

"Yes."

"I'll buy the wine."

"Fine."

"Fine." Just then the bell dinged again.

Austin looked around the shop warily. He knew they were just starting out, but nonetheless it would have been nice to see a few people here, and Issy may be moving her butt a bit to get things done rather than sitting up at the counter mooning with her girlfriend.

Darny was at a play program, and Austin was having one of those realizations he had with wearying predictability, when he got the horrible feeling he'd forgotten something important and had to struggle to remember what it was. After their parents died, Austin had been advised by the social worker handling the guardianship that he should talk to a therapist. The therapist had suggested that being disorganized was at some level a cry for help for his parents to come back and sort him out, and recommended he didn't look for a life partner to do the same. Austin suspected this was total bollocks, but that still didn't help when, as had happened half an hour ago, he realized that he'd lost his copy of the shop rental agreement and if he didn't get it for the files Janet was going to have his guts for garters.

"Uh, hi there," he said.

Issy jumped up guiltily. What would be nice, she figured, would be if people involved with her business would come along when there were lots of people in. She wished obscurely that Helena wasn't there; it didn't look very professional. Especially with Helena nudging her and raising her eyebrows like Groucho Marx.

"Hello!" she said. "Would you like a cake for Darny?"

"Giving away cakes?" said Austin with a twinkle in his eye. "I'm sure that's not in the business plan."

"You can't have read it right," said Issy, suddenly feeling flustered. It was that grin of his. It was distractingly un-bank-like.

"That's right, I didn't," agreed Austin. "How's it going?"

"Well, this is our soft launch," said Issy. "You know, obviously, it's going to take a while to build up."

"I have full confidence in the business plan," he said swiftly.

"The one you haven't read," said Issy.

Austin would have smiled more if he had actually read it, but he had totally followed his gut as he always did when lending. It usually worked in his favor. If it was a good enough method for murder detectives, he liked to think, it was good enough for him.

"You know, I know someone who does a marketing workshop," he said, and wrote the details down for Issy. She pored over them carefully and asked some questions; it felt like he was genuinely taking an interest. Well, protecting his investment, obviously, she realized.

"Thanks," said Issy to Austin. It was odd to hear him talk so much sense when he was wearing his stripy jumper inside out. "Your jumper's inside out."

Austin glanced at it.

"Oh, yes, I know. Darny decided that all clothes should have their labels sticking out, that's how you know you're wearing the right clothes. And I couldn't seem to convince him logically otherwise, so I decided to just, you know, play along till he figures it out. He should probably have grown out of that now, huh?"

"And how's he going to figure it out if you've got it all wrong?" asked Issy, smiling.

"That is a very good point," said Austin, and in one gesture he pulled off the sweater. Inadvertently he pulled up some of his forest-green shirt with it, exposing a trim tummy. Issy caught herself staring at it, then realized Helena was staring at her, muted mirth in her eyes. Her old habit came back: she felt her cheeks flushing a deep, horrifying red.

"I don't know," said Austin, who hadn't stopped talking. "I was just trying to get him to jungle gym on time. I assume the other kids will call him horrible names and make him cry till he eventually falls into line, stamps out his individuality and conforms like a sheep."

He pulled his jumper back on properly and looked for Issy, but she'd disappeared downstairs.

"Uh, I'll get those rental agreement papers you need!" she shouted up the stairwell. Helena gave him a knowing smile.

"Stay for coffee," she said.

Issy threw cold water on her face from the catering sink downstairs. This was absolutely ridiculous. She had to pull herself together; she had to work with him. She wasn't twelve.

"Here." She reappeared, only mildly flushed. "A cupcake for Darny. I insist. It's…what would your marketing people call it? A sample."

"Giving samples to people who get a pound a week pocket money probably wouldn't pass a cost/benefit analysis," said Austin, "but thank you." He took the cake and found his fingers holding on to it just a second too long, as if reluctant to give up the traces of her touch.

● ● ● ●

"And then," said Helena, pouring the last of the wine, "then you dragged him downstairs into your store cupboard and—"

Issy bit her lip. "Shut up!" she said.

"He pulled you into his manly, calculator-wielding arms and—"

"*Stop it!*" said Issy. "I will throw cushions."

"Throw all the cushions you like," said Helena. "I already like him nine thousand percent more than Graeme."

As usual, at the mention of Graeme's name, Issy went a little quiet.

"Oh, come on, Iss, I'm only teasing. Don't be so sensitive."

"I know, I know. Anyway, Austin came in to get those rental papers signed. And to give me a telling-off for slacking; you could see it on his face when he walked in the door."

"On a Saturday?"

"He's local. He lives around here. Knows the area inside out."

"That's because he's so clever and wonderful. Smooch smooch smooch."

"Shut up!" Issy hurled her pillow direct at Helena's head. "And I need an early night. I've got stuff to do tomorrow."

"Is it smooching?"

"Good night, Helena. You need a hobby."

"You're it!"

• • • •

The Sunday train was absolutely packed with weekend travelers; lots of men coming back from the match yesterday, loudly spilling cans of beer and hollering at their friends across the aisles. Issy found a quiet corner seat with her book and half gazed at her tired-looking reflection in the window, thinking back over her visit to Grampa Joe.

"Well, you didn't half perk him up with that party," Keavie had said when she arrived. "He's been tired since though. And maybe a little…distracted."

"It's starting again, isn't it?" Issy had said, stricken. "It's taking hold."

Keavie looked pained, and touched Issy briefly on the arm.

"You know…I mean, this is why he's here, you know that," she said.

Issy nodded. "I know. I know. It's just…he's seemed so well."

"Yes, well, often just the security of being looked after can help people for a few months."

Issy looked down. "But not forever."

Keavie looked sad too. "Issy…"

"I know, I know. It's incurable. It's progressive."

"He has his moments," said Keavie. "He's had a good few days actually, you might be lucky. And he always likes it when you visit."

Issy rearranged her face by an effort of will, for the second time in as many days, and marched into the room.

"Hello, Gramps!" she said loudly. Joe half opened his eyes.

"Catherine!" he said. "Margaret! Carmen! Issy!"

"Issy," said Issy gratefully, wondering briefly who Carmen was. She gave him a hug, felt the whiskery skin that seemed to droop off his bones even more every time she came. "How are you doing, Gramps? Been outside much? They feeding you all right?"

Joe waved his hands.

"No, no, no," he said. "No. Not that."

He leaned forward as far as he could toward Issy. The effort made his chest rattle.

"Sometimes," he said, slowly. "Sometimes I don't always get things right these days, my Issy."

"I know, Grampa," said Issy, clasping his hand. "Nobody does really."

"No," he said. "I know. But it's not that…"

He seemed to lose his train of thought and stared out of the window. Then he came back to himself.

"I…I was thinking, Issy, but sometimes I get things wrong, sometimes I just dream things…"

"Go on."

"Have you…has my little Issy got a bakery?"

He said bakery like he might have said Kingdom of Gold.

"Yes, Grampa! You've seen it, remember? You came to a party there."

Joe shook his head.

"The nurses read those letters out to me every morning," he said, "but I never remember a thing."

"I do have a bakery," said Issy. "Yes. Well, more a patisserie really. Cakes and things. I don't make bread."

"Making bread is a fine profession too," said Joe.

"I know. I know it is. This is more like a café."

Issy noticed her gramps's eyes go watery. This wasn't ideal; it didn't do to get him too emotional.

"My little Issy. A baker!"

"I know! Well, you taught me everything I know."

The old man clasped her hand hard.

"And is it doing well? Is it making a living?"

"Hmmm," said Issy. "Well, it's early days. I'm finding it…well, I'm finding it all a little tricky, to be honest."

"That's because you're a businesswoman now, Issy. It's all on your shoulders…Do you have children?"

"No, Gramps. Not yet," said Issy, a little sadly. "No. I don't have any children."

"Oh. So you only have to provide for yourself. Well, that's good."

"Hmmm," said Issy. "But you know I still have to get people through the door."

"Well, that's easy," said Joe. "People just have to smell a bakery and they're there."

"That's the problem," mused Issy. "They can't smell us. We're too far away, tucked away."

"That is a problem," said Joe. "Well, are you taking your products to the people? Getting out on the street? Showing people what you have?"

"Not really," said Issy. "Mostly I'm busy in the kitchen. It would feel a bit…desperate, don't you think, to shove food at people in the street? I'm sure I wouldn't take anything people offered me in the street."

Joe's face grew perturbed.

"Have you learned nothing from me?" he said. "It's not all cream horns and French cakes, you know."

"I thought if the cakes were big enough…"

"When I started in Manchester, it were 1938. Right before the war. Everyone terrified and not a spare penny in their pockets for fancy cakes."

Issy had heard this story before but was always happy to hear it again. She settled back in her chair, like she was a little girl and Gramps was tucking her up in bed rather than vice versa.

"And my father had died in the first war, and the bakeries in those days, they were fierce places. Black bread and mice droppings and who knew what, as long as you could get what you were after for a far-thing and feed your mites. People didn't care. There weren't no market for fancy cakes in that part of the world, no. But I started young, and there weren't no one hungrier than me. I were up at four, sweeping floors, sifting flour, kneading; kneading? I had biceps like a boxer's, no joke, my Isabel. People used to remark on it. The ladies especially."

Joe looked like he was about to fall asleep, so Issy leaned closer.

"Course there was one good thing about working there, with the early starts and the big bags of flour…when it was that cold in the winter. And I mean proper cold." Joe looked around. "It's never cold in here. They always stuff you up with scarves and dressing gowns till you think you're going to pop like a sausage.

"But on those cold mornings, when you came in—and the ovens never went out, you know, they ran all night so the bread was always fresh, aye. So you'd wake up and man, my ma's house—your great-grandma Mabel—oh, it was absolutely cold. Ice on the blankets, ice on the windows. You couldn't dry a thing in the wintertime, so you just kept it on.

"I'd build the fire up in the morning and I wouldn't be able to light the kindling without trembling. We had some harsh winters then. But you stepped into that bakery and suddenly you could feel the warmth in your bones, feel it through your wet clothes and your damp wool and your chapped hands. The kiddies used to come in, Isabel, and you could see it in their faces; they loved the warm and the smell of it. There were real poor folks then, Issy, not like now when they've all got flat screen TVs."

Issy let this pass and patted his hand.

"Kind of like the pub is for me, I think," said Joe. "Warm and friendly and something to sup. That's how you've got to be. Welcoming like." He leaned forward.

"And if a woman had a babbie at home she could barely feed, or someone was a bit short of a coupon, or there were just too many mouths to feed—those Flahertys, I remember, they had a babbie a year and Patrick never could hold down a job. Well then, you'd slip them a bit extra. A loaf that didn't turn out true or a few buns a couple of days old. And word would get around. And sure, some folks turn up to see if they'll be getting something for nothing. But some folks just turn up because you do right by them. And I tell you, every single Flaherty child—and there were gone thirteen of them, you had to stop counting about then. Well, every single Flaherty child, and their children when they all grew up and got jobs, and then their children came along and went to college and everything, and every single one of them got their bread from Randall's for their whole lives. I could have run that bakery off of Flahertys alone. And that's how it is in business. Some'll rob you blind, some'll kick you when you're down, but you spread some good feeling and some warmth about, and people like that. Aye."

Joe sat back, looking tired out.

"Gramps," said Isabel, leaning over and kissing him square on the nose. "You're brilliant."

The old man looked up with watery eyes.

"What is it now? Who are you? Is that you, Marian?"

"No, Gramps. It's me. It's Isabel."

"Isabel? My wee lass Isabel?"

He peered closer.

"What are you doing these days, my sweet?"

11

A little taste of sunshine to take out into the world

strawberry meringue cupcakes

• • • •

For 24 cupcakes

* 16 tbsp unsalted butter, at room temperature
* 1 cup superfine sugar
* 4 eggs
* 1 cup self-rising flour
* 4 tbsp milk (whole or semi-skimmed, not skimmed)
* 6–8 tsp strawberry jam

For the Swiss meringue buttercream
* 8 egg whites
* 2 cups superfine sugar
* 32 tbsp unsalted butter
* 4 tsp vanilla extract
* 8 tbsp seedless strawberry jam

Preheat the oven to 370°F/convection oven 340°F/gas mark 5.

Beat together the butter and sugar until pale and fluffy. Add the eggs, flour, and milk, and beat until well combined and smooth. Spoon the mixture evenly into the 24 paper cases.

Spoon a little jam onto each cake and, using a cocktail stick, swirl the jam into the batter.

Bake for 15 minutes or until a skewer comes out clean.

To make Swiss meringue buttercream:

Place the egg whites and sugar in a bowl over a pan of simmering water. Stir pretty much constantly to prevent the egg from cooking. After five to ten minutes, when the sugar has dissolved, remove the bowl from the pan of simmering water and whisk until the meringue has puffed up and the mix is cool.

Add the butter and vanilla to the meringue and whisk until the butter has been completely incorporated into it. At first, it will look a disaster—it will collapse and look curdled but don't worry! Stop when the mixture is smooth, light, and fluffy.

Beat the jam into the buttercream. If you want it pinker, add a little food coloring. Spoon the buttercream into a piping bag and swirl onto each cupcake. Finish off with some sugar sprinkles or decorations.

Quarter the cakes and put the pieces into tiny cases with cocktail sticks poking out. Attempt to get passersby to try them and be knocked out by your genius so they then come and spend lots of money at your shop and save you from bankruptcy.

Won, *doo, free!*" Louis, hands carefully washed, was allowed to put the mini cupcakes into their special tin. There were considerably more than three, but that was as far as his counting went. Issy was in a whip of excitement that morning, making up free samples for everywhere she could think of.

"We're changing our whole strategy," she said to Pearl.

"So instead of throwing our cupcakes away at the end of the day we're throwing them at people instead?" Pearl had said, but didn't want to rain on Issy's parade; a big surge of positivity couldn't be a bad thing this early in the game. Issy had called up Zac and complimented his hairdo until he'd drawn her up a pretty flyer and she'd made copies at the all-night Liverpool Street Kail Kwik when she couldn't sleep with excitement at 5:00 a.m.

MEET ME AT THE CUPCAKE CAFÉ!

Busy day? Stressful time?
Need five minutes of peace, quiet, and
Some heavenly cake and coffee?
Then come on in and soothe your soul at
4 Pear Tree Court, off Albion Road.
Free cupcake and relaxation with every
cup of coffee and this flyer.

Then the menu was printed underneath.

"Now, make sure you hand these out to everyone at the nursery," said Issy strictly.

"*Iss,*" said Louis.

"Uh, yeah," said Pearl, wondering. The nursery hadn't turned out at all like she'd expected. Although it was nominally a government-run scheme for young disadvantaged children—and she couldn't deny it had beautiful facilities, clean, new toys, and unripped books—it wasn't, as she'd imagined, full of mothers like herself, struggling to get by and make a living, maybe on their own too. There were lots of yummy mummies, affluent women who double-parked and blocked the road in huge 4×4s, who all seemed to know each other and discussed interior decorators and hiring children's party entertainers at full volume across the room.

Their children weren't dressed like Louis, who Pearl always thought looked smart in his little tracksuits and sparkling white trainers. These children wore old stripy Breton shirts and baggy knee-length shorts and had long hair and looked like children from long ago. It couldn't be practical, Pearl thought, considering how dirty kids got—those shirts would get holes in them in no time, they were only cotton, and think of the ironing. Mind you, these women didn't really look like they did their own ironing. And Pearl couldn't help but notice that when the party invitations came around, or the playdates, Louis—who played beautifully with whoever was there; who shared his toys and cuddled the play leader, Jocelyn, every day; Louis at whom the other women directed pleasant but nonspecific smiles and truisms of "isn't he adorable?"—was never invited. Her gorgeous, beautiful, delightful son.

And Pearl knew it wasn't, as her younger self would have once loudly asserted, because of the color of his skin. There were Chinese and Indian children; mixed race, African, and every shade in between. All the little girls wore sprigged muslin tops and immaculate white linen trousers, with polka dot Wellingtons when it rained outside, their hair long and lustrous or cut into little French bobs with bangs. The little boys looked hardy and ruddy, used to running about and watching rugby with their dads—there was much talk of fathers and husbands at the nursery. There had been much less back on the estate in Lewisham.

It was her, Pearl knew. Her clothes, her weight, her style, her voice. Rubbing off on Louis, her perfect boy. And now she had to go and hand out Issy's sodding leaflets and her sodding free samples, like some kind of *Big Issue* seller, to all those immaculate women, just so she could confirm every single thing those women already thought about her. She stomped out rather crossly into the lightly drizzling spring morning.

● ● ● ●

Issy had rather the easier task; she strolled down to her old bus stop, a large tin tucked under her arm, the drizzle not dampening her buoyant mood. Off to the bus stop. It felt almost like the old days.

Sure enough, the lineup of familiar faces, peering around for the big red bus, was still there: the angry young man with the loud iPod;

Mr. Dandruff; the bag lady trundling by. And Linda, whose face was wreathed in smiles when she saw her.

"Hello, dear! Have you got a job? You know, it's a shame you never got into feet like my Leanne. I was thinking that."

"Well," said Issy, smiling, "I have done something. I've opened a little café…just up there!"

Linda turned around, and Issy enjoyed her astonishment.

"Oh how *lovely*," Linda said. "Do you do bacon sandwiches?"

"Nooo," said Issy, making a mental note that, if the business ever took off, they must look into serving up bloody bacon sandwiches if everyone wanted them so much. "We do coffee and cake."

"Like your hobby?" said Linda.

Issy bit her lip. She didn't like her baking being referred to as a "hobby," especially not now.

"Well, they do say follow your passion," she said, smiling through gritted teeth. "Here! Have a cake. And a flyer."

"I will," said Linda. "Oh, Issy, I'm so pleased for you! And what about that nice young man of yours with the fancy car?"

"Hmmm," said Issy.

"Oh well, soon you'll be able to give up your hobby, and you'll be down in haberdashery to pick out some voile for your veil."

"Please pop in for a coffee sometime," said Issy, trying to keep the smile on her face. "Would be lovely to see you."

"Well, yes, of course. For as long as you're there," said Linda. "It's great to have a hobby."

Issy managed not to roll her eyes but headed up the line, and as the bus arrived, even the young man who never took his iPod out grabbed a cake and gave her a thumbs up. She popped her head inside the bus and offered a cake to the driver, but he fiercely shook his head and Issy withdrew, slightly flattened.

Well, she said to herself, we've got to start somewhere.

Issy bit into a frankly heavenly cappuccino cake, where she'd whipped the icing so fine it was practically foam. It was exquisite. Or just a cake, she supposed.

Hobby my bum, she said crossly to herself. She returned slowly to the shop, just in time to see two schoolkids charging out, each clutching two cakes in grubby paws.

"Get out of it, you little bastards!" she screamed, relieved at least that she had locked the till.

The man from the ironmonger's walked past, looking at her strangely.

"Hello!" said Issy, trying to get back her normal voice. He stopped.

"Hello," he said. He had a slight accent Issy couldn't place.

"We're the new shop," said Issy, somewhat redundantly. "Would you like a cake?"

He was dressed fastidiously, she noticed, suit, a narrow tie, a topcoat, a scarf, and even a homburg. The effect was very old-fashioned. She'd have expected him to be in brown overalls, if anything.

He bowed his head over her cake tin and selected the most perfect of the cappuccino cakes, picking it up daintily between two fingers.

"I'm Issy," she offered when he'd made his choice.

"Delighted," said the man and headed on back toward his shop, which, as always, had the shutters tightly closed. Peculiar.

•   •   •   •

"I am undaunted," vowed Issy, even as Pearl returned from dropping off Louis, uncharacteristically bowed. She still had more than half the cakes in the tin. "Joshua isn't allowed sugar," she reported, "and Tabitha has food intolerances. And Olly's mother wanted to know that the flour was fair trade."

"Everything's fair trade," said Issy, exasperated.

"I told her that, but she said she was going to say no just to be on the safe side," said Pearl dully.

"Never mind," said Issy. "We soldier on!"

• • • •

The following morning Issy headed up to Stoke Newington High Street, aiming to leave flyers and free samples in every shop. This wasn't as easy as it sounded. Every little shop already had every spare centimeter of space taken up with flyers for yoga classes, baby gyms and massage, circus school, jazz concerts, tango lessons, home delivery organic vegetables, knitting circles, library events, local theatre shows and nature walks. The world seemed papered in flyers, thought Issy, and Zac's beautiful, elegant designs seemed suddenly limp and colorless going up against neon oranges and bright yellows. The people in the little shops seemed listless and uninterested, although they accepted the cakes of course. Issy took the opportunity to study them. These were people, like her, who'd had a dream of running their own business and had gone for it. She wished they looked a little less exhausted and unhappy.

About a third of the way down the street an angry-looking woman in a tie-dye T-shirt with messy hair came storming up to her with a bumptious look on her face.

"What are you doing?" she demanded peremptorily.

"I'm handing out samples for my new café," said Issy bravely, proffering the tin. "Would you like one?"

The woman made a face. "Full of refined sugar and trans fats, designed to turn us into obese TV slaves? Not bloody likely."

Issy had encountered lack of interest, but this was the first open hostility she'd faced over the café, she realized.

"OK, never mind," she said, replacing the lid.

"But you can't just go handing stuff out," said the woman. "There's other cafés on this street! We've been here a lot longer than you, so you just have to butt out of our way."

Issy turned around, and sure enough, at the doors of several coffee houses and tea shops, people were standing and watching, their eyes hostile.

"And we're a cooperative," said the woman. "We all work together in partnership. Everything is wholesome, and everything is fair trade. We're not poisoning children. And that's what the community wants around here. So you can just back off."

Issy felt herself shaking with upset and rage. Who was this horrible bloody woman with her horrible long gray greasy hair and ugly spectacles and hideous T-shirt?

"I think there's room for everyone," she managed, her voice shaking.

"Well, there's not," said the woman, who'd obviously spent a lifetime standing up and shouting at gatherings and, as far as Issy could tell, was thoroughly enjoying this. "We were here first. We're helping communities in Africa; you're not doing anyone the least bit of good. Nobody wants you. So just piss off, OK? Or at least the next time ask before you come up trying to steal people's livelihoods."

Someone in a doorway muttered, "Hear, hear," loud enough so that Issy caught it. She stumbled off, half-blinded with tears, conscious of the eyes of the other café owners on her back—wearing that silly floral dress, they must think her a completely stupid priss. Hardly knowing where she was going, just that she couldn't turn back through that crowd—feeling she could never ever walk that street again—she headed straight to the main road where she could lose herself in the mass of humanity, of all colors and types, thronging the Dalston Road, where no one would notice a crying woman in a vintage dress.

• • • •

Austin was fighting his way to the pound shop to see if they had something good for Darny to wear to a costume party—he'd like to buy him that Spiderman costume with the muscles he really wanted, but when he'd paid for after-school care plus the mortgage his parents had thoughtlessly not paid off before they died, plus the day-to-day living expenses, plus the late fees on all the bills he always meant to move on to direct debit but never seemed to manage, there was precious little left, and there seemed no point in buying anything pricey as Darny rarely came home without huge rents in filthy clothing. (He had horrified a putative girlfriend of Austin's a few years ago by answering the question "What do you like doing?" with *"Fighting!"* Then he had jumped on her and pummeled her to show exactly what he meant. Austin hadn't seen much of Julia after that.) As he'd nearly made it across the road he saw Isabel Randall standing by the *Wait* sign but not crossing.

"Hello," he said. Issy looked up at him, blinking back tears.

She couldn't help it; she was glad to see a friendly face. But she didn't trust herself to speak, in case she suddenly broke down.

"Hello," Austin said again, worried she hadn't recognized him. Issy swallowed hard and reminded herself that crying in front of her bank manager was possibly the worst look imaginable.

"Um. Er. Hello," she managed finally, trying not to trumpet a huge wall of snot at him.

Austin was used to being taller than everyone around him and having to make a real effort to peer down and check out people's faces, and he didn't like to look as if he were staring. On the other hand, she sounded really weird. He looked into her face. Her eyes were shiny and her nose was red. In Darny, that was rarely a good sign.

"Are you all right?" he said. Issy wished he didn't sound so kind. He was going to set her off again. Austin could see quite a lot of restraining going on. He put a hand on her shoulder. "Would you like to get a coffee somewhere?"

He cursed the words as soon as they were out of his mouth. To Issy's credit she managed not to actually burst into tears, but one lone drop did trickle slowly and obviously all the way down her cheek.

"No, no, no, of course you wouldn't…of course not. Um."

For want of anywhere better to go, they ended up in a horrible pub, full of morning drinkers. Issy ordered a green tea and dredged the scum off the top with a spoon, and Austin looked around nervously then ordered a Fanta.

"I'm sorry," said Issy several times. But then, somehow—and she was sure she would regret this—she ended up telling him the whole thing. He was just so easy to talk to. Austin winced.

"And now I'm telling you," concluded Issy, worried she was going to start crying again, "you're going to think I'm totally rubbish and too wimpy for business, and you're going to think I'll fail, and you know, it might fail. If they all gang up on me…it'll be like the mafia, Austin! I'll have to pay protection money, and they'll come around and put a horse's head in my oven!"

"I think they're all vegetarians," said Austin, draining his Fanta and spilling some on his shirt. Issy gulped and tried a tentative smile.

"You've spilled some of your drink," she pointed out.

"I know," said Austin, "but I look stupid when I use a straw."

He leaned forward. Issy was conscious, suddenly, of how long his eyelashes were. Having his face so close to hers suddenly felt strange and intimate.

"Look, I know those guys up there. They came to us on a campaign to make us do more ethical banking and then we pointed out to them that banking isn't terribly ethical and that we couldn't absolutely promise that some of our investments weren't in the defense industry, seeing as it is, you know, Britain's biggest industry, and they screamed and called us all fascists and stormed out and then called us back later and asked for a loan. And there were about sixteen of them too. Their business plan included the four-hour weekly meeting they have to make the cooperative fair. Apparently it frequently ends up in physical violence."

Issy smiled weakly. Of course Austin was only trying to cheer her up—he would do this for anybody—but nonetheless it was definitely helping.

"And don't you worry a bit about 'café solidarity.' They all hate each other's guts on that street. Honestly, if one of the cafés burned down they'd be absolutely delighted. So don't think they're all going to gang up against you, they can't even manage to gang up to clean their own toilet, as I noticed when I had to take Darny in there one day in an emergency. Does dreadful things to the digestion, too much vegan food."

Issy laughed.

"That's better."

"You know," said Issy, "I'm not always like this. I actually used to be quite a fun person, before I got into the whole running-a-business thing."

"Are you sure?" said Austin gravely. "Maybe you were even worse and this is you lightening up."

Issy smiled again. "Oh yes, you're totally right—I remember now. I was a goth and didn't leave the house. And I listened to a lot of very serious music and sighed a lot like this."

She sighed loudly. Austin sighed too.

"So you thought you'd get into happy cakes…" he said.

"Which you never eat."

"For very sound reasons."

"And yes, this is me ecstatic now," said Issy.

"I knew it," he replied.

Issy really did feel better.

"OK," said Austin, heaving another big sigh. "You've talked me into it. Give me one of your depressive cupcakes."

"Ha!" said Issy. "No!"

"What do you mean, no? I'm your banking adviser. Give me one immediately."

"No, because I can't," said Issy, indicating the red-nosed, ruined faces of the morning drinkers lining the bar. "I handed them out when you went to the loo. They looked so hungry and they were so appreciative."

Austin shook his head as they got up to leave, happily toasted by the line of poor old men along the bar.

"You are a very soft touch, Miss Randall."

"I'll take that as a compliment, Mr. Tyler."

"Don't," said Austin suddenly and fiercely as he opened the door for her. He was shocked to find, suddenly, how much he wanted to…no, he mustn't think that way. Really, he just so wanted Issy to succeed. That was it. She was a nice person with a nice café, and he really wanted things to start going right for her. And the wash of inexplicable tenderness that had come over him, looking at that lone tear roll down her pink cheek—that was just simple fellow feeling. Of course it was.

For her part, Issy looked up into his handsome, kind face and found herself slightly wishing that they could stay in the world's grottiest, smelliest pub for a little longer.

"Don't what?"

"Don't be too nice, Issy. Not in business. Just assume everyone around you is as much of an arse as that woman was—whose name, you may be interested to know, is Rainbow Honeychurch, although her birth certificate says Joan Millson—"

"I *am* quite interested to know that," added Issy.

"—and you know, if you are going to survive, if this is going to work, Issy, you'll just have to toughen up."

Issy thought of the tired, discontented faces of the shopkeepers along the street and wondered if that was what they'd had to do: toughen up. Tough it out. Take the shit on board.

And Austin, even as he was saying the words, wondered if he meant them. Obviously Issy should toughen up—toughen up and fight for this business. But he wondered if she wasn't a better, sweeter person the way she was.

"I will," said Issy, with a worried look on her face.

"Good," said Austin, shaking her small hand gravely. She smiled and squeezed his hand back. Suddenly, neither of them wanted to be the first to take their hand away.

Fortunately Issy's phone rang—it was the shop number, Pearl wanting to know where she was, no doubt—so she could, slightly flustered, move away first.

"Um," she said. "But is it OK if I go the other way back to the café? Just this once? I don't want them to start throwing things at me."

"You don't," said Austin. "Their flapjacks are rock solid."

brandy and horlicks
get well cake

• • • •

A good strong healing cake will make you feel better, like the time you were coming home from a terrible day at school and it was getting dark and you were cold in your blazer and you came around the end of your road and you saw the light on in your house and Marian was still there and she gave you a cuddle and something to eat and everything was much better. This cake tastes like that. It should not be too heavy, so it works well for invalids. Please send me a batch, Issy dear, so I can get out of this place.

* 16 tbsp butter, softened
* ½ cup superfine sugar
* 5 eggs
* ½ cup sweetened condensed milk
* 8 oz Horlicks (malted milk powder)
* 1 cup plain flour
* ½ tsp vanilla extract
* 2 tbsp cognac

Crease the small square tin and line the base and sides with baking paper. Allow the baking paper to extend over the top by about an inch if using the shorter tin.

Beat the butter and sugar until pale and fluffy. Beat in the eggs, one by one, until well combined. Beat in the sweetened condensed milk until well mixed. Stir in Horlicks. Fold in flour. Finally stir in vanilla and cognac.

Pour the batter into the prepared tin (the batter will fill the tin to almost 90 percent, but the cake will not rise up too much, so don't worry, darling). Cover the top loosely with a piece of aluminum foil.

Steam over high heat for 30 minutes. Fill up with more hot water if the steamer is low on water after 30 minutes. Turn heat down to medium and steam for another 60 minutes, or until cooked (may steam for up to 4 hours in total if desired—this, according to wisdom, allows the cake to be kept for up to a month). Remember to replenish steamer with hot water whenever it is drying up.

Mrs. Prescott the accountant was having strong words with Issy that week on cash flow. It was mid-April, and the weak evening sun was filtering through the basement blinds. Issy was dead tired and couldn't even remember where they kept the steamer. Her feet hurt from standing up all day serving a total of sixteen customers, and she'd let Pearl go early when she got a phone call from the nursery saying Louis was upset.

"It's those horrible kids," she'd said, cursing. "They just stare at him. Then they play stupid games he doesn't know like Ring a Ring o' bloody Roses so he can't join in."

Issy had wondered at this.

"Stupid snobs," said Pearl.

"Can't he learn Ring a Ring o' Roses?" Issy said. "I'll teach him if you like."

"That's not the point," said Pearl. Her voice went quiet. "They're calling him names."

Issy was shocked. She had noticed that Louis was lingering longer and longer over his morning muffin, sitting on the counter singing sad little songs to himself. He didn't fuss or throw tantrums, but his normal ebullience seemed to seep away the closer it got to nursery time.

Sometimes Issy picked him up, and he would cling to her like a little huddling cub, and then Issy didn't want him to go to nursery either.

"What kind of names?" Issy asked, surprised by how furious she was.

Pearl's voice started to choke. "Fatty bum-bum."

Issy bit her lip. "Oh."

"What?" said Pearl defensively. "There's nothing wrong with him! He's perfect! He's a gorgeous, plump baby."

"He'll be fine," said Issy. "He's just settling in. Nursery's a new world."

But she'd let Pearl take the afternoon off anyway. It didn't matter that they didn't have many customers, or that many of their tables and chairs hardly got used; every day Pearl scrubbed out the toilets, made the tables shine and washed down the arms and legs of the chairs. The place gleamed like a new pin. Maybe that was the problem, Issy thought in an idle moment. Maybe people were scared to mess it up.

"The thing is," said Mrs. Prescott, "you have to watch your stock levels. Look what's going out in ingredients. I know it's not really my place to comment on how you run your business, but you're making too much stock and as far as I can tell just throwing it away. Or giving it away."

Issy looked down at her hands and mumbled, "I know. The thing is, my grandfather...my grandfather says if you do, kind of, good turns, and send things out in the world, then it will come back to you."

"Yes, well, it's very difficult to account for good deeds," sniffed Mrs. Prescott. "It's quite hard to pay a mortgage from good deeds as well."

Issy was still looking at her hands.

"My grandfather was successful," she said, biting her lip. "He did all right."

"These are harder times, maybe," said Mrs. Prescott. "People's lives are faster, their memories are shorter, do you think?"

Issy shrugged. "I don't know. I just want to run a good place, a nice place, that's all."

Mrs. Prescott raised her eyebrows and didn't say any more. She made a mental note to start looking for another client.

● ● ● ●

Pearl had gotten home that night upset enough before she saw him, sitting casually on her back step as if he'd merely forgotten his key. She felt, suddenly, Louis's little paw start to tremble in her hand with excitement. Just as well he was still in nappies, he'd have peed his pants for sure about now. She knew that half of him wanted to run up to the man in glee, but he knew already that this would not please his mother. And also that sometimes he received a welcome, and presents and promises from this man, and sometimes he didn't.

Pearl swallowed hard. It was only a matter of time before word got around that she was earning a wage, she supposed. She guessed he wanted some of it.

He was, she thought, regretfully, still such a handsome man. Louis got his sweet smile from her, but the rest of his beautiful face came from his dad; the long-fringed eyes and high cheekbones.

"Hey there," said Ben, as if he hadn't been completely off radar for the last five months and missed Christmas.

Pearl gave him one of her looks. Louis was clutching tight to her hand.

"Hey, little man!" said Ben. "Look how big you're getting!"

"He's big-boned," said Pearl reflexively.

"He's gorgeous," said Ben. "Come say hi to your dad, Lou."

•   •   •   •

Of course it had started to rain. So what could Pearl do except invite him in for a cup of tea. Her mother was on the sofa, watching the early evening soaps. When she caught sight of Benjamin, she simply raised her eyebrows and didn't bother to greet him. Ben had said, "Hello, Mrs. McGregor," in a slightly fake over-the-top fashion but didn't look too surprised when he didn't receive a reply. Instead, he knelt down next to Louis, who was still struck completely dumb. He reached into his pocket. Pearl switched on the kettle in the little strip of kitchen in the corner of the room, watching the pair closely. She bit her lip. She had a speech prepared for Mr. Benjamin Hunter, absolutely she did, for the next time she saw him. She had thought it over in her head and she had a lot to say—as did her friends—about his messing about, staying out late, sending her not a penny for Louis, even when he was working. And he had a good job too. She was going to give him a proper lecture about his responsibilities, to her, and to his boy, and tell him to grow the hell up, or stop bothering Louis.

Then she caught sight of Louis's eyes, wide open in amazement and adoration, as his dad brought out of his pocket a bouncy ball.

"Watch this," said Ben, and he bounced it hard off the cheap plastic linoleum. The ball bounced up, hit the low ceiling, came whooshing back down again and did this twice more. Louis erupted in a screaming giggle.

"*Do again, Daddy! Do again!*"

Ben duly obliged, and within five minutes the ball was bouncing all over the tiny flat and Louis and Ben were rolling and tumbling after it, getting in the way of Pearl's mother's programs and steady stream of cigarette smoke, and killing themselves laughing. Finally, they sat up, panting. Pearl was frying sausages.

"Do you have enough of those for a hungry man?" said Ben. He tickled Louis on the tummy. "Do you want your daddy to stay for tea, young man?"

"*Yesh! Yesh!*" hollered Louis. Pearl's brow darkened.

"Louis, go sit with your grandma. Ben, I want a word. Outside."

Ben followed her out, lighting a cigarette as he went. Great, thought Pearl. Another brilliant role model for Louis.

They stood by the wall of the alleyway, Pearl avoiding the eyes of neighbors coming to and fro who could clearly see them both there.

"You're looking well," said Ben.

"*Stop it*," said Pearl. "Stop it. You can't…you can't just walk in here after five months and pretend nothing has happened. You can't. You *can't*, Ben."

She had lots more to say, but, strong as she was, Pearl could feel the words choking in her throat. Ben, however, let her finish—that wasn't like him. Normally he was defensive, full of excuses.

Pearl pulled herself together, with some effort.

"It's not even about me," she said. "It's not about me. I'm over it, Ben. I'm absolutely doing just fine. But for him…can't you see how awful it is? Seeing you and getting all excited, then not seeing you again for ages? He doesn't understand, Ben. He thinks it's his fault that you leave, that he's not good enough."

She paused, then spoke quietly. "He is good enough, Ben. He's wonderful. You're missing it all."

Ben sighed. "You know, I just…I just didn't want to be tied down."

"Well, you should have thought of that before."

"Well, so should you," said Ben, with some justification, Pearl knew. He was just so handsome, so nice; he had a job, which was more than you could say for some of the men she met…She'd let herself be carried away. She couldn't blame him for everything. On the other hand, that didn't mean he could just zip in and out whenever he wanted.

"I mean, I figure some of me is better than nothing, right?"

"I'm not sure," said Pearl. "Some of you on regular days…when he knows you're coming…yes, that would be a wonderful thing for him." Ben scowled. "Well, I can't always plan ahead that far." Why not? thought Pearl mutinously. She had to. Ben finished his cigarette and crushed it out on the big wheelie bin. "So can I come back in or not?"

Pearl weighed up the alternatives in her head. To deny Louis the chance to spend some precious quality time with his father…versus teaching him a lesson Ben would probably ignore anyway. She sighed.

"OK," she said.

Ben headed in the door. Brushing past her, he brusquely handed her an envelope.

"What's this?" she said, surprised. She fingered it. There was cash inside. Not much, but certainly enough to get Louis a new pair of trainers. Ben shrugged, embarrassed.

"Your mum told me that place you're working isn't going to last the month. Figured you could do with it till your benefits come back on stream."

Pearl stayed outside a second or two longer in amazement, clutching the envelope and listening to Louis doing tiger-roaring inside, till the sausages started to burn. God, even Ben knew the business was doomed.

• • • •

"What would you say," Austin was saying the following day, trying to finish off an email to his grandmother in Canada while also transporting a petulant Darny down the busy street. "What would you say your favorite things are right now, D?"

Darny thought about it for a bit.

"Ancient martial arts secrets of jujitsu," he said finally. "And the Spanish Inquisition."

Austin sighed. "Well, I can't tell your grandmother that, can I? Can't you think of something else?"

Darny thought some more, dragging his heels on the pavement. "Snowboarding."

"What do you mean, skiing? You've never been snowboarding."

"All the kids at school love snowboarding. They say it's totally rad. So I suppose that's the kind of thing you'd like me to like. So just say that, it hardly matters."

Austin looked at him warily. Darny's school was good, and the area they lived in had gotten markedly posher in the last few years. There were more and more children who had more than Darny, and the older he got, the more he was starting to notice.

"You probably would like it," he said. "We should try it one year."

"Don't be stupid," said Darny. "One, you'd never take me, two, I'd hate it, and three, you have to wear moronic hats. Mo-*ron*-ic," he said, enunciating clearly in case Austin had missed the point.

"OK," sighed Austin, just typing in "skiing" on his BlackBerry. It wasn't like his grandmother could make it over to check. She was old, he realized, that was true, and devastated by the loss of her only son, but after that, it was as if she'd had the great tragedy of her life and therefore was excused from doing anything else: she hadn't ever seemed to be the least bit interested in the progress of her grandchildren, apart from the occasional passing query and a very small check at Christmas. Austin had given up trying to understand it. Families were funny things, no matter what size. He squeezed Darny to his side.

"*Hey!*" said Darny. Austin turned his head. "Sirens!" shouted Darny. "Fire engines! I think we should go see. I want to see."

Austin smiled. Every time he thought Darny was turning into a sullen teenager way too quickly, the ten-year-old in him reared its head. As ever, though, Austin wanted to hold back. Once upon a time, those sirens had been for their parents. He lived in constant dread of witnessing it happening to someone else.

"We shouldn't, D," he said, trying to steer him in the direction of a local sweet shop.

"Fire engines," said Darny. "You can tell Grandma it's fire engines I like the best."

Pearl, deep in thought, and Issy, likewise, felt the crumping sound as well as heard it; it was extremely loud and startling in the quiet Saturday morning air. A large, twisted metal noise, punctuated with shattering glass, then sudden screams, and car alarms, and horns beeping and tooting furiously.

Along with the two customers, both young studious males who had plugged their laptops into the walls and had been enjoying the free Wi-Fi and electricity for over forty-five minutes, one on a small latte and one with a bottle of sparkling mineral water, they charged outside to the entrance to Pear Tree Court.

"Oh no," said Issy, stopping dead in her tracks.

Pearl was grateful Louis was home with her mother and felt her hand fly to her mouth.

Strewn right across the road, as if dropped from the sky by a bored child, the bulk of the number 73—the huge, elongated, unloved bendy bus—lay smashed and on its side. It blocked the road completely, its true size suddenly laid bare, as wide as the height of the house, and as long as half the road; the smell of wrecked machinery was horrifying; smoke rose from the undercarriage, a mass of exposed metal and piping.

A cab with its roof bashed in had come to a stop, skewed at a crazy angle across a reservation. Behind it could just be glimpsed a dirty white Ford Escort that had ploughed straight into the back of it. And most ominously of all, several meters in front of the top right corner, as if hurled there, was a twisted, bent bicycle.

Issy felt sick, her heart pounding in her chest. "Christ," she could hear one of the laptop boys saying. "Christ."

Issy felt in the pocket of her apron for her mobile phone. She glanced, lightheaded, at Pearl, who had already found hers and was prodding 999 into the handset.

"Quick," said the other man. "Come on! We have to get them out."

And Issy glanced up, as if in slow motion, and saw the bus was full of people—shouting, waving, clawing people. Others were already running from shops, from the bus stops, from houses, to help. In the far distance, the first siren could be heard.

Issy picked up her phone again.

"Helena," she gasped into it. She knew her flatmate had a day off—a precious day off—but she was two streets away.

"Hmmm?" said Helena, obviously still half-asleep. But within two seconds she was wide awake and pulling on her clothes.

• • • •

At one end of the bus, people were hammering on the window; it didn't seem to be breaking. With the smoke seeping out of the pipework, Issy wondered—everyone wondered—if the engine was going to explode. Surely not. But there had been stories about these buses catching fire, everyone knew it. Anything could happen. In the middle of the bus, a tall man was desperately trying to open the doors from the inside, above his head. One of the men from the coffee shop was already clambering up the side of the bus—what had been the roof, but was now the side— and other people were anxiously shouting guidance to him. From inside the bus Issy could hear screaming; the driver looked unconscious.

There was a scream from a woman halfway down the road. A young man—obviously a cycle courier, in skintight Lycra, now ripped, with a huge walkie-talkie still on his hip—was lying, eyeballs rolling, in the gutter, his arm at a very strange angle. Issy looked over her shoulder and was relieved to see Helena tearing down the road at full pelt.

"Over here!" she shouted, then ushered Helena through. "She's a nurse! She's a nurse!"

Helena ran to the boy as the sirens grew louder.

"I'm a medical student," volunteered a young man standing watching on the curb.

"Come with me then, sonny," said Helena grimly. "And don't give me any cheek."

Issy glanced around. Suddenly, she noticed a very calm, quiet figure. While everyone else was either stock still in shock or tearing about like a wild thing, the figure was approaching steadily from Pear Tree Court. It was the strange man from the ironmonger's; the man who hadn't even bothered to acknowledge them when they moved in. He was carrying an enormous metal box. It must have weighed a ton, but he hoisted it effortlessly.

Her eyes followed him as he headed toward the bus, knelt down by the windscreen away from the driver's side, opened his box and selected a heavy mallet. Indicating to the panicking passengers inside to stay well back, he hit the glass sharply three or four times until it shattered. He then carefully selected a pair of pliers and lifted out the large, dangerous shards from the black rubber rim of the window frame. Then and only then did he beckon the people inside to come forward; first a screaming baby, which he handed to the person nearest to him, who happened to be Issy.

"*Oh*," said Issy. "There, there."

The baby screamed, her hot wet face buried in Issy's shoulder, the great peanut shape of her mouth seeming oddly wider than her head. She had thick, straight black hair, and Issy stroked it soothingly.

"Shhh," she said, and two seconds later the baby's mother was out, her hands flapping and outstretched, the buggy twisted and discarded behind her.

"Here you are," Issy said. The mother could barely articulate her distress.

"I thought she was...I thought we were..."

The baby, back in the familiar scent of her mother's arms, hiccupped and gulped and let out another experimental wail but then seemed to decide that the danger had passed, and snuggled her damp face into the crook of her mother's neck, peering around to gaze at Issy with huge dark eyes.

"It's OK," said Issy, patting the mother on the shoulder. "It's OK."

And as she could see other people clambering out behind her—some clutching their heads, some with rips in their clothing, all sharing a similar expression of shock and bemusement, Issy thought that it just might not be too bad…Nobody seemed to be horribly injured. Except for the cyclist—she glanced back, but all she could see was the wide form of Helena bent low over him, gesticulating at the young medical student. Her throat constricted. Whoever he was, he'd left home that morning without a worry in his head.

The bus driver too was still lying contorted across the huge steering wheel.

"Everyone, get away from the bus!" the ironmonger said loudly, in a tone that brooked no argument. The bystanders and rubberneckers were hanging about the pavement, watching; no one seemed to know what to do for the confused commuters with their cut lips and twitching eyes.

"Perhaps," said the ironmonger to Issy, "you might be able to make these people a hot drink. And I've heard sugar can be good for shock."

"Of course!" said Issy, stunned that she hadn't immediately thought of it herself. And she ran back as fast as she could to get the urn heated up.

By the time they started feeding tea and cake to the victims, five minutes later, the ambulances and fire engines had arrived; the police were ushering everyone away from the bus and had cordoned off the road. Everyone was absolutely delighted by the hot tea and buns Issy and Pearl had rounded up, and the bus driver, already beginning to stir, had been loaded into the ambulance.

Helena and the medical student, whose name was Ashok, had

stabilized the cycle courier and been congratulated by the ambulance crew, who had grabbed a couple of cakes to enjoy once they'd delivered their patient to A&E. The survivors of the crash were already bonding, sharing stories of where they'd been on their way to, and hadn't everyone always been sure that these bendy buses were going to cause trouble one day; the joy and luck that no one, it appeared, had been too seriously injured or killed made people quite voluble and a bit overexcited, like they were at a cocktail party, and everyone rounded on Issy to express their thanks. One or two people pointed out that they lived just around the corner and they hadn't even known she was there, so when the photographer from the local paper turned up, as well as taking pictures of the shattered bus from every angle (the ironmonger had disappeared as smoothly as he'd arrived; Issy hadn't even noticed him go), he also took a shot of her smiling with all the passengers. When the *Walthamstow Gazette* came out the following week, the headline to part of their crash coverage was LOCAL CAKES BEST MEDICINE; after that, things started to change quite a lot.

• • • •

Before that, though, there was the simple fact that the entire stock was sold out. Half they'd given away to the tumbled and bruised and shocked; half they'd sold to the nosy and curious. Either way, every crumb was cleared, the milk all finished, the big, unwieldy coffee machine was jarred into life—obviously, Issy thought in retrospect, it was made to be used all the time. It didn't like stopping and starting, and who could blame it?

Exhausted, she looked over at Pearl, who was washing the floor.

"Shall we go for a drink?" she asked.

"Why not?" said Pearl, smiling.

"Hey!" Issy yelled to Helena, who was, uncharacteristically, mooning out of the window. "You coming for a drink?"

They went to a nice wine bar and the three girls relaxed around a bottle of rosé. Pearl had never tried it before and thought it tasted like vinegar, but she gamely sipped along, trying not to notice how fast the other two downed their glasses.

"What a day," said Issy. "Cor. Do you think those people will come back?"

Helena raised her glass to Pearl.

"I gather you've already seen the glass-half-empty side of your boss then?"

Pearl smiled.

"What do you mean?" said Issy. "I'm very optimistic."

Helena and Pearl swapped glances.

"Well, it's not so much pessimistic," said Helena. "I suppose...timid."

"I've started my own business!" said Issy. "That feels pretty optimistic to me."

"And you still think Graeme's going to make an honest woman of you one day," said Helena, starting in on her second glass. "That's pretty optimistic."

Issy felt herself color.

"Who's this?" said Pearl.

"No one," said Issy. "My ex."

"Her ex-boss," explained Helena helpfully.

"Ouch," said Pearl. "That doesn't sound too good."

Issy sighed. "Well, I'm moving on now. Taking control of my life."

"Was he nice?" asked Pearl, who didn't feel in any position to tell people who they should and shouldn't be taking back.

"No," said Helena.

"He was!" protested Issy. "You just didn't see that side of him. He had a sensitive side."

"That came out when he wasn't summoning you by taxi halfway across town in the middle of the night to make him Super Noodles," said Helena.

"I knew I should never have told you about the Super Noodles."

"No, you should have done," said Helena, helping herself to a packet of crisps. "Otherwise I might have been sitting here saying, 'Oh yes, he is terribly handsome; you must turn yourself into a total doormat to get him back just because he looks like he should be in a razor commercial.'"

"He is handsome," said Issy.

"That's why he preens himself in every polished surface," said Helena. "It's brilliant you're over him."

"Hmmm," said Issy.

"And have that banker to pash on."

Issy shot a look at Pearl. "*Helena*," she said.

Pearl smiled back at Helena. "Oh, I know."

"I am not. And for your information, just because I don't dribble on about it all the time, I do still miss Graeme."

Pearl patted her hand. "Don't worry," she said. "I know it can be hard to get over people."

"You?" said Issy. "You look like you never worry a day in your life about that kind of stuff."

"Do I?" snorted Pearl. "What, I'm completely sexless?"

"No!" said Issy. "I mean, you just seem so sorted."

Pearl's eyebrows shot up. "That's right, Issy. Oh, and there's Louis's dad, Barack Obama, sending the helicopter to give us a lift home."

"Is Louis's dad still around?" asked Helena, forthright as ever.

Pearl tried not to let a little smile cross her face. She was being tough. If even Issy could show her no-good lover the door, the least she could do was put up a bit more resistance to Benjamin. On the other hand, what time was it…

"Well, he sees his boy," she said, conscious that she sounded a bit proud.

"What's he like?" asked Issy, anxious to change the subject to someone else's romantic travails.

"Well," said Pearl reflectively, "my mother always used to say that handsome is as handsome does…but I was never very good at listening to my mother."

"I didn't want to listen to mine," said Issy. "She said, 'Don't get tied down.' But I would really like to be tied down…"

"Or up," added Helena.

"And nobody wants to. So I am Not Tied Down." Issy sighed and wondered if more rosé would help. Probably not, but worth a shot under the circumstances.

"Well, look at you now—owning your own business, which actually sold some cakes today," said Helena. "Not reliant on some lantern-jawed eejit for snogging. And men love a woman who can bake and look nice in a flowery dress, they think it'll be like the fifties and you'll mix them a martini. You're at the start of a pulling bonanza. Trust me." She raised a glass.

"Now you are glass-half-full," said Issy, but she felt mildly cheered nonetheless.

"What did your mother tell you, Helena?" asked Pearl.

"Never to get involved in other people's business," said Helena promptly. And the three women laughed, and chinked glasses.

Where's my little man Chunks?" asked Issy as Pearl turned up—a little late, but frankly she was so grateful to Pearl that she was going to overlook the small things. "I miss him."

Pearl smiled tightly and rushed in to grab the Hoover and mop so she could run around before they opened up.

"He just loves being with his grandma," she said, realizing as she did so what an idyllic cake-baking, duck-feeding picture that presented, rather than the cheerless, fuggy little flat. "Anyway, let me just get around here quickly, the morning rush will be on soon."

They smiled at each other, but it was true that since the accident there had been a steady stream of people—the ambulance men, the bystanders, the mother with the lovely baby girl, and Ashok, who had popped in to ask for Helena's phone number, which made Issy's eyebrows rise so much he'd apologized instantly. Issy had taken his and passed it on, fully expecting Helena to drop it in the hospital incinerator.

The council had replaced the long bendy buses with the original double-deckers, which looked nicer coming down the street (and moved at more of a clip) but held far fewer passengers than the bendy buses. As a result, a lot of people couldn't get on during rush hour and found themselves popping in for a coffee to pass the time; Issy had started buying in croissants. Short of growing another pair of hands, she sadly admitted to herself, she had to buy them in; anyway, the very best croissant-making was an art all to itself, so rather than her straining for a new goal, she'd sourced the most wonderful boulanger, courtesy of François, who'd pointed her in the direction of a company who delivered an exquisite mixed box of pains au chocolat, croissants and croissants aux amandes at seven a.m. sharp every day; there was never a single one left by nine.

Then came the morning coffee; Mira, with little Elise, had managed to find herself some new friends among other mums, and they came often and chattered loudly in Romanian on the gray sofa, which was beginning to take on the soft, well-used sheen Issy had hoped for it. Some of the yummy mummies had started to make their way down from the crèche; if they recognized Pearl, she would smile briefly then busy herself (now not difficult) fetching organic lemonades and juices. Lunchtime was a rush, then the afternoon was a little more meditative, with office girls and women organizing children's parties coming in to buy boxes of half a dozen or even a dozen cakes; Issy was considering getting a sign up to invite personalizing and special orders. In between there were endless lattes, teas, raspberry specials; vanilla-iced blueberry cakes; slices of thick apple pie; cleaning up, wiping, signing for suppliers, invoices; post; cleaning up spills, smiling at children and waving to regulars; chatting to passers-by and opening more milk, more butter, more eggs. By four, Issy and Pearl would be ready to lie down on one of the huge sacks of flour in the storeroom, where Pearl fearlessly scratched out the inner corners with her mop to make sure they were as sparkling as the areas of the shop people actually saw.

The Cupcake Café was afloat. It had launched; it was sailing, tipping slightly from side to side, all hands working her—but it was afloat. It felt to Issy like a living, breathing entity, a thing that was as much a part of her as her left hand. It never went away; she sat poring over the books with Mrs. Prescott late at night; she dreamed in buttercream and icing, thought in keys and deliveries and sugar roses. Friends called and she begged off; Helena snorted and said it was like she was in the first grip of a romance. And although she was tired—exhausted—from working all out six days a week; although she desperately wanted to go out and have a few drinks without knowing how much she would suffer for it the next day; although she would have liked to just sit and watch some TV without wondering about stock levels and expiry dates and disposable bloody catering gloves, she shook her head in complete disbelief whenever she heard people mention the word "holiday." Yet she was happier, she realized, deep down, than she'd been in years; happier every day, when she earned the rent money, then the utilities, then Pearl's salary, then, finally, finally, something of her own, from something she was turning over with her own two hands, made to cherish and make people feel good.

At 2:00 p.m., a large group of mothers entered, tentatively at first, many with huge three-wheeled buggies. The shop was so small, Issy would have liked to ask them to leave the buggies outside so they didn't kneecap other customers, but frankly she was a little frightened of these Stoke Newington women, who were in incredible shape, despite the fact that they all had two children and had perfectly high-lighted hair and wore very tight jeans with high heels all the time. Issy sometimes thought it must be a little exhausting, having to look identical to all your friends. On the other hand, she was delighted with their business.

She smiled a warm hello, but they glanced past her and their gazes alighted on Pearl, who looked semipleased to see them.

"Um, hi," said Pearl to one of the mums, who glanced around.

"Now where's your *darling* little Louis?" she said. "He's usually here somewhere! I'd think a cake shop was a perfect environment for him."

Issy glanced up. She recognized that voice. Sure enough, with a slight stab of nervousness she saw that it belonged to Caroline, the woman who had wanted to turn the café into a wholefood center.

"Hello, Caroline," said Pearl stoically. She sweetened her voice considerably to talk to the serious-eyed blond girl and small boy still in the buggy at the bottom of the table.

"Hello, Hermia! Achilles, hello!"

Issy sidled up to say hello, although Caroline seemed to be ignoring her quite competently.

"Oh, don't listen to them," said Caroline. "They have been absolutely foul all morning."

They didn't look foul to Issy. Tired, maybe.

"And you know Kate, don't you?"

"Well, this is just charming!" said Kate, looking around approvingly. "We're doing up the big house across the road. Something like this is just what we need. Keep the house prices going in the right direction, you know what I mean. *Haw!*"

She had a sudden, expectorating laugh that took Issy slightly by surprise, and two girls who were obviously twins, sitting holding hands on the same stool. One had a short bob and was wearing red dungarees, and one had long blond curls and was wearing a pink skirt with a puffed-out underskirt.

"Aren't your girls lovely!" exclaimed Issy, moving forward. "And hello, Caroline, too."

Caroline nodded regally to her. "I'm amazed this place appears to be taking off," she sniffed. "Might as well see what all the fuss is about."

"Might as well!" said Issy cheerfully, bending down to the little ones. "Hello, twins!"

Kate sniffed. "They may be twins, but they are individuals too. It's actually very damaging to twins not to be treated as separate people. I have to work very hard to build their separate identities."

Issy nodded reassuringly. "I understand," she said, even though actually she didn't understand for a second.

"This is Seraphina." Kate indicated the little girl with the long blond curls. "And this one here," she pointed to the other one, "is Jane."

Seraphina smiled prettily. Jane scowled and hid her face in Seraphina's shoulder. Seraphina patted her hand in a maternal fashion.

"Well, welcome," said Issy. "We don't normally do table service, but as I'm here, what would you like?"

Even though Pearl had now made her way back across the room to stand behind the counter underneath the pretty bunting they'd draped on the wall, Issy could, she swore to Helena later, *feel* her eyes roll in their sockets.

"Well," said Kate, after deliberating over the menu for some time, "now." Seraphina had prompted Jane, and the two girls, who must have been four, walked up to the cake cabinet, rose on their tiptoes, and pressed their noses to the glass.

"You two! Snot off the glass, sweethearts," said Pearl, firmly but kindly, and the girls withdrew immediately, giggling, but stayed mere centimeters away where they could examine the icing carefully. Hermia looked at her mother.

"Please may I—" she risked.

"No," said Caroline. "Sit nicely please. *Assieds-toi!*"

Hermia looked longingly at her friends.

"Oh, are you French?" asked Issy.

"No," said Caroline, preening. "Why, do I look French?"

"I shall have a mint tea," said Kate finally. "Do you do salad?"

Issy couldn't bring herself to meet Pearl's eyes.

"No. No, at the moment we don't do salad," she said. "Cakes mostly."

"What about, you know, organic flapjacks?"

"We have fruit cake," said Issy.

"With spelt flour?"

"Um, no, with real flour," said Issy, wishing she was out of this conversation.

"Nuts?"

"Some nuts."

Kate let out a long sigh, as if it was unbelievable what kind of hardship she had to go through on a regular basis.

"Can we have a cake, Mummy? *Pleeease!*" begged Jane from the counter.

"It's 'can *I* have a cake,' Jane. I."

"Can I have a cake then please?"

"*Me too! Me too!*" yelled Seraphina.

"Oh, darlings…"

Kate looked on the brink of giving up. "You don't…you don't have any little boxes of raisins, do you?"

"Um, no," said Issy.

Kate sighed. "Well, that's a shame. What do you think, Caroline?"

Caroline's face didn't move—her eyebrows were very pointy—but Issy still got the sense she was disappointed. She glanced at Hermia, who was gazing at her friends, one tear dripping slowly down her face. Achilles sorted it for her.

"*Mummy! Cake! Now! Mummy! Cake! Cake! Mummy!*" He went red-faced while wrestling with the buggy straps. "*Now!*"

"Now darling," Caroline said, "you know we don't really like cake."

"*Cake! Cake!*"

"Oh dear," said Kate. "I'm not sure we're going to be able to come in here again."

"*Cake! Cake!*"

"They do say the sugar makes them hyperactive."

Issy didn't want to point out that everything in her shop was all-natural and that they hadn't even had any yet.

"Fine," said Caroline, desperate to stop her son screaming. "Two cakes. I don't care which ones. Hermia, little bites please. You don't want to blow up like—" Caroline immediately stopped.

"Yes!" shouted the twins by the counter.

"I want pink! I want pink!" they both yelled simultaneously, in voices so similar Issy wondered how you really did tell them apart.

"You can't both have pink," said Kate absentmindedly, picking up the *Mail*. "Jane, you have the brown."

Later, Caroline came over to chat.

"This is actually quite quaint," she said. "You know, I love to bake too…obviously, much healthier than this, and mostly we eat raw, of course, but I was like, now I must have a central island for my little messes…In fact, you know," she peered down the stairwell, "I think my oven is probably bigger than yours! My main oven of course; I have a steam oven and a convection oven too. But no microwave. Terrible things."

Issy smiled politely. Pearl let out a snort.

"I am dreadfully busy with everything now…I've taken on a lot of charity work, my husband's in the City, you know…but maybe one day I could bring you one of my recipes! Yes, I create recipes…Well, it's hard when you have a creative side, isn't it? After children?"

She looked at Issy as she said this, and Issy tried to look polite to a customer, even an idiot, and even an idiot who was clearly implying that Issy looked old and dumpy enough to have loads of children. Caroline of course weighed about the same as a fourteen-year-old.

"Well, I'm sure that would be fascinating," said Pearl, before Issy's mouth drooped open any further. "Uh, Caroline, is that your son taking off his nappy and putting it in your Hermès bag?"

Caroline turned around with a squeal.

● ● ● ●

"They're all like that?" asked Issy after they'd left, Achilles screaming, Hermia sobbing quietly, and the twins having perfectly cut their cakes into two halves, swapping them then squeezing them together again, so their cakes would be exactly the same, to Kate's voluble disgust.

"Oh, no," said Pearl. "Lots are miles worse. One says she won't potty train till the child decides to do it himself."

"Well, that makes total sense," said Issy. "Keep them in nappies till eleven. Saves a lot of time. Does she let the child do the cooking too?"

"Oh, no, Orlando only eats raw vegetables and sprouting things," quoted Pearl. "Except when I caught him stealing Louis's Mars bar."

Issy raised her eyebrows but didn't say anything. Neither had she asked about Pearl's distracted demeanor all day. If Pearl wanted to tell her, she would.

• • • •

By 4:30 that Friday, after their busiest week ever, they were utterly exhausted. Issy locked the door and turned the sign to *Closed*. Then they went downstairs to the cellar and Issy took from the catering fridge their now ritualistic end-of-the-week bottle of white wine. Saturday was a quiet day—although it too was picking up, especially around lunchtime—so they could indulge a little on a Friday without suffering too badly.

As had also become a habit (and would be severely frowned upon by health and safety, Issy knew, if they ever found out), after counting up the day's takings they would slump down on the big flour sacks in the cellar, using them like gigantic bean bags.

Issy poured Pearl a large glass.

"That," she said, "was our best week so far."

Pearl wearily raised her glass. "I'll say so."

"Compared, obviously, to not very much," said Issy. "But projection-wise…"

"Oh," said Pearl, "I forgot to say. I ran into your fancy bloke at the bank." Pearl did the banking.

Issy's interest was piqued. "Oh yes? Austin? Uh, I mean, really? Who?"

Pearl gave her a very Pearlish look. Issy sighed.

"OK. How is he?"

"Why are you asking?" said Pearl.

Issy felt herself color and buried her face in her glass. "Just politeness," she squeaked.

Pearl sniffed and waited.

"Well?" said Issy after a minute.

"Ha!" said Pearl. "I knew it. If it really was politeness, you wouldn't be that bothered."

"That is not true," said Issy. "It's an entirely professional…relationship."

"So it's a relationship?" teased Pearl.

"Pearl! What did he say? Did he ask about me?"

"He was surrounded by about fifteen lingerie models and getting into a Jacuzzi, so it was hard to say."

Issy harrumphed until Pearl relented.

"He was looking quite smart. He'd had a haircut."

"Oh, I liked his hair," said Issy.

"I wonder who he got his hair cut for?" mused Pearl. "Maybe it was you."

Issy pretended not to be pleased with that remark, but men like Austin always had girlfriends. She was probably really pretty too, and really, really nice. That tended to be how it worked. She sighed. She just had to come to terms with it now; she was a career girl for the moment. She would worry about it later. Shame though. She found herself imagining, just for one second, gently stroking the back of his neck, where a wisp of hair had been left behind, and…

"*And*," said Pearl loudly, noticing Issy had vanished into a reverie and assessing, correctly, that she was fantasizing about the handsome young banking adviser, and not for the first time, "*and* he said he had a message for you."

"A what?" said Issy, startled.

"A message. Just for you."

Issy sat bolt upright on her sack.

"What was it?"

Pearl tried to get it exactly right.

"It was…'Tell her, "You showed 'em."'"

"'You showed them?' I showed them what?…Oh," said Issy as she realized he meant the other café owners of Stoke Newington. "Oh," she said, going pink. He had thought about her! He was thinking about her! OK, maybe only from the point of view of his business investment, but still…

"Oh, that's nice," she said.

Pearl was looking at her.

"Private joke," said Issy.

"Oh is it?" said Pearl. "Well, on the plus side, I suppose you're keeping him sweet."

Issy glanced at Pearl. "What about you?" she said. "How's your love life?"

Pearl grimaced. "Is it that obvious?"

"You cleaned the same toilet four times," said Issy. "I don't want you to think I'm not grateful, but…"

"No, no, I know," said Pearl. "Ach. Well, Louis's dad…he came around."

"Oh," said Issy. "And is that good, bad, fine, terrible, or all of the above?"

"Or (e) I don't know," said Pearl. "I think (e) I don't know."

"Oh," said Issy. "Is Louis pleased?"

"Ecstatic," said Pearl grumpily. "Can we change the subject?"

"*Yes!*" said Issy. "Um. OK. Right. OK. Well, here we are having wine, so I might as well go for it. I hate to ask a delicate question, but…are you losing weight?"

Pearl rolled her eyes.

"Maybe," she said. "Not on purpose," she added defiantly.

"You know I don't mind you eating stock," said Issy, worried she'd offended.

"You know," said Pearl, "don't tell the customers, and you are a baking genius, but…"

Issy looked at her. There was a glint of mischief in Pearl's eyes.

"I seem to…I seem to have gone off sweet things altogether. I'm sorry, Issy! I'm sorry! It's not you! Don't sack me!"

Issy opened her mouth and started to laugh.

"Oh God, Pearl, please, please don't."

"What?" said Pearl.

"I haven't eaten a cake in six weeks."

They both made horrified faces, then burst into fits of laughter.

"What are we like?" said Pearl, helpless. "Next time, can we open a chip shop?"

"Absolutely," said Issy. "Chips and crisps."

"I am dreaming about this place," said Pearl. "Every second of every day. I'm not saying it's not great, Issy, honestly. But the hours…the hours are filling me up."

"Me too," said Issy. "Me too. For me to admit I don't like eating cake anymore…it's a complete denial of me. As a person."

"This is bad," said Pearl. "Could be bad for quality control."

"Hmmm," said Issy. "Maybe we need a new member of staff."

Pearl made a quiet fist of triumph underneath the sack.

"Hmmm," she said noncommittally, as if she didn't care one way or the other.

• • • •

Of all things, Issy hadn't expected finding someone else to help out the least bit difficult. Times were hard and people were desperate for jobs, weren't they? As soon as she'd put a sign up in the window, she figured she'd get the whole thing organized in ten seconds flat—in fact a little bit of her wondered whether she might manage to poach a top pâtissier down on their luck a bit from one of the big hotels, who didn't want to work nights and, er, didn't mind minimum wage plus tips.

Instead, the stream of people who responded to the card—and later, the ad they took out in the *Stoke Newington Gazette* extolling the success of the café and thanking the supportive community—were all unsuitable. (As she drafted the ad, Issy couldn't help the faintly spiteful gleam in her eye when she thought of the other cafés reading it. It was mean of her, she realized, and she tried to suppress it immediately.

But it was a lovely ad, beautifully designed; she would absolutely have to start paying Zac one of these days.) Finding a new member of staff wasn't anything like as easy as she'd expected. Some people came in for a chat and did nothing but criticize their last employers; one person announced they would need Tuesday and Thursday afternoons off to visit their therapist; one asked when the salary would be going up and at least four had never baked in their lives but didn't think it could be that difficult.

"It's not that difficult," Issy had explained to Helena, who was putting on makeup. "It's that they can't even be arsed to pretend they love cakes. It's like me expecting them to be even vaguely interested in the job is somehow uncool. God, it's been weeks."

"You sound five thousand years old," said Helena, smoothing some thick, shimmery greeny-gold stuff on her eyelids that made her look goddess-like rather than tarty. Not that Ashok wouldn't treat her like a goddess anyway. Madly, it was Issy being so busy that had finally swayed her in his direction. She missed her best mate and having someone to go out with. It was all right both of them being single together. It was rubbish sitting watching *America's Next Top Model* repeats every night by herself.

One day Ashok, looking very dashing in a pink shirt under his white coat that set off his huge dark eyes, had casually sidled up to her in A&E while she was clearing up a pile of puke. (There were meant to be cleaners to do that kind of thing, but finding one meant phoning central services and being put on hold for half an hour while they connected you to the contracted-out team, and frankly it was easier just to do it yourself before someone slipped on it and broke their coccyx, plus it gave a good example to the junior nurses.) He had said, "Now I suppose you are very busy on Thursday evening. However, just in case you aren't, I took the liberty of reserving a table at Hex, so do let me know."

Helena had stared after him down the corridor. Hex was the coolest new restaurant in London, in the papers every day. It was meant to be nearly impossible to get a reservation. Although, of course, she couldn't go. This kind of suppliant behavior wasn't her kind of thing at all. Definitely not.

"You do look gorgeous," said Issy, focusing on her friend for the first time. "How do you do that thing with your eyes anyway? I'd just look like I'd had an accident in the bronzer factory."

Helena gave a Mona Lisa smile and kept blending.

"What are you doing anyway? Where are you going?"

"Out," said Helena. "It's a kind of place and it's not your house and not your shop. Things happen there that people talk about called current affairs and social life."

Normally she'd have told Issy straightaway what she was up to. But she was torn—partly because she felt it needed a longer conversation, but also because she didn't want to take the teasing she would get for going against all her dearly held principles to date a nervy, sweaty-palmed, underpaid first-year junior doctor. The junior doctors had been a standing joke between them for years. They arrived in two tranches, green as grass, in February and September, and ended up so grateful for Helena and her good advice, strong leadership and magnificent bosoms that at least one of them always trailed around after her for weeks with flowers and sorrowing looks. Helena never gave in. Ever.

"When you're back in the social world," said Helena, "then you can find out."

Issy reddened.

"Oh, don't blush!" said Helena, genuinely surprised she'd upset her friend. "I didn't mean it! In fact, I was thinking recently of how much tougher you've been getting."

"Sod off!"

"No, really, all this running-your-own-business stuff. You have a spring in your step, Ms. Randall. You are no longer the girl I met who was too scared to go see the student med service about a finger wart."

Issy smiled at the memory. "I thought they'd make me take my knickers off."

"Even if they had, was it anything to be scared of?"

"No."

"And now look at you! Entrepreneur! If you were a bit more annoying and a bit of a nobber, you could go on *The Apprentice*. If they had a cake-based task. If they only had cake-based tasks."

Issy raised her eyebrows. "I will take that as a semicompliment, which coming from you is pretty good. You're right, I have gotten boring though. I just never think about anything else."

"What about that hot scruffy bloke from the bank with the horn-rimmed glasses?"

"What about him?"

"*Nothing*," said Helena. "It's just good to know you're not sitting around waiting for Graeme to come back."

"No," said Issy suddenly, "no. I'm not. Hey, I know—why don't I come with you?"

Helena started putting on mascara. "Um, you can't."

"Why not? Shake off my working day a bit."

"None of your beeswax."

"Lena, have you got a *date*?"

Helena calmly went on layering her mascara.

"You have! Who is it? Tell me everything."

"I would have done," said Helena, "if you'd stopped going on about the Cupcake Café for one second. As it is, I'm late."

And she kissed Issy firmly on the cheek and swept out of the room in a haze of Agent Provocateur perfume.

"Is it a greenhorn?" said Issy, running after her. "Tell me. Come on. There must be some reason you're not telling me."

"Never you mind," said Helena.

"It is! It's a baby doctor!"

"It's none of your business."

"Nice of him to take you out in between accidentally killing pensioners."

"Shhh!"

"I hope you're going Dutch."

"Shut up!"

"I hope you've got a book for when he falls asleep at the table."

"Bog off!"

"I'll wait up for you," hollered Issy to her disappearing back.

"Like hell you will!" came the reply, and sure enough, Issy's eyelids were already half-closed by the end of *Location, Location, Location.*

●　●　●　●

The next morning the croissant rush was just about finished, and Pearl was making up the new boxes they'd ordered. Candy-striped, with their name blazoned across the front, they fitted a dozen cakes perfectly and were then wrapped up in pretty pink ribbon before being handed to the customer. They were absolutely lovely, but it was taking a bit of time to get the hang of folding them up, and Pearl was practicing to try to make herself a wizard at it.

The doorbell went and Pearl glanced up at the railway clock; just a few minutes' peace before the 11:00 a.m. sugar rush kicked off. She wiped her brow. Boy, it was lovely to be busy, but it was full-on too. Issy was downstairs, trying to make the world's first ginger beer cupcake. The scent of cinnamon, ginger, and brown sugar filled the shop and smelled absolutely intoxicating; people kept asking to try one and then, when told they weren't ready, camping by the stairs. One or two were striking up conversations with each other, which was nice, Pearl thought, but really right at the minute she needed everything cleared out of the way, so she could get to the leftover coffee cups. The duck-egg and teal had been joined by a very pale yellow as they'd gotten busier, and she wanted to stack the dishwasher. A delivery of eggs had just arrived fresh from the farm, with feathers still on them, and she had to sign for that, pick the feathers off, and put them away downstairs while still serving the ongoing queue, which she couldn't because she had no cups, and "*Issy*," she yelled. There was a clatter from downstairs.

"Ouch! Ooh, hot hot hot!" shouted Issy. "I'm just going to run my finger under a tap!"

Pearl heaved a sigh and tried to look patient as two teenage girls kept changing their minds in an agony of cake-related indecision.

Suddenly the door banged open. It was raining outside, a steady spring downpour, but still the tree was tentatively, nervously budding, tiny, furled-up little shoots just showing on its branches. Pearl occasionally sneaked some coffee grounds out and spread them around its base; she'd heard they were good for trees, and she felt quite protective of this one. Into the shop crashed someone she recognized immediately, and her heart dropped. It was Caroline, health-food Nazi of Louis's nursery, original bidder for the Cupcake Café.

Caroline marched straight to the front of the queue. As she got closer, Pearl noticed she wasn't her normal immaculate-looking self. Her blond hair had grayish roots showing through. She wasn't wearing makeup. And she had lost weight, taking her always very slender form into the realms of extreme thinness.

"Can I speak to your boss please?" she barked.

"Hello, Caroline," said Pearl, trying to give this incredibly rude woman the benefit of the doubt in case she just hadn't recognized her.

"Yes, hello, em…"

"Pearl."

"Pearl. Can I speak to your boss?"

Caroline glanced around the shop, wild-eyed. On the sofa were camped a group of young mothers cooing over each other's babies while clearly preferring their own; two businessmen with laptops and papers spread everywhere were having a meeting near the big window; a young student reading an old gray Penguin Classic was having trouble concentrating on it and was instead eyeing up another student by the fireplace, who was scrawling notes on a pad while tossing her long lusciously curly hair over her shoulders, presumably on purpose.

"*Issy*," bellowed Pearl down the stairwell, with such force it made Issy jump. She came up the stairs sucking her burnt finger. Caroline propped herself against the wall, tapping her foot anxiously.

She leaned in toward Pearl. "You know, my son is going to school in September. He's got all these cast-off clothes I was just about to get rid of, but I wonder if your wee chap would like them? He's about the right age, and it's nice stuff—lots of White Company, Mini Boden, Petit Bateau."

Pearl recoiled behind the counter.

"No thank you," she said stiffly. "I think I can clothe him, thanks."

"Oh, OK," said the blond, completely unperturbed. "Just thought I might save myself a trip to Oxfam! Not to worry."

"I don't need any charity," said Pearl, but the woman had turned to see Issy coming up the stairs, and her hands erupted in a flurry of nerves.

"Oh...oh, hello!"

Issy wiped her hands warily. Caroline and Kate hadn't been back to the café since that first day; Issy had taken it rather personally. Still, local business was local business.

"You know," said Caroline. "Uh, you know when I didn't get the site?"

Pearl went back to serving the other customers.

"Yes," said Issy. "Have you...did you find anywhere else?"

"Um, well, obviously I weighed up lots of offers. It's like totally an idea whose time has come..." said Caroline, her voice trailing off.

"Oh. Right." Issy wondered where this was leading. She needed to get back down to check on that ginger beer cupcake. "So, nice to see you again," she said. "Would you like a coffee?"

"Actually." Caroline lowered her voice as if this was a terribly funny secret of some kind. "No. Er, OK. Well, here's the thing. Ha, I know this will sound absolutely crazy and everything but…" Suddenly, her haggard but still beautiful face seemed to crumple. "That bastard. My bastard husband has finally left me for that stupid bint in the press office—and he's told me that I need to get a bastard *job*!"

• • • •

"No way," said Pearl afterward. "No no no no no."

Issy bit her lip. Of course it had been an unorthodox approach. But on the other hand, without a doubt Caroline was a smart cookie. She had a degree in marketing and had worked for a prestigious market research outfit before giving it all up for the children, she'd sobbed bitterly, while her husband nobbed some twentysomething publicist. But once she'd stopped bawling, over about a pint of tea and some hazelnut tiffin, it transpired that she did in fact know loads of people in the area; she could turn the café into the place to get your baby-shower cakes, your birthday icing; she could work just the hours they were looking for, she lived around the corner…

"But she's *horrible*," Pearl pointed out. "That's really important."

"She's maybe just a bit wrapped up in herself right now," said soft-hearted Issy. "It's awful when someone leaves you," her voice tailed off momentarily, "or things don't work out."

"Yes, it makes you really rude and selfish," said Pearl. "She doesn't even need the job. It should go to someone who needs it."

"She says she does need it," said Issy. "Apparently her husband told her if she wants to keep the house without a fight she needs to get off her arse and start working."

"So she wants to swan about here being snobby to people," said Pearl. "*And* she'll want to introduce whole meal flour and raisins and wheatgrass juice and talk about BMIs and yap on and on all day."

Issy was torn. "I mean, it's not like we've seen loads of wonderful candidates," she argued. "No one we've had in has been right at all. And she'd be covering a lot of your time off, it's not like you'd have to see her that much."

"This is a very small retail space," Pearl said darkly. And Issy sighed and put off making the decision for a while.

• • • •

But things didn't ease off—which was fantastic, but also brought its own problems. Now it was phones constantly ringing, and lists, and Issy falling asleep during dinner, and Helena being out all the time, and she hadn't seen Janey since she'd had the baby, and Tom and Carla had moved into their new place in Whitstable and she hadn't even made it to their housewarming, and God, when she had five minutes she was still missing Graeme, or even just missing someone, anyone, to hold her hand occasionally and tell her that everything was going to be all right, but she didn't have time for that, didn't have time for anything, and everything was just building up and up.

She pushed her feelings back down inside herself and worked even harder, but the day Linda pushed her way through the door, she was very close to her wits' end.

It was a lovely Friday in late spring, and the warm air gave out the promise of a summery, light London weekend to come. People were thronging the streets looking cheerful, and they were doing a roaring trade in boxes of light lemon-scented cupcakes with a velvet icing and a little semicircle of crystallized fruit on the top; workers wanted to spread a little of the lovely day around their offices. Issy, though half bent over with exhaustion, was also taking huge pride in watching the enormous pile of cakes she'd started so early that morning—a mountain so big she couldn't believe they would possibly all be sold by the end of the day—steadily diminish in sixes and dozens. And people were buying more cold drinks too, which took pressure off the coffee-making routine. Even though Issy could now make a flat white or a tall skinny latte with effortless grace and speed (the first nineteen times she'd usually spilled something), it was still more time-consuming than grabbing some elderflower juice from the fridge. (Issy had stuck to prettier drinks rather than fizzy ones. They fitted better, she felt, with the ethos of the shop. And also, Austin had pointed out, the profit margins were better.)

Then, best of all, at 4:00 p.m., just as they were calming down, the door pinged open to reveal Keavie, pushing her grandfather in a wheelchair. Issy rushed up and flung her arms around his neck.

"Gramps!"

"I don't think," the old man said, heavily, "you quite know what you're doing with a meringue."

"I totally do!" exclaimed Issy, affronted. "Taste this."

She set in front of him one of her new miniature lemon meringue tarts, the curd so thick and fondant it sank right into the thin pastry. You could scoff the whole thing in two seconds, but the memory of it would stay with you all day.

"That meringue is too crunchy," pronounced Grampa Joe.

"That's because you have no teeth!" said Issy, indignant.

"Bring me a bowl. And a whisk. And some eggs."

Pearl made a hot chocolate for Keavie and they looked on as Joe and Issy gathered together the ingredients, and Issy sat on a stool next to him. With her dark curls next to his wispy pate, Pearl could see instantly how they must have looked together in her childhood.

"You've got the elbow action all wrong," said Gramps, even at his age cracking the eggs one-handed without even glancing at them, and separating them in the blink of an eye.

"That's because..." Issy's voice trailed off.

"What?" said Gramps.

"Nothing."

"What?"

"That's because I use an electric whisk," said Issy, blushing, and Pearl laughed out loud.

"Well, that proves it," said Gramps. "No wonder."

"But I have to use an electric whisk! I have to make dozens of these things every day! What else can I do?"

Gramps just shook his head and carried on whisking. At that moment the ironmonger passed by the window, and Joe beckoned him in.

"Did you know my granddaughter uses an electric whisk on meringues? After everything I've taught her!"

"That's why I don't eat here," said the ironmonger, then when he saw Issy's shocked face, he added, "Apologies, madam. I don't eat here because, lovely though your shop is, it's a little out of my price range."

"Well, have a cake on us," said Issy. "One without meringue."

Pearl obediently handed one over, but the ironmonger waved it away. "Suit yourself," said Pearl, but Issy pressed it on him till he relented.

"Very good," he said, through a mouthful of chocolate brownie cupcake.

"Imagine how good she'd be if she hand-whisked," said Gramps. Issy smacked him lightly on the head.

"This is *industrial* catering, Gramps."

Grampa Joe smiled.

"I'm just saying."

"Stop just saying."

Grampa Joe handed over the bowl of perfectly crested egg whites and sugar, standing up stiff and glazed.

"Stick it on some greaseproof paper, give it forty-five minutes..."

"Yes, I know, Gramps."

"OK, I just thought you might be putting it in the microwave or something."

Pearl grinned.

"You're a hard taskmaster, Mr. Randall," she said, leaning down to his wheelchair.

"I know," said Grampa Joe in a stage whisper. "Why do you think she's so brilliant?"

● ● ● ●

Later, after they'd eaten Gramps's amazing meringues with freshly whipped cream and a spoonful of raspberry coulis over the top, Keavie had taken Gramps—and a huge box of cakes for the residents—off to the van, and the cleaning up was finally done.

Issy could feel a solid bone-weariness deep down, but there would be wine tonight, and they didn't open till 10:00 a.m. on a Saturday, which felt like a huge lie-in, then early closing and the whole of Sunday off, and maybe it would be warm enough to push Gramps into the garden in his wheelchair (even though he was always cold, these days), and she could lie on a rug and read him bits of the paper, then maybe Helena would be around for a curry later on and a good natter. She was enjoying this little dream, and the way the late afternoon sun came through the clean panes of the windows, the ever-dinging bell of fresh customers and the happy faces of people on the brink of cake, when the door burst open, once more, in a panicky way.

Issy glanced up. At first she didn't recognize the woman who crashed into the room. Then she realized it was Linda, haberdashery Linda, normally so composed, whose life was never upset or the least bit disorganized.

"Hello!" Issy said, pleased to see her. "What's up?"

Linda rolled her eyes. She glanced around the shop and Issy realized with a slightly annoyed pang that this was the first time Linda had ever been in. She'd thought she might have been a bit more supportive, seeing as she was local and everything, and they'd stood together in rain and shine.

Issy's irritation was swept away in an instant, however, when Linda stopped and took a breath.

"Oh dear, it's lovely in here. I had no idea; I thought it was just a little sideline. I'm so sorry! If only I'd known."

Pearl, who'd leafleted her at least three times, harrumphed, but Issy nudged her to stop it, and Pearl went back to serving the postman, who came in after his rounds far too often. (Issy was worried eating cupcakes twice a day wasn't terribly good for him. Pearl reckoned he was just after her. They were both right.)

"Well, you're here now," she said. "Welcome! What would you like?"

Linda looked anxious. "I have to…I have to…Can you help me?"

"What is it?"

"It's…it's Leanne's wedding—tomorrow. But her cake company…A friend said she would make her cake and then she got it all muddled up or something, and anyway, Leanne's paid hundreds of pounds, but she doesn't have a wedding cake."

Issy later realized what it must have cost Linda to utter these words about her perfect daughter who never put a foot wrong. She looked close to breaking down.

"No cake on her wedding day! And I still have five hundred things on my checklist."

Issy remembered that this was the wedding to end all weddings, the wedding Linda had been talking about for over a year and a half.

"OK, OK, calm down. I'm sure we can help you," she said. "How many are we talking about? Seventy?"

"Um…" said Linda, and mumbled something so quietly Issy missed it.

"What's that?"

"…" said Linda again.

"That's odd," said Issy, "because it sounded like four hundred."

Linda raised her red-rimmed eyes to Issy.

"It's all going to fall apart. My only daughter's wedding! It's going to be a disaster!" And she burst into sobs.

• • • •

By seven thirty, when they'd only got the second batch in, Issy already knew they weren't going to make it. Pearl was a saint, a hero, and an absolute trooper and had stayed on without a second thought (and Issy knew the overtime couldn't hurt), but they couldn't use today's cakes. They had to start absolutely afresh, as well as designing some kind of structure to hold the cupcakes in the shape of a wedding cake.

"My arm hurts," said Pearl, stirring in ingredients for the mixer. "Shall we have the wine first, then get started?"

Issy shook her head. "That would turn out very poorly," she said. "Oh God, if only I knew someone who wants to…" She stopped short and looked at Pearl. "Of course I could phone…"

Pearl read her mind instantly.

"Not her. Anyone but her."

"There's nobody else," said Issy. "Nobody at all. I've called them all."

Pearl sighed, then looked back at the bowl.

"What time is this wedding?"

"Ten a.m."

"I want to cry."

"Me too," said Issy. "Or phone someone who might be a bit of a time-and-motion specialist."

• • • •

Pearl hated to admit it. But Issy had been right. The scrawny blond woman had marched in in an immaculate professional chef's uniform—she'd bought it for a week's cooking in Tuscany, she informed them, a gift from her ex-husband, who'd celebrated her absence by spending the entire time with his mistress—and immediately organized them into a production line, timed with the dinging of the oven.

After a while, once they were in the swing of things, Pearl put on the radio and they found themselves suddenly dancing in a row to Katy Perry, adding sugar and butter, baking and icing, tray after tray after tray without missing a moment's beat, and the pile in front of them steadily grew. Caroline improvised a cake stand out of old packaging and covered it beautifully with wedding paper they picked up from the newsagent, all the while telling them about the £900 cake she'd had specially made for her wedding by an Italian pâtissier from Milan, which in the end she didn't get to eat because she spent the entire day talking to one of her dad's friends who wanted to know how to get his daughter into marketing, while the evil ex got drunk with all his college friends, including his ex-girlfriend, and didn't even bother to come and rescue her.

"I should have known it was doomed," she said.

"Why didn't you?" asked Pearl, quite shortly. Caroline looked at her.

"Oh, Pearl. You'd understand if you'd ever been married."

And Pearl growled at her, quietly, behind the dairy fridge.

The cupcakes they smothered in a pure creamy vanilla icing, seemingly whipped effortlessly by Issy to perfection, with silver balls marking out the initials for Leanne and Scott, her groom-to-be. This was the worst job. By 11:30, Pearl was dotting the balls on anyhow and insisting they spelled L/S. But still the cakes grew and balanced and turned into, indeed, a magnificent wedding cake dusted with pink sparkly icing sugar.

"Come on, chop chop," shouted Caroline. "Stir like you mean it."

Pearl glanced at Issy. "I think *she* thinks she works here already."

"I think maybe she does," said Issy quietly.

Caroline beamed and momentarily stopped production.

"Oh," she said. "Thank you. This is…this is the first good thing that's happened in a while."

"Oh good," said Issy. "I was a bit worried about you, you're looking terribly thin."

"OK, the second good thing to happen," said Caroline. Pearl rolled her eyes. But when they finally got to go home just after midnight, she knew they couldn't have done it without her.

"Thanks," Pearl said grudgingly.

"That's all right," said Caroline. "Are you catching a cab home?"

Pearl grimaced. "Cabs don't go where I live."

"Oh really?" said Caroline. "Are you out in the country? How lovely."

Issy ushered Caroline out before she could get herself in more trouble and asked her to start off by covering a good lunch hour for Pearl and herself, before increasing her hours, all going well, to make them all happy.

"Absolutely," said Caroline. "I'm going to order my book group to start meeting here. And my Stitch 'n' Bitch. And my Jamie at Home Tupperware party. And my rotary club. And my Italian Renaissance art evening class."

Issy hugged her. "Have you been terribly lonely?"

"Dreadfully so."

"I hope you start to feel better."

"Thank you." And Caroline accepted the large bag of cakes Issy pressed on her.

"Don't give me that look," said Issy to Pearl, even though Pearl was standing behind her. "You are *mostly* right, I'll give you that. That's not the same thing as *always* right."

• • • •

The next morning was glorious; the entire city felt like it had dressed in green for a wedding day. Pearl and Issy inched across town in a cab, terrified their confection would wobble apart, but it held firm. They arranged it as the centerpiece of a huge table covered in pink stars and balloons.

Linda and Leanne came running up to meet them. When the bride, young and pink in her strapless dress, caught sight of the hundreds of delicately snow-iced soft pastel cupcakes, her mouth dropped open, showing newly whitened teeth.

"Oh," she said. "It's so beautiful! It's so beautiful! I love it! I love it! Thank you! Thank you so much!" And she hugged them both.

"Leanne!" hollered Linda. "I can't believe we're going to have to do your eye makeup again. We're paying this makeup artist by the hour, you know."

Leanne dabbed frantically under her eyes.

"Sorry, sorry, I've done nothing but burst into tears for about four hours. Everything is, argh, just so crazy. But you guys…you have totally saved my wedding."

A woman rushed into the assembly room and started fiddling about with Leanne's hair.

"The car's on its way," said somebody else. "Wedding minus forty-five."

Leanne's mouth opened in a paroxysm of panic. "*Oh my Gawd*," she yelled. "*Oh my Gawd*." She clasped Pearl and Issy. "Will you stay? Please? Stay."

"We would love to," said Issy, "but—"

"I have to get back to my boy," said Pearl firmly. "But the best of luck to you."

"You are going to have a *wonderful* day," Issy added, pressing a pile of business cards on the table next to the cake.

And Linda threw her arms around them both. Then they emerged at the top of the steps, out into a beautiful London day with pigeons sunning themselves on the pavement, and people passing on their way to coffees and markets and to buy cloth for saris and meat for barbecues and beer for football and goat's cheese for dinner parties, and papers for the park, and ice creams for children. Already Leanne's friends were gathering on the steps, young and gorgeous, with carefully set hair and bright dresses like peacocks; high strappy sandals and bare shoulders, a little ambitious for a May wedding. They were squealing in excitement and complimenting each other on their outfits and playing nervously with small bags and cigarettes and confetti.

●　●　●　●

Always the caterer, never the bride, thought Issy to herself, a tad ruefully.

"Well, enough of that," said Pearl cheerfully, whipping off her apron. "I'm off to give my boy a cuddle and tell him he might be able to see his mother occasionally from now on, now the Wicked Witch of the West has started work."

"Stop it!" said Issy teasingly. "She's going to be fine. Now, scoot."

Pearl kissed her on the cheek.

"Go home and get some rest," she said.

But Issy didn't much feel like getting some rest; it was a gorgeous afternoon, and she felt antsy and unsettled. She was considering hopping on a bus at random and going for a wander, when she spotted a familiar figure at the bus stop. He was bent over, fiddling with the laces of a small skinny boy with sticky-up auburn hair and a cross look on his face.

"But I *want* them like this," the boy was saying.

"Well, they're impossible knots that you keep tripping over!" The man sounded exasperated.

"That's how I *want* them."

"Well, at least try and trip over a paving stone and then we can sue the council."

Austin straightened up and was so surprised to see Issy there, he nearly stepped backward into the road.

"Oh, hello," he said.

"Hello." Issy tried to make sure she didn't go red. "Uh, hi."

"Hi," said Austin. There was a pause.

"Who are you?" said the small boy, rudely.

"Hello. Well, I'm Issy," said Issy. "Who are you?"

"Duh. I'm Darny," said Darny. "Are you going to be one of Austin's drippy girlfriends?"

"Darny!" said Austin in a warning tone.

"Are you going to come around at night and cook horrible suppers and use a silly voice and say, 'Oh, so *tragic* for Darny to lose his mummy and daddy, let me look after you,' kissy kissy kissy smooch smooch yawn stop telling me when to go to bed?"

Austin wanted the ground to open and swallow him up. Although Issy didn't look offended; rather, she looked like she was about to laugh.

"Is that what they do?" she asked. Darny nodded, mutinously. "That *does* sound boring. No, I'm nothing like that. I work with your dad and I live up this road here, that's all."

"Oh," said Darny. "I guess that's all right."

"I guess so too." She smiled at Austin. "Are you well?"

"I will be once I have this ten-year-old surgically removed."

"Ha ha ha," said Darny. "That wasn't me really laughing," he said to Issy. "I was pretending to laugh and being sarcastic."

"Oh," said Issy. "Sometimes I do that too."

"Where are you off to?" asked Austin.

"In fact I've been working all night, you'll be pleased to hear," she said. "Catering for a wedding at a nearby town hall. *And* I've taken on a new member of staff. She's great…slightly evil, but on the whole…"

"Oh, that's terrific," said Austin, and his face broke into a large smile. He was genuinely, truly happy for her, Issy realized. Not just from the bank's point of view, but personally.

"No, where are you going now?" said Darny. "That's what he asked you. Because we're going to the aquarium. Would you like to come?"

Austin raised his eyebrows. This was totally unprecedented. Darny made a point of disliking all grown-ups and being rude to them to forestall their mooning all over him. To spontaneously invite someone somewhere was unheard of.

"Well," said Issy, "I was thinking of going home to bed."

"While it's *light*?" said Darny. "Is someone making you?"

"In fact, no," said Issy.

"OK," said Darny. "Come with us."

Issy glanced at Austin.

"Oh, I probably should…"

Austin knew it wasn't professional. She probably wouldn't even want to. But, he couldn't help it. He liked her. He was going to ask her. And that was that.

"Come," he said. "I'll buy you a Frappuccino."

"Bribery," said Issy, smiling. "That's what'll get me to spend my Saturday looking at fish."

And at that moment the bus rounded the corner and, after a second, all three of them got on it.

• • • •

The aquarium was quiet—the first lovely sunny day of the year had prompted most people out of doors—and Darny was utterly transfixed by the tanks of fish; little quicksilver shoals, or huge great coelacanths that looked left over from the age of the dinosaurs. Austin and Issy talked; quietly, because the dark, warm underground environment seemed to encourage a quiet tone of voice; small revelations; and it was easier, somehow, to talk in the half light, barely able to see one another except for the outline of Issy's curls backlit by jellyfish, pink and luminous, or the tankful of phosphorescence that shimmered and reflected in Austin's glasses.

Issy found the worries and cares of the café, which had lain on her relentlessly for months, it felt, somehow get soothed away in the strange underwater tranquility, as Austin made her laugh with stories about Darny at school or touched on, without a trace of self-pity, how hard it was to be a single parent who wasn't even a parent. And in return, Issy found herself talking about her own mother—normally when she spoke of her family, she talked about how amazing her grandfather was, and how they'd all lived together, and made it sound cozy. But talking to someone who knew how it felt to lose a parent, absolutely and irrevocably, made it easier somehow to talk about how her mother had danced in and out of her life, trying to make herself happy but not succeeding in making anyone happy.

"Were your parents happy?" she asked.

Austin thought about it. "You know, I never considered it. Your parents are just your parents, aren't they? It never even occurs to you till you grow up, whatever they're like, that they aren't completely normal. But yes, I think they were. I used to see them touch all the time, and they were close, always physically close, holding hands, close to one another on the sofa."

Without thinking, Issy glanced down at her own hand. It was silhouetted in front of a gently glowing tank filled with darting eels, not far from Austin's. It crossed her mind: how would it feel if she was to take his hand then and there? Would he pull away? She could almost feel her fingers tingle in anticipation.

"And of course, there was the fact of them being completely and utterly ancient and having another baby when all their friends were becoming grandparents. So, you know, something must have gone all right. Of course at the time I thought it was totally disgusting…"

Issy smiled. "I bet you didn't really. I bet you loved him from the get go."

Austin glanced over at Darny, whose eyes were wide; his gaze following the shark around its tank, completely hypnotized.

"Of course I did," mumbled Austin, and turned away slightly, his hand moving further from Issy's, who felt embarrassed suddenly, like she'd gone a little too far.

"I'm sorry," she said. "I didn't mean to be so personal."

"It's not that," said Austin, his voice a little muffled. "It's just…I would have liked to know them, you know? As a grown-up, not an overgrown teenager."

"You're making me want to go phone my mum," said Issy.

"You should," said Austin.

Now it was Issy's turn to glance away.

"She's changed her number," she said quietly.

And almost without realizing he was doing it, Austin put out his hand to take hers, at first in a gentle squeeze, but then suddenly he didn't want to let it go.

"*Ice cream!*" came a very loud voice from below them. Immediately they dropped each other's hand. It was too dark down here, Issy found herself thinking. Like a nightclub.

"I spoke to the shark," said Darny importantly to his brother. "He said that I would make a very good marine biologist and also that it would be OK for me to have some ice cream now. In fact he thought it was quite important. That I got some ice cream. Now."

Austin looked at Issy, trying to read her face, but it was impossible in the gloom. It was very awkward, all of a sudden.

"Um, ice cream?" he said.

"Yes please!" said Issy.

The three of them sat by the river, watching the boats go by and the great wheel of the London Eye overhead, and were still enjoying each other's company, so much so in fact that Issy hardly noticed the time. When Darny finally came off the high jungle gym and grabbed Issy's hand with his sticky paw as they left the park, she didn't mind a bit—was pleased in fact (Austin was stupefied)—and they decided as a special treat to take a cab back to Stoke Newington, whereupon Darny, having attempted to press all the buttons, curled up in the back and fell asleep on Issy's shoulder. When Austin glanced over two minutes later as the cab trudged slowly through the traffic, he saw Issy, too, fast asleep, her black curls tangled with Darny's spikes, her cheeks pink. He stared at her all the way home.

• • • •

Issy couldn't believe she'd fallen asleep in the cab. OK, she'd had no rest the night before, but still. Had she dribbled? Had she snored? Oh God, horrific. Austin had just smiled politely and said good-bye…Oh God, that meant she must have then, because surely otherwise…wouldn't he have asked for another date? Although that wasn't a date, was it? Was it? No. Yes. No. She thought again of the moment when he'd held her hand. She couldn't believe how much she'd wanted him to go on holding it. Putting her key in the door, Issy moaned. Helena would know what to do.

She caught sight of herself in the filigree mirror that hung in the tiny hallway, over the flower-sprigged retro wallpaper she was so proud of. She hadn't realized till then that she must have had that big white streak of wedding cake flour in her hair all day.

"*Helena?! Lena! I need you,*" she bawled, stalking into the sitting room and marching over to the fridge, where she knew they had a couple of bottles of rosé left over from something. Then she stopped and turned around. There on the sofa, sure enough, was Helena. And beside her on the sofa, someone she thought she recognized. They were in the exact positions of people who'd suddenly jumped apart in an effort to look completely innocent of any wrongdoing.

"Oh!" she said.

"Hello!" said Helena. Issy looked at her carefully. Could she…? She couldn't possibly. Could she be blushing?

Ashok was pleased. Meeting Helena's friends was definitely a good step forward. He jumped up immediately.

"Hello, Isabel. How lovely to see you again," he said politely, shaking her hand. "I'm—"

"Ashok. Yes, I know," she said. He was much handsomer than she'd remembered, out of his rookie-looking short white coat. Over the top of his head she waggled her eyebrows furiously at Helena, who was pretending to ignore her.

"So what is it you need to ask me?" said Helena, trying to change the subject.

"Um, not to worry," said Issy, moving over to the fridge. "Who'd like some wine?"

"Your gramps called," said Helena, when they were all ensconced in the sitting room. Ashok made for very easy company, Issy noted, pouring wine and adding comments when needed.

"Oh, lovely," said Issy. "What's he up to? Apart from, um, lying in bed."

"He wanted to know if you got his cream of soda scone recipe."

"Ah," said Issy. She had gotten it. But the thing was, she'd gotten it four times, all copied out in the same wavering hand. She'd forgotten about that.

"And," said Helena, "he didn't recognize me on the phone."

"Oh," said Issy.

"He knows me quite well," said Helena.

"I know."

"I don't have to tell you what that means."

"No," said Issy quietly. "He seemed fine yesterday."

"It can ebb and flow," said Helena. "You know that."

"I'm sorry," said Ashok. "The same thing happened to my grandfather."

"Did he get all better?" asked Issy. "And then everything went back to how it used to be and it was fine again, just like when you were little?"

"Um…not exactly," said Ashok, and he offered her a little more wine, but Issy suddenly found herself overwhelmed with tiredness. She bade good night to them both and stumbled off to bed.

• • • •

"I'm calling the home," said Issy, after a long, luxurious lie-in the next morning.

"Good," said Helena. "What was it you wanted to ask me before?"

"Ooh," said Issy. "Well." And she told her about her day with Austin.

Helena's smile got wider and wider.

"Stop that," said Issy. "That's exactly the look Pearl gets every time his name comes up in conversation. You two are totally in cahoots."

"He's an attractive man…" said Helena.

"Whom I owe lots and lots of money," said Issy. "I'm sure it's not right."

"Well, you haven't *done* anything," said Helena.

"Nooo…"

"Apart from the dribble."

"I didn't dribble."

"Let's hope he loooooves dribble."

"Stop it!"

"Well, at least he's seen you at your dribbliest. It can only get better from now on in."

"Shut up!"

Helena grinned. "I reckon he's going to phone you."

Issy felt her heart beat a bit faster. Even just talking about him was the most…well, it felt nice.

"Do you think?"

"Even if it's just to bill you for the dry cleaning."

• • • •

Austin did phone. First thing Tuesday morning.

But it wasn't the kind of phone call he really wanted to make.

224

It wasn't the kind he liked making to anyone. The fact that he had to make it to Issy really made him think that, once and for all, and however sweet she might be and however interesting he found her and however pretty she looked, these kinds of things were pointless and he couldn't mix business with pleasure, and that was that. Which was incredibly annoying, given that he was still going to have to call her. And it didn't help that Darny kept mooning around the place, asking when he could see her again.

Well, it had to be done. He sighed, then picked up the phone.

"Hello," he said.

"Hello!" came the warm tones immediately. She sounded really pleased to hear from him. "Hello! Is that Austin? How nice to hear from you! How's Darny? Can you tell him I have been looking for fish cake-shapes to make fishy cakes but apparently nobody likes fishy cakes and I can't find any. Well, they like fishcakes, you know what I mean, but not…anyway, do you think dinosaurs would do and…" Issy was aware she was babbling.

"Um, fine, he's fine. Um, look, Issy…"

Her heart sank. That tone of voice was one she recognized. In that instant she knew that whatever she thought might have happened on Saturday was not really on the agenda; that he'd reconsidered, if he'd ever considered it in the first place. OK. OK. She took a deep breath and pulled herself together, putting down her spatula and pushing her hair away from her face. She was surprised just how acute her disappointment was: she'd thought she was still getting over a broken heart, but this felt much more painful than thoughts of her old boss.

"Yes?" she said, in a clipped way.

Austin felt cross with himself, stupid. Why couldn't he just say, look, would you like to meet for, you know, a drink? Somewhere nice. Late at night. Where nobody had to get up in the morning and be at work at 7:00 a.m., and no one still wet the bed if they'd been watching *Doctor Who* and needed his bunk bed changed at peculiar hours;

somewhere they could have a glass of wine, and maybe a bit of a laugh, and a dance and then afterward…God. He felt like smacking himself on the head. Concentrate.

"Look," he managed. He was going to keep this short and terse, make absolutely sure he didn't say anything inappropriate. "I've had Mrs. Prescott on the phone…"

"And?"

Issy was ready for good news. Earnings were marching steadily upward, and she fully expected Caroline to make a huge difference; when she wasn't bursting into tears or tut-tutting over the butter order, she was already proving herself an icon of efficiency.

"She says there's a…she says she needs to send out an invoice and you won't let her."

"Well, I've explained it totally to Mrs. Prescott," said Issy stiffly. "I was doing a wedding favor for a friend."

"She says there was no mention of this at all. She found there was an unaccounted-for amount of ingredients missing that would add up to about four hundred cakes…"

"God, she's good," said Issy. "Four hundred and ten, actually. In case some got squashed."

"That's not funny, Issy! That's a week's profit for you!"

"But it was a wedding gift! To a friend!"

"Well, the invoice should still have gone through, even at a heavy discount. You have to charge for raw materials."

"Not for a gift," said Issy stubbornly. How dare he take her out and be all soft and mooshy on Saturday, then three days later phone her up and think he could give her a bollocking. He was just as bad as Graeme.

Austin was exasperated.

"Issy! You can't run a business this way! You just can't! Don't you understand? You can't just shut up the shop unannounced, and you can't go giving stock away like that! Apple don't hand out free iPods, and exactly the same principle applies to you. Exactly."

"But we're loads busier these days," said Issy.

"Yes, but you've taken on more staff and you're paying overtime," said Austin. "It doesn't matter if you have a million people a day; if you don't take in more cash than you spend you're going to the wall, and that's the end of it. You didn't even open on Saturday."

That was a step too far and they both knew it.

"You're right," said Issy. "Obviously on Saturday I made a mistake."

"I didn't mean it like that," said Austin.

"I think you did," said Issy.

There was a pause. Then Issy said, "You know, my grandfather… My grandfather ran three bakeries at one point. He supplied huge amounts of bread in Manchester. He was a success, and he knew everyone. Of course all his money's gone now…Nursing homes, you know. Getting good care is expensive."

"I do know, yes," said Austin, and Issy heard the simple pain in his voice, but didn't want to feel sympathetic.

"Anyway, he was famous when I was growing up; everyone got their bread from him. And if they were sick or couldn't make the bill that week, he'd help them out, or if a hungry child was passing by, he'd always have a cake for them, or a sickly mum, or an old soldier. Everyone knew him. And he was a huge success. And that's what I want to do."

"And I think that's wonderful," said Austin. "He sounds like a wonderful man."

"He is," said Issy fervently.

"And that's how businesses worked for hundreds of years—then the big boys came in and built huge shops, not in town, and made everything loads cheaper and invented central distribution and however much everyone liked the little shops and knew the people, they all went to the big shops. That's just what happened."

Issy stayed silent. She knew that was true. The local stores had nearly all gone by the time Gramps retired; the city center was almost deserted. People didn't want a chat with their bread anymore, not if it cost them a few pence extra a loaf.

"So if you're going to offer personal service, and a small shop with all the overheads involved in single-service marketing, you do, I'm afraid, have to fight a bit harder than your grandfather did."

"Nobody fights harder than him," said Issy defiantly.

"Well, that's good. I'm glad you've inherited his spirit. But please, please, Issy. Apply it to the modern age."

"Thank you for the business advice," said Issy.

"You're welcome," said Austin.

And they hung up, both upset, both frustrated, at opposite ends of Stoke Newington.

• • • •

Telling herself she had been foolish to think that anything might have happened over the weekend, Issy took Austin's words to heart. She submerged herself in the business; paid her bills on time, kept on top of the paperwork; used Caroline's new hours to organize and streamline everything. She was even at risk of wringing a smile out of Mrs. Prescott. She was in early to bake cupcakes—the standard favorites, orange and lemon, double chocolate and strawberry and vanilla, plus a constantly rotating menu of new recipes to keep the regulars coming back for more. Most of these were tested on Doti the postman, whose visits were almost getting embarrassing for everyone except Pearl, who smiled at him and teased him no more nor less than she did everyone else who crossed her path.

Caroline and Pearl were continuing to clash.

"I *must* do those windows," Caroline murmured to Issy on her way out one day.

Pearl rolled her eyes. "Well, I'll do them."

"No, no," said Caroline. "I'll come in on my day off."

So of course the windows got washed by Pearl, immediately.

"I think we'd better tell Issy there's too much cinnamon in the cinnamon rolls, don't you?" Caroline would say chummily. "I'll do it of course."

So Pearl was always left feeling like the junior partner. One day, when Pearl was alone in the shop, Kate marched in with the twins.

"I'm here for the order."

Seraphina was wearing a pink ballet tutu. Jane was wearing blue dungarees. Pearl tried to focus on what Kate was saying, but she was distracted by the sight of Seraphina holding open the tutu waistband and Jane attempting to climb inside, while simultaneously pushing a dungaree strap over Seraphina's little shoulder.

"What's that?" she said, pleasantly.

"For the cakes with messages. Caroline said it was a brilliant concept and she'd get you right on it."

"Did she?" said Pearl. Kate was saved from a classic Pearl snort by the two little girls suddenly falling over.

"Seraphina! Jane! What are you doing?"

The girls were all tangled up in each other's clothing and were rolling around the floor in hysterics.

"*We not Jane an Sufine! We Sufijane!*"

They dissolved in giggles again, cuddling one another, the two blond heads identical.

"Get up," shouted Kate. "Or it'll be the naughty step for you, Seraphina, and the naughty corner for you, Jane."

The two girls slowly disentangled themselves, heads hanging.

"Honestly," said Kate, shaking her head at Pearl.

"They're adorable," said Pearl, missing Louis. She couldn't believe how much you could miss someone you were going to see in a few hours. Sometimes after he was asleep she had to go and look at him at night because she couldn't wait to see him in the morning.

"Humph," said Kate. "So, can you do it?"

"Do what?" said Pearl, hating the idea of Caroline subcontracting on her behalf.

"I want letters piped on the cakes."

"Oh," said Pearl. It would be time-consuming but they'd be able to charge a premium, she supposed. Would it be worth her while?

"I'd want it professional standard," said Kate. "None of this local amateur nonsense."

And would it be worth having to do it to Kate's standards?

"Can we have cake, Mummy?" Seraphina was asking sweetly. "We'll share."

"We *like to share*," shouted Jane.

"No, darlings, this is all junk," said Kate absentmindedly. Pearl sighed. Kate took a quick phone call while Pearl stood there, cursing Caroline and all her friends, then Kate turned off her phone.

"All right," she said briskly. "I want lemon cupcakes, orange icing, and 'H-A-P-P-Y-B-I-R-T-H-D-A-Y-E-V-A-N-G-E-L-I-N-A-4-T-O-D-A-Y.'"

Pearl wrote it down. "I think we can manage," she said.

"Good," said Kate. "I hope Caroline was right about you."

Pearl privately thought she was not. "Good-bye, twins!" She waved.

"*Buh bye!*" called the twins in one voice.

"Actually it's Seraph—"

But Pearl had already disappeared downstairs to give the good news to Issy.

•   •   •   •

They both worked late to finish, and Helena popped in for a chat and a catch-up, and they teased her unmercifully about Ashok and she refused to answer any questions, turning them around by asking Pearl repeatedly about Ben, but she ably deflected them by complaining to Issy about Caroline, when Issy was absolutely not in the mood to listen.

But Helena and Pearl gradually fell silent, just watching Issy at work. It was so instinctive, what she did—she didn't measure or weigh anything out, simply tossed, almost unthinkingly, the ingredients into a bowl, a fine, careless toss to the arm as she spun the mixture, spooning it up in the blink of an eye, twenty-four perfect measures into the baking tins she'd greased without looking at them; spinning the sugared icing then whipping it on and shaping it with a knife, every one perfect and delicious, a miniature work of art, even before she started the delicate piping of each individual letter. Helena and Pearl exchanged glances.

"That is quite cool," said Helena finally.

Issy, engrossed in what she was doing, looked up, surprised. "But I do this every day," she said. "It's like you stitching up someone's glassed arm."

"I am good at that," confirmed Helena. "But it doesn't look quite so delicious at the end."

The cakes, laid out in a row, were stunning. Issy was going to pop them in on her way home.

"They are better than that lady deserves," said Pearl crossly.

"Behave yourself," said Issy, sticking out her tongue.

● ● ● ●

Dashing in one morning to get the temperamental coffee machine warmed up before what was rapidly becoming the morning rush, Pearl realized she hadn't even opened yesterday's post. "*Won! Doo! Free! Hup!*" Plonking Louis on one of the high stools they'd recently got to line the mantelpiece and give people somewhere extra to sit when they were busy, she passed him a pain au chocolat and opened up the letter from the nursery. Then she stared at it in disbelief.

The doorbell tinkled. Issy was meeting a sugar rep that morning and was going to be in a little later, so Caroline was opening up.

"*Buens deez*, Caline!" shouted Louis, who had been learning how to say hello in different languages at nursery and thought that that was splendid.

"Good morning, Louis," enunciated Caroline carefully, who thought Louis's diction was absolutely dreadful and that she was the only person who could save him from a life of sounding lower class. She wished Pearl would be a teensy bit more grateful, not that she could see past that enormous south London chip she had on her shoulder. "Good morning, Pearl."

Pearl didn't utter a peep. Well, that was just great, thought Caroline, who was, nonetheless, used to girl-on-girl spats ever since she'd been sent to the terribly fraught and highly competitive girls' school she planned on one day making Hermia sit the exams for. She had learned pretty much everything she needed to know about falling out with other women at that school. She could hold a sulk like nobody's business, so this wasn't going to worry her. She had a divorce going on, for crying out loud. Nobody cared about her.

But when she turned to hang up her Aquascutum raincoat, she noticed that Pearl wasn't wearing her customary look of slightly hang-dog suspicion. That in fact Pearl was holding a letter in her hand, staring into the middle distance—and she was crying.

Caroline felt the same instinct within her as when one of her dogs got sick. She crossed the room instantly.

"Darling, what is it? What's the matter?"

"*Mamma?*" said Louis in alarm. He couldn't get down from the high stool on his own (the benefits being, once up there, he couldn't get his fingers in anything either). "*Mamma? Boo-boo?*"

With some effort, Pearl pulled herself together. In an only slightly shaky voice she said, "Oh, no, darling. Mamma doesn't have a boo-boo."

Caroline touched her lightly on the shoulder, but Pearl, hands trembling, could only give the letter to Caroline as she crossed in front of the counter to pick up Louis.

"Come here, baby," she said, cradling his face into her wide shoulder so he couldn't see her eyes. "There we go," she crooned. "Everything's fine." *"Me not go nursery,"* said Louis decisively. *"Me stay Mamma."*

Caroline glanced at the letter. It was formally marked North East London Strategic Health Authority.

Dear Mrs. McGregor,

Your son **Louis Kmbota McGregor** has recently undertaken a medical test at **Stoke Newington Little Teds Nursery**, 13 Osbadeston Road, London N16. The results of this test show that for his age and height, Louis falls into the **overweight to obese** category.

Even from very early days, a child who is overweight or obese can suffer serious damage to their health and fitness in later life. It can cause heart disease, cancer, fertility problems, sleeping disorders, depression, and early mortality. Taking a few simple steps to improve your child's diet and exercise program can be all that is needed to ensure that your child **Louis Kmbota** will grow and live to his full potential. We have arranged for you an appointment with Neda Mahet, nutritionist counselor at the Stoke Newington Practice, on June 15...

Caroline put it down.

"This letter is absolutely disgusting," she announced, her nose twitching. "They're all horrible bossyboots nanny-state socialist interfering cruel bloody left-wing idiots."

Pearl blinked at her. Caroline couldn't have said a better thing to cheer her up. "But...it's their official letter."

"And it's officially a total disgrace. How dare they? Look at your adorable boy. Well, yes, he is too plump but you know that anyway. It's none of their business. Would you like me to rip it up for you?"

Pearl looked at Caroline with something close to amazement. "But it's official!"

Caroline shrugged. "So what? We pay taxes. The fewer nosy busybodies they employ to do this kind of thing, the better for everyone. Shall I?"

Shocked and feeling naughty, Pearl nodded. Normally, anything official she paid very close attention to. In her world, you did what those letters said or bad things happened. They cut your benefit. They reassigned where you lived, and you just had to go, even if it was somewhere awful. They came and pawed at your children and if you didn't like it, they could even, she was sure, take your children away. They asked you how much you drank and how much you smoked and how many hours you worked and where was the baby's father, and if you got the answer wrong, even a tiny bit, then you weren't going to be buying shoes in the foreseeable future. Seeing Caroline rip up the letter like it was nothing—something stupid to be ignored—worked a surprising change in her. She was still cross at Caroline for not having to care about this stuff. But she felt oddly liberated too.

"Thank you," she said to Caroline quietly, with a hesitant admiration.

"You know," said Caroline, daintily sweeping up the scraps, "you don't *look* like you're the kind of person who would let anyone push you about."

Pearl sat Louis back up on the high chair. Was he plump? He had round little baby cheeks and an adorable pot belly, and a high little round bottom and chunky kissable thighs and fat pudgy fingers. How could he be fat? He was perfect.

"You're gorgeous," she said, looking at him. Louis nodded. His mum told him this a lot and he knew how to respond in a way that normally got him a sweetie.

"*Louis is gojuss,*" he said, grinning merrily and showing all his teeth. "*Yis! Louis is gojuss! Now sweeties.*"

And he put out his chubby hand and made a beckoning gesture.

"Mm," he added for emphasis, just in case anyone had missed the reference, licking his lips and rubbing his tummy. *"Louis does do like sweeties."*

Caroline was rarely demonstrative even with her own children—in fact, had she stopped to think about it she would probably have categorized her mood with them as mostly peevish—but she moved toward Louis on the chair, who eyed her warily. He was universally benevolent, but this woman never gave him sweeties, he knew that much.

Caroline prodded him in his fat tummy and he giggled and wriggled obligingly.

"You are gorgeous, Louis," she said. "But you shouldn't have that."

"It's just a baby tummy," protested Pearl strongly.

"No, it has rolls," said Caroline, whose contemplation and understanding of human body fat in all its permutations bordered on the maniacal. "That's not right. And I never see him without a cake in his paws."

"Well, he's a growing boy," said Pearl defensively. "He's got to eat."

"He does," said Caroline thoughtfully. "It all depends on what."

A tap at the door alerted them to their first customers—the laborers who were working on Kate's house on Albion Road. Now Kate directly blamed the work's slow progress and tardy completion on Caroline selling them coffee and cakes all day and encouraging them to hang about chatting rather than getting on with the job and taking five minutes of their own time to throw down a homemade cheese sandwich underneath the roof slats. Her annoyance was making Stitch 'n' Bitch increasingly uncomfortable.

As they handled the morning rush, and Louis sat cheerfully greeting the regulars, who found it hard to pass him without tweaking his sticky cheeks or rubbing his soft shorn head, Pearl kept sneaking glances at him in the faded antique mirror that hung over the room. Sure enough, there was old Mrs. Hanowitz, who liked a huge mug of hot chocolate and a proper kaffeeklatsch, scratching his roly tum as if he were a dog— then she popped the marshmallow from the top of her chocolate into his mouth. And Fingus the plumber, with the huge belly and builder's bum spilling out of the side of his white dungarees: he high-fived his little mate, and asked as he did every day if Louis had brought his spanner yet, seeing as he was going to be his apprentice. Issy didn't help matters by running in from her early meeting to get started on the baking, but not without going up to Louis for her morning cuddle and announcing loudly, "Good morning, my little chub-chubs." Pearl's brow furrowed. Was this what he was? Everyone's plump pet? He wasn't a pet. He was a person, with the same rights as everyone else.

Caroline caught her looking, and bit her lip. Well, quite right, she didn't want her child to end up the same way as her, did she? And Pearl's distress had given her an idea…

● ● ● ●

"Well, maybe she's right," said Ben, lounging against the kitchen counter. "I dunno. He looks all right to me."

"And me," said Pearl. Ben had "popped in" on his way home, even though he was working in Stratford, which was right across the other side of town. Pearl pretended that he was just passing; Ben pretended he didn't really want to stay the night (although Pearl's cooking was worth it on its own. It was odd, Pearl had found. When she wasn't working, she couldn't really be bothered with cooking and they'd lived off chicken and fish fingers. Now, even though she was tired when she got home, she quite liked sticking Louis on the counter and putting a meal together. She was a good cook, after all), and Louis nearly expired with happiness.

The little boy bumbled past them entirely covered in a blanket.

"Hey, Louis," said his dad.

"*I not Louis. I turtle*," came a muffled voice. Ben raised his eyebrows.

"Don't ask me," said Pearl. "He's been a turtle all day."

Ben put down his cup of tea and raised his voice.

"Any turtles around here who would like to *go outside and play some football?*"

"*Yaaayyyy,*" said the turtle, getting up without taking off his blanket and bumping his head on the cooker. "Ouch."

Pearl looked at her mother in amazement as Ben led his boy outside.

"Don't think it," said her mother. "He comes for a bit then he goes again. Don't let the boy get too fond."

It might be too late for that, Pearl found herself thinking.

bran and carrot cupcake surprise

● ● ● ●

* 1½ cups whole wheat pastry flour
* ½ tsp baking soda
* 2¼ tsp baking powder
* ¼ tsp salt
* ¾ cup oat or wheat bran
* egg replacement for 2 eggs
* 1 cup rennet
* ½ cup brown rice syrup
* ¼ cup applesauce
* ¼ cup safflower oil
* 1½ cups grated carrot
* ½–¾ cup crushed dates
* ½ cup raisins
* ½ cup chopped walnuts or pecans

"I just wanted to try out something new," said Caroline, trying to look suitably humble and helpful the next morning when she turned up with a Tupperware box. "It's nothing really, I just tossed them together."

"What the hell is brown rice syrup when it's at home?" said Pearl, glancing down the recipe. "Safflower oil?"

"They're perfectly easy to source," lied Caroline.

"Don't call it 'surprise,'" said Issy over her shoulder. "Every child knows that 'surprise' means hidden vegetables. Call it 'white sugar chocolate toffee delight.'"

"It's simple, wholesome fare," said Caroline, trying to make a Jamie Oliver face. In fact, it had taken her five hours slaving over her Neff faux-aged pale cream country kitchen table and much cursing to get the mixture right and make the cupcakes stick together. How did Issy make it look so damn easy, throwing ingredients together to produce cakes that tasted light as air and melted in the mouth? Well, of course she was using evil refined ingredients that would send her to an early grave. But as she'd mixed and reworked them, Caroline had had an image in her head—of her wholesome treats outselling the sugary rubbish and becoming famous; eclipsing the Cupcake Café with Caroline's Fresh Cooking; converting children all over the world to the benefits of a healthier, slenderer lifestyle…She wouldn't be the part-time member of staff then, no sirree…

Pearl and Issy looked at one another, their hands wavering by their mouths.

"Well?" said Caroline, still half-demented from lack of sleep. Her cleaner was going to have a lot of scrubbing to do that morning. "Give one to Louis."

"*Iss please!*"

Pearl put her hand down. "Yes, in a minute."

Issy fought an urgent desire to scrape the bits of raw carrot off her tongue. And what was that custardy aftertaste that hinted at broccoli?

"Here, little man." Caroline took the box over to him.

"Um, he's not hungry," said Pearl desperately. "I'm trying to cut down, you know."

But Louis had already cheerfully stuck his fat little paw in the box. "Ta, Caline."

"Thank you," said Caroline, unable to help herself. "Don't say ta, say thank you."

"I don't think he'll be saying either in a minute," muttered Pearl to Issy, who was surreptitiously slurping coffee and rolling it around her mouth to try to remove the taste. Pearl had simply scarfed some of Issy's brand new batch of Victoria sponge cupcakes to change the taste and Issy didn't blame her for a second. Caroline fixed her eyes on Louis expectantly.

"This is *much* nicer than your normal silly old cakes, darling," she said insistently. Louis bit into the cupcake-shaped object confidently enough, but gradually, as he started to chew, his face took on a confused, upset expression, like a dog chewing a plastic newspaper.

"There we go, darling," she said encouragingly. "Yummy, huh."

Louis signaled his mother with his eyes desperately, then simply, as if it wasn't connected to him in any way, let the lower half of his jaw drop open so that the contents of his mouth started to fall out and crumble to the floor.

"Louis!" shrieked Pearl, dashing over to him. "Stop doing that immediately."

"*Yucky, Mummy! Yucky! Bleargh bleargh bleargh!*"

Louis began frantically shoving his hand over his tongue to scrape off any remaining pieces of the cake.

"*Yug, Mummy! Yug, Caline! Yug!*" he cried accusingly, as Pearl gave him a drink of milk to calm him down and Issy fetched the dustpan and brush. Caroline stood there with a pinkish blush at the top of her very high cheekbones.

"Well," she said, when Louis was quite himself again, "obviously his palate has been completely ruined by junk."

"Hmmm," said Pearl crossly.

"*Caline*," said Louis seriously, leaning over to make his point. "*Bad cake, Caline.*"

"No, yummy cake, Louis," said Caroline tightly.

"No, Caline," said Louis. Issy hastily got in the middle before it turned into a genuine argument between a forty-year-old and a two-year-old.

"It is," she said, "a brilliant idea, Caroline. Absolutely great."

Caroline eyed her beadily. "Well, I still own copyright on the recipe."

"Um, well..." said Issy. "But obviously, well, yes. Of course. We could call them Caroline's cupcakes; would that work?"

Caroline was reluctant to hand over the rest of the cakes (Issy didn't want her sneaking them to a customer; she trusted Caroline absolutely with money, stock, and hours but didn't trust her one iota in terms of thinking she knew best when it came to their clients' tastes), but Issy insisted she needed them for an experiment, and, well, it was true that they hadn't stuck together as well as Caroline had hoped. Rennet wasn't quite as good for making delicious firm cakes as the all-natural cookbook had assured her it would be. Issy wasn't even sure the cakes would be all right for the compost she'd started handing over to the Hackney City Farm, but subtly got rid of them anyway.

And there were two good effects immediately: Caroline was absolutely right about one thing. There was a market for "healthy" cupcakes.

"Caroline's cupcakes," as amended by Issy, little applesauce, raisin and cranberry muffins in tiny baking cases with fire engines or pink umbrellas on them, were an instant hit with mothers who were anxious to avoid their children getting stuck into icing once a day, and Issy faithfully added a kilo of carrots to their stock order every week then took some home each night. Caroline genuinely believed they had gone into the recipe. Helena and Ashok, who appeared to have practically moved in (Helena explained that the doctor's single-person digs left a lot to be desired and would leave a lot to be desired even if one were a dog, ferret or rat), ate a lot of soup. But Issy never did find a use for the rennet.

The second good result was that Louis became entirely suspicious of every cupcake in the shop and refused to eat a second breakfast there. It did him no harm at all, and with Caroline working more hours and Louis skipping to the bus stop with his mum every day, his second weigh-in went without a hitch. Which didn't matter to Pearl and Caroline, who cheerfully tore up the health authority's letter regardless.

• • • •

Three weeks later, Pearl came in to find Caroline bent over the counter, stock still.

"What's up?"

Caroline couldn't answer. She was stiff as a board.

"What's the matter, sweetheart?"

"I'm…I'm fine," stuttered Caroline.

Pearl gently but firmly turned her around.

"What's happened?"

Caroline's usually immaculately made-up face was tear-stained and tragic, mascara pouring down.

"What is it?" said Pearl, who was familiar with how the pain, sometimes, of losing your man could come in and hit you at the most unexpected moments, even when you hadn't thought of him in days. Like she'd gone past Clapham Common on a bus and remembered a picnic they'd had there, when she was just pregnant with Louis and enjoying looking pregnant, rather than just big, although her boobies had grown utterly gigantic (Ben had liked that). They had sat in the park and eaten chicken as Ben talked about what his future son would do and what he'd grow up to be, and she'd looked at the blue sky above and felt as safe and happy as she could ever remember. She never went to the common now.

Caroline choked and indicated her trouser zip. She was wearing a pair of very closely draped cigarette pants, clearly expensive. The zip, however, had burst and pulled off a button at the top to boot.

"Look!" she wailed. "Look at this!"

Pearl squinted and examined it.

"You've bust the zip…Are you scarfing ginger cookies in secret when we're not looking?"

"*No!*" said Caroline emphatically. "No, definitely not. It caught on a door."

"If you say so," said Pearl, who found Caroline's obsession with self-denial quite amusing. "So, what's the problem?"

"These are D&G Cruise 10," said Caroline, a sentence which meant absolutely nothing to Pearl. "I…I mean, they cost hundreds of pounds."

Pearl thought she could easily get a pair down Primark for a tenner, but didn't say.

"And I won't…I won't be able to buy any more now. That's it for me. The Bastard says he's not paying for my lifestyle." Her voice tailed away in sobs.

"I'm going to have to wear…high street." Caroline's sobs grew louder. "And color my own hair!"

She dropped her head in her hands.

Pearl couldn't see the problem. "Well, there's nothing wrong with that. You know what they say, as long as you have a roof over your head and enough to eat…"

"I never have enough to eat," said Caroline defiantly.

"Let me take a look at it," said Pearl. "It's only a busted zip. Can't you fix it in your Stitch "n" Bitch?"

"Ha!" laughed Caroline. "No. That's just for patchwork and gossip, not real sewing."

"Well, I can fix it for you," said Pearl.

Caroline blinked her wide blue eyes. "Really? You'd do that for me?"

"What would you do otherwise?"

Caroline shrugged. "I suppose…just buy another pair. In the old days. Of course I'd give them to the charity shop."

"Of course you would," said Pearl, shaking her head. Hundreds of pounds for a pair of trousers, thrown out because of a zip. The world made no sense.

The doorbell rang and Doti the postman came in, with his normal hopeful smile.

"Hello, ladies," he said politely. "What's going on here?"

"Caroline is out of her trousers," said Pearl, unable to help herself.

"Oh good," said Doti.

"*Why* is that good?" spluttered Caroline.

"You need a bit of meat on your bones," said Doti. "Skinny women look…sad. You should eat some of these delicious cakes."

Caroline rolled her eyes. "I do not look sad. Does Cheryl Cole look sad? Does Jennifer Aniston look sad?"

"Yes," said Pearl.

"I don't know who they are," said Doti.

"I look in shape, that's all."

"Well, you look nice," said Doti.

"Thank you," said Caroline. "Although I'm not sure about taking fashion advice from a postman."

"We postmen don't miss much," said Doti, completely unoffended and putting their few letters down on the counter, as Pearl simultaneously handed him an espresso. They smiled at one another.

"You, on the other hand," said Doti, necking his espresso as if to give himself courage. "*You* look beautiful."

Pearl smiled and said thank you as Doti left, and Caroline's mouth fell open.

"What?" said Pearl, still pleased enough by Doti's compliment not to be too bothered by Caroline's unflattering amazement. "You don't think he meant it?"

Caroline looked her up and down, taking in, Pearl knew, her rounded hips, her large bosom, the curve of her back and her hips.

"No," she said, in a humbler voice than Pearl had ever heard before. "No. You are beautiful. It's my fault. I didn't even notice. I don't," she added, her voice becoming more mournful, "I don't always notice much."

So Pearl took Caroline's trousers home and replaced the zip, and the button, and turned up a trailing hem and was slightly disappointed, actually, at the quality of the rest of the sewing on trousers that cost hundreds of pounds, and Caroline was so genuinely grateful she wore them twice in a week, which was a record for her wearing anything, and didn't pick Louis up on his pronunciation for almost four full days, until he said "innit" and she absolutely couldn't help herself.

best birthday cake ever

· · · ·

* 8 tbsp Breton soft butter, first churn
* 1 cup white superfine sugar, sifted
* 4 large fresh free-range eggs, beaten
* ¾ cup self-rising flour
* ¾ cup plain flour
* 1 cup fresh milk
* 1 tsp vanilla essence

Icing

* 8 tbsp Breton soft butter, first churn
* 2 cups icing sugar
* 1 tsp vanilla essence
* 4 tbsp milk
* 2 tsp essence of roses

Grease three small cake pans. Cream the butter until as smooth as a child's cheek.

Add sugar very gradually. No dumping like you normally do, Isabel. This has to be fluffy, properly fluffy. Add a grain at a time through the whisk.

Add the eggs slowly. Beat well at all times.

Mix the sifted flours and add a little milk and vanilla; then some flour, then some milk and vanilla and so on. Do not rush. This is your birthday cake for you, and you are very special. You deserve a little time.

Bake for 20 minutes at 350°F/gas mark 4.

For the icing, add half the icing sugar to the butter. Add milk, vanilla and essence of roses. Beat thoroughly, adding sugar till the icing reaches the desired consistency.

Ice layers and top of cake. Add candles. Not too many.

Add friends. As many as you can.

Blow candles out while making a happy wish. Do not tell anyone (a) your wish, (b) your recipe. Some things, like you, are special, my darling.

Love, Gramps

I ssy put the birthday card up in the window. The sun came through the shop so strongly on June 21, Issy felt herself turn almost pink and wondered if you could get a suntan through glass. It was, undoubtedly, the only way she'd get a suntan this year.

"It's burst into summer without me noticing," she said.

"Hmmm," said Pearl. "I always notice. I hate weather where I can't wear tights. My wobbly bits don't know what they're doing and start moving in different directions. I hope we get another freezing summer."

"Oh no you don't!" said Issy in dismay. "We want to be outside, all our clients sitting about for ages. It's a shame we can't get a license."

"Drunks as well as sugar addicts," said Pearl. "Hmmm. Anyway, it wouldn't be right." She indicated a table by the window, currently occupied by four old men.

"Oh yes!" giggled Issy. It had been the oddest thing. One day two old men had trudged in the door, quite late in the day. They had looked, frankly, a bit like drunken tramps. They already had a local tramp, Berlioz, who came by most days for a couple of bits and bobs to eat and a cup of tea when it was quiet (Pearl also let him empty the Royal Society for the Protection of Birds charity tin by the till, but Issy didn't know about that, and Pearl had justified it to her pastor, and they had decided to keep quiet about it), but these chaps were something new.

One came shuffling up.

"Um, two coffees, please," he asked in a croaky, cigarette-ruined voice.

"Of course," Issy had said. "Do you want anything with them?"

The man had dragged out a brand new ten-pound note and Austin's card had fallen out too.

"No," he said. "Oh, but we're to tell you Austin sent us."

Issy squinted for a minute, then remembered. They were the all-day drinkers from the pub Austin had taken her to.

"Oh!" she said in surprise. She had been avoiding Austin completely; she was still embarrassed about having thought he was interested in her rather than just her business, and things were going so much better there was no reason for the bank to complain. She did think of him sometimes though, wondering how Darny was doing. She hadn't used the dinosaur molds yet. And she wasn't sure about her new customers.

But from that day on, they came in three times a week, gradually joined by more furtive-looking characters. One day, cleaning up around them, Pearl had realized they were holding an informal AA-type meeting. Issy, shaking her head, wondered how Austin had managed to persuade them to do that. And made a vow not to walk past that pub again. She suspected the landlord wouldn't be terribly pleased. That made about five places she didn't dare walk around. In fact, had she only known, people who now came to Stoke Newington to buy cupcakes often wandered up to the other shops and cafés on the high street too. And the landlord was delighted to get rid of all his old soaks; he had installed Wi-Fi, opened up the windows, and was doing a roaring trade in hearty breakfasts and tea for a pound; patrons were much happier sitting in a light, toast-scented room that wasn't haunted by the wrecks of early morning drinkers. But Issy kept out of their way nonetheless.

"Longest day, longest day of the year," one of the old men was singing. The others laughed heartily and told him to pipe down on the rude old rhyme.

"Is that the date?" said Issy suddenly, checking her watch. Once they'd gotten past the financial year-end deadline, she'd slightly lost track of the days; now, finally, the Cupcake Café seemed to be on a reasonably even keel and earning its keep. It looked like, mortgage money aside, there was a possibility that she could start drawing a salary from it. Which was kind of ironic, Issy thought, seeing as she'd been so all-focused on the shop that she hadn't actually done any shopping for herself in months. And anything she wore was covered in an apron all day, so it scarcely mattered. She really ought to get her roots done though, she thought, catching sight of herself in the mirrored edges of the cake cabinet. Ten years ago, having slightly messed-up, different colored hair was kind of sexy and cute and beach style. Now, she risked looking like an old crazy person. She crumpled up her face in the distorted mirror. Where did that furrow between her brows come from? Did she always have it? That expression she caught sometimes, of a woman with too many things in her brain, always one step behind. She smoothed it out with her fingertips, but the faint lines it had left were still there; perturbed at them, she watched her face go into exactly the same expression as before. She sighed.

"What's up?" said Pearl, who was cutting out templates for the cappuccino chocolate. She didn't know why customers liked little flowers on top of their foam so much, but they did, and she was happy to oblige.

"Hmmm. Nothing," said Issy. "It's…it's my birthday coming up, that's all."

"Oh, a big one?" said Pearl.

Issy looked at her. Did she mean thirty? Or forty?

"How old do you think I am?" she asked.

Pearl sighed. "I can't answer that question. I can never tell how old people are. Sorry. I'd just get it wrong and insult you."

"Unless you aimed really low," said Issy.

"Well, that would be insulting too, wouldn't it? If you thought I had to say you were twenty-eight just to flatter you."

"So I can't pass for twenty-eight?" said Issy sadly. Pearl threw up her hands.

"What do I need to do to get out of this conversation?"

Issy sighed. Pearl glanced at her. Wasn't like Issy to be down.

"What?"

Issy shrugged. "Oh, nothing. It's just…Well, you know. It's my birthday. On Thursday in fact. It's just…it must have crept up on me. Normally I never forget my birthday."

Issy called Helena.

"Uh, Lena. You know Thursday is my birthday?"

There was a pause.

"Oh, Issy, that's three days away!"

"Yes, I know. I, er, forgot."

"You're in denial, more like."

"Yeah, yeah. Shut up."

"OK, well, will we do something on the weekend? I'm on night shift Thursday and I've already swapped once, I can't do it again. I'm so sorry."

"That's all right," said Issy, feeling dejected.

"Want to do something on Sunday? Ashok's off too."

"The weather might be gone by Sunday," said Issy, conscious she sounded like she was moaning. Plus, what was she expecting? She'd been ignoring her friends pretty much solidly for months while she got the shop up and running; she could hardly complain now that they wouldn't drop everything at a second's notice to celebrate her special day when she couldn't even remember to send cards for their first babies or house moves.

She was a little sharper than usual in saying no to Felipe when he came in politely, as he did once a week, to ask her if he could serenade her customers on the violin. She knew Stoke Newington was bohemian and a bit exotic, but she still wasn't entirely convinced as to the wisdom of having a wandering troubadour getting into people's faces when they were trying to enjoy a quiet cake and the paper. Felipe never seemed remotely insulted or perturbed, merely spinning a few notes and moving on, tipping his black hat as he went.

"Sometimes," said Pearl, watching him depart, his cheery dog at his heels, "I think this is a very peculiar neighborhood. And you should see where I come from."

• • • •

The sun was still shining on Thursday morning, that was one good thing. Issy swallowed: she couldn't help thinking back to a year ago. They'd all gone out to the pub after work to celebrate her birthday and it had been a total laugh: she and Graeme had kept pretending to sneak out for a cigarette, though neither of them smoked, then snogging up the alleyway like teenagers. It wasn't like Graeme to be so romantic and demonstrative, not like him at all. It had been an amazing evening. She'd been so happy with the idea of being swept off her feet by the boss, full of plans, she remembered. She'd thought…she'd thought there might even be a ring by this year. That seemed absolutely ridiculous now. Stupid. He certainly wouldn't be thinking about it now, that was for sure.

She knew when Graeme's birthday was: September 17. She'd signed his office card like everyone else but liked to think she'd put special meaning into the line of kisses she'd written underneath his name; or at least that he would understand what they meant. He was a Virgo, with finicky habits and a perfectionist streak; all of that made perfect sense to Issy too. She liked to check his horoscope; it made her feel protective, like it gave her ownership. But of course he'd never have remembered hers. Anyway, he'd even told her once that he thought girls were idiots when it came to presents and stuff like that. He wouldn't have cared even if they had still been together. She sighed.

In fact she was suddenly wishing she'd never mentioned the birthday thing to anyone, just completely ignored it. It was embarrassing in front of Helena and Ashok, like they were her only friends; and a horrid reminder that, however hard she worked, and whatever new face creams she bought, and the fact that she still shopped in Forever 21, nonetheless, time was ticking away. She bit her lip. No. She wouldn't think like that. Thirty-two was *nothing*. Nothing at all. Helena wasn't the least bit worried about her age, and she'd been thirty-three for ages. Just because some of her friends were insisting on flaunting big bumps all over the place, just because all those yummy Stoke Newington mummies didn't seem any older than her when they hung out with their precious little Olivias and Finns. So what? She was definitely getting her life sorted; she was definitely in a better place than she'd been a year ago; she had a proper job. At least the Cupcake Café made her happy. The phone rang. For a tiny, fluttery second, she found herself wondering if it was Graeme.

"Hello?" said an old voice, a little crackly down the line. "Hello?"

Issy smiled to herself. "Gramps!"

"Are you going to have a lovely day, darling?" came her grandfather's voice. It sounded weaker than of late; breathier, as if he was getting lighter and lighter; untethering himself.

Issy remembered birthdays above the bakery. Grampa would make her a special, huge cake, far too big for herself and the handful of friends who would visit her house and ask where her mother was, or, if her mother was there, ask why her mother was wearing twigs in her hair, and sitting very quietly with her legs crossed, one mortifying year when Issy turned nine and her mother was deep into transcendental meditation and had told Issy if she practiced hard enough, she could learn how to fly.

But mostly they were good memories: the pink icing, the candles, the lights dimmed, Gramps's full table of goodies—no wonder she had been such a plump child—and everyone in the bakery popping their heads around the door to say happy birthday, warned as they had been in advance by her proud grandfather. There had been plenty of gifts—not big gifts, just felt-tip pens and notebooks and bits and pieces, but she had felt like a princess and rich with it all. If someone had told her then it was entirely possible to feel lonely on your birthday, she wouldn't have believed them. But she did.

Issy took a deep breath.

"Yes," she lied stoutly. "I'm having a big party with all my friends in a lovely restaurant; we're going out for a meal and they've all clubbed together to buy me a fantastic present." She tried not to let a wobble escape into her voice. That she would go to work, open up, bake, serve customers, cash up, lock up, come home, eat carrot soup, watch TV, and go to bed.

Oh no…She heard a knock at the door and knew instantly that it was the Parcelforce man, delivering her annual box of Californian wine from her mother. Well, that was even worse. She would drink some wine then go to bed, thus ensuring herself a hangover as well as everything else.

"Gramps, someone's at the door," she said. "I have to go. But I'm going to get up to see you on Sunday."

"Hello? Hello?" her grandfather said into the phone. He sounded like he'd been connected to a different line altogether. "Hello? Can you hear me? Who am I speaking to?"

"It's Issy, Gramps."

"Hmmm. Issy. Yes. Good," he said.

Issy felt a cold grip of fear on her heart. The door buzzed again, loudly. If she didn't get it, the man would go away and she'd need to pick up the parcel from the depot and that was definitely time in her day she could not carve out right now.

"I have to go. I love you."

"Yes. Hmmm. Right. Yes."

Issy wrapped her ugly but comfy dressing gown around her and answered the door. Yup, it was the delivery man with her box of wine. She'd thought, just for a split second, just for a tiny moment, that Graeme might have...Maybe flowers...No. Anyway, everyone knew she was in the café all day. She signed for the box and peered inside. Yup, Californian red again. Her mother must know on some level that Issy only drank white and pink wine, mustn't she? That whenever they'd been out, she had never ever ordered red wine, as it gave her a headache? Maybe it was her mother's way of encouraging her not to drink too much. Maybe it was her way of showing she cared.

• • • •

Meanwhile, up in Edinburgh, Graeme woke up in the Malmaison Hotel and came to a decision. He'd been thinking about it for a long time and now he knew. He was a decisive man, and a forceful one, he told himself, and it was time to go and get what he wanted.

• • • •

At the shop, Louis cheered her up a little by giving her a huge cuddle and a card he'd made, covered in orange splotches.

"Thank you, darling," she said, grateful and enjoying the feeling of his little arms around her neck. He gave her a wet sloppy kiss.

"*Happee birdee, Auntie Issy,*" he said. "*I is five!*"

"You're not five," said Pearl indulgently. "You're two."

Louis gave Issy a mischievous look as if they were sharing a secret. "*I is five*," he said, nodding his head emphatically.

"Well, I am a *bit* older than five," said Issy, admiring the card and hanging it up in the café.

"Happy birthday, boss," said Pearl. "I would offer to bake you a cake, but…"

"I know, I know," said Issy, strapping on her apron.

"So…" said Pearl. She turned around and reached into her bag and pulled out a Tupperware box. Opening it up, Issy squealed with delight and stuck her hand in front of her mouth.

"We *cannot* show anyone who comes in," said Issy.

"No," said Pearl, smiling. "Anyway, it would fly away."

There was, tentatively hanging together, a little cake shape. But instead of sponge, it was made of interlocking crisps; a net of Nik Naks, piled up on top of a base of square crisps, crowned with a Hula Hoop tower, with a chipstick flag sticking out the top.

"I got some very odd looks on the bus," said Pearl. "It's held together with Marmite."

Issy threw her arms around her. "Thanks," she said honestly, feeling her voice getting slightly choked up. "For everything. I wouldn't…I don't know how I'd have managed without you."

"Oh, you and Caroline would be expanding to Tokyo by now," said Pearl, patting her on the back.

"What's that about me?" said Caroline, marching in. The girls turned to look at her. Caroline wasn't due on till lunchtime, and she *never* got her shifts wrong.

"Yes, yes, I know, I'm early. Is it your birthday?" she said to a dumbfounded Issy. "OK, this is my present for you. It's a morning off. I've outsourced the bloody children."

"You mean, they're at school?" Issy asked.

"Yes," Caroline said. "Pearly Gates and I can hold the fort, can't we?"

Issy knew this was meant to be an affectionate name for Pearl, but she could feel her colleague bristle. Everyone knew the Pearly Gates were gigantic.

"Are you sure?"

"Of course," said Pearl. "We can hold the fort. Off you go!"

"But I won't know what to do with myself!" said Issy. "Time to myself...I just don't..."

"Well, it finishes at one thirty when I have my Reiki session," said Caroline. "So I'd get on with it if I were you."

• • • •

The sun was already warm on her back as Issy marched up the road, feeling oddly light and free—nobody knew where she was! She should get a bus to Oxford Street and go shopping! Hmmm, maybe she didn't have enough money to go shopping; she really needed to check with Austin. She had no idea what shape her personal finances were in. She felt incredibly uncomfortable having to ask him about it. He'd probably only give her another bollocking. But why should she care? They had no personal relationship at all, so she shouldn't worry about it: she could ask him a professional query. He'd made it 100 percent clear that was where he thought they should stand, and anyway, she didn't care. She cared a little bit about having to walk past all the other cafés on Stoke Newington High Street though. She hadn't forgotten what happened the last time. It had been horrible, but they hadn't come around to bother her since.

Well, bollocks to that too; she wasn't going to care about anything today. It was her birthday, and if she wanted to walk up past all the other cafés on the high street, then she would. Head in the air, hoping to render herself unrecognizable, she strode up the road, careful to avoid eye contact and feeling a bit nervous, but also defiant. Whether everyone else liked it or not, she was part of this community now and that was an end to it. She belonged.

At the pub opposite the bank, she sat down on one of their new outside tables. Maybe one day she could order some for the café too: no one had formally complained about clients sitting under the tree, but it felt rude, and the ironmonger looked at them crossly as he scurried past at odd times of day. She asked for a coffee. It was horrible, but it was only one pound fifty. Issy could live with that. At ten past nine he appeared, scurrying as usual, with his shirt untucked and coming out from his trousers—over, Issy couldn't help noticing, rather a nice bum. It must be the sunshine. She never normally noticed anyone else's bum, not compared to Graeme's gym-hardened buttocks of which she sometimes thought he was unpleasantly proud. Anyway, she wasn't looking at Austin's bum. She needed to ask him a professional question, that was all. It wasn't that she was desperate to see him, even if the blue shirt went beautifully with his eyes. Not at all.

"Austin!" she called tentatively, waving her newspaper. He turned around then, seeing her, and looked at first very pleased, then anxious for a second. Issy felt cross. He didn't have to look like she was some kind of scary stalker person.

He crossed the road. Inside, he was annoyed with himself about how pleased he was to see her. It would be a business proposition, for sure.

"Don't look so frightened, it's just a business proposition," said Issy. She'd meant it to sound lighthearted, but now she felt it had come out terribly weird-sounding.

"Hooray," he said, sitting down. Issy felt disappointed. "OK then. Can we have coffee and I'll call it a business meeting?"

Issy watched as Austin called Janet. "Yes, I forgot to mention… really? I'm double-booked? Oh, please tell them I'm terribly sorry…"

Issy shook her head. "How does Janet cope with you?"

"She makes a face like this," said Austin, giving a stern scary look. "I've told her the wind will change, but she won't listen. Nobody listens to me."

Austin's coffee arrived.

"This place has gotten better," he noted.

"Really?" said Issy, sipping the bitter dregs of the factory "beverage."

"Oh God yes, this is luxury compared to what you used to get."

"I'll take your word for it," said Issy. She was glad to feel that at least there wasn't any residual awkwardness. Even though there probably ought to be; he didn't really deserve her being nice to him, she thought. She didn't ask about Darny. Too personal. "Now, I need to know...do I have any money?".

"Well, that depends," said Austin, stirring in four sugars. When he spotted Issy staring at this, he poked his tongue out at her and put another one in. Sometimes, with Issy, he just couldn't help himself.

"You are such a peculiar banking adviser," sighed Issy.

"No I'm not. The other ones play golf, can you imagine? How weird is that? Golf!"

"Depends on what?" said Issy.

"The money? It depends what you want to do with it. Are you planning on packing it all in and retiring to South America?"

"Can I?"

"No. So I was just pointing out, you know. Not that."

"OK," said Issy. "Actually, I was wondering...can I go shopping?"

Issy had moved her personal accounts to Austin's branch shortly after the shop opened; as she was funding so much of the café herself, it seemed to make sense to have everything under the same roof. It felt odd that Austin should know so many personal things about the state of her bank account, when they'd seemed to somehow agree that they weren't going to get any more personal with one another.

"For what?"

Issy felt a bit embarrassed suddenly.

"Well...the thing is...it's my birthday."

Austin looked half-surprised, half-guilty. "Cheers! What a surprise!" he said. "Oh no, hang on, that sounded a bit phony. I knew that. It's on all your application forms," he said, feeling himself getting a bit flustered. "Um, I happened to be filing them away just recently. So. Kind of. I know. But I didn't want to make a big thing of it in case you were ignoring it. You know. Except you wouldn't, of course, so: happy birthday."

He smiled weakly and not entirely successfully.

"I should have ignored it," admitted Issy. "Honestly. It's a bit of a shit one. Well, apart from work. Work's been nice. But that means," she said fervently, "that just shows that I've based my entire life around my job rather than finding my work/life balance! It means I get all my emotional sustenance from work and I'll never be able to move on..."

"I think that means you've been reading too many self-help books," said Austin.

"Oh yes," said Issy, calming down a bit. "That's possible too."

"You should be so proud of yourself at this stage of your life," said Austin. "Look at you, businesswoman all afloat."

"I know," said Issy.

"What were you doing last birthday?"

"Well, I just went out with the people from my office..."

Austin rolled his eyes. "See?"

"Well, what did you do for your last birthday?" asked Issy.

"Well, Darny and I went to a hot-dog festival," said Austin.

"Whose idea was that?"

"Well, maybe it was Darny's."

"Uh-huh. And how did that turn out?"

Austin winced at the memory.

"Well, OK, I would say we saw some of the hot dogs again. Splashed on the pavement." Then he smiled. "But Darny insisted it was all worth it. And I still have the card he gave me, look."

Austin slipped his hand into his suit pocket and rooted around. Then he pulled out some dry cleaning receipts, a small plastic cowboy, and a voter registration form.

"That's where that went," he said to himself. "Well, I did have it. And it was brilliant. Darny drew a picture of me and him fighting off a giant poo monster. And we had a lovely day, apart from the spew. We got over the spew with ice cream."

"Was that wise?" said Issy, smiling.

"Holds things down better than you'd think," said Austin. "You learn a thing or two in this substitute-parenting lark."

Suddenly, Issy decided something. OK, so she'd been rebuffed before. She'd sworn she wouldn't do this. Yet somehow her feet had taken her here…She could easily have rung Janet for the balance on her accounts. But she hadn't, had she? She was going to do it. She was going to ask him. She swallowed.

"Um," she said, "would you…and Darny I suppose, or maybe you can get a babysitter? Or maybe no, obviously no, it would be a stupid idea, forget I mentioned it."

"What?" said Austin, suddenly feeling a little prickly around the ears and nervous.

"Um, it doesn't matter," said Issy, conscious that her deep blush was back, and as she felt it, realizing how long it was since she'd done so. Was that progress?

"What?" Austin needed to know what she was going to say. This dancing around was agonizing. But did she mean it? And what was she really after? Issy was now staring at the floor, looking absolutely tortured.

"Did…I was going to ask if you fancied a drink tonight, but obviously that's daft, don't listen to me. I'm just being stupid because I should have told my friends—and I have loads of friends actually—"

"I'm glad to hear it," interjected Austin.

"—well, anyway, it doesn't matter. Never mind."

Issy glared at her lap, miserably.

"OK," said Austin. "Actually, I'd have loved to. I have something on tonight though."

"Oh," said Issy, not looking up.

They fell silent. Issy was too humiliated—what on earth was she thinking? Was she asking her banking adviser for a drink? After he'd already made it clear he wasn't interested? And now, as if to rub it in even more, he'd just *turned her down*, and now they'd have to work together for ages and he'd think she totally fancied him. Great. This was turning into a super day. Best birthday ever.

"Well, I'd better get on," said Issy quietly.

"OK," said Austin. Then they both awkwardly stood up at the same time and turned to cross the road.

"Uh, bye," said Issy.

"Bye," said Austin. Then in a clumsy gesture he raised his arms as if to kiss her on the cheek, and Issy leaned in, equally clumsily, before she thought that maybe that wasn't what Austin was doing at all and tried to lean back again. But it was too late and Austin had realized that Issy seemed to be moving in for one of those social kisses he found so absolutely awkward, so he tried to do what was expected of him and leaned in to kiss her cheek, just as she dodged around to reverse and accidentally got the side of her mouth by mistake.

Issy leaped back, pasting a broad fake smile on her face to cover her consternation, while Austin couldn't help his hand, briefly, flying to his mouth.

"*Bye*," said Issy brightly again, feeling her face as hot as the sun—and, just momentarily, and tantalizingly, the feel of his surprisingly soft lips against hers.

Austin was even more distracted than usual that morning in his late meeting. God, this girl.

• • • •

Issy didn't go shopping in the end. Instead, she bought a cream cheese and smoked salmon bagel, and a tiny bottle of champagne with a

MEET ME AT THE CUPCAKE CAFÉ

straw—which might be a bit off for midmorning, she figured, but she didn't really care—and a magazine, and went to sit in the sunny park. She tried to enjoy the yells of other people's happy children throwing bread to the ducks, and the slightly jolty, unnerved sense she got whenever she thought of Austin's accidental near-kiss.

Lots of friends were sending remote regards via Facebook, which, while she realized it wasn't exactly as good as everyone coming to celebrate her birthday, was better than nothing and made her phone ping cheerily every time another one came through. After the bagel, she bought an ice cream too, and lay down and looked at the clouds for a bit and reflected that truly, from last year to this, she had come a long way, she really had. So she must stop being so grumpy and be more positive and…nope. It didn't help. She felt queasy from the champagne and, suddenly, in the midst of the bustling park and the noisy people, terribly lonely.

• • • •

"Cheer up, love," said one of Kate's builders.

Issy turned to Pearl. She was back in the shop; she'd sent Caroline away again, noticing that Caroline had been telling Pearl a convoluted story, punctuated by customers, about her holiday in the Dominican Republic, which Issy could tell Caroline thought in some completely mad way would impress and endear her to Pearl and it was doing neither of those two things.

"Nine," Issy said.

"Nine what?" asked the builder, who was already slurping the Smarties off his cinnamon cupcake. "Mm, these are great."

"Nine times someone has come in and said, 'Cheer up, love.'"

"And three 'It might never happens,'" added Pearl helpfully.

Issy glanced around the café. It was bustling nicely; she'd spontaneously bought a bunch of lilies on her way back from the park to cheer herself up, and the scent was permeating through the room; with the windows thrown open and the door held wide (totally against fire regulations, Pearl had pointed out, but they had had so very little summertime), the café felt fresh and summery, filled with the chink of china and the sounds of conviviality. She'd introduced some new floral plates too, to set off the lighter lemon and orange sponges with the candied peel on top that sold so well during the warmer days, and they looked absolutely beautiful. The two students who'd spent the wet spring finishing up their theses off the free Wi-Fi were, she noticed, cuddled up together, alternately typing and kissing. She suspected they were sharing more than the Wi-Fi now. Well, it was nice that at least some people weren't lonely on her birthday, she thought mournfully.

"What's up then?" asked the builder, taking a slow sip from his cappuccino. Issy bit her lip. Kate was going to have her guts for garters. She'd actually asked Caroline "as a friend" to stop serving them cappuccino. Caroline had explained that on a cost/benefit analysis, no marketing expert worth their salt would ever run a business on that basis and Kate had lost her temper and told her that before she'd given up her entire life to care for two ungrateful individual children, she'd had an MBA, thank you very much, and didn't need a lecture from some ex-wife, and Issy had to step in before Kate took her sewing circle somewhere else and she lost some much-needed income. She too, however, took Caroline's approach and would serve anyone who walked in the door, whatever someone else thought they should have been doing.

"Lost a tenner and found a fiver?" went on the builder.

"Actually my entire immediate family has just died," said Issy, more waspishly than usual. But really, it was such an annoying thing for people to say. The builder looked wounded.

"Oh, sorry, I didn't mean it," said Issy. "It's just—it's my birthday today. And I'm single, and my friends are away and I'm feeling a bit lonely, that's all."

"Yeah?" said the builder, who was about twenty-eight and had a cute cheeky look about him. "You can come out with me and the lads if you like. We're off for a bit of a bevvy."

Issy quickly restrained herself from saying, "On a Thursday? Kate will be furious," and merely smiled.

"What—me and a bunch of builders?"

"Some girls might like that," said the builder.

"It's your lucky day," said Pearl. "Shoo, builders! Out of the shop, you're getting my nice floor all dirty."

"Don't ban us from the shop, Nana!" begged the builder. "Please!"

But Pearl was already shooing him backward.

"You finish that nice lady's house, we'll sell you cakes. Understand?"

"She's not a nice lady!" said the builder. Issy was inclined to agree with him, having had Kate very deliberately walk up and down outside the shop tapping her foot and huffing on more than one occasion when she felt the men were lingering too long.

"That's not the point," said Pearl. "Paid for a job, then do a job. Then there'll be more cake for you. Out you go!"

The builder winked at Issy. "Just as well the cakes are good—the welcome's a bit rubbish."

"Off you go," said Issy. "Be nice."

"We'll be at the Fox and Horses!" yelled the builder as a parting shot. "From four thirty!"

Pearl shook her head and turned to serve the girl from the temp agency up the road.

"I mean it, I'll bar them."

Issy sighed. "I just can't believe it's the best offer I've had today." She turned to Pearl. "Thanks though. I wouldn't want to lose Kate's group."

"Happy birthday," said the girl from the temp office, who always looked like she'd had about two hours' sleep and needed an extra shot of caffeine in everything she bought, including the coffee cake.

"Birthdays are crap. My last one I spent watching the *Ghost Hunters* marathon on Living. I couldn't sleep," she added. "I'm an insomniac."

"I'd be an insomniac if I watched *Ghost Hunters*," said Pearl.

"Oh dear," said Issy, thinking desperately about what she could possibly find to do that wasn't just watching TV that night. "Extra shot?"

"Yes please. Happy birthday."

●   ●   ●   ●

Issy wasn't even that keen to close up at the end of the day; she didn't chivvy the hang-backers fiddling with their laptops, or bundle up the newspapers for recycling. She held back, straightening everything up for the following day. Pearl looked at her.

"I have to go get Louis now, OK?"

"OK."

"Would you…would you like to come for supper with us?"

Issy couldn't bear Pearl feeling sorry for her. Which wasn't attractive, she realized; it meant she felt that she should feel sorry for Pearl. But that was just the way it was.

"No, no…well, yes I *would*, obviously," she added quickly. "Yes, please. But, you know. Not tonight."

Pearl nodded. "OK. Bye then!"

And the bell dinged, and she was gone. It was still a beautiful afternoon outside, the shadows lengthening. Sod it, thought Issy, turning the sign to *Closed* and locking the door. This was ridiculous. She had done nothing but mope about all day. Well, that was going to stop. Almost without thinking, she propelled herself out of the shop and up to the high street again. A little boutique had opened up, run by a friend of Caroline's. Even if she was still slightly nervous about the high street, she was going in to have a look, and that was that.

The shop, just called 44, was packed tight with clothes, and smelled beautiful and expensive. Issy tried not to feel intimidated by the elegant blond saleswoman with the perfect red lipstick and fifties sunglasses sitting behind the counter.

"Hello," she said. "I was looking for…well, a dress."

"You've come to the right place," said the woman, eyeing her up and down in a professional manner. "Evening? Or just something kind of smart but not too over the top?"

"Yes. That." Issy glanced about. "And not *too* expensive."

The woman raised a beautifully plucked eyebrow. "Well, you know, quality does show."

Issy felt her face go a little pink again, but the woman bustled away through the back. "Stay there!" she yelled, and Issy stayed rooted to the spot, looking around at the Aladdin's cave—beautiful chiffon cocktail dresses in hot pinks and deep reds hung on the wall, looking as if they demanded to be drenched in perfume and taken out to dance; little bags with shiny patent bows that were large enough only for an invitation and a lipstick; extraordinarily beautiful shoes. It was so lovely it reminded Issy how long it had been since she'd got dressed up for something, or someone.

The woman returned, bearing just one garment.

"Come on then." She harried her into the tiny dressing room. "Are you wearing a decent bra? Nope, thought not."

"You're as bossy as Caroline," said Issy.

"Caroline! That woman is a pushover," said the shop owner. "Now, bend down."

Issy did. And when she straightened up, the soft mossy-green jersey of the dress rippled down her as the silk slip fitted her skin.

The dress skimmed her curves, gave her a tiny waist, and the full skirt swooshed out and swung every time she moved. The green brought out her eyes and contrasted wonderfully with her black hair; the boat neck showed off a hint of white shoulders and the elbow-length sleeves fitted perfectly. It was a dream of a dress.

"Oh," said Issy, looking in the mirror, then doing a spin. "It's lovely."

"Yes, I thought it would work," said the lady, peering over her specs. "Very good then."

Issy smiled. "How much is it?"

The woman named a figure that was almost, but not quite, more than Issy would ever have dreamed of paying for a dress. But as Issy turned and twisted to catch sight of herself once again, she realized: this would be hers. Because it was lovely, yes, but because every penny it would take to pay for it wasn't a wage, or a credit card bill, or something random and untouchable. This was her money, earned by her, every penny, fair and square.

"I'll take it," said Issy.

• • • •

She went back to the café then, conscious she'd dashed out without finishing up, but utterly thrilled that she had. Once she'd let herself in, she ran the coffee machine one more time, made herself a large foamy latte, covered it in chocolate powder, selected one of the few leftover cakes—a chilly chocolate, possibly too advanced for their clientele, but a wonder nonetheless—selected the evening paper and collapsed onto the sofa, her head well down and her back to the window so no one would see her over the arm of the chair and think they were still open for business. She had nothing to do and no one to do it with, so she wasn't going to hurry to get everywhere. She would just sit for a few minutes, that was all. It was very comfortable here, and she'd had a busy time of it and there was lots to do tonight as well, sign off her insurance and do her stocktake and check to see if anyone had sent any flowers to the house and maybe she'd have some of that awful wine of her mother's in the bath and…

When Issy woke up again, the shadows had lengthened in the

courtyard, the tree casting its shade right into the shop itself, and she blinked, not at all sure where she was. Also there was a noise that sounded vaguely familiar...yes, it was Felipe playing his violin. But why would he bother at this time of night, when everything was closed? It wasn't the next morning, was it? She checked her watch. No, she'd only been asleep for an hour and a half. So what was all that noise? She turned around, stretching out her arms sleepily, and...

"*Surprise!*"

At first Issy thought she'd fallen asleep again. This made no sense. Outside, in the just fading daylight, she saw the little stumpy tree, with fairy lights strung from branch to branch. The lights were lit; it reminded her of the lantern in Narnia. But what surrounded it was even more surprising. Felipe, dressed in a rather disheveled dinner jacket and bow tie, was playing "Someday" and standing around him was...everyone.

• ◦ • ◦

Helena was there, with Ashok of course, who had his arm around Helena's shoulders and was displaying her as if she were the finest piece of china. Ashok firmly believed that dedication was what had gotten him into medical school and on to a tough rotation and would one day propel him toward a top surgical career. Dedication was all it took. And he had taken the same path to Helena. Finally, it appeared to be paying off. He was trying not to grin like a Cheshire cat, but inside he felt ten feet tall. Zac was there with his girlfriend, Noriko. Pearl and Louis of course, laughing their heads off, and Hermia and Achilles bounced excitedly next to Caroline. But more than that, all her friends were there—her real friends. Tobes and Trinida from college, all the way from Brighton. And Tom and Carla from Whitstable. And Janey, looking utterly exhausted, her friend since that ill-favored play in freshers' week, had managed to drag herself away from her new baby. Paul and John were there, still loved up obviously; Brian and Lana, whom she'd entirely resigned herself to having a Facebook relationship with, if that; even François and Ophy from her old office… Issy's heart flooded. She rushed out of the shop then realized she had locked it behind her, and had to fumble around to find the keys. Everyone still outside laughed heartily, and when she finally let them in, launched into a rousing chorus of "Happy Birthday to You" that brought instant tears to Issy's eyes, as did the thoughtful, lovely gifts, as did the hugs and kisses that greeted her.

"This is your last chance," said Zac, with a half smile. "Stop neglecting all your friends."

"OK," said Issy, nodding frantically. Everyone came into the café who hadn't been there before and oohed and ahhed, and Helena unleashed the crates of champagne they'd hefted over from the house, after they'd all hidden in the cupboard for three-quarters of an hour and realized she wasn't coming home. Pearl had figured it out first and rung Helena, then they'd crept into the square one by one, giggling heartily. And now it was time to party! And she even had the perfect new dress.

Felipe played up a storm as the friends and family, clients and random people (Berlioz turned up to eat the snacks) mingled and chatted. The evening was wonderfully warm, and the soft lighting of the Cupcake Café blended with the fairy lights of the tree and some candles Helena had brought put a magical glow over the whole of Pear Tree Court, turning it into an enchanted space, a private paradise full of laughing friends, cheerful toasts, birthday cake, spice cake, hunter's cake, Paris cake and every kind of cupcake. Louis danced with everyone who passed and the sounds of companionship and gaiety spread up through the brick houses; anyone passing in the street would have wondered about the little oasis of sparkling light under the darkening sky.

As old friends often do when they come together again, everyone grew quite tipsy quite quickly, so that by the time Austin had finally settled Darny with the babysitter and could consider leaving the house (crossing his fingers, and failing to mention to the babysitter that unless she had a PhD in dinosaurs she might be in for a rocky evening), Issy was pink in the face and entirely overexcited, talking babies, other friends, old incidents and the shop to anyone who strayed into her orbit, regardless of where she knew them from. Pearl had called him up and insisted with some severity that he came along, and he wasn't going to risk her wrath. As soon as he arrived, he noticed immediately that everyone was a bit squiffy. So he'd have to keep playing sensible banking adviser then. He sighed.

"*Austin!*" Issy yelled when she saw him, a glass of champagne or two to the wind. What the hell, she found herself thinking. So he didn't like her—it didn't matter. But he was here! Graeme wasn't here; no one had even mentioned him. It was her birthday. She was looking lovely in her green dress, and suddenly she felt absolutely wonderful; full of happiness and love and joy. This was the party her grandfather had wanted her to have and she wanted to share it with everyone.

She waltzed up to him. "You *knew* about this!" she said accusingly. Austin thought how pretty she looked with her hair curly and full and her cheeks and lips pink with excitement. "You knew!"

"Well, of course I knew," he said mildly, accepting with some surprise her arms thrown around him. He was sure there was something in the banking manual about not getting too close to your clients. Of course he'd never read the manual. He remembered back to their near-miss kiss that morning and glanced around. A very skinny blond woman was staring at him, hungrily.

"*Who* is that?" said Caroline, reflexively dropping Achilles's hand, who immediately set up a wail.

"Back off," growled Pearl.

Caroline gave a little laugh. "What, him and Issy…?"

A warning look from Pearl stopped her from going any further, but inside Caroline felt completely uncowed.

Austin smiled. "Pearl told me. Well, I say told me, Pearl ordered me here. And when Pearl tells you to do something…"

Issy nodded fervently. "Oh yes. If you know what's good for you."

Pearl, standing on the other side chatting to friends of Issy's who were telling her a little more about their new baby's bowel movements than perhaps she had specifically requested, glanced over. The lights gleamed off Issy's hair as she stretched up on tiptoes to hear what Austin was saying; he was so tall and messy-looking. Whatever it was, Issy had opened her mouth in laughter, grabbing Austin's arm as she did so. Pearl smiled to herself. Well, yes. She thought that one looked about right.

"*Ahem*," said Helena, suddenly standing next to Issy. Issy jumped away from Austin slightly suspiciously.

"Yes?" she said. Then, "Oh, Lena. I can't believe…I can't believe you did all this. I'm so, so, *so*…"

"Yes, yes," said Helena quickly. "Well, you were working so hard, and I knew you wanted to see people, so…"

"It was a lovely thing to do."

Helena looked pointedly at Austin.

"Oh." Issy felt her blush rising. "This is—"

"Are you Austin?" asked Helena, to cause maximum embarrassment. Oh great, thought Issy, now he'd know she'd been talking about him. "Hello there."

"Hello," said Austin gravely. Helena reckoned Issy had talked too much about the reddish hair and not enough about the stunning gray eyes and broad shoulders. This guy was miles better looking than Graeme. But she didn't want Issy throwing herself in it too much and getting blown out again. Twice in a year would really be pushing it.

"You need to mingle more," said Helena to a pink Issy. "All these people have come a long way. *He* works across the road."

Issy smiled apologetically at Austin.

"Oh, yes, I suppose…"

"Get Issy another drink," ordered Helena to Ashok, and he immediately scuttled off to do so.

"You've got him under control," said Issy in admiration. "I thought you wanted a man to take charge of everything, like a kind of hot Simon Cowell?"

"Simon Cowell is a hot Simon Cowell," said Helena crossly, with the air of a woman tired of repeating herself. "Anyway, I thought that too," she added.

Ashok glanced at her back across the room. He loved a woman who knew what she wanted.

"But sometimes you never know what's right for you." Helena lowered her voice almost apologetically and in a near-whisper said, "I've never been happier."

Issy hugged her.

"Thank you," she said. "Thank you, my dear friend. It's wonderful. It's just fantastic. I'm so glad you're happy."

And she hurried off to chat to her long traveling, long-suffering friends, while Austin skulked in the shadows, chatting to Des the estate agent, which wasn't his ideal notion of where this party was headed, but still, the babysitter hadn't rung yet and this was a personal record.

At 9:30, suddenly, there was a bolt of noise. Helena had been expecting a bit of complaining from neighbors and had been quite prepared to move the party back to the flat, but this was the familiar rattle of a shop grille coming up with a noisy snap. It was the ironmonger's. He couldn't, Issy thought. He couldn't still be here at this time of night. But he was. With solemnity and funereal speed, the ironmonger emerged from the shop, which was in pitch darkness, and glided toward Issy. Issy, slightly the worse for wear, suddenly envisaged him in a top hat, like something out of Dickens. He was wearing, instead, a dark three-piece suit and a fob watch. She smiled a welcome to him, and offered him a glass of fizz, which he refused. Instead, he stood in front of her.

"Happy birthday, my dear," he said, and gave her a very small, wrapped parcel. Then he nodded his head (he should have tipped his top hat, thought Issy tipsily; or topped his tip hat—ooh, she had to stop drinking), and vanished out of the little passageway and into the dark night.

Everyone gathered around as Issy opened the parcel, which was wrapped in brown paper. Inside was a small cardboard box, which Issy opened with slightly shaky, overexcited fingers. Then she drew out, to gasps of admiration, a tiny key ring; a fine filigree of metal, twisted exquisitely into the shape of the logo of the Cupcake Café, with, next to it, an exact representation of the pear tree they were currently underneath. It was utterly exquisite.

"Oh," said Issy, suddenly feeling quite faint.

"Let me see! Let me see!" said Zac, anxious to hold a 3D representation of his design. It was absolutely lovely; pure craftsmanship and quite beautiful.

"That is far too lovely to be a key ring," said Pearl straightaway, and Issy nodded.

"I know," she said. "It's lovely. I think I'll hang it in the window."

And although everyone else's gifts—Jo Malone smellies, and Madeleine Hamilton scarves, and Cath Kidston cake tins—would be treasured, somehow Issy knew that the key ring was the most special gift of all. There was something about it being metal—not like cake, good for a day, or paper menus, good for a couple of weeks. This would last for many, many years. Which made her think that the café might, too.

There was one person missing. She knew it, she couldn't deny it. She knew if he'd been well enough, nothing would have kept him away. And in the midst of all her happiness, Issy felt a cold chill blow through her.

● ● ● ●

Even though the evening stayed warm, people started to drift away after that; friends who'd come from far away and were facing late trains; those with babysitters to relieve, and long commutes in the morning, and Pearl with Louis, who had fallen fast asleep under the tree. Issy turned around at one point to realize that most people were gone, and there were only a scattering, slightly drunk now, dotted around the courtyard. Felipe was playing a winding-down kind of a song.

She looked up and realized that, one, she was in front of Austin, and two, she was very drunk. Very drunk and very happy, she realized. Was it because she was in front of Austin? Could that be the connection? She always seemed happier after she saw him, that was true. But maybe that was because he was lending her money. It was all very confusing.

Austin bit his lip and looked at Issy. She did look so pretty, and so sweet, but she was obviously quite drunk, so it was definitely time for him to go home. He had quite a lot of success with women—some of whom were intrigued and some very much not by the plethora of Batman-related merchandise they found when they got back to his house; either they wanted to move in and play mummies and daddies, or backed off at the speed of light. Austin enjoyed playing the field on his rare nights off, and was absolutely adamant that he didn't want to introduce more upset into Darny's life until the boy was a little more…well, just a bit more stable. It didn't stop him, though. From wanting someone around a bit. Short-term dalliances were easy to find; especially when people had been drinking. But sometimes he thought he might be ready for something a bit more solid; he was over thirty after all. Normally he felt he had enough grown-up stuff in his life without going to the bother of an adult relationship. But sometimes—like now—he thought it might be nice.

"Hey," said Issy.

But Issy, thought Austin to himself, forgetting instantly a lot of other evenings. She was…she'd gotten under his skin. He couldn't deny it. It was her eager face; the slightly wounded look it took on if she thought anyone was in trouble; the optimism of her little pink-iced cakes, and the dogged man hours she had put into making the shop a success; he liked it. He had to be honest. He liked all of it. He liked her. And here she was, face rosy and tentative, pointed up toward him. The fairy lights glowed in the tree, and the stars shone brightly overhead and after her "hey" neither of them spoke: it didn't seem to be in the least bit necessary. Issy was gazing up at him, biting her lip. Slowly, almost without even thinking what he was doing, he took his large hand and gently, with a feathery touch, ran it delicately down the line of her jaw.

Issy shivered under his touch and he saw her eyes widen. He brought his hand up now, and cupped her face with a firmer grasp, all the time staring straight into her wide green eyes. Issy felt her heart pound with excitement as if she'd been jump-started by a defibrillator. For the first time in what felt like months, the blood began to pump faster in her veins. She leaned into his warm dry hand, feeling its embrace on her skin, then looked at him with a message that was very clear: yes.

• • • •

Graeme stepped out of the cab. His flight had been late getting in from Edinburgh, but he didn't care; he had no time to waste. It was entirely possible she was still hanging about her stupid shop, icing buns or whatever it was she did, and if she wasn't, he could just go straight to the flat. He slammed the cab door, not forgetting to ask for a blank receipt. He could see there were people outside the café, though it was hard to make out in the dim light. Issy must be among them. He walked out of the shadows and into the throng. The ones who knew Graeme immediately fell silent.

Issy, caught up in Austin's eyes, only felt the change in the air around her. She turned her head, as Graeme, handsome as ever, beautifully dressed, stood underneath the streetlights.

"Issy," he said, quietly. Issy leaped back from Austin as if she'd been stung.

Austin looked up. Although they'd never met, he took one look at Graeme, and decided to leave.

• • • •

Graeme had been doing a lot of thinking in Edinburgh. There was just something about that place. Lot of expensive real estate too. It definitely felt like there was something in the air, something was picking up again. But it was just so bloody quaint, that city; full of little alleyways and hidden squares and cobblestones and back streets. And everyone was completely mad for it. You could see it; the tourists, the students, the people coming up for a look, or the people who wanted to live there. It was all about character nowadays. People didn't want a skyscraper or a brick-walled loft or a cool box to live in, although he didn't understand why—he thought all of these things, with their air conditioning and security keys, were obviously better than old places. But not everyone agreed with him. People wanted quaint old places, with "personality." Graeme thought this was bollocks—people should go for stuff that worked and places that were comfortable. But on the other hand, if they were prepared to pay over the odds for it—he reasoned as he lounged in his expensive turret room, in his expensive boutique hotel—if they were prepared to pay over the odds for properties that looked cute, then who was he, Graeme, to stand in their way?

And that was when he'd had his brilliant idea. He was incredibly impressed with himself. And it would work for everyone. He had to get back to London right away, it was so brilliant. The Pear Tree Condominiums.

He knew *condominium* only meant *flat*, but it sounded American, and in his experience American was always better. Live/work spaces in a quaint old courtyard, only steps from Stoke Newington High Street, but lovely and peaceful and away from the road. But the clever bit—the *really* clever bit—was that they would look old, but in fact that would just be the frontage. They'd redo the whole thing. They'd tear out all those stupid little windows with the glass you couldn't see through, and the draughty old wooden doors, and replace them with proper PVC frames and metal doors with a fingerprint entry system (the financiers loved those), and security cameras perched above them—in fact, his heart had really started to beat fast at this bit. Maybe they could even put a gate across the alleyway, so it was like you had your own private compound! That would be ace! And you could park in the courtyard, they'd just cut down the tree. It would be fantastic. And it would all look cute but be full of the latest hi-tech gizmos—air conditioning, and wine fridges, and state-of-the-art entertainment systems.

The best thing was, he congratulated himself, he could cut Issy in on the deal. After all, it was only fair; she'd brought the area to his attention, which deserved a finder's fee. She could come back and work with him—but not taking the minutes now; she could be a proper agent if she wanted. That would be a huge leg up for her. *And* he was going to…he couldn't believe he was going to do it. If anyone had said Graeme, you old sap, you are going to turn into a house cat, get under the whip, he wouldn't have believed them.

But there were things, he had come to realize since they'd been apart, that were good about Issy, when she wasn't flaying her fingers to the bone in that stupid café. Her cooking. Her interest in him. The way she made everything feel slightly softer, slightly easier and gentler in his life when he was out fighting like a tiger all day. He liked it. He wanted it around. He was prepared to make the biggest sacrifice, while also improving her life immeasurably—no more 6:00 a.m. starts—*and* making a huge pile of money into the bargain. It was so obvious. He had solved everything. He was going to be top dog at the firm again. He was going to take his mates' teasing about the fact that he'd settled for a woman who, OK, wasn't exactly a size six Swedish underwear model. He could handle it. He knew what he wanted. And of course she'd agree.

"Issy," he said again, and she looked at him. She seemed slightly nervous, he realized. She must be expectant and excited; she must know something was up. He was going to blow her mind, right from the start.

"Iss...I've been an idiot. I was a total idiot to let you slip through my fingers. I've really missed you. Can we get back together?"

•   •   •   •

Issy's mind was an absolute hive of confusion. Helena was shaking her head. Graeme stepped forward, noting quickly the cards and gifts piled up and coming to the obvious conclusion. Why, this was even better!

"Happy birthday, darling," he said. "Did you miss me?"

•   •   •   •

Austin loped home, kicking himself. Would he never learn? Crossly, he unlocked his front door, freed the babysitter from Darny's under-table pirate prison, paid her double time as usual, and listlessly hailed her a cab. Bugger it.

•   •   •   •

Issy stood frozen to the ground. She couldn't believe it. The very thing she'd dreamed of happening; wept over; wished for more than any-thing: Graeme, here, begging forgiveness, for another chance.

Graeme fumbled in his bag and pulled out his airport purchase. "Uh, here," he said.

Graeme! Bringing her a present! Wonders would never cease! Issy could feel Helena's eyes boring into her back. Still unable to speak, she drew the gift out of the plastic bag. It was a bottle of whisky.

"Finest malt," said Graeme. "Costs two hundred quid normally." Issy forced her face into a smile.

"I don't drink whisky," she said.

"I know," said Graeme. "I thought you might like to put it into your cakes or something. For your very important, very successful business."

Issy looked at him.

"I'm sorry," he said again. "I didn't take you seriously. I was wrong. Can I make it up to you?"

Issy stood, hugging herself. It felt like the wind was rising, it was definitely getting a little colder. Graeme peered into the darkened windows of the Cupcake Café, then glanced up at the empty properties around it. He did a full circuit of Pear Tree Court, tapping his fingers meditatively.

"You know," he said, "I always knew this place would come good."

"You big fat liar!" said Issy before she could stop herself. "You thought I was going to starve to death."

"Hmmm. Reverse psychology," said Graeme. "Yeah, that's what it was."

"Was it?" said Issy.

"Anyway, it's come good. Good for you."

"Good for Issy!" said Helena loudly, and raised her glass, then the few remaining party people raised their glasses too, and it felt like the party was over after that, and Issy didn't know what to do. Helena was no help, setting off home with Ashok, which meant she didn't really want to go back there with Graeme, the walls not being all that…and so on.

"We need to talk," she said to Graeme, buying time.

"We do!" said Graeme cheerfully, hailing a cab to take them both to Notting Hill, and quietly, confidently, slipping a breath mint into his mouth.

helena's secret doughnuts

• • • •

Buy real ginger. It looks like a knobby root thing. You can ask someone if you can't figure it out. Not that fruiterer who always asks you if you want any melons. He's disgusting. Right, now, nick one of those medicine-measuring thingies from work. I know they're the only ones you can figure out as long as it's in centiliters or whatever. So do it from that. OK, now grate it.

Stop looking in the mirror on the extractor fan. You're gorgeous, and if you don't keep stirring the mix, it's going to set solid and you'll get ginger biscuits.

OK, here it is. And the answer is, lime curd. Mrs. Darlington's, from Penrith. You'd never have guessed in a bazillion years.

* 2½ cups plain flour plus additional for dusting
* 4 tsp baking powder
* 2 tsp baking soda
* 1½ tsp salt
* 1½ tsp grated ginger
* 1 cup sugar
* 4 tbsp crystallized ginger, coarsely chopped

* 2 cups well-shaken buttermilk
* 3½ tbsp unsalted butter, melted and cooled slightly
* 2 large eggs
* 1 tbsp vegetable oil
* 2 cups lime curd

Whisk together flour, baking powder, baking soda, salt, and ¾ teaspoon grated ginger in a large bowl. Whisk together ¾ cup sugar and remaining ¾ teaspoon grated ginger in a shallow bowl. Pulse remaining ¼ cup sugar with crystallized ginger in a food processor until ginger is finely chopped. Transfer this to a bowl and whisk in buttermilk, butter, and eggs until smooth. Add buttermilk mixture to flour mixture and stir until a dough forms (dough will be sticky). Turn out dough onto a well-floured surface and knead gently just until it comes together, 10 to 12 times, then form into a ball. Lightly dust work surface and dough with flour, then roll out dough into a 13-inch round (about ⅓ inch thick) with a floured rolling pin. Cut out rounds with a floured cutter and transfer to a lightly floured baking sheet. Gather scraps and reroll, then cut out additional rounds. (Reroll only once.) Heat oil in a wide heavy pot until a splash would result in third-degree burns. Working in batches of seven or eight, carefully add rounds, one at a time, to oil and fry, turning over once, until golden brown, one and a half to two minutes in total per batch. Transfer to paper towels to drain. Cool slightly, then dredge in ginger sugar. Gently slice doughnuts in half and spoon lime curd on the bottom half; top with the second half of the doughnut. Serve three or so to a plate, garnished with slices of crystallized sugar.

Well, that took you five blooming seconds," said Helena.

"Stop it," said Issy, looking to Pearl for backup.

"Yeah," said Pearl. "More like four."

"They don't respect you if you go running back," said Caroline. "I haven't spoken to the Bastard in months."

"How's that working out?" said Pearl.

"Fine, thank you, Pearl," sniffed Caroline loudly. "Actually, the children see more of him now than they did when we were still together. One Saturday afternoon a fortnight. I'm sure he hates it; he's taken them to the zoo three times. Good."

"Well, nice to know what I've got to look forward to," said Issy, who'd been expecting people to be slightly more positive about the fact that she had a boyfriend again.

"What about that gorgeous man from the bank?" said Helena.

"That is strictly professional," said Issy, lying. But Austin had disappeared at the speed of light. She knew he didn't want a relationship, and he had Darny. It was stupid to fantasize about things she couldn't have, like dreaming about a pop star. Whereas having Graeme come back to her…

"Plus, I have my eye on him," said Caroline.

"What for, fostering?" said Helena.

"Sorry, do you work here?" said Caroline. "I only hang about because I get paid."

"Well, I think it's kind of amazing he's realized he was wrong and come crawling back," said Issy. "No? Nobody?"

The other women looked at each other.

"Well, if you're happy," said Pearl, encouragingly. "He is nice, that man from the bank though."

"Shut up about the man from the bank," said Issy. "Oh. Sorry. I didn't mean to shout. But I've just…it's been so lonely. Even with all of you guys, I know. But setting everything up and sorting everything out myself and then going home alone because Helena's smooching up a doctor…"

"Who adores me," added Helena.

"…and now he's back, and he wants to make a real go of it, and that's all I ever wanted."

There was a pause.

"Five seconds though," said Helena. Issy stuck her tongue out at her. She knew what she was doing. Didn't she?

• • • •

Issy sat up, hugging her knees, several days later as Graeme got ready for an early morning squash match. "What's with you, Iss?" he said, smiling. She still couldn't believe how handsome he looked: his chiseled chest, with a light sprinkling of dark hair; his broad shoulders and white-toothed smile. He winked at her staring. Ever since she'd come back with him that night he'd been like a different person: romantic, thoughtful, always asking her questions about the bakery and Pear Tree Court and how she liked it there.

But still, a bit of her was cross with herself. She wasn't at his beck and call. She didn't run back to him just because he happened to be around. She hadn't even rung Helena, who had texted eleven times to ask if she would (a) come back, (b) get in touch, or (c) let Helena have her room. Issy hated to think that all he had to do was wiggle his eyebrows and she would jump into bed.

But she had missed it so much. She'd missed the human touch, the companionship; going home to someone at the end of the day. She had gotten so lonely she'd nearly made a complete fool of herself in front of her banking adviser, for goodness' sake. It was embarrassing. She went pink just thinking about it. She had risked turning into a crazy spinster. And when she saw how happy Helena and Ashok were, or Zac and Noriko, or Paul and John or any of her friends, all coupled up, all cheery (or so they seemed) at her party—well, why couldn't she have a bit of that? She wished they could see her now, all loved up and sweet, like in a toothpaste advert. Graeme, she mused dreamily, would probably get a job in a toothpaste advert.

"I'm fine," she said. "Just wish we didn't have to get up today."

Graeme leaned over and kissed Issy on her lightly freckled nose. It all seemed to be going well. He was delighted she'd come back to him, if not that surprised. He was about to unleash the next stage in the campaign. By the time he came to getting her to give up the bakery, he was going to have a very grateful girlfriend indeed. And a lot of money, and more prestige at the firm. No wonder he was so cheerful.

"I have a question for you," he said.

Issy smiled cheerfully. "Oh yes?"

"Um…Well. Um." Issy looked up. Graeme was being uncharacteristically reticent. He was not, as a rule, one of life's hemmers and hawers.

• • • •

Graeme was putting it on, of course. He thought a show of shyness might go down well.

"Well, I was thinking," he continued. "I mean, we seem to be getting on all right, don't we?"

"For the last five days, I suppose, yes," said Issy.

"I was going to say, I really like having you here," said Graeme.

"And I like being here," said Issy, a curious sensation—a mixture of happiness and nerves—stealing over her as she tried to fathom what he was getting at.

"Well, I was going to say…and I've never asked anyone this before…"

"Yes?"

"Would you like to move in with me?"

Issy stared at Graeme in shock. Then she felt shocked that she was shocked. After all, it was absolutely everything she'd ever imagined. Everything she'd ever dreamed about—living with the man of her dreams, in his lovely flat, sharing his life, cooking, hanging out, chilling on the weekend, planning their future—here it was. She blinked.

"*What* did you say?" she asked again. This didn't feel right.

She should be ecstatic, bouncing with happiness. Why was her heart not leaping and pounding with joy? She was thirty-two years old and she loved Graeme, goddamnit, of course she did. Of course she did. And when she looked at him, his face was so excited, nervous too. She could see, as she very rarely could, what he must have looked like as a little boy.

Then she saw on his face again a slight puzzlement, as if he'd been expecting her (as indeed he was) to throw herself into his arms with sheer delight.

"Um, I said," said Graeme, now stuttering slightly for real as he hadn't got the anticipated reaction. "I said, would you like to come and live here? You could, I don't know, sell the flat or rent it out or whatever…"

Issy realized she hadn't even considered that. Her lovely flat! With its pink kitchen! OK, she didn't spend much time there nowadays, but still. All the happy times she'd had with Helena; all the cozy evenings; the baking experiments that succeeded or otherwise; the times she'd spent poring over her relationship with Graeme and every tiny sign he gave out—she felt another pang, realizing that she'd missed doing exactly the same in return over Helena and Ashok, she'd been so immersed in the café—the pizza nights, the large bottle of pennies in the hallway that at one point Issy had thought she was going to have to break open in order to pay the Cupcake Café's buildings insurance…all of those things. Gone forever.

"…or we could have a trial period…"

Graeme hadn't been expecting this. He'd been expecting wild gratitude, excited plans; he'd anticipated having to tell her to slow down and stop measuring for curtains, not to think too much about marriage just yet, then being the joyful recipient of grateful sex, before explaining how he was also going to make her rich and release her from the shackles of her tiny shop, for which he was also expecting grateful sex. This look of consternation and air of distraction weren't all what he had planned. He decided to play the hurt card.

"Sorry," he said, making his eyes droopy and sad-looking. "Sorry, but…I might be wrong but I thought this was getting quite serious."

Issy couldn't bear to see him—her Graeme—looking sad. What was the matter with her? This was ridiculous. Here was Graeme, whom she loved, whom she'd dreamt of for so long, her heartthrob, her crush. He was offering her everything on a plate and here she was, being stupid and churlish; who on earth did she think she was? Issy rushed to his side and clung to him.

"Sorry!" she said. "Sorry! I was just—I was just so surprised I didn't know what to think!"

Wait till you hear what else I've got up my sleeve, thought Graeme, pleased his tactics had worked. He returned her embrace gladly.

"Can we…? What about…?" attempted Issy.

Graeme stilled her mouth with a kiss. "I have to get to squash," he said. "Let's talk through the details tomorrow," he added smoothly, as if she was a prevaricating customer.

• • • •

Pearl and Ben were laughing, Louis running ahead, as he picked her up from the bus stop. Pearl could see a tiny bit of Ben's tightly coiled chest hair over the top of his shirt. Her mother had been haranguing her again, saying she'd move to her sister's till Pearl had her man back, and that he couldn't just drop in whenever he wanted…Was he going to be a man about it or not?

"What would you think," she said, as casually as she was able, "about moving back in?"

Ben made a noncommittal noise and immediately changed the subject, dropping her politely at her door with a peck on the cheek. It wasn't quite what she'd been hoping for.

• • • •

"*Mummy sad, Caline,*" announced Louis boldly at work.

"Mummies do sometimes get sad, Louis," said Caroline, giving Pearl a sympathetic look that wasn't terribly welcome, but better than nothing, Pearl supposed.

"*Doan be sad, Mummy! Mummy sad!*" Louis announced to Doti, who was coming in with the post.

"Is she now?" said Doti, crouching down so he was at Louis's height. "Did you try giving her one of your special kisses?"

Louis nodded seriously then whispered, loudly, "Gave Louis kisses. But still sad!"

Doti shook his head. "Now that is a conundrum." He straightened up. "Maybe I could make Mummy happy and take her out for coffee sometime."

Pearl sniffed. "In case you haven't noticed," she said, "I'm surrounded by coffee."

"I'll go!" said Caroline, then her hand flew to her mouth. "Uh, I mean, I'll just be working quietly over here."

They both ignored her.

"Maybe a drink sometime then?"

"Maybe," said Pearl.

"I knock off early."

"I don't."

"Lunch?" parried Doti. "Next Tuesday?"

Pearl affected to gaze out of the window. Issy, finally exasperated, popped her head up from down below.

"She says yes!" she hollered.

• • • •

Issy went straight over to the flat after work. Helena was there, as was Ashok, whom Helena immediately dispatched to get coffee. Issy groaned. "No! No more coffee, please. Could you pick me up some Fanta? And some Hula Hoops?"

"You *are* bad," said Helena, popping the kettle on. "So, how's the new life with the old man? Fun?"

Issy threw her arms around her. "Thank you so much for the party," she said. "It was…it was *amazing*. I can't thank you enough for doing it for me."

"You can actually," said Helena. "After the first four hundred times you thanked me on the night."

"OK, OK. But listen, guess what happened?"

Helena raised an extremely well-plucked eyebrow. She had been expecting something like this, and was worried Issy seemed so jittery. After all the trouble she'd gone to, to make sure Austin would be there, and then, of all things, Graeme turning up. She hoped Issy didn't think she'd asked him. Although even a lunkhead like Graeme, Helena had to regretfully concede, was going to notice Issy's good points sooner or later.

"Go on then," she said.

"Graeme's asked me to move in with him!"

At this even Helena was surprised. Told her he loved her maybe, offered to let her meet his parents or be his official girlfriend. But living together was a big step; even when they'd been together a few months it had hardly seemed that serious, and Helena just didn't see Graeme as the warm, naturally hospitable type. But then she'd thought Ashok was a shy, retiring sort rather than the most amazing man ever, so what did she know.

"Well!" she said, trying not to sound fake. "This is great!"

Helena also looked at her friend's face. Her tone was upbeat but…was it real? Was she genuinely over the moon? Three months ago she would have been in paroxysms of joy, but now she seemed…

"And you're happy?" said Helena, realizing with a wince that she sounded a little sharper than she'd intended to.

"Um, shouldn't I be?" said Issy, fishing. "I mean, you know…it's Graeme. Graeme. Who I've been mad about for ages and ages and ages, and he's asked me to move in with him."

Helena paused to pour the tea. They both waited a long moment, fussing with cups and spoons, until Helena spoke up.

"You know, you don't have to. If you don't feel like it. There's plenty of time."

"But I do want to," said Issy, sounding agitated, as if she was trying to convince herself. "And there isn't plenty of time, Lena, don't pretend there is. I'm thirty-two. I'm not a child. I mean, everyone's settling down, I must have looked at nine thousand baby photos the other night. And I want that, Lena. That's what I want. A good man who loves me and wants to share my life and do all of that. I'm not a bad person to want that, am I?"

"Of course not," said Helena. And it was true; that nice chap from the bank, well, he couldn't be trusted to put his underpants on the right way around, never mind look after Issy, could he? And he already had a child to look after. Graeme was an earner, he was good-looking, he had no other baggage hanging over his head—by anyone's standards he was a catch, of course he was.

And Issy was right; Helena had seen it happen a million times. Just because someone wasn't absolutely perfect for you, you threw them over and expected someone better to come around the corner, but they didn't always. Life just wasn't like that. She knew too many friends and colleagues feeling marooned and terrified at forty, forty-one, and wishing with all their hearts they hadn't thrown over Mr. Nice but Not Quite Perfect when they were thirty-one. So he had taken a while to take Issy seriously—that didn't make him a bad guy, did it?

"It's great," said Helena. "I'd propose a toast if I didn't think you'd probably had enough booze this week."

"Stop nursing me."

"We had this woman in, younger than you, turned yellow, liver failure."

"Sharing a bottle of wine with Graeme is not liver failure."

"I'm just saying."

But somehow it felt better to be back bickering. They finished their tea, though, in silence. Issy felt slightly embarrassed and a little crestfallen. She'd rather expected Helena to dive in with her usual alacrity, and say don't be ridiculous, of course she couldn't live with Graeme, she had to stay here and nothing would change and it would all be fine and there were a million fantastic guys and fantastic things waiting to happen, just around the corner. But Helena hadn't said that. At all. Which meant that Issy was being a total idiot; of course this was the right thing to do. It was wonderful. And she was excited deep down, of course she was. It was natural to feel a little nervous, that was all.

Helena smiled at her, hopefully. "And, you know…well, just say no if this is all too sudden or anything like that, but, well…"

"Spit it out," said Issy. It wasn't like Helena to be nervous about anything.

"Well," said Helena, "I might know someone who might like to rent your room."

Issy raised her eyebrows.

"Might he be a…*doctor* by any chance?"

Helena looked pink. "The doctors' digs are horrendous, really awful. He was looking for a flat but your place is so nice and—"

Issy held up her hands. "You've been plotting this!!"

"I haven't, I swear." Helena was biting her lip to stop the grin from bubbling up.

"And you think I would stand in the way of true love?" said Issy.

"Do you mean it?" said Helena. "Oh my God! Oh my God! That's brilliant! Oh my God! I'll just phone him quickly! Ooh! Look at us!" she announced. "The cohabitees! Oh my God!"

She kissed her erstwhile flatmate and rushed to the phone.

Issy couldn't help contrasting how unbelievably thrilled Helena was with her own doubts. Almost imperceptibly, it felt like something was moving between them and their friendship; paper-thin, a crack that was opening up. She knew what this was like. When your friends had boyfriends, it was fine to discuss their plus points and shortcomings. But when the relationship became serious, then it was too late. Then you had to pretend they were totally perfect in every way in case they got married, and while it was nice to see your friends happy and everything, it did mean that the dynamic changed. And Issy was delighted to see Helena so happy, she was. But the dynamic had definitely changed. They were both moving on, that was all, she told herself.

They arranged to meet for drinks that night so Issy could pack up some of her stuff, and they went out and had a few glasses of hair of the dog and pretended it was just like the old days, but as one bottle turned into two, Helena put her cards down on the table.

"Why?" she said. "Why did you go back to him so fast?"

Issy looked up from where she'd been surreptitiously glancing at her phone—she'd texted to say she'd be a bit late, but hadn't heard from him. She felt her face stiffen.

"Well, because he's great, and he's available, and I really, really like him. You know that," she said.

"But he picks you up and drops you whenever he feels like it. And coming back into your life like this…I mean, you don't know what he's up to."

"Why does he have to be up to anything?" said Issy, feeling her face getting hot.

"Well, you know, with my Ashok…"

"Oh, yes, it's fine with your Ashok, your perfect Ashok, oh, look at my gorgeous handsome doctor whom everybody loves and who adores me and I'm so in love, blah blah blah. But then when it's Graeme you're all snooty."

"I'm not *snooty*. I'm just saying, he's put you through an awful lot of heartache and—"

"And I'm not good enough to have someone love me the way Ashok loves you, is that what you're saying? That it's so unlikely that any man would want me that he has to have some sort of ulterior motive?"

Helena wasn't used to seeing Issy so riled up.

"I didn't mean it like that…"

"Really? That's how it sounded. Or maybe you just think old Issy won't answer back, is that it? That I'm completely spineless?"

"No!"

"Well, you got one thing right. I'm not completely spineless."

And she got up and walked out of the bar.

• • • •

Across town, Pearl was staring at Ben.

"This isn't fair," she said.

"What?" he said. Louis was happily playing with his trains at his feet. "I just came over to get your mother to stitch on a button."

"Hmmm," said Pearl. The fact that Ben was sitting there shirtless, lit only by the newly acquired reading lamp her mother was using to pore over the sewing which Ben's own mother could easily have done, or in fact Ben himself if he wasn't so damn lazy…She knew his game.

"Why don't you two go out for a drink while I finish this," said Pearl's mother, managing to smoke a cigarette and stitch a shirt at the same time, quite a feat. "Louis will be fine."

"*Louis come have drink*," said Louis, with one of his emphatic nods.

"Bedtime," said Pearl, who would not have admitted it in a million years, but had been taken aback by Caroline's shock that Louis normally went to bed at the same time as she did and was trying to improve matters.

"*No no no no,*" said Louis. "*No no no no. Fanks,*" he added as an afterthought. "*No bed, fanks, Mummy.*"

"You go," said her mum. Louis looked like he might work himself up into a state if they hung about while he had to lie quietly in the corner. "I'll see him off."

"I've got a T-shirt in my bag," said Ben. "Or I could just go like this."

"You can't just go hot and cold on me all the time. And I have other options, you know!"

"I know," said Ben. "Put that red dress on. The one that makes your hips sway."

"I will not," said Pearl. The last time she'd worn that dress out with Ben…well, she already had one extra mouth to feed.

He offered her his arm when they left the little flat. Pearl's mother's eyes were on them all the way, Louis vocalizing very loudly and clearly why he didn't think his parents should be going out without him. Pearl didn't take any notice.

• • • •

"What's up, princess?" said Graeme, as Issy got home. Issy looked at the ground.

"Oh, girl stuff," she said.

"Oh," said Graeme, who didn't have the faintest idea what to do about girl stuff, and didn't really care either. "Don't worry about it. Come to bed for some boy stuff."

"OK," said Issy, although she hated to think of her friend going back to her house and the two of them having fallen out. Graeme stroked her dark curly hair.

"Come on," he said. "Oh, and I thought...now we're shacking up and everything...want to come and meet my mum sometime?"

And those were Issy's last thoughts before she fell asleep: he did love her. He did care for her. She lived with him, she was meeting his family. Helena was wrong about him.

Graeme lay awake a little longer. He had meant to tell her about the development tonight—he'd pitched it in the office and they'd gone mad for it. A keen landlord with an eye for a sound deal, apparently, and no problem tenants—the whole thing was going to be perfect. Too easy.

• • • •

This is too easy, thought Pearl, as Ben's hand brushed hers on the short walk back from the pub. Too easy. And it was what had gotten her into too much trouble before.

"Let me stay," said Ben wheedlingly.

"No," said Pearl. "We've only got one bedroom, and that's Nana's. It's not right."

"Well, come to my place. Or we could get a hotel."

Pearl looked at him. In the light of the streetlamp, he was even handsomer than she remembered. His broad shoulders, his beautiful curly hair, his handsome face. Louis was going to be so like him. He was the father of her child; he should be the center of their family. He leaned forward, very gently under the streetlights, and kissed her, and she closed her eyes and let him. It felt so familiar and yet so strange at the same time; it had been a while since she'd been touched by a man.

• • • •

Issy rolled out of bed with the sun the next morning, confusedly pulling clothes out of bags.

"What's the rush, babes?" said Graeme, sleepily.

Issy squinted at him. "I'm going to work," she said. "Those cupcakes don't bake themselves."

She stifled a yawn.

"Well, come give me a cuddle anyway."

Issy nestled into his hairless chest comfortably. "Mm," she said, mentally ticking down how much time she had, now she needed to cross north London to get to the café.

"Why don't you skip work today?" said Graeme. "You work too hard."

Issy smiled. "You of all people, saying that!"

"Yes, but wouldn't you like to slow down a bit? Work a bit less? Go back to a nice cozy office with sick pay and lunch breaks and office parties and someone else doing all the paperwork?"

Issy rolled onto her stomach and clasped her hands under her chin.

"You know," she said. "You know, I really don't think I would. I don't think I could go back to working for someone else for all the tea in China. Not even you!"

Graeme looked at her in consternation. He would tell her later, he thought. Again.

● ● ● ●

Pearl was actually humming coming in the doorway.

"What's with you?" said Caroline suspiciously. "You seem oddly cheerful."

"Can't I be cheerful?" said Pearl, getting out her broom as Caroline polished the temperamental cappuccino machine. "Are only middle-class people allowed to be cheerful?"

"Quite the opposite," said Caroline, who had received a particularly nasty solicitor's letter in the post that morning.

"Quite the opposite to what?" said Issy, coming up the stairs to greet Pearl and grab a coffee, with her eyebrows covered in flour.

"Pearl thinks middle-class people are jolly."

"Not now I don't," said Pearl, reaching out her finger to dip it in Issy's bowl.

"Stop that!" said Issy. "If the health inspector saw you he'd have a fit!"

"I have my plastic gloves on!" said Pearl, showing her. "Anyway, all chefs taste their own produce. Otherwise how would you know?"

Pearl tasted Issy's concoction. It was an orange and coconut cream sponge, soft, mellow and not too sweet.

"This tastes like a piña colada," she said. "It's wonderful. Amazing."

Issy stared at her, then glanced at Caroline.

"Caroline's right," she said. "What's up with you? Yesterday you were miserable, and today you're Rebecca from Sunnybrook Farm."

"Can't I be happy once in a while?" said Pearl. "Just because I don't live in your neighborhood and have to take the bus?"

"That's not fair," said Issy. "I am a bus connoisseur."

"And I'm going to have to move out of the neighborhood," said Caroline. She sounded so gloomy, the other girls looked at her in some amazement as she too dipped her finger in Issy's bowl.

"Fine," said Issy exasperated. "I'll throw this lot out and make a new batch, shall I?"

Pearl and Caroline took this as an invitation to get stuck into the batter in earnest, and with a sigh, Issy put down the bowl, pulled up a chair, and joined them.

"What's up?" said Pearl.

"Oh, my evil bloody ex-husband," said Caroline. "He wants me to move out of the home. The home that, by the way, I renovated almost all by myself; furnished all eleven rooms including his study, managed the building of the all-glass back wall *and* oversaw the construction of a fifty-thousand-quid kitchen, which by the way is no picnic."

"Although it comes with, obviously, an integrated picnic unit," said Pearl, before realizing from Caroline's face that this was no time for levity. "Sorry," she added, but Caroline had hardly heard her.

"I thought if I got a job, showed willing…But he says it means I obviously can work, so I can manage by myself! It's so unfair! I can't possibly keep my staff and the house and everything on what I earn here! This barely keeps me in pedicures."

Issy and Pearl concentrated on the cake mix.

"Sorry, but it's true. So I don't know *what* I'm supposed to do."

"He wouldn't force you to move out with your children, surely?" said Issy.

"There's probably room at my project for you," said Pearl, at which Caroline choked back a sob.

"Sorry," she said. "No offense meant."

"Oh, none taken," said Pearl. "I'd like to live in your house too. Or maybe just your kitchen."

"Well, the letter says 'steps may be taken,'" said Caroline. "Oh God."

"But surely he can see you're trying?" said Issy. "Doesn't that count for anything?"

"He doesn't want me to try," hissed Caroline. "He wants me to disappear. Forever. So he can keep getting it on with Annabel fucking Johnston-Smythe."

"How does she even get that on her credit card?" wondered Pearl.

"Anyway, let's change the subject," said Caroline testily. "Why *are* you so happy, Pearl?"

Pearl looked embarrassed and said a lady never kissed and told, which made both of them squeal so much Pearl got quite cross, particularly when Doti the postman turned up and told her she was looking particularly beautiful this morning, and they realized there was a queue of barflies at the door, looking hungry and anxious, but unwilling to intrude on the girls' morning catch-up.

"*I* have work to do," said Pearl stiffly and got up to leave.

"You take it nice and easy," said Issy, heading downstairs hastily as the first client of the day asked to try out the coconut and orange she had already chalked up on the specials board.

"Soon, soon," she said to the customer.

"Don't you deliver?" said the woman. The girls looked at each other.

"We should do that," said Pearl.

"I'll put it on the list," said Issy.

She felt cheered by Pearl's good humor—the fact that she wouldn't admit to the identity of the chap made Issy wonder if it wasn't Louis's dad, but she would never dream of asking something so personal. She worried about Caroline's divorce, partly for her and partly for selfish reasons, because she didn't want to lose her. She was prickly and snobbish, but she also worked hard and had an ability to present the cakes in the most beguiling of styles; she'd also improved the room in ways that were hard to pinpoint—tiny floating candles that emerged after dusk; cozy cushions in awkward corners that softened the place. She had an eye; there was no doubt about it.

But, mixing a new batch of cakes, sprinkling the coconut with a light hand and switching the white sugar to brown to intensify the depth of flavor, she couldn't help thinking about Helena. They'd never fallen out, not even when she'd asked Helena to save that one-legged pigeon. They'd always just got on; she couldn't bear the idea of not sharing with her what Pearl was up to and all the other gossip. She thought about phoning, but you couldn't phone Helena at work, it was awkward, she always had her hand up someone's bottom or was holding a severed toe or something. She'd go around. And take a gift.

● ● ● ●

Issy met Helena on the way.

"I was just coming over…" said Helena. "I'm so, so so—"

"No, I am," said Issy.

"I'm happy for you, honestly," said Helena. "I just want you to be happy."

"Me too!" said Issy. "Please, let's not fight."

"No," said Helena. The two girls embraced in the street.

"Here," said Issy, handing over the piece of paper she'd been carrying about all day.

"What's that?" said Helena. Then, as she stared at it, she understood. "The recipe! No way! Oh my God!"

"Well," said Issy. "Now you have your heart's desire."

Helena smiled. "Come back," she said. "Come and have a cup of tea. It's still your flat."

"I should get back," said Issy. "Got to see my man, you know."

Helena nodded. She did know. Which didn't make it any less odd, as they hugged tightly once again and parted, for them to head off home, but going in different directions.

● ● ● ●

Helena had given her her mail too. And Issy's heart had sunk. More recipes; but they were ones she'd already had, or things that didn't make sense. She'd spoken to Keavie on the phone, who'd said yes, he had been on good form when she'd seen him, but overall things weren't good, and to pop in whenever she could, which she did the next day.

To her surprise, when she reached the hospital, someone was already in the room; a short man with a hat on his knee, sitting on the chair next to the bed, chatting away. When he turned around she realized she knew his face but for a second she couldn't place him. Then she did: it was the ironmonger.

"What are you doing here?" she said, rushing over to kiss Gramps, so very pleased to see him.

"A darling girl!" said Gramps. "I am mostly but not completely sure which one. This delightful man has been keeping me company."

Issy eyed him shrewdly. "Well, that's kind of you."

"Not at all," said the man. He put out his hand. "Chester."

"Issy. Thank you for the key ring," she said, suddenly shy. The man smiled back, shy too.

"I met your grandfather through your shop. We've become good friends."

"Gramps?" said Issy.

Her grandfather smiled weakly. "I just asked him to keep an eye on you."

"You asked him to spy!"

"You use a microwave! What next, margarine?"

"Never," said Issy vehemently.

"It's true," said Chester. "She has never had a margarine delivery."

"Stop spying on me."

"All right," said Chester. There was that trace of a Middle European accent she couldn't place. "I won't."

"Or…well, if you must," said Issy, who rather liked the idea of having someone looking out for her. It hadn't happened before. "At least come in and try one of the cakes."

The man nodded. "Your grandfather warned me off eating your profits. He said you were too kind not to feed me for nothing and that I wasn't allowed to ask for anything."

"It's still a business," said Grampa Joe weakly from the bed.

Keavie popped her head in. "Hi, Issy! How's the love life?"

"So you know everything too!" said Issy, stung.

"Give over! Anyway, he does your grandfather a power of good. Perks him right up."

"Hmmm," said Issy.

"And I like it," said the ironmonger. "Selling spanners is a lonely road."

"And we both know the shop trade," said Gramps.

"All right, all right," said Issy. She'd been used to being the only person her gramps would turn to for so long, she wasn't sure about him having a friend. Now, though, Gramps was looking around, confused.

"Where is this?" he said. "Isabel? Isabel?"

"I'm here," said Issy, as Chester made his good-byes and left. She took Gramps's hand.

"No," he was saying. "Not you. Not Isabel. That's not who I meant. That's not who I meant at all."

He grew more and more agitated, and his grip on Issy's hand grew stronger and stronger, till Keavie came in with a male nurse, and they persuaded him to drink some medicine.

"That'll calm him down," said Keavie, looking straight at Issy. "You understand," she went on, "that calming him down, making him comfortable…that's all we can really…"

"You're saying he's not going to get any better," said Issy miserably.

"I'd say his lucid moments are going to get fewer and farther apart," said Keavie. "And you need to prepare yourself for that."

They looked at the old man settled back into the pillows.

"He knows," Keavie whispered. "Even patients with dementia… Everyone is so fond of your grandfather here, you know. They really are."

Issy squeezed her hand in gratitude.

●　●　●　●

Two Saturdays later, Des, the estate agent, popped his head around the door. Jamie was squawking his head off.

"Sorry," he said to Issy, who was enjoying the *Guardian Guide* before the Saturday shoppers' lunchtime rush arrived. Her Cupcake Café key ring was sparkling in the summer sunlight through the polished windows.

"Oh, that's all right," said Issy, jumping up. "I was just enjoying a quiet moment. Hang on, what can I get you?"

"I wondered if you'd seen Mira?" said Des.

Issy glanced at the sofa. "Oh, she normally comes in around this time," she said. "She should be here any moment. They've got a proper flat now, and she's got a job."

"That's brilliant!"

"I know! I'm trying to persuade her to send Elise to the same nursery as Louis, but she's having none of it and keeping her in a Romanian nursery."

"I didn't even know they had such a thing," said Des.

"Stoke Newington has everything…Aha," said Issy as Mira and Elise arrived. "Speak of the devil."

Mira immediately took Jamie off Des and, as was his wont, he stopped howling to regard her with his large round eyes.

"Ems has kicked me out of the house…for a bit," added Des hastily, in case they imagined she'd kicked him out once and for all. (It was rather worrying, Issy thought, if you had to correct people's impression of your marriage like that.) "He's been right as rain, Mira, since he got over that colic, absolutely a splendid…he's a great wee man." His voice grew slightly emotional as he regarded his son. "Yes," he said, "anyway, right. The thing is, the last couple of days have been just awful, just terrible."

Mira raised her eyebrows.

"The doctor said it's nothing, just teething."

"So you brought him to the baby whisperer!" said Issy cheerfully, lining up a tea, a babycino for Elise, and a large cappuccino with plenty of grated chocolate. Jamie, previously content, was now opening his mouth in preparation for a huge wail, as Mira poked her fingers in his soft gums.

Des looked sheepish. "Uh, well, something like that."

Mira gave him a stern look as Jamie screamed.

"In this country they think it is so hilarious that nobody knows anything about babies, and the grandmothers, they say, 'Oh, I will not interfere with the babies,' and the aunties, they say, 'Oh, I am too busy to help with the babies,' and everybody ignores the babies and buys stupid books about the babies and watches stupid television about the babies," she said fiercely. "Babies are always the same. Adults, not so much. Give me a knife."

Issy and Des looked at each other.

"Uh, what?" said Issy.

"Knife. I need a knife."

Des put up his hands. "Honestly, we can't take much more of this at home. Ems is sleeping at her mum's as it is. I'm going bananas. I've started to see ghosts out of the corner of my eye."

"*You're* not having a knife," said Issy. Somewhat nervously, she handed Mira a serrated knife. Quick as a flash, Mira stuck Jamie down on his back on the sofa, pinned down his arms, and made two little darts inside his mouth with the knife. Jamie screamed the place down.

"What…what have you *done*?" said Des, grabbing Jamie up from the sofa and cradling him in his arms. Mira shrugged. As Des glared at her, he noticed that Jamie, once the initial shock and pain had passed, was gradually calming down. His great heaving gulps of air grew slower and slower, and his tense, infuriated little body started to relax. He nestled his head lovingly into his father's chest, and once again, no doubt utterly exhausted from his painful, sleepless nights, his eyelids started to droop.

"Well," said Des. "Well."

Issy shook her head. "Mira, what did you do? How did you do that?"

Mira shrugged again. "He has teeth coming. They are pushing through the gum. Very painful. Now I cut through the gum. Teeth through now. Not sore. Not rocket science."

"I have never heard of that," said Des softly, so as not to disturb his now snoozing baby.

"Nobody here has heard of anything," said Mira.

"You should write a baby book," said Issy admiringly.

"It would be one page," said Mira. "It would say, 'Ask your grandmother. Do not read a stupid baby book. Thank you.'"

She accepted the tea, and Elise, who had been sitting very quietly with a book, murmured a little thank-you for the babycino. Des rushed to pay for them.

"This has saved my life," he said. "Actually, can I have mine in a takeaway cup? I'm going to go straight home and attempt a nap."

"Of course," said Issy.

Des looked around. "So…ahem…I hear rumors on the grapevine."

"What's that then?" said Issy pleasantly, ringing up the sale.

"About this place…Oh, must be wrong then."

"What?"

"I heard something about you selling up…assumed you were off somewhere bigger." Des looked around appraisingly. "You've done a really good job with this and no mistake."

Issy handed him his change.

"Well, you've heard totally wrong," she said. "We're not going anywhere!"

"Excellent," said Des. "I must have misheard. Sleep deprivation, you know. OK, well, thanks again."

Suddenly there was a loud scraping noise outside. Issy rushed out; Des stayed inside in case Jamie woke up again. In the bright summer sunlight, the ironmonger was dragging two wrought iron chairs past the tree. Next to that was a beautiful table, freshly painted cream. Issy stood and stared.

"That's amazing," she said. Doti came around the corner, still dejected because Pearl hadn't made the lunch. While she was still caught up with an undecided Ben, she'd explained to Issy, she wasn't going to complicate things. Issy rushed to help drag the furniture into position. There were two sets, each with three seats, and two heavy chains to stop them being stolen in the night. They were absolutely lovely.

"Your grandfather ordered the whole thing," said Chester, putting up his hands as Issy gave him a hug. "And paid for it, so don't worry about it. He reckoned you needed them."

"I do," said Issy, shaking her head. "What a stroke of luck you turned out to be. You're our guardian locksmith."

Chester smiled. "You have to look out for each other in the big city," he said. "And I know he told me not to but…"

"Coffee and cake?"

"That would be lovely."

Pearl came out with a tray all ready, smiling shyly at Doti, and sitting down to admire the new view.

"Perfect," she said. Louis scampered beneath her feet.

"*I is lion in lion cage*," he growled. "*Grrr.*"

"And we can keep a guard lion to get rid of anyone we don't like," said Issy.

"*I likes everyone*," announced the guard lion from underneath the table.

"That's my problem," said Pearl, taking the empty cups back inside.

• • • •

Any day now, thought Issy. Any day now she was going to stop feeling like a guest in someone else's home. She would be able to stop tiptoeing everywhere, terrified of making a mess. She hadn't realized Graeme's commitment to minimalism was so…so absolute.

Yes, the flat was lovely, but it was all hard edges. The sofas were uncomfortable, the television/Blu-ray/stereo combo fiendishly difficult to work; the oven was a tiny concealed afterthought in an off-plan hi-tech bachelor pad, obviously not intended for people to cook in, although the instant boiling water tap was nice, after the first few agonizing blisters. It was more the habits: getting into the habit of taking off her shoes, never putting anything down, not even a coat, not even for a second. Of having no magazines lying around, of lining up the remote control, of trying to find a tiny space for a chest of drawers to take her clothes, as Graeme's were all hung up, still wreathed in their plastic wrappers from the dry cleaner's. His bathroom cabinet was full of every sort of product imaginable, for skin, for hair, all of it immaculate.

The cleaner scuttled in twice a week and scrubbed down absolutely everything, and if Issy happened to be around when she did so, she didn't dare touch anything afterward. Toast had become a happy memory—too many crumbs on the shiny glass surfaces of the kitchen—and they were eating a lot of easy-to-clear stir-fry, even though Issy chafed a little in a kitchen that bothered with a boiling water tap, a wok flame and a wine fridge, but not a proper bloody oven to bake anything in. Would it ever really feel like home?

Graeme, on the other hand, was already feeling he could get used to this. As long as he gave her a bit of a sharp look whenever she left stuff on the floor—why were women always so messy? Why did they need bags to keep all their stuff in? He'd given her a chest of drawers but he'd noticed her shampoos and hair serums—inferior brands, he reckoned, waste of money most of them—creeping into his black-tiled bathroom. He would have to have a word about that.

Apart from that, it was nice to have someone there at the end of the day—she finished so much earlier than he did. It was nice to have someone ask him how his day had been, to produce a home-cooked dinner rather than the Marks & Spencer ready meals he usually lived off; to pour him a glass of wine and listen to the litany of his day. It was really good actually; he was surprised he hadn't thought of it before. She'd asked him whether she could bring her books over and he'd had to say no; he didn't have bookshelves, it would spoil the layout of the double-height sitting room, and he absolutely didn't want her kitsch cooking gear in here. But she didn't seem to mind that. All of that was fine.

But there was something else playing on his mind. The London office was gung ho for him to go full steam ahead on this Pear Tree Court idea now. They saw it as a move from just letting offices to actually selling lifestyles, and if it went well, he could see a seriously major future for himself in lifestyle development. It was big-time stuff.

But now it was becoming clear to him that actually, like a total nut job, she really liked running this stupid little shop, getting up at sparrow's fart and being treated like a housemaid all the time. The more they sold and the harder she had to work, the happier she seemed to be. And the money was still total rubbish. Surely she'd see sense when he explained it…

Graeme scowled to himself and turned again to make sure the smooth planes of his face had the perfect shave. Twisting to see his reflection from all angles, he was pleased. But he wasn't 100 percent sure this Issy situation would resolve itself quite as easily as he'd believed.

• • • •

As the summer progressed, the shop showed no signs of slowing down; quite the opposite, in fact. Issy made a mental note for next year to think about stocking some proper homemade organic ice creams; they would have sold brilliantly. Perhaps they could have a barrow outside for people wandering past. Maybe Felipe could staff it, and play his violin in quiet times. More forms, of course, for the council, to run an outdoor food concession, but she sent them in anyway. It was amazing, she thought, how the paperwork, which had once seemed so daunting, was now so easy to handle. She realized, with a start, that—apart from the night when Graeme had turned up and she was with Austin (which she had decided to deal with by never thinking about it or going to the bank ever again—well, obviously she'd have to go in at some point, they were paying back their loan, but until it was absolutely essential Pearl could do it)—she was blushing less too. What a funny side effect of baking for a living.

Coming in from a quick break in the park (complete with ice cream), she could hear Pearl and Caroline squabbling. Uh-oh. They'd seemed to be on pretty good terms recently; Pearl was mostly cheerful, and Caroline had taken to wearing tiny vest tops that on someone twenty years younger would have looked cute but on Caroline emphasized her jutting collarbones and Madonna-like arms. Issy was aware that the builders made rude comments about her and Pearl together, but ignored them. Pearl anyway was looking miles better; simply coming to a job every day instead of staying indoors had meant she'd dropped a couple of dress sizes and now, to Issy's eyes, looked very much the size she was born to be, perfectly in proportion in every way.

"We'll have his aunties around, and everyone will bring a bottle, and that will do," Pearl was saying stubbornly.

"A *bottle*? To a child's third birthday party? No, it *won't* do," Caroline was saying. "He needs a proper party like everybody else."

Pearl bit her lip. Louis, eventually, due to his unstinting good nature, and the mothers' desire to look inclusive and nonprejudiced, had started to receive a party invitation or two, but Pearl had looked at them and worriedly turned them down. They all seemed to be held in really expensive places like the zoo, or the Natural History Museum, and she just wasn't sure she could afford them yet. Now the shop was doing better, Issy had increased her wages (against Mrs. Prescott's advice, she knew), but Pearl was using the money to pay off catalogues for stuff she really needed—a proper bed for Louis, new sheets and towels, not buying expensive gifts and going to expensive parties. She didn't know that the child's parents were paying for the partygoers' entrance to these places; it would have shocked her even more if she had. She'd managed to distract Louis, but he was getting older now; there would come a stage when he'd begin to understand, and realize he was different, and she didn't want it to come sooner than it had to.

And anyway, when he started school in a year or so, he wouldn't be different anymore. Pearl shuddered sometimes when she thought about the primary school nearest the estate. The council was doing their best but it was still graffiti-strewn, with high gates covered in barbed wire, and since the change in government it had gotten markedly worse. Her friends around the place spoke of bullying and disaffected teachers, but grudgingly admitted the school tried hard. Pearl wasn't sure trying hard was good enough for Louis. She might find the nursery awkward, but there was absolutely no doubt that he was flourishing; he could count to twenty, solve jigsaw puzzles, sing songs that weren't just commercial jingles and ride a tricycle, and he wanted more library books than she could keep up with. She sometimes had the creeping horrors of him going to school and getting all of that intimidated out of him. On the other hand, she didn't want to breed some kind of sissy boy who had themed birthday parties and posh friends and would get the crap ripped out of him for that too.

"It will be a proper party," she said. On top of all that, she didn't like Caroline being right about anything. "There'll be plenty of presents."

"Why don't you have his friends around?" persisted Caroline in that annoyingly blinkered way of hers. "Just invite ten or so."

Pearl tried to imagine ten Harrys and Liddies and Alices and Arthurs clambering up and down her mother's bed settee and failed.

"What's this?" asked Issy cheerfully, coming back with Graeme's dry cleaning. It obviously made more sense if she took care of it, even if he was traveling by car.

"We're planning Louis's birthday party," said Caroline brightly.

Pearl shot her a look. "Maybe."

"Well, I'll ask him if he wants a proper party," said Caroline.

Pearl looked at Issy with desperation in her face. Suddenly Issy had an idea.

"I've been thinking about this for a while," she said. "You know how quiet we are on Saturdays? I was thinking about shutting then, but Mrs. Prescott will kill us and then Austin will kill us too, etc. So, one thing I thought we might do is have…cupcake-themed birthday parties. Mostly for little girls, of course. But the idea is that the kids come and they have to bake and decorate their own cakes, and we have little aprons and mixing bowls for them, and we charge for the hire of the place. It could be quite a nice little money-maker. And good for kids, no one learns to bake anymore."

Issy didn't know how much she sounded like her granddad when she said that.

"That is brilliant," said Caroline. "I shall tell my gals immediately and insist that they do it. And we can serve the grown-ups tea. Although," she added thoughtfully, "I personally have never got through one of those wretched children's parties without a strong drink or two. It's the noise, you see."

"We're not getting a license," said Pearl. "I promised my pastor."

"No, no, of course not," said Caroline, still looking regretful.

"You can do what the Prince of Wales does and bring a hip flask," said Issy. "So, Pearl, we could have Louis and his friends as a test case to see if it's going to work. Take some sweet photos of them all covered in flour, use them as publicity, that kind of thing."

"So it will be just like every working day, except more so," said Pearl.

"Oh Christ, all children's birthdays are like that," said Caroline. "Hell on wheels!"

• • • •

Graeme tried to feel as confident as he knew he looked—he'd checked himself out in the mirror of the BMW just before he stepped out of the car, ignoring a passing child who jeered at him as he did so. Nonetheless, although normally he felt like a tiger at meetings, aggressive and confident that he would be the top man, today he was nervous. Undoubtedly, nervous. It was getting ridiculous. He was Graeme Denton. He didn't get silly about a girl, ever. He still hadn't told Issy his plan. But every day Kalinga Deniki wanted to know his progress, were pushing for planning applications and the green light. They had already had preliminary surveyor's reports and now he was meeting with Mr. Barstow, the landlord for most of Pear Tree Court.

Mr. Barstow didn't bother with the formalities when he walked in. He extended his small plump hand and grunted. Graeme nodded, ordering his new assistant, Dermot, to start up the PowerPoint. Dermot, nine years younger, a total squirt who dressed like he read too many men's magazines and kept trying to get onto all of Graeme's projects, reminded Graeme of himself when he started out. Graeme began his presentation, talking about how a bulk buyout of both occupied and vacant space would be a great thing for Barstow, at some bulk discount to KD. By the third graph, Mr. Barstow's eyes were glazing over. He waved his hands at them.

"OK, OK. Write the figure down on a piece of paper."

Graeme paused and decided to do exactly that. Mr. Barstow glanced at it contemptuously and shook his head. "Nah. Anyway, got someone in number four. Running a little caff. Making not a bad fist of it either. She's bringing up the prices around the place."

Graeme inwardly rolled his eyes. This was all he needed; Issy was actually making his job harder for him.

"She's coming to the end of her six-month contract though. We'll make it worth your while."

Graeme felt a momentary twinge. He shouldn't know when Issy's contract was up, but he did of course. Mr. Barstow raised his eyebrows. "So you've talked to her about it then? Well, I suppose, if she's amenable…"

Graeme didn't change his expression, either to imply he'd spoken to her or not. It was none of Mr. Barstow's business.

"Don't know how I'll get that ironmonger out though. He's been there longer than I have," reflected the landlord. He rubbed one of his chins. "Don't know how he turns a dime."

Graeme didn't care either way. "I'm sure we can make him an offer he can't refuse."

Mr. Barstow looked doubtful again.

"I think you'd better keep writing on that envelope, mate."

some scones.

scones, issy. scones.

* * * *

* 32½ cups all-purpose flour
* ½ cup flour
* sprinkle of flour
* 6¼ cups white sugar
* ¾ cup brown sugar
* ¾ cup salt

Issy put the letter down and sighed. It was heartbreaking. Awful. She was heading up there with some baking of her own; maybe the sight of some fresh cakes would help. Issy knew it was going to be a pain to carry them all up there on the bus but she didn't care. There were forty-seven residents (although the numbers changed quite often, she knew) and thirty staff at the home, and she was taking them each a cupcake and that was that. She had thought of asking Graeme if he wanted to drive her up and meet her grand-dad, but when she'd gone into the sitting room he'd immediately closed down the window on the computer he'd been working on and been so short with her that she'd retreated instantly—once more, she thought crossly, a visitor in what was now supposed to be her own home. If Graeme wasn't so grumpy all the time she'd have considered suggesting that they start to look for somewhere new. On the other hand, it wasn't like she was bringing in such a fortune that they could massively upgrade together. And she wasn't sure she was ready to sell the old place, even though she suspected that when she was, Helena would buy it in a heartbeat.

When she viewed these problems it was almost like she was thinking about someone else's life, so disconnected did it seem—sell her flat, buy somewhere new. On the other hand, she had moved. Issy thought back to last Sunday, when she'd finally met Graeme's mum. His parents had split up when he was small—he was an only child—and she'd been really curious to meet his mother, especially after the phone call she'd had from her own.

"Issy!" Marian had hollered, as if she was talking to her from Florida without a telephone. "Isabel! Listen! I'm not sure how your granddad is. Could you pop in and see?"

Issy had swallowed back everything she might have said: actually she spent every Sunday there already, and had been warning her mother for weeks via email that he wasn't himself at all.

"I've seen him, Mum," she settled on.

"Oh, *good*. Good. That's good."

"I think...I think he'd really like to see you. Are you coming back? Any time soon?" Issy tried not to sound sarcastic, but it was completely wasted on her mother anyway.

"Oh, I don't know, darling, Brick is so busy at work..." Her mother's voice trailed off. "And how are *you*, sweetheart?"

"I'm fine," said Issy. "I've moved in with Graeme."

Marian had never met Graeme. Issy thought she would keep it like that for as long as possible.

"Oh, wonderful, darling! OK, be careful! Bye!"

So it was little wonder Issy was looking forward to meeting her possible future mother-in-law. In her mind's eye she was a nice, slightly rounded, eager-to-please lady with Graeme's handsome dark hair and twinkling eyes, and they could share recipes and bond. Maybe she'd have liked a daughter in her life. At any rate, it was with some excitement that she'd dressed up in a pretty summery frock, and taken along her lightest Victoria sponge as a gift.

Mrs. Denton lived in an immaculate modern townhouse on a group of streets that looked exactly alike in Canary Wharf. The house was tiny with low ceilings, but had all mod cons—Graeme had found it for her off-plan.

"Hello," said Issy warmly, looking past her at the pristine hallway. There were no pictures on the walls, apart from an enormous one of Graeme as a schoolboy, and no clutter of any kind anywhere. "Ooh, I can see where your son gets his tidiness from!"

Graeme's mother smiled, seemingly lost in thought for a moment.

"I brought you some cake," Issy went on cheerfully. "Did Graeme tell you I was a baker?"

Carole felt rooted to the spot. She had been so excited—this was the first girl Graeme had brought home in four or five years. She was so proud of him for being out there and doing so well—he was something big in property, as she liked to tell all her friends. Without actually saying as much, she implied that he'd bought her the house. The last couple of girls—well, they'd been terribly, terribly pretty, especially that one with the blond hair all down her back. Of course they'd been gorgeous, look at her son. But she'd known it wouldn't be serious. Graeme had his big career to establish first, of course, and he didn't have time for all that settling down.

But recently she'd started to lose bragging rights to her friends when they discussed their children's weddings—the size of the marquee, the number of guests, the arrays of presents—and worse, she'd had to go to these weddings, smile happily and compliment her friends' good taste, even if the cold salmon tasted of nothing and they had those loud discos with DJs. Finally, the worst thing of all had happened: she'd been upstaged by Lilian Johnson, of all people, pathetic little mouse Lilian Johnson, whose daughter Shelley who'd gone off to university all lah-de-dah then come back and ended up a social worker, and everyone knew how rubbish they were. Well, Shelley had gotten married. The chicken had been disappointing at the reception, but she supposed it was all right if you liked that kind of thing, and Lilian had looked quite fetching in mauve. And now Shelley was pregnant. Lilian was going to be a grandmother. Carole couldn't bear it. So she'd been quite impatient for a while now for Graeme to get moving.

She'd thought maybe one of those delicate, pretty girls—a Gwyneth Paltrow type—very clever and so on, but utterly ready to give up her career and look after her boy, and desperate for some good advice on Graeme's likes and dislikes, how to cook his favorite things, and some guidelines on taste—from her. She pictured them going to the department store John Lewis together, and the girl saying, "Oh, Carole, you do know him inside out," and then perhaps they could pick out nursery things together and the girl would say, "Now, Carole, I don't know anything about having a baby, you're just going to have to fill me in on everything." And Graeme would say, "Well, I couldn't find another you, Mum, I just had to make do with the next best thing." Not that that was the kind of thing Graeme was prone to saying, but she liked to imagine him thinking it.

So yes, that was what she was expecting, after Graeme had called and said, rather briskly, that he was bringing "Issy" to tea. Isabel—that sounded like rather a smart name too, nothing common. Not that her Graeme would ever have gone for anyone common of course. He had good taste, like her.

So when she opened the door to see this diminutive, rounded, rosy-cheeked brunette—who had to be at least, what, thirty-four? Thirty-five? Could she even still *have* children? What on earth was

Graeme thinking? It couldn't be this girl. Graeme was so handsome, everyone said so. Since he was a little boy. Her ex might have been a total bastard, but he was a good-looking bastard, that was the truth, and it had all come out in the boy. And so smart, with his smart car and his smart suits and his smart flat. There was absolutely no way... Maybe she wasn't his girlfriend. Maybe she was...Carole clutched at straws. Maybe someone who needed a visa to stay in the country. Maybe she was a friend of a friend passing through London and Graeme was kindly letting her stay at his flat. But then...why would he bring her? He wouldn't.

"Cake!" said Issy again. "Um, I don't know if you like cake."

Issy felt the familiar blush spreading across her cheeks and grew hot and cross with herself. She felt dully, stupidly, like she wasn't what Carole had been expecting. She glanced hurriedly at Graeme, who normally ignored his silly mother, but even he could see that her behavior could be construed as quite rude. He gave Issy's hand a quick squeeze.

"Issy's my girlfriend," he said, and Issy was grateful to him. "Uh, Mum, can we come in?"

"Of course," said Carole weakly, standing back and letting them cross the threshold onto the cream shag pile carpet. Without thinking Issy walked straight in, then froze as she realized that, behind her, Graeme had bent down and taken off his shoes. Of course he had.

"*Ah*," said Issy, taking off her sandals and realizing as she did so that she could do with a pedicure—but really, when did she have the time? She noticed Carole checking out her feet too.

"Shall I put this cake in your kitchen?" said Issy brightly. Carole gestured ahead. The kitchen was utterly spotless. Laid out on the side were three neat bowls with prewashed salad, a small pile of neatly trimmed white-bread ham sandwiches, and a jug of lemonade.

Issy put the cake down with a sigh. This could turn into a long afternoon.

• • • •

"So do you work?" asked Issy politely when they sat at the obviously rarely used round table to eat lunch. It was a glorious day, and Issy had looked longingly at the immaculately tended garden but Carole had announced loudly that she was terrified of wasps and flying insects and never ever sat outside. Issy had complimented her on her skin, which Carole had totally ignored, and now they were all sitting indoors with the windows shut and the television on so that Graeme could watch the game.

Carole looked surprised at the question, but Issy had rarely asked Graeme about his mother; early in their relationship they were far too casual for it to be appropriate, and more recently she had sensed he rather avoided the topic. Carole couldn't believe he hadn't mentioned her to this girl...Well, woman, girl was pushing it a bit. Maybe the relationship wasn't that serious after all.

"Well, presumably Graeme's told you about my charity work?" Carole said stiffly. "And of course, the Rose Growers Association keeps me busy. Although I mostly do the admin for that. Insects, you see. They never seem very grateful."

"The insects?"

"The rose growers." Carole sniffed. "I slave over the minutes for them."

"I know what that's like," said Issy sympathetically, but Carole didn't seem to hear her.

"Do they all still love you in the office, darling?" she cooed to Graeme. Graeme grunted and indicated that he was trying to watch the television. "He's ever so popular there," she said to Issy.

"I know," said Issy. "That's where we met."

Carole raised her eyebrows. "I thought he said you worked in a shop."

"I run my own business," said Issy. "I'm a baker. I make cakes and so on."

"I can't eat cakes," said Carole. "They interfere with my digestion."

Issy thought with some regret of the lighter-than-air sponge sitting in the kitchen. They'd already eaten the ham sandwiches—it had taken two minutes—and she now felt trapped and unsatisfied, still sitting at the table, waiting for the tea to cool.

"So, er," said Issy, desperate to get this conversation on track. Graeme was whooping a goal; Issy didn't have the faintest idea who was playing. But this was, potentially, her future mother-in-law sitting in front of her. Potentially, the grandmother...Issy stopped herself thinking along those lines. It was far too early, and far too precarious, to think along those lines. She decided to stick to the safest possible ground.

"So, Graeme was totally the most popular at work. He's doing brilliantly there, I think, still. You must be very proud."

Carole almost softened for a second before remembering that this chubby, aging harpy sitting in front of her had had the temerity to show up with a cake, implying that she, Carole, didn't bake for her own son, and had swanned in here with her shoes on like she owned the place already.

"Yes, well, he always did go for the best, my son," she said, larding the comment with as much double meaning as she could manage. Issy had been completely crestfallen.

There had been another long, uncomfortable silence, punctuated only by Graeme cheering or sighing along with his football team.

"She hates me," Issy had pointed out mournfully in the car on the way home.

"She doesn't hate you," said Graeme, grumpy because his team had lost again. In fact, Carole had taken him into the kitchen to tell him in no uncertain terms that she wasn't happy. Wasn't Issy terribly old? And just a baker? Graeme, unused to his mother questioning his judgment on anything, had tuned out. He didn't need Issy nipping his head about it too. Issy hadn't deliberately tried to overhear the conversation in the kitchen, but figured the very fact that Carole had decided she and Graeme needed a private chat was probably all the information she needed. "She just thinks you're a bit old."

Graeme turned up Radio 5 Live. Issy stared out of the car window, into a rainstorm coming in from the east, over Canary Wharf. The raindrops came down thick and heavy and started hitting the window.

"That's what she said?" said Issy quietly.

"Mm-hm," said Graeme.

"Do you think I'm a bit old?"

"For what?" said Graeme. He had the distinct sensation that this was a conversation he didn't want to be in, but here he was stuck in a car with it, and no way out.

Issy closed her eyes tightly. So close, she thought. So close; she could just ask him now. Was this her happy ever after? Get it sewn up. Signed, sealed, and delivered. But what if she did ask and the answer was no? And what if she did ask and the answer was yes?

If both the answers were going to make her unhappy, well, what did that mean? What did that make her? Suddenly she saw the years stretching ahead…Graeme, marching forward with his career, using her, maybe, as a sounding board if he needed to vent, but otherwise as a general slave…ignoring her to watch TV, the way he did his mother. An easy, nondemanding doormat.

Well, maybe she had been a bit like that—Helena, she was sure, would agree. But she had changed. The café had changed her. For the better. And this time it wouldn't be shouting and histrionics or an optional go-and-come-back whenever he wanted a hot meal. She would do it properly.

"Graeme…" she said, turning to him in the rain-flecked car.

• • • •

"What do you mean?" Graeme had said. He'd been more upset than Issy had expected, but of course she didn't know what this meant for him at work.

"I don't think…I don't think this is going to work out, do you?" said Issy, as calmly as she could, reflecting, as she did so, on the fine profile and tight jaw, as he cut off another car splashing out of a roundabout. After swearing repeatedly, he had shut up like a clam and refused to speak to her anymore. As soon as was legally possible, he had simply stopped the car and dropped her by the side of the road. It felt oddly fitting somehow, thought Issy, watching the sports car zip away. Allow him his petty little victory; in fact, it wasn't cold outside in the rain, she didn't even mind too much; and when a cab cruised past, its yellow light shining like a friendly beacon, she hailed it to take her home.

Helena shrieked when she came in and demanded all the details of her disastrous visit to Graeme's mother.

"It just became obvious," said Issy, "that, regardless of *what* is out there…well, it was doing me no good. Although," she said, with slightly wobbly bravado, "I would have liked to have a baby."

"You'll have a baby," said Helena reassuringly. "Maybe freeze some eggs just in case."

"Thanks, Lena," said Issy, and her friend took her in her arms and gave her a long, reassuring hug.

• • • •

Issy felt much better after a night's sleep. After dispensing the goodies—which were met with considerably more enthusiasm than her Victoria sponge had been the day before—she flopped onto her grampa's bed like she needed it more than he did.

"Hello, Gramps."

Her grandfather was wearing his little half-moon reading glasses. They were the same style he had worn when she was a child. She wondered if they were the same actual pair. He was from that generation—the type who didn't change things just because they were tired of them, or they were outdated. You bought something, or married someone, and stuck with it.

"I'm just writing a recipe to my granddaughter in London," he announced. "She needs to know this stuff."

"Great!" said Issy. "Gramps, it's me! I'm here! What is it?"

Joe blinked several times, then his vision cleared and he recognized her. "Issy," he said. "My girl," and she hugged him.

"Don't give me my letter," she said. "You've no idea how much it cheers me up to get them in the post. But I've changed my address again—I'll give it to the nurse."

But Joe insisted on taking it down; he pulled from his bedside cabinet an old battered leather address book that Issy remembered sitting next to their rotary-dial green telephone on the hall table for years and years. She watched as he turned the pages. Page after page was full of names, old addresses crossed out, over and over again; numbers starting short—Sheffield 4439; Lancaster 1133—and becoming longer and more complicated. It was a melancholy document, and her grandfather started to mutter over it too.

"He's gone," he would say. "And them—the both of them. Died within a month of each other. I can't even remember who this is."

And he shook his wispy head.

"Tell me," said Issy quickly to cheer him up, "tell me about my grandmother again."

When she was little she had always loved to hear stories about her glamorous granny but it hurt her mother too much, so her grandfather had waited till it was just the two of them.

"Well," started Joe, and his crumpled face relaxed slightly as he took on the familiar tale. "Well, I was working at the bakery, and she came in one day for a cream horn."

He paused for appreciative laughter, which Issy duly supplied. One of the nurses, passing, popped her head in and stayed to listen.

"And I knew her of course—you knew everyone then. She was the youngest daughter of the farrier, so quite posh, you know. Wouldn't look at a simple flour boy like me."

"Mm-hm."

"But I noticed that she'd started coming in quite a lot. Nearly every day in fact, even though people still had a woman then who would do that for you. And it got so that, well, I'd stick a little extra in her bag maybe. A little bit of jam tart that I happened to have spare or some Bath buns.

"And I began to notice—oh, it was a lovely thing. I mean, in those days, the women were little things of course, not like those big cart-horses who stomp up and down the halls all day and night now," he added fiercely, as Issy shushed him, and the nurse, who was generously proportioned, shook her head and laughed.

"But she started to put a little flesh on—just a little bit, in all the right places, you know, up top, around the derrière. And I thought to meself, that's my cakes that are doing it. She's fattening herself up for me. And that's how I knew that she was interested. If she were after some other fella, she'd have been watching her weight."

He smiled contentedly.

"So I says to her, 'I've got my eye on you.' And she looked back, pert as you like, and said, 'Well, that's just as well, isn't it?' and she sashayed out of that shop like Rita Hayworth. And so that's when I knew. So when I saw her at the Royal Air Forces Association dance on the Saturday night, all dressed up, and me and my friends are hanging around for some of the latest shopgirls, you know, but I saw her with all her smart friends, laughing and standing around with some posh boys, I said to my friends, I'm going to ask her anyway. Normally I would never see her at the dance halls we went to. Oh no. It was a stroke of luck that night. So I went up to her and she said—"

"'I thought you had white hair,'" chorused Issy, who had heard the story a hundred times.

"Then she put out her hand and touched it. I reckon I knew about then."

Issy had seen photos of her grandparents' wedding day. He'd been a handsome man, tall, with a thick head of curly hair and a shy smile. Her grandmother was a knockout.

"And I said, 'What's your name then?' although of course I knew perfectly well. And she said…"

"Isabel," said Issy.

"Isabel," said her grandfather.

● ● ● ●

Issy played with her skirt like a little girl.

"But did you just know?" she asked forcefully. "I mean, did you just know straightaway? That you were going to fall in love and get married and have children and you were going to love her forever and everything was going to be all right? Well, you know, until…"

"We had twenty years together," said Joe, patting Issy's hand. Issy had never known her namesake; she'd died when Issy's mother was fifteen. "They were wonderful, happy years. A lot of people in here, they were married sixty years to someone they couldn't abide. I know people in here who were relieved when their spouses died. Can you imagine?"

Issy didn't say anything. She didn't want to imagine.

"She was a wonderful woman. She always was cheeky, you know. And confident, whereas I was a bit shy. Apart from that one night. I still don't know how I found the courage to go up to her. And yes, I knew straightaway."

He chuckled at the memory. "Took a while to talk her old dad around though. Oh, he was a stickler. He perked up a bit when I opened the third shop, I remember that much."

Joe touched Issy's cheek. "She'd have loved you too."

Issy held his old hand to her face. "Thanks, Gramps."

"Give me a cake then."

Issy raised her eyebrows at the nurse; it wasn't Keavie today. The nurse walked her to the door.

"Where have all the romantics gone these days?" the nurse mused. "It wouldn't be like that now. He'd kiss her then, not ring her the next day. Not your grandfather," she hastened to add. "I mean, a bloke. In general. I don't think a man would ever come up to me in a nightclub and think, right, babe, let's get married and have children. Or if he's going to, he'd better hurry up."

Issy smiled in sympathy.

"Good luck. Would you like another cake?"

"Go on then."

17

Graeme looked at the post and sighed. He didn't even want to open it. He'd been through this before; it was a big envelope, stuffed with leaflets and information. With planning, a big envelope was good. A small one was bad, it meant "no." A big envelope meant, "Please fill in all these forms for the next stage." It meant printed signs to put up on the lampposts around Pear Tree Court. He didn't even have to open it. He just had to do it. He sighed.

A blond head poked around the door. It was Marcus Boekhoorn, the Dutch owner of Kalinga Deniki along with about a hundred other companies, who was over on a tour of his UK bases.

"Our rising star," he said, striding into the office. Marcus did everything quickly. He never stopped moving, like a shark. Graeme jumped up immediately.

"Yes, sir." He was glad he was wearing his tight-fitting Paul Smith suit. Marcus was in great shape, and was rumored to like his lieutenants lean and hungry-looking.

"I like this local project," said Marcus, tapping his teeth with his Montblanc pen. "This is exactly the way I think our business should be going. Local business, local clients, local finance, local builders. Everyone is happy. You understand?"

Graeme nodded.

"You get this right, I think there is a big future for you. Anywhere you would like to go. Local development. It is the new thing. I'm very pleased."

He glanced at Graeme's desk. Even upside down, and in another language, he too recognized the envelope immediately. Not much got past him.

"You have it?" he said joyfully. Graeme tried to forget that he had been putting off opening it.

"Looks like it," he said, trying to seem cool and laid-back.

"That's the business," said Marcus, patting him on the shoulder. "Good for you."

Billy the pushy salesman rushed in after the boss had departed for the heliport in Battersea.

"You're in the good books," he said, not altogether pleased. Kalinga Deniki wasn't a place that encouraged good co-working skills. It was winners and losers in this game.

Graeme felt cross when he looked up and saw Billy standing there, in his flash loafers and gold signet ring, carefully cultivated stubble on his jutting chin.

"Mm," said Graeme, reluctant to reveal anything to this little shit-head who would only use the information to his own advantage.

"It's sweet," mused Billy. "This local stuff. Just as well, you know. You've got to sort out the mortgage with the local bank. The leases up there are a mess, and you're going to have to get your money out of them."

"I know all that," said Graeme, pretending to be nonchalant, even though it was a pain in the arse not to be able to go to the big merchant banks like he usually did.

"Good," said Billy. "It's just, I don't know, seems to me you aren't all that keen on this project. Your heart's not in it. Figured it might be the legwork. So if you need someone else to take it on…I mean, I know you're really overworked."

Graeme narrowed his eyes.

"Keep your sticky fingers off my project please," he said. He'd meant to sound jovial, but it came out sharper than he'd intended.

"Ooh, touchy," said Billy, raising his hands. "Fine, fine. I just didn't want you to bite off anything more than you could chew, that's all."

"Thanks for your concern," said Graeme, staring at Billy stonily until he left the room and closed the door. As soon as he'd done so, Graeme testily threw the envelope at the wall.

18

children's cooking party cupcakes

• • • •

* 10½ tbsp butter, softened
* ⅔ cup superfine sugar
* ¾ cup self-rising flour
* 3 eggs
* 1 tsp vanilla extract
* icing, marshmallows, chocolate buttons, sprinkles, edible stars, orange and lemon jelly slices, food coloring (all colors); edible gold and silver foil, candy footballs, M&Ms, candy flowers, licorice allsorts, ground almonds, toffee and chocolate sauce, jelly worms

Preheat the oven to 355°F/gas mark 4.

Line a 12-cupcake pan with cupcake papers.

Crack the eggs into a cup and beat lightly with a fork.

Place all the ingredients in a large bowl and beat with an electric mixer for two minutes, until light and creamy. Divide the mixture evenly between the cake cases.

Bake for 18 to 20 minutes until risen and firm to the touch. Allow to cool for a few minutes and then transfer to a wire rack. Um, decorate.

A s Issy buried herself in work to deal with her conflicting sense of sadness and relief at breaking up with Graeme, and Graeme tried to figure out a strategy to win back Issy's trust, at least until the deal went through, and Pearl tried to get a straight answer out of Ben about his intentions, and Helena started checking out flats for sale, Austin found himself languishing. He read the proposal again and again. There was no doubt about it: Kalinga Deniki was trying to unravel the complex banking arrangements of the block, take out another loan and rebuild the entire thing. Sod the ironmonger's, the newsagent's. Austin thought back to Issy's birthday present from the funny little man next door. She'd seemed so genuinely pleased, so touched and happy to be accepted into the community. But for what? The duplicity, that was what amazed him. She'd seemed an honest, straightforward, genuine person. And it wasn't until now, when he understood how much she wasn't what he'd hoped, that he realized how much he'd liked the person she'd seemed to be.

● ● ● ●

Louis's birthday finally arrived.

"You are bouncing this morning," observed Pearl, folding up Buzz Lightyear napkins.

"Of course I am," said Issy. "It's beautiful Louis's birthday, isn't it."

"*Is ma birfday*," agreed Louis, who was sitting on the floor making his new Iggle Piggle and Tombliboo (gifts from Issy) kiss each other and bake imaginary cupcakes. "*I likes been five.*"

"You're not—" Issy decided that no one should have their illusions shattered today. "Five is a wonderful age," she agreed. "What I especially like about it is how many cuddles and kisses you give everyone when you're a big boy of five."

Louis realized he was being played but was such a benevolent soul, he didn't mind too much.

"I gives *yooo* kiss and cuddle, Issy."

"Thank you, Louis," said Issy, throwing her arms around him. If Louis were the closest she ever got to having a small person around the place, she had decided, she was going to make the most of it.

"And are you having a birthday party today?"

"Iss. All mah frens is coming to Louis party."

Issy glanced at Pearl, who nodded. "Well, they all said yes," she said, looking faintly surprised.

"Why wouldn't they?" said Issy.

Pearl shrugged. She still felt forced into this. It was one thing asking the kids at playgroup to Issy's safe, well-known cupcake shop, right next to their homes. It would have been a different story altogether if she'd invited them to her home. Then it would have been excuses and murmurs about swimming lessons and long-standing grandparent visits. Being the first kid in the area to get exclusive access to a baking party was one thing. Doing it for Louis was quite another.

"Who else is coming?" asked Issy. She rather liked the idea of becoming a whizz at children's parties.

"My mum," said Pearl. "My pastor. A couple of people from the church."

She didn't add that she'd hardly asked any of her friends. It wasn't that she was ashamed of where she worked, or that Louis was in with a group of new people. A lot of her friends couldn't work anyway; they had more than one child at home, or no help with childcare like she had with her mum. She just didn't want them to think that she was showing off, throwing a big extravagant party for Louis like she didn't think the local Mickey D's was good enough for her child (which she didn't), and she didn't want anyone to imagine she was getting above herself. Louis had to go to school soon, after all. Life where they lived was hard enough.

Most of all, she didn't mention Ben. She couldn't. He had been, though, so sweet. So lovely. She'd seen him so much. She had actually begun to…Well, he was working up this way. Up at the Olympic site. He was earning. Her mother could stay in the council property, but there was nothing to stop them…well, maybe renting a place. Just a little place around here. Not too far from Ben's work, and close enough so that Louis could still go to the same nursery…and then, maybe next year, one of the wonderful schools they had around here, filled with light and art and happy children in smart uniforms. She'd seen them. It didn't feel, to Pearl, in the scheme of things, such a big dream. It was more than she could possibly have envisaged only a year before. And she was terrified of jinxing it. But Ben knew where the party was. And he'd promised to be there.

"Well, it'll be fantastic," said Issy, sorting out the raw ingredients into little bowls. She'd also invested in a dozen tiny aprons, which she'd been sighing and cooing over. Pearl looked at her with narrowed eyes. Something was definitely up.

"*Ish my birfday!*" announced Louis loudly, seeing as no one had mentioned it for at least three minutes.

"Well, is it there, little man?" said Doti, coming through the door. "Just as well I have some cards for you then."

And he opened his bag and revealed half a dozen bright-colored envelopes. The girls and Louis gathered around. Some were addressed just to him, others simply to "the little boy at the Cupcake Café." Pearl squinted.

Issy picked him up. "Have you been telling everyone it's your birthday?" she asked him solemnly.

Louis nodded. "*On Satday. Mah birfday Satday. I say, 'Come to my birfday pahty Satday. Ah have mah birfday pahty in shop!'*"

Pearl and Issy exchanged slightly worried glances.

"But I'm already closing the shop for a dozen toddlers," said Issy.

Pearl put her head next to Louis.

"*Who* did you ask to your birthday, baby?" she asked gently.

"Well, me for one," said Doti. "Thought I'd come by when I've finished my rounds. I have quite the present for you, young man."

"*Yay!*" said Louis, rushing up to the postie and throwing his little arms around his knees. "*Ah do laike presents, Mr. Postman.*"

"Well, that's good."

Doti checked his bag. "Oh, there's another couple here."

"Oh God." Pearl rolled her eyes. "He's invited half the town."

"Are you an irrepressible socialite?" said Issy to Louis, rubbing his nose.

"*I is ipress slite!*" said Louis keenly, nodding his head. Pearl watched the two of them together, meaningfully, until she almost didn't notice the postman leaning over.

"Heavy bag this morning," he said. "Maybe I should have a coffee. And one of your gorgeous cakes."

Pearl gave him her usual amused look.

"What about a green tea?" she said. "I might even come drink it with you. Seeing as you appear to be such a good friend of my son."

The postman's face lit up, and he immediately dropped his bag.

"I would like that," he said, just as an Owl City song came on the radio. It was such a beautiful morning. Pearl and the postman sat down, and Issy spun Louis around in a dance, feeling his little heart close to hers. She hugged him so hard, she nearly squeezed the breath out of him.

"*Hip hip h'ray!*" yelled Louis.

● ● ● ●

"*Bugger* it. Ow. *Ow. Ow.* Darny!" Austin crumpled over onto the floor.

"Well, you didn't stay still," came the small, furious-sounding voice.

"I bloody did," said Austin, pulling his hand away from his face. As he'd expected, there was blood on it. "Back to bears!"

"I am *never* going to become Robin Hood if you won't let me practice," huffed Darny. "And Big Bear said no more arrows."

"Why did Big Bear say that?" said Austin, marching upstairs to the bathroom.

"Um, because it is…so sore," said Darny, his voice trailing off.

"*Exactly!*"

Austin looked at himself in the bathroom mirror—which, he noticed belatedly, was horribly smeared. He had just about enough money to pay a cleaner, but not enough to pay a good one. He sighed and wiped it with a towel. Just as he'd thought, there was a perfect hole in his forehead—not much blood, but deep enough to leave a mark. He groaned. Obviously he shouldn't have let Darny shoot that arrow at him but it was only meant to be a toy, and Darny had been so persuasive…He rubbed the sore spot. Sometimes this parenting lark was a steep learning curve. Dabbing it with tissue, he came back downstairs. There was also a mountain of work mail that he had thrown in his satchel the previous evening before he left the bank. He absolutely had to look at it; it wasn't—as he repeatedly told his overdraft clients—going to go away.

"OK," he said, going back downstairs and opening the sitting room door. An arrow narrowly missed his head. "You can watch that Japanese strobe-y thing you like on TV. I have work to do."

"And we have a party this afternoon," said Darny laconically. Austin looked at him suspiciously. Darny didn't get asked to many parties. Darny had explained to him that it was because he wore cheap sneakers, but had also said he didn't care because cheap sneakers were a stupid reason not to like someone. In fact, they did get invited to a few, but it was no coincidence, Austin quickly realized, that it was all the single mothers who invited him along, whether their kids were boys, girls or sometimes not even in Darny's class. Darny complained about this most vociferously of all and hated "being a pimp," as he called it.

"The problem is," as Mrs. Khan, his form teacher, had put it, "he has an extremely advanced vocabulary for his age. Which is both good and bad."

"Whose party?" asked Austin doubtfully. "Oh, and don't shoot any more arrows in the house."

"You're not the boss of me," said Darny.

"I am, for the thousandth time, the boss of you," said Austin. "Shut up or I won't take you to this party. Whose party?"

"Louis's party," said Darny, firing an arrow into the light fixture. It stuck there. Both Austin and Darny regarded it with interest.

"Hmmm," said Darny.

"I'm not getting it," said Austin. "Who's Louis?"

"The boy in the café," said Darny.

Austin squinted. "What, little Louis? The baby?"

"You're very prejudiced," said Darny. "I would hate to only have friends from my own age range."

"It's his birthday today? And he's invited you to his party?"

"Yes," said Darny. "When you went in with the bank bags."

Austin had popped in the previous week. After Issy's party he had wanted to see her, even if just to make sure things were all right between them and not too embarrassing. Also, even though it was tough to admit it to himself, he missed her. Whenever he went past the now-thriving old men's pub, he remembered her, all sad, or excited, or just generally emotional at breakfast. He liked spending time with her; there was no getting around it. He had liked spending time with her. He supposed that was coming to an end now; she certainly wasn't popping around at breakfast time anymore.

At any rate, when he'd gone to the shop after school one day, she wasn't there, just Pearl and that scary-looking woman with the prominent jawbone, who'd done a funny breathy voice when she was serving him and stared deeply into his eyes, which might have been meant to be sexy or was maybe just hungry, he couldn't tell. And sure enough, Darny and Louis had been on the floor together, playing. Louis had announced that he'd seen a mouse, and Pearl was mortified—apparently they'd had a story about a mouse at nursery, but shouting "Mouse, mouse!" in a catering establishment was frankly bad for business. Darny had shouted, "Mouse, mouse!" the next five times they'd gone out, in every café or fast food restaurant they'd been in, and sure enough, nobody liked it.

"Hmmm," said Austin. Well, it was a beautiful July day, and he didn't really have a plan for them that afternoon.

"We'll have to cut your hair," he said to Darny.

"No way," said Darny, who had to continually flip it back now to see.

Austin sighed. "I'm going to work in the front room, OK? Don't turn the music up too loud."

"Mouse, mouse," said Darny sulkily.

● ● ● ●

Austin was worrying about whether he had time to get Louis a birthday present when he opened the first of the work mail he'd brought home in a rush. He had to stare at it for a couple of minutes before he got his head around it. It was a loan application for a property development initiative marked Kalinga Deniki…all properly filled in, all up to date. He looked at the address. Then he looked at it again. It couldn't be. It couldn't be right. Pear Tree Court. But not one number in it: the whole of it. "A new paradigm in work/life style, conveniently situated in the heart of buzzing Stoke Newington," it said.

Austin shook his head. It sounded horrible. Then he glanced at the name at the bottom of the paper and shut his eyes in dismay. It couldn't be. It couldn't. But there it was. Graeme Denton.

Austin lowered the paper in total shock. Surely not? Surely not Issy's Graeme. But, of course, it was. Graeme. Which meant, as he had clearly seen at the birthday party, Issy and Graeme. Together.

So they must have planned the whole thing. This must be their little scheme. Posh up the area with a little cupcake shop, then cash in on it. It was, he had to admit, very clever. The cachet would certainly add value to the properties. Then the two of them would scarf the profits and move on and do it somewhere else. Unbelievable. He was almost impressed. He glanced at the architect's plans enclosed with the applications. There it was; a great big gate across the entrance to Pear Tree Court. Making it a private road. Blocking off that lovely little courtyard and the tree from everyone else. Austin remembered it just a few weeks ago, with the fairy lights in the tree and Felipe playing his violin. It had seemed such a happy place. He wondered how they'd managed to persuade the ironmonger to move. Well, people as ruthless as that…He supposed they'd stop at nothing.

He couldn't help remembering, though, how eager, how keen Issy had seemed about her business; how hard she'd worked, how convincing she'd been. He'd been completely taken in. She must think he was a fucking idiot.

Austin realized he was pacing the room. This was stupid. Stupid. She was someone who'd needed a bank loan and was well on the way to paying it back, and now they needed another and had good security and backing. It was a simple business proposition, and one that technically he'd support. Graeme's company was a respectable one, and raising money from a local bank rather than a City titan made good practical sense for everyone and would definitely impress the planners.

But he couldn't believe his instincts about Issy had been so far off base. It made him doubt himself completely. She wasn't what he'd thought at all, not a tiny bit of it. Amazing.

● ● ● ●

"OK, so that's Amelia, Celia, Ophelia, Jack 1, Jack 2, Jack 3, Jacob, Joshua 1, Joshua 2, Oliver 1, and Oliver 2," said Issy, counting from her list. "Harry can't come."

"*Harry gaw chin pox,*" said Louis. Pearl rolled her eyes. That meant they'd almost certainly all have it in a week.

"*Get ice cream chin pox,*" Louis told Issy importantly.

"Well, when *you* have chicken pox, you will get frozen yogurt," said Issy, planting a kiss on his head.

"*Iss ogurt,*" said Louis. Outside it was a glorious day, and Issy and Louis had already had a long game of running around the tree. Pearl looked on. Issy had told her everything that had happened. She thought it was for the best. Graeme had seemed such a petulant man. And when children came along, you didn't want two infants to deal with.

She let her thoughts flicker briefly to Ben. But people could change. She was sure of it. Of course they did. Boys grew up. Became men. Did what men were supposed to do. But still, in Issy's case, she thought it was probably for the best.

Pearl set her jaw. And even without Ben—she glanced over at Issy tickling Louis on the tummy—sometimes you took your family where you could get it. Still. She heaved a sigh. That nice scruffy young man from the bank. Yes, he was a little zany, but there was a real man. There was a man who knew how to look after his family.

"OK!" said Issy, spotting the first 4×4 pulling up on Albion Road and a slightly nervous, beautifully groomed young mother emerge, with a spotless child in a button-down shirt and chinos clutching a large gift. Louis dashed out to meet them.

"*Jack! Ayo, Jack!*"

"*Hahyo, Louis!*" hollered Jack. Louis looked at the gift expectantly.

"Give the present to Louis," said the mother briskly. Jack looked at the present. Louis looked at the present.

"Hand it over now, Jack," said the mother, slightly tight-jawed. "Remember this is Louis's birthday."

"*Mah birfday,*" said Jack, burying his head in the present.

"It's not your birthday, Jack," said the mother. "Hand it over please."

"*Mah birfday.*"

"*Iss mah birfday!*" chimed in Louis. Jack's lip wobbled. Issy and Pearl dashed out.

"Hello, hello," said Pearl. "Thank you so much for coming."

"Look what I've got for you," said Issy, leaning down next to Jack and Louis with two tiny aprons. "Do you want to be a top chef and come and make cakes?"

"Going to eat cakes?" said Jack suspiciously.

"Yes we are! We're going to make our own cakes then eat them," said Issy.

Jack reluctantly allowed himself to be taken by the hand, as other children started to arrive behind him. But not just children: Mrs. Hanowitz was there, dressed up in a smart purple hat; then three builders, who'd brought their own children; Mira and Elise, of course; Des, the estate agent, and Jamie; the young students who were meant to be working on their theses but had obviously run off with each other instead; two firemen; and Zac, Helena and Ashok.

"Louis invited you?" said Issy, delighted to see them. Ashok and Helena were entwined in each other's arms.

"He certainly did," said Helena. "We bought him a doctor's kit. It's a real doctor's kit with all the sharp bits taken out."

"I thought the NHS was underfunded," said Issy, turning on the coffee machine. They'd pushed all the tables together so there was a long workbench, and as soon as everyone was here and Oliver had stopped crying in the corner and his mother stopped telling him off for crying in a corner, they were going to start.

• • • •

Graeme had woken up at 5:00 a.m. that morning, sat bolt upright, then lain staring at the ceiling, feeling his heart race. What was he thinking? What had he done? This was a disaster. An absolute disaster.

How had he let Issy break up with him already? She could do whatever she liked once the deal was done.

He canceled his squash game; the idea of having to trade quips with Rob about how sexy or moose-like the girls passing in the gym were seemed just too much to face. Maybe he'd go for a run instead, get it out of his system.

He returned to the flat, sweating—partly from his run, partly from sheer nerves. There was a message in his inbox. It was from the bank where they'd put in for a loan, asking him to go in for a meeting on Monday. Fuck. Fuck fuck fuck, they were going to say yes too. Of course they were. You spend half your life trying to get things done when nothing moves and everyone is bloody slow, then the one thing you don't want to happen gets done in the blink of an eye. Graeme was moving toward the shower when he saw something that made his blood run cold. The bottom of the email…Where did he know that name from?

Austin Tyler.

He shook his head. Fuck. It was that lanky friend of Issy's. The same guy. God, obviously it was meant to be confidential but…he'd been at her birthday party, he'd seen him. If they were mates…If Austin had read the application, he would almost certainly tell Issy about it. He did her banking, didn't he? It would be weird if he didn't ask her about it. And if she found out from someone other than him… Graeme's blood ran cold. She wouldn't like it. Not one little bit. And the consequences for him, for them, for his job, if Issy didn't like it…Graeme showered in double-quick time then threw on the first clothes he came to—very unlike him—and ran to the car.

●　●　●　●

"OK!" said Issy, once everyone finally had a coffee. There were people squeezed against the back walls. It was ridiculous in here. Even Louis's nursery teachers had come, and Issy couldn't believe that after having the children all day for five days the staff would voluntarily come out on a Saturday, but here they were. It was nice when you thought about it. A really lovely nursery. The other mothers had spotted it too and were asking themselves why they hadn't thought to invite the nursery staff. It smacked of favoritism, they sniffed.

Pearl sniffed back in their general direction. Of course it was favoritism. Who wouldn't want her radiant Louis over Oliver, who had now wet his pants and the floor and whose mother was almost as close to hysteria as he was? She looked around. There was one person missing.

"OK," said Issy, and everyone settled down. She even turned down the ear-splitting volume of Louis's favorite party hits tape, which included "Cotton-Eyed Joe" nine times on a loop.

"Now, first of all, has everyone washed their hands?"

"*Ye-es*," chorused the little ones, although the amount of snot on show definitely made it appear as if the cakes would be more than moist enough.

"Well, first we take the flour…"

• • • •

Tosser, thought Graeme to himself, as a white van refused to let him cut in coming over the Westway. This was a totally bloody ridiculous journey right across London every day; nobody in their right mind would commute this. The traffic was horrific, and the sunny weather meant everyone was out on the streets, wandering across pedestrian crossings or hanging about on street corners, cluttering the place up. He was in a hurry, goddammit.

• • • •

"*Austin!*"

"No."

"I want to go to the party!"

"I said no."

"I've been *totally good.*"

"You shot me with an arrow."

"I'm going on my own," said Darny. "You can't stop me. I'm ten."

Darny sat down and started lacing up his shoes. This could take a while, but even so. Austin didn't know what to do if Darny insisted. He'd never physically admonished his younger brother, never, not even once, not even the time Darny had held his wallet over the toilet and emptied it in slowly, card by card, while staring right at him. And it was true: Darny had been behaving absolutely fine, or at least no worse than normal, and didn't deserve punishment. But Austin just didn't want to see Issy right now. He was cross; he felt let down and hoodwinked, even though he realized he had no right to feel that way. She'd never promised him anything. But she had taken a tiny corner of the area he'd grown up in, an area he loved, and she'd made it lovely; put flowers in the square, and a colored canopy over the windows, and pretty little tables. It was a nice place to be, to go; to see other people enjoying some peace and quiet, or a good chat, over a slice of absolutely heavenly cherry pie. And now she was closing up shop; shutting it all off, for the sake of a few measly quid. He was totally not in the mood for a children's party. They weren't going. He was jerked out of his reverie by a slamming door.

● ● ● ●

"Now," said Issy. "This is the tricky part. Could the mummies help with the eggs, please?"

"Nooo!" said a dozen little voices simultaneously. "*Do it self!*" The mothers swapped looks. Issy raised her eyebrows.

"Well, I did bring along lots of extra eggs. How about we get another mummy to help you? All the mummies move one child along."

Sure enough, the toddlers were happy to be helped by someone who wasn't their mother. Issy took note of this and filed it away for future reference. A ray of sun beamed through the windows and lit up a happy tableau: the adults, chatting and making friends around the periphery of the shop, and in a row the little boys and girls, focusing intently on their wooden spoons and mixing bowls. At the top of the table, wearing a special chef's birthday hat, was Louis, banging happily and commenting on everyone else's work—"*Veh good*, Alice, *gooh cake*"—like the café authority, which, Issy supposed, he probably was by now.

Kate's twins were trying to make identical cakes by mixing them at the same time, and Kate was splitting them up and making a mess of them overhead, while saying in a piercing voice, "Of course, we would be baking cakes in our *own* kitchens by now if we didn't have such lazy, useless builders."

"Speak for yourself, love," said the head builder, who had his own three-year-old mixing away like a demon right next to the twins. Seraphina leaned up and gave the little boy a kiss. Kate's mouth fell open. If her eyebrows could have moved they would have shot up. Then Jane came around the boy's other side and leaned up to kiss his cheek.

"*I yuv you too, Ned*," she said, and the builder beamed complacently as Kate pretended to stare out of the window at something new and interesting.

"Achilles darling," came a trilling voice from behind the counter. "Stand up straight! Good posture is the key to good health."

Little Achilles's shoulders went rigid, but he didn't turn around. Issy patted him on the head as she went past. Hermia was standing shyly to one side.

"Hello, darling," said Issy, crouching down. "How's school?"

"She's doing wonderfully!" came Caroline's booming voice. "They're thinking about putting her in the gifted and talented program. And she's doing marvelously on the flute!"

"Really," said Issy. "I was terrible at music. Clever you!"

The little girl beckoned Issy down to her level and whispered in her ear, "I'm terrible too."

"That's OK," said Issy. "There's lots of other things to do. Don't worry about it. Would you like to make a cake too? I bet you'll be good at that."

Hermia smiled gladly and, standing next to Elise, rolled up her sleeves cheerfully.

•   •   •   •

Issy moved on to make sure everyone had something to drink. Deep inside, listening to the clink of cups and the chatter of conversation and the squeaks and snuffles of the children, she suddenly felt a sensation of great peace; of accomplishment; of something created with her bare hands out of nothing. I made this, she thought to herself. Suddenly she felt almost teary with happiness; she wanted to hug Pearl, Helena, everyone who'd helped her make this a reality, given her the privilege of earning money by getting herself covered in flour for a three-year-old's birthday party.

"Very good mixing, everyone," she said, biting her lip. "Very good."

•   •   •   •

Darny burst into the shop, pink in the face, partly from running and partly from crossing the road without waiting for Austin, who was going to go absolutely nuts. Darny was counting on him not wanting to go nuts in front of all the people in here. He might save it for later, but being Austin, he might also forget all about it. It was a risk worth taking.

"Hello, Louis," he announced cheerfully.

"*Dahnee!*" said Louis adoringly, and not pausing to wipe the cake mixture off himself, he threw himself on Darny, covering Darny's already dirty shirt with flour.

"Happy birthday," said Darny. "I brought you my best bow and arrow."

He solemnly handed it over.

"*Yay!*" said Louis. Pearl and Issy exchanged glances.

"I'll just put that somewhere safe," said Pearl, deftly lifting it from Louis's fingers and sticking it on the fruit-tea shelf well out of reach.

"Hello, Darny," said Issy, welcomingly. "Do you want to bake?"

"Yeah, all right," said Darny.

"OK then," said Issy. "Where's your brother?"

Darny stared at the ground.

"Um, he's coming…"

Just as Issy was about to question him further, the doorbell tinged. Austin entered, his face pink.

"*What did I say to you?*"

Theatrically, Darny turned around and indicated the room full of people. At the sound of Austin's raised voice, Oliver curled himself back up into a ball and started to cry again.

"OK, outside," said Austin, looking stressed.

"Oh, can't he stay?" said Issy, without thinking. "We're just doing some baking…"

Austin looked at her. It was almost impossible to believe. Here she was, in a flowery apron, her cheeks pink, her eyes sparkling, with a bunch of rug rats, baking cupcakes. She didn't look anything like an evil property developer. He tore his gaze away.

"I told him he couldn't come," Austin muttered, feeling disgruntled, with everyone's eyes upon him.

"*I vite mah fren Dahnee to mah pahtee,*" came a small voice from down by his knees. Austin glanced down. Oh great, this was all he needed. No one could refuse Louis anything.

"*Is mah birfday. I free, not five!*" said Louis. "*Not five, no,*" he said again wonderingly, as if he couldn't quite believe it himself. Then he added, "*Dahnee give me bown arrs.*"

Austin blinked while he translated this. Then he glanced at Darny in some surprise.

"Did you give him that bow and arrow?" he asked in surprise.

Darny shrugged his shoulders. "He's my friend, innit."

"Don't say innit," said Austin automatically. "Well, well done. Good. That was good."

"Does that mean he can stay?" said Caroline from behind the counter. "Oh good. *Hello*, Austin darling, can I get you anything?"

Darny skipped off to the end of the long tables where Pearl was helping everyone spoon their cake mix into the cupcake baking cases.

"Now you guys are going out to play Ring a Ring o' Roses around the tree," she was explaining, "and when you've finished the games and come in again, the cakes will be ready."

"Yay!" yelled the little ones.

"No thanks," said Austin, then reconsidered. "Yes, get me a latte. Last chance of a decent cup of coffee for a while."

Issy was surprised by how jolted she was when he said this.

"Why?" she said. "Going somewhere?"

Austin stared at her. "No," he said. "You are."

"What do you mean?" said Issy, conscious that down the other end of the table one of the children had dropped their cake mix and Oliver was licking it up like a dog. She felt for Oliver's mother.

She refocused. "You mean, you're not going anywhere?"

That was such a relief. Why did she feel it was such a relief? And why was Austin staring at her like that? It was a strange look, full of curiosity, but also something a little like contempt. She stared back at him. It was odd, she thought, how little she'd noticed him when they first met—beyond seeing how scruffy he was, but she'd rather gotten used to that. Whereas now, when he looked a little fierce, she noticed what she'd missed: he was gorgeous. Not man-in-a-razor-blade-advert gorgeous, like Graeme, all sharp lines, Action Man jaw, and perfectly gelled hair. Gorgeous in an open, honest, kind, smiling way, with a wide forehead, those shrewd gray eyes always narrowed as if thinking of a private joke; the wide, dimpled grin; the tousled, schoolboy hair. Funny how one didn't notice these things always, not at first. Well, there you go. No wonder she wanted—had wanted, she told herself firmly—to kiss him at her party.

"Unbelievable," said Austin, turning around. "Forget the coffee, er…"

"Caroline!" trilled Caroline.

"Yeah, whatever. Darny, I'll be back to pick you up in an hour. Meet me outside."

Darny waved vaguely, as excited as the three-year-olds by the enormous oven Pearl was leading them down to see, with many dire warnings as to what would happen if they so much as wiggled a finger near it.

"That man," breathed Caroline by Issy's left ear as Austin moved toward the door, "is unbelievably hot. Smoking hot."

"*Smoking* hot?" said Issy, cross. "Have you been watching those shows about cougars again? Cougars aren't real, you know."

"I'm not a cougar!" said Caroline, sounding hurt. "I'm a modern woman who knows what she wants. And when it comes down to it, he's still a banker. You know, for introducing at dinner parties."

"Well, you seem to have it all worked out," said Issy absentmindedly, trying to figure out why Austin was so upset. Could it be because he'd seen her with Graeme? Her ego couldn't help being a little excited by the idea; that he actually did like her, that it wasn't just a drunken flirt at a birthday party. But if that was the case, what should she do? She couldn't avoid him forever.

As she was thinking this, the door was pushed open, almost into Austin's face. He had to jump back. Graeme didn't give him as much as a second glance as he stormed into the café.

• • • •

Graeme looked around in consternation. Who were all these people? Normally there was nobody here on a Saturday afternoon. He looked at Issy, who looked horrified to see him. Austin found himself trapped between the door and a crocodile of tiny children in aprons, who were now being shepherded out into the sunshine by Pearl and the postie, en route to playing Ring a Ring o' Roses around the tree. Seeing Issy with children, reminded Graeme of his mission. Then he caught sight of Austin.

"You," he said.

Austin shoved the door closed. "Our meeting's not till Monday," he said quietly.

"What meeting?" said Issy. "What are you talking about?"

Austin turned to Issy. The entire room was watching what was happening intently.

"You know," he said. "The meeting on Monday. When you come to borrow money for the development."

"What development? What the hell are you talking about?"

Austin stared at her for a long time. Issy felt panicky and confused.

"What's going on?"

"You mean you don't know?"

"I *don't* know. Do I have to start throwing cakes at people to get some answers around here?"

Austin looked back at Graeme. This man was even more of an arsehole than he'd taken him for. Unbelievable. He shook his head.

"You haven't told her?"

"Told me *what?*"

There was silence in the café.

"Um," said Graeme, "can we go somewhere quiet and discuss it?"

"Discuss what?" said Issy. She found she was shaking. Graeme looked so strange—both men did. "Tell me here. Tell me now. What is it?"

Graeme rubbed the back of his hair, nervously. It stuck up. It normally did, unless he used quite a lot of taming gel. He didn't know Issy liked it better that way.

"Uh, Issy. Actually, it's great news. For us. We've been granted planning permission to turn Pear Tree Court into apartments!"

"What do you mean, 'us'?" said Issy, her blood running cold. "There's no 'us.'"

"Well, you, me, Kalinga Deniki, you know," said Graeme, hurrying his words. "This whole space is going to be an amazing flagship development for Stoke Newington."

"We don't want a flagship development," said someone at the back. "We want a café."

Issy stepped closer to Graeme. "You mean you were thinking of doing something that involves…closing the café? Without *telling* me?"

"But listen, sweetie," said Graeme, leaning in close and giving her the special crinkle-eyed intense look that always made the temps work extra hours for him. He spoke quietly so the rest of the café couldn't hear, though Austin caught the gist of it. "Listen. I thought you and I could do the deal together. We were so good together, we could be again. We can make a lot of money. Buy a bigger house of our own. And you won't have to get up at six in the morning anymore, or spend all night doing paperwork, or haggling with suppliers, or getting yelled at by that accountancy woman. Huh?"

Issy looked up at him. "But…" she said. "But…"

"You've done such a great job here; it's going to give us real financial independence. Really set us up. Then you can work on something much easier, huh?"

Issy gazed at him, half-disbelieving, half-furious. Not with Graeme—he was a shark; this was what he did. With herself. For staying with him as long as she had; for letting this snake into her life; for stupidly believing that he could change; that the man she had met—sharp, selfish, attractive, not interested in commitment—would suddenly turn into the man she wanted him to be, just by her blindly wishing for it to be so. After all, how would that happen? It didn't make any sense. She was such a total idiot. Such a cretin.

"But you can't!" she said suddenly. "I have a lease! I rent this place."

Graeme looked regretful. "Mr. Barstow...he's more than happy to sell out to us. We've already spoken. You're nearly at the end of your six months."

"And you'd have to get planning—"

"That's already in process. It's not exactly an area of outstanding natural beauty."

"It bloody is!" said Issy. Infuriatingly, she felt tears sparking in her eyes and a huge lump in her throat; outside the window, the children were laughing and playing around their beloved, stumpy, twisty, unbeautiful tree.

"Don't you see?" said Graeme, desperately. "This is for us! I was doing it for us, darling! We could still work it out."

Issy glared at him.

"But...but don't *you* see? I love getting up at six a.m. I love doing the paperwork. I even love that old cow Mrs. Prescott. And why? Because it's mine, that's why. Not yours, not somebody else's, and *not* bloody Kalinga Deniki's."

"It's not yours," said Graeme softly. "It's the bank's."

At this Issy turned to Austin. He held out his hands toward her and was shocked to see the rage in her face.

"You *knew* about this?" she yelled at him. "You knew and you never told me?"

"I thought you knew!" protested Austin, taken aback by her fury. "I thought it was your little plan all along! To tart up this joint then sell it to some dumb financiers!"

At this, something inside Issy cracked. She didn't know how much longer she could dam the flood of tears.

"You thought I would do that?" she said, all anger gone and pure sadness taking its place. "You thought I would do that."

Now it was Austin's turn to feel awful. He should have trusted his instincts after all. He stepped toward her.

"Stay away from me," Issy yelled. "Stay away from me. Both of you. Go. Get out. Get out of here."

Austin and Graeme shot each other a glance of mutual loathing, and Austin hung back to let the shorter man leave first.

"Hang on!" Issy shouted suddenly. "How long…how long have I got?"

Graeme shrugged. Dumpy, blushing Issy, plucked out of the bloody typing pool, for fuck's sake—that she dared to say he wasn't enough for her…bloody cow. How dare she dump him. How dare she get in the way of his plans. He suddenly felt coldly furious that she would cross him like this.

"Planning goes up tomorrow," he said. "You've got a month."

The café went silent, as the oven pinged. Louis's cakes were ready.

● ● ● ●

Pearl looked at the tears flooding down Issy's face and the crowd of concerned well-wishers around her as she ushered the littlies back in and decided it was time for the emergency white wine to be deployed, license or no license. Two of the mums, excited to be caught up in such a drama, sorted out the children's cakes, which they could decorate, as soon as they cooled a little, with blue or pink icing, sprinkles, and tiny silver balls. There were also bowls set out of chopped fruit, sesame seeds, carrot sticks, hummus and Twiglets.

Caroline had managed this side of the catering "as a gift to darling Louis." Louis had given her one of his Hard Stares when he'd seen what was on offer. They were keeping it all to one side.

Pearl and Helena bundled Issy downstairs.

"Are you all right?" said Pearl, worriedly.

"That *snake*," shouted Issy. "I'll kill him. I'll sort him out. We'll establish a fighting fund! We'll start a leafleting campaign! I'll bury him! You'll help, won't you, Helena? You'll get on it with us?"

Issy turned to Helena, who was suddenly looking rather distracted and biting her lip, having left Ashok behind upstairs. Issy explained everything again. She started to cry a little as she did so, particularly at the point where she talked about Austin thinking she'd done it on purpose. Pearl was shaking her head.

"I mean," Issy protested, "they can't do that. They can't just march in here, can they? Can he?"

Pearl shrugged. "Well, it belongs to Mr. Barstow."

"You'll find another property," said Helena.

"Not like this," said Issy, looking around at the immaculate storeroom, the tiny view of the cobbles in the street; her beautiful, perfect oven. "It won't be like this."

"It might be better," said Helena. "Get somewhere bigger. You know you can do it. Maybe it's time to expand. They're queuing out the doors here now."

Issy stuck out her bottom lip. "But I'm happy here. And it's the principle of the thing."

Helena snorted. "Well, it's not like you ever listened to me when I told you what a shit Graeme is."

"I know," said Issy. "I know. Why do I never listen to you?"

"I do not know."

"She doesn't listen to me either," said Pearl. Helena lifted her chin meaningfully.

"And I want to show him," said Issy. "I want to show him that you can't just buy and sell people when it suits you. You can't just tell people to up and leave. Oh," she said, "Lena. Are you sure you're all right with us all living together for a while longer? This could take a bit of unraveling."

"Actually," said Helena, looking uncharacteristically nervous, "no, I think we really are going to have to move."

"Why?"

Helena seemed nervous and excited and full of anticipation, and she glanced up the stairwell for Ashok.

"Well," she began, "it's been a bit quicker than we'd have planned, but…"

Issy stared at her, completely confused. Pearl was delighted and guessed immediately.

"A baby!"

Helena nodded, looking demure for the first time in her life. It was going to take some getting used to, she thought.

Issy summoned up every reserve of courage, every tiny brave part of her. She almost made it. Her lips almost made it into the smile she so wanted to give, that Helena so deserved. But at the very end, her strength deserted her. Her throat clogged up and her eyes stung.

"Con—" she stuttered. Then, suddenly, she was in floods of tears. She had nothing, and Helena had everything. It felt so hard, so unfair.

"Oh, Issy…what? I'm so sorry, I thought you'd be pleased," said Helena, dashing to her friend. "Oh, darling. Sorry. We'll need to find a new place, of course, but you won't be on your own…It was an accident but we're both delighted, but…"

"Oh, dear Lena," said Issy, "you know, I am absolutely thrilled for you." And the girls hugged again.

"Course you are," said Helena. "You're going to be the best god-mother ever. Teach it to bake."

"You'll be able to deliver the baby yourselves!" said Issy. "Oh God, someone get me a tissue."

A mum appeared at the top of the stairs.

"Um, shall we sing 'Happy Birthday'?"

"My baby!" said Pearl. "I'm coming, I'm coming."

As Issy emerged from the cellar to join in a rousing chorus for

Louis, who beamed, then looked at his three candles and said, "*Wan faive candles,*" and Pearl shone with pride at her little boy, only three and he knew how to count, she was surrounded by a sea of people, commiserating about the shop, offering support and threatening to write to planning, or host a sit-in, or boycott the estate agents. (Issy wasn't sure how helpful that one would be.) It was overwhelming.

"Thanks, everyone," Pearl said finally, addressing the room. "We will—well, we don't know what we can do but we will try everything, I promise, to keep the café open. And now, let's enjoy Louis's party!"

And she turned up the music again and watched the children dance around, sticky oblivious faces filled with happiness, Louis at the center of it all. She didn't want this to go either. This wasn't just a job. This was their lives now. She needed it.

● ● ● ●

It was utter torture for Issy to last until the final child had been sent home with a bouncing ball and an extra piece of cake in a bag; to politely wave good-bye to clients and friends and thank them for their concern; to collect the debris and clean up the mess; to pack away all of Caroline's uneaten snacks for Berlioz. She scarcely knew how to endure it. But what had to come next was worse. Pearl saw her face.

"Must you go now?" she asked Issy. "Darling, it isn't going to change if you pick your stuff up later."

"No," said Issy. She felt like she had a huge hole in her stomach, tangled up and cramped and filled with anxiety. "No. If I leave it at Graeme's, I'll just have it in front of me to dread. I'll have to do it fast. Just get in. There's hardly anything there anyway. He was always a bit tight with cupboard space. Needed a lot of room for his hair gel."

"That's the spirit," said Pearl. They looked at Louis, who was happily exploring his presents on the floor.

"You know," said Pearl, "I wouldn't change a thing about my life, not a tiny little thing. But sometimes…well, I would say it is probably easier breaking up before. Rather than after. If you know what I mean."

Issy nodded her head slowly.

"But Pearl…I'm thirty-two. Thirty-two. What if that was my last chance to have a baby? If I have to go and work somewhere else now…how will I ever meet anyone? If I'm stuck in someone's back kitchen, working for a chain…I can't build it up again, Pearl. I can't. This place took everything I have."

"Course you can," Pearl urged her. "You've done all the hard stuff. Made all the mistakes. The next one will be a breeze. And thirty-two is nothing these days. Of course you'll meet someone. What about that handsome banking adviser? I reckon he'd be a far better fit for you."

"Austin?" Issy's face tightened suddenly. "That I can't believe. I can't believe he thought I was behind all this, that I'd sell out in five minutes. I thought he liked me."

"He does like you," said Pearl. "There you go. Of course you'll meet someone. I know things seem a *little* bleak now…"

They looked at each other. Then, stupidly, they both started to laugh. Issy got a little hysterical, tears standing in her eyes.

"Yes," she gasped when she could catch her breath. "You could say a little bleak."

"Oh, you know what I mean," protested Pearl.

"Yes, just a *bit* of a bad day."

Pearl laughed more. "There have been better days."

"Yes," said Issy. "My last cervical smear was more fun than this."

Louis wobbled up to them, wanting to know what all the laughter was about. Issy looked at him ruefully.

"Hello, pumpkin."

Louis stretched his hands out to his mother.

"*Best birfday*," he said proudly. "*Louis best birfday.*" Then he went a little quieter. "Weah Daddy, Mummy?"

Ben, in the end, hadn't shown. Pearl's face was completely impassive.

• • • •

Graeme's flat had no windows facing the street, so Issy had no way of knowing whether he was in or not, short of ringing the intercom, and she had no intention of talking to him unless it was absolutely necessary. She swallowed hard, unwilling to get out of the taxi.

"All right, love?" asked the cabbie, and she nearly confided in him there and then, but stepped out nonetheless. The heat had mostly gone out of the day, but it was mild enough for just a cardigan.

"Yes," she said, reflecting that this was the last time she would ever get out here. Surely he'd have gone out. It was Saturday night after all. He'd be out with his mates, having a few beers, trying to score someone new in a nightclub, probably. Laughing it off, talking about being free at last, and how much money he was going to make with this new deal. She swallowed hard. He didn't give a shit about her. He never had. It had always been about the money for him, always. He'd strung her along like an idiot, and she'd fallen for it completely.

She was so convinced he would be having a wonderful time in a cocktail bar, seducing a blond right at that very minute, that Issy wasn't at all expecting to see Graeme when she entered the dimly lit hallway. In fact, she nearly missed him. He was sitting in his fake Le Corbusier armchair, in his dressing gown—Issy hadn't known he owned a dressing gown—glass in hand, staring out of the window at the minimalist courtyard garden nobody ever visited. He started when she entered, but didn't turn his head. Issy stood there. Her heart was thumping painfully.

"I'm here to get my stuff," she announced loudly. After the hubbub of the day, the flat was deathly quiet. Graeme clutched at his glass. Even now, Issy realized inside, she was waiting for a sign…for something that would show he had been fond of her, that what they'd had had meant something, that she had pleased him. Something more than just being that girl from the office who happened to be handy. Someone to use, to get what he wanted.

"Whatever," said Graeme, not looking at her.

Issy packed up her bits and pieces into a small suitcase. There wasn't much. Graeme didn't move a muscle the entire time. Then she marched into the kitchen, which she'd stocked up with supplies. She took one cup of flour, five eggs, an entire tin of treacle, and a small sachet of sprinkles and whipped them up with a wooden spoon.

Then she brought the whole lot into the living room and, with a practiced flick of the wrist, poured it all over Graeme's head.

• • • •

Her flat felt different. Issy couldn't put her finger on it. It was the sense not just of someone new living there that she'd had for a couple of weeks—Ashok was interesting, serious, and entirely charming—but of a shifting dynamic. They had piles of estate agents' details and a copy of *What to Expect When You're Expecting*.

It felt like the entire world was moving on, except for Issy. And she felt less comfortable striding into her pink kitchen and collapsing on the huge squishy settee—like a stranger in her own home. Which was ridiculous, she knew. But more than anything else it was the shame of her first, her only experiment in cohabitation ending so quickly and so badly.

Helena knew that pointing out Graeme had always been a wrong'un wasn't particularly useful but being there probably was, so she did her best to do that instead, even if she tended to fall asleep every five minutes.

"What are you going to do?" she asked, ever practical. Issy sat, staring unseeingly at the television.

"Well, I'm going to open up on Monday morning…After that, I'm not so sure."

"You've done it once," said Helena. "You can do it again."

"I'm just so tired," said Issy. "So tired."

Helena put her to bed, where Issy thought she wouldn't be able to get to sleep at all. In fact, she slept halfway through Sunday. The sun pricking through her curtains made her feel a tiny bit more optimistic. Just a little bit.

"I can try and get a baking job," she said. "The problem is, the hours are even worse than what I have now, *and* there's a million brilliant pâtissiers in London, *and*—"

"Hush," said Helena.

"Maybe everyone else was right all along," said Issy. "Maybe I should have become a podiatrist."

• • • •

On Monday morning, she picked up an envelope off the mat. Yes, there it was. A notice to quit once her lease was up, from Mr. Barstow. Tied with white cord to lampposts around the court were plastic laminates with the outlines of the planning application. Issy could hardly bear to give them a second glance. She started off the day's baking on autopilot, making her first cup of coffee; going through the motions of normality in the hopes that it would quell her rising panic. It would be fine. She'd find something. She'd speak to Des, he'd know. In her confusion, she called him before realizing it was still only just after seven in the morning. He answered immediately.

"Oh, sorry," said Issy.

"It's all right," said Des. "Teeth. I've been up for hours."

"Oh dear," said Issy. "Have you called a dentist?"

"Um, Jamie's teeth. More."

"Yes, yes, of course." Issy shook her head. "Um…"

"I'm sorry," said Des instantly. "I'm sorry. Did you call me up to yell at me?"

"What about?" said Issy.

"About we might have to handle the apartment sales. Sorry. It wasn't my decision, it's just…"

Issy hadn't even thought about this, she was only calling to ask about vacant properties. But of course.

"…business," she said dully.

"Yes," said Des. "I thought you knew."

"No," said Issy, dully. "I didn't."

"I'm sorry," said Des, and it sounded like he truly meant it. "Are you looking for another property? Would you like me to ring around a few people? I'll ring around everyone, OK? Try and find something just right for you, OK? It's the least I can do. It's just, often these speculative things don't come to anything…I didn't want to freak you out unnecessarily. I really am sorry."

Jamie started to wail into the phone.

"Jamie is sorry too."

"It's OK," said Issy. "You can stop apologizing now, it wasn't your fault. And yes, if you see anything…yes please."

"OK," said Des. "OK. Sorry. Right. Yes."

He was still apologizing as Issy hung up the phone.

● ● ● ●

Pearl was looking gloomy. "Cheer up," said Caroline. "Something will come along."

"It's not that," said Pearl. Ben hadn't returned for two days. He'd been out with his friends, and one thing had led to another and he was having a good time, and he didn't see what the big deal was, Louis was going to have loads of birthdays and he'd bought him a present (in fact a huge racing-car track that wouldn't fit in the apartment). Pearl had heard him out then closed the door in his face.

"I can't believe he would miss his kid's birthday," she explained to Caroline, who harrumphed.

"That's nothing," she said. "My ex didn't make a single birthday, carol concert, school play, sports day…not a single one. 'Working,'" she sniffed. "My bum."

"Well, exactly," said Pearl. "That's why he's your ex."

"That's not why he's my ex," said Caroline. "None of the dads here do that stuff. They're too busy working to pay for the big swanky houses. None of the kids knows what their dad looks like. I dumped him for sleeping with that gruesome tart. Showed he had absolutely the worst taste imaginable. Ha, if you dumped a man for neglecting his children…"

The door pinged. It was the builder, the one who'd brought his son to Louis's party.

"Cheer up, love," he said, his traditional greeting.

Caroline gave him an appraising look, up and down, noting his nicely honed pecs, cheeky grin and clear lack of a wedding ring.

"You *do* cheer me up," she said, and leaned right over the front counter, which would have exposed her cleavage, had she had any. "Bit of cheering up once a day…I do like it."

"Posh birds," said the builder under his breath, then smiled happily. "Give us a bit of froth, love."

Pearl rolled her eyes.

But on reflection, there had been lots of nannies and some dressed-up mummies at the party, and Austin of course, but no dads, not really. She sighed.

"Has he embarrassingly slept with any of your friends?" asked Caroline, when the builder had left with a wink and a telephone number.

"Not yet," admitted Pearl.

"Well, there you go," said Caroline. "I wouldn't give up on him right away." She brandished a letter. "You won't believe what I got this morning."

"What?"

"From his lawyers. Apparently if I could have guaranteed my employment here, he'd have kept me in the house, local enough not to need a nanny to pick up the kids." Caroline shook her head. "But now I'm back to square one. No job, but I've proved I can work, so I have to. So I'll have to move. God. No wonder I need a bit of flirting in my life."

She sighed.

"Hmmm," growled Pearl, going back to her sheets of paper.

"What are you doing?" Issy asked her, coming up the stairs.

"I'm writing to the planning commission of course."

"Oh," said Issy.

"Don't you think that's a good idea?"

"Unlikely. Plus, I know Kalinga Deniki. They never move with this kind of thing unless they know they've already got it in the bag."

"OK, well, do nothing then," said Pearl, going back to writing. It was the quiet part of the morning, after the morning rush but before the midmorning mummies.

Issy stared out of the window some more and heaved a sigh.

"And stop that sighing, it's doing my head in."

"OK, as opposed to you snorting every five minutes?"

"I do *not* snort."

Issy raised her eyebrows, but took her coffee cup and went out into the courtyard, regarding the shop critically. Since the warm weather had arrived, they'd done some upgrading. Now they had a pink-and-white-striped awning, which looked fresh and pretty in the sunlight, and matched Gramps's tables and chairs. In the sunshine, the shade of the awning looked incredibly inviting, the key ring glinted in the sun, and the plants Pearl had set either side of the door only added to the effect. She blinked away tears. She couldn't cry anymore. But neither could she imagine creating her little oasis anywhere else; this was her corner of the world; her little kingdom. And it would be closed up again, and chopped to bits, and turned into some lame garage for stupid overpriced executive apartments...

Issy meandered up to the ironmonger's shop. What was he doing about all this? Had they got rid of him too, or would he somehow escape the bullet? She didn't even know if Mr. Barstow was his landlord.

The metal grille was still closed, at 10:00 a.m. Issy screwed up her face and tried to peer through. What was in there? There were little holes in the grille, although the bright sunshine stopped her from seeing much. She kept focusing in. As her eyes adjusted, she started to make out shadowy shapes on the other side of the glass. Suddenly a pale shape moved.

Issy let out a yelp and jumped back from the grille. With a deafening noise, it began to open automatically. Someone must be inside—someone, presumably, whom she'd already seen. She swallowed hard.

After the grille was wound up fully, the door was opened from within, out toward her. The ironmonger was there. Wearing pajamas. Issy was struck dumb. It took her a second to collect herself.

"You...you live here?" she said in amazement. Chester nodded his head in that formal way of his. He bade her enter.

For the first time, Issy went into the shop. And what she saw took her aback completely. At the front were pots and pans, mops and screwdrivers. But in the back of the shop was an exquisite Persian carpet, and laid out on it, a carved wooden Balinese double bed; a small bedside table piled high with books and a Tiffany lamp; a large mirrored armoire. Issy blinked twice.

"Oh my," she said, then again, "You...you live here."

Chester looked embarrassed. "Um, yes. Yes I do. Normally I have a little curtain to hang during the day...or I shut the shop whenever it looks like anyone is coming in to buy something. Coffee?"

Through the back Issy saw a small, immaculate galley kitchen. An expensive Gaggia coffee pot was bubbling away on top of the stove. It smelled wonderful.

"Um, yes," said Issy, although she had already had far too much caffeine that morning. But this little Aladdin's cave felt completely unreal. The man directed her to a floral-upholstered armchair.

"Please, sit down. You've made my life very difficult, you know."

Issy shook her head. "But I've been passing by this alleyway for years, and this shop has always been here."

"Oh yes," said the man. "Oh yes. I've been here for twenty-nine years."

"You've lived here for twenty-nine years?"

"Nobody's ever bothered me before," said the man. "That's the beauty of London."

As he spoke, Issy noticed his accent again.

"No one knows your business. I like it like that. Until you came of course. In and out, leaving me cakes, wanting to ask me things. And customers! You're the first person ever to bring people into the alley."

"And now…"

"Now we have to go, yes." The man looked at the notice to quit in his hand. "Ah, it would have happened eventually. How's your gramps?"

"Actually, I was going to go and ask him."

"Oh good, is he up to having a conversation?"

"Not really," said Issy. "But it makes me feel better. I know that's selfish."

Chester shook his head. "It's not, you know."

"I'm so sorry," said Issy. "I brought the developers here. I didn't mean to, but I did."

Chester shook his head.

"No, you didn't," he said. "Stoke Newington…you know, it used to be considered half a day's ride from London. A lovely village, nice and far out of town. And even when I arrived, it was always a bit raffish and run down, but you could do what you wanted here. Have things your way. Be a bit different, a little off the beaten track."

Chester served up the coffee with cream in two exquisitely tiny china cups and saucers.

"But things get sanitized, gentrified. Especially places with character, like around here. There's not much of old London left really."

Issy cast her eyes down.

"Don't be sad, girl. There's lots good about new London too. You'll go places, look at you."

"I don't know where though."

"Hmmm, that makes two of us."

"Hang on, are you squatting?" said Issy. "Can't you just claim residency?"

"No," said Chester. "I think I have a lease…somewhere."

They sat there sipping their coffee.

"There must be something I can do," said Issy.

"Can't stop progress," said Chester, setting down his coffee spoon with a light tinkle. "Believe me, I should know."

● ● ● ●

Austin was early for once. And smartly dressed, or as smart as he could manage while not letting Darny get a glimpse of where he kept the iron. He ran his hands through his thick hair nervously. He couldn't believe he was doing this. He could risk everything. And for what? Some stupid business that would probably move anyway. Some girl who wouldn't look at him.

Janet was there of course, bright and efficient as ever. She'd been at the birthday party too, and she knew what was on his schedule. She glanced at him.

"It's horrible," she said, with unusual ferocity. "It's horrible what that man wants to do."

Austin looked at her.

"To that nice girl and that lovely shop and to turn it into more

featureless rubbish for more stupid executives, it's horrible. That's all
I want to say."

Austin's mouth twitched.

"Thank you, Janet. That's helpful."

"And you look nice."

"You're not my mum, Janet."

"You should call that girl."

"I'm not going to call her," said Austin. Issy wouldn't touch him with
a bargepole now, and he supposed, with a sigh, that she had good reason.

"You should."

Austin reflected on it, drinking the coffee Janet had gone all the
way down to the Cupcake Café to get for him. It was cold, but he
fancied he could still smell the sweet essence of Issy clinging to it
somewhere. Checking no one could see into his office, he inhaled it
deeply, and very briefly closed his eyes.

Janet knocked.

"He's here," she said, then led Graeme in with an uncustomary
frostiness of manner.

• • • •

Graeme didn't notice. He just wanted to get this over and done with.
Stupid local microfinancing, he hated local banking and piddling
mortgage snarl-ups more than any other part of his business.

Fine. Well, he needed to rubber-stamp this money, call Mr.
Boekhoorn and get the hell out of it. Maybe take a holiday. A lads'
holiday, that's what he needed. His mates hadn't been very sympathetic when he told them he was single again. In fact a lot of them
seemed to be settling down and getting all boring and cozy with their
girlfriends. Well, fuck that. He needed somewhere with cocktails and
girls in bikinis who could respect a guy in business.

"Hey," he said, scowling, as he shook Austin's hand.

"Hi," said Austin.

"Shall we keep this short?" said Graeme. "You hold the existing mortgages on the extant properties, and we need to combine them so you can give me a new rate on the amalgamated loan. Let's see what you can do, shall we?"

He scanned through the documents quickly. Austin sat back and took a big sigh. Well, here went absolutely nothing. It would probably ruin his career if his bosses took a proper look at it. It shouldn't really matter to him one way or another whether his corner of the world got more and more corporate and homogeneous and white bread. But it did. It did. He liked Darny having lots of different friends, not just ones called Felix. He liked being able to buy cupcakes—or falafel, or hummus, or mithai, or bagels—whenever he felt like it. He liked the mixture of hookah cafes, and African hair-product shops, and wooden toy emporiums and diesel fumes that made up his neck of the woods. He didn't want to be taken over by the stuffed shirts, the quick bucks, the Graemes of this world.

And, more than anything, he couldn't get out of his head the image of Issy's face, sparkling and flushed and joyous in the fairy lights. When he'd thought she was one of them, out for herself and anything she could get, it had upset him so much. Now he knew that she felt the same as him, that she believed in the same things he did...now he had finally realized that mixing business with pleasure was exactly what he wanted to do, he found it was all too late.

Ah, fuck it, thought Austin to himself. There was one thing he could do for her. He leaned over his desk.

"I'm sorry, Mr. Denton," he said, trying not to sound too pompous. "We have a local community investment guidance program" (they did, although no one from the bank ever read it), "and I'm afraid your scheme goes against that. I'm afraid we won't be able to unbundle the mortgages."

Graeme looked at him as if he couldn't believe what he'd just heard.

"But we've got planning," he said sullenly. "So it obviously is in the interests of the community."

"The bank doesn't think so," said Austin, mentally crossing his fingers and hoping the bank never got to hear of him turning down an absolutely sound investment. "I'm sorry. We're going to continue to hold on to the mortgages as they stand."

Graeme stared at him for a long time.

"What the hell is this?" he burst out suddenly. "Are you just trying to screw with me? Got the hots for my girlfriend or something?"

Austin tried to look as if he'd never heard of such a thing.

"Not at all," he said, as if offended. "It's just bank policy, that's all. I'm sorry, you must understand. In the current financial climate…"

Graeme leaned over. "Do. Not," he enunciated very slowly, "Tell. Me. About. The current financial climate."

"Of course, sir," said Austin. There was a silence. Austin didn't want to break it. Graeme lifted up his hands.

"So you're telling me I'm not going to get this loan here."

"That's right, sir."

"That I'd have to bring in another bank and pay them commission to take on and untangle all your stupid loans which have probably been packaged in with some bunch of junk and sold up some untraceable river somewhere?"

"Yup."

Graeme stood up.

"This is bullshit. *Bullshit.*"

"Also, I've heard there's actually quite a lot of late opposition to the planning. Enough that might even make them go back on their decision."

"They can't do that."

"Planning officers can do whatever they like."

Graeme was turning pink with fury.

"I'll get the money, you know. You'll see. Then you'll look the fricking idiot in front of your bosses."

Austin reflected that he did already, and was surprised to find he wasn't too concerned. Maybe it didn't always matter what your bosses thought, he figured. He wondered who had taught him that.

Graeme eyed Austin one more time before he left.

"She'd never go for you, you know," he sneered. "You're not her type."

Well, neither are you, thought Austin mildly, as he filed the paperwork in the bin. But he felt a tugging sadness in his heart.

There was no time for that, however. He grabbed the phone and dialed the number he had in front of him on the desk. He sent his instructions through as soon as he was connected. A chorus of swearing reached him from the other end. Then a pause, and a sigh, and a barked command that he had fifteen minutes to stop arsing around and go back to spending time on serious businesses.

Then he had to make the other call. He used the bank phone to call Issy's mobile. She'd have to pick up now. Fingers crossed.

His heart racing, he tapped in the numbers...numbers he realized he'd actually memorized. What an idiot he was. Issy picked up straightaway.

"Hello?" she said, her voice sounding unsure and nervous.

"Issy!" said Austin, his voice coming out rather strangulated. "Um, don't hang up, please. Look, I know you're angry and stuff, and I know, and I think I rather slightly fucked that up, but I think...I think I might be able to do something. For the café, I mean, not you. Obviously. But I think...argh. I don't have time for this. Listen. You have to go out onto the street right now."

"But I can't," said Issy, panic in her voice.

●　●　●　●

She had hardly recognized the old man on the bed; he was a wraith. Her beloved grandfather; so strong, his huge hands pushing and kneading and molding great lumps of dough; so delicate when shaping a sugar rose, or intricate when cutting a long line of Battenberg.

He had been, truly, mother and father to her; always there when she needed him; a safe haven.

Yet now, at her lowest ebb, when Issy felt her dreams about to slip through her fingers, he was powerless. As he lay on the bed while she told him her story, his eyes had widened, and Issy felt a terrifying clutch of guilt around her heart as he tried to sit up.

"No, Gramps, don't," she'd insisted, in anguish. "Please. Please don't. It's going to be fine."

"You can do it, sweetheart," her gramps was saying, but his breathing was ragged and labored, his eyes rheumy and bloodshot, his face an awful gray.

"Please, Gramps." Issy rang the bell for the nurse, holding on to her grandfather with all her might, trying to calm him down. Keavie came in, took one look at him, and her normally stolid face grew intent and she immediately called for backup; two men came in with an oxygen cylinder and struggled to get a mask over his face.

"I'm so sorry, I'm so sorry," Issy was saying, as they worked on without her. That was when her mobile rang, and Keavie ushered her outside while they fought to stabilize him.

● ● ● ●

Issy went back into the room after Austin had hung up, terror clawing at her, but Gramps was there, with the mask on, his breathing much quieter.

"I'm so sorry," said Issy in a rush. "I'm so, so sorry."

"Hush," said Keavie. "It wasn't you. He's been having these episodes."

She held Issy's arm very tightly and pulled her around until they were face to face.

"You have to realize, Issy," she said, speaking kindly but firmly. It was a voice Issy had heard Helena using when she had to pass on bad news. "This is normal. This is part of the process."

Issy stifled a sob, then went and held Gramps's hand. The color had come back to his cheeks and he was able to take his mask off.

"Who was that on the phone? Was it your mother?"

"Uh no," said Issy. "It was…it was the bank. They think they know a way to save the café, but it had to be done right then and there, and I'm sure they missed it…"

Issy felt her grandfather's pressure on her hand grow extremely strong.

"You go!" he said, sternly. "You go and save that café right now! Right now! I mean it, Isabel! You go and you fight for your business."

"I'm not leaving you," said Issy.

"You bloody are," said Grampa Joe. "Keavie, you tell her."

And he let go of her hand and turned his face to the wall.

"Go!"

"Will it really save your café?" said Keavie. "With all those lovely cakes?"

Issy shrugged. "I don't know. It's probably too late."

"*Go!*" said Keavie. "*Go!*"

● ● ● ●

Issy tore down the road to the station, and for once, just for once, the world and London Transport were on her side, and the stopping train that would let her out at Blackhorse Road was right there waiting for her. She flung herself on board and phoned Austin.

"I'm stalling it," said Austin grimly, not wanting to let on how much danger he'd just put himself in. "Be as quick as you can."

"I'm doing that."

"How's…how's your grampa?"

"Well, he's well enough to be cross with me," said Issy.

"That's something," said Austin.

"We're coming into the station."

"Run like the wind! Whatever he offers you, take it! One year, two years, whatever it is!"

Issy raced the beautiful new shiny double-deckers sidling down Albion Road. Linda was in one, she saw, sitting on the top deck. She waved, and Linda waved back excitedly. Then, right in front of her, a huge black car drew to a halt. She glanced at it. Could this be what Austin meant? The tinted windows made it impossible to see in, but very slowly the back window came down. Issy bent over, squinting in the bright sunlight.

"You! Girl with the cakes! Give me a cake!" came a gruff voice. Issy automatically passed over the powdered honey-blossom she found she still had in her hand. Mr. Barstow took it in his fat paw, and for a few seconds all she could hear was contented chewing. Then he looked out at her, wearing large black sunglasses.

"I hear the developers are having some trouble getting the money," he said. "Well, I can't be buggered with that. Give me my money. Here. Sign."

He passed her over a contract. It was an increase in rent—but not an impossible one. And it was an increase in the lease, to eighteen months. Eighteen months! Her heart leaped. It wouldn't make it hers, but it would be enough time, surely, to get on more of a secure footing. And if they did well...perhaps, at the end of eighteen months, even she might be happy to look for bigger premises. Unless...

"Stay here," she said, then dashed across the courtyard and pounded on the ironmonger's door. She dragged him over to the car.

"Him too," she said, pushing him up front. "I'll sign for him too. Or he can sign for me."

Mr. Barstow sighed and lit a cigarette.

"I can't stay here," protested Chester. "It's over for me."

"No," said Issy. "Don't you see? I can take over the ironmonger's too. We need room to expand, look." She gestured at The Cupcake Café, a queue spilling out into the warm square full of hungry, laughing customers, all anxious to stock up on Issy's sweet treats in case they got taken away.

"I've already had four more bookings for children's parties. If we take both…" She lowered her voice. "I suspect we'd need a night watchman. Seeing as we haven't got a security gate. Someone who could keep an eye on the premises at night. Of course, it wouldn't pay very well…"

Chester scribbled on the paperwork excitedly. And ten seconds later, they were standing on the pavement, watching the sleek black car pull away into the thickening traffic, staring at each other in disbelief.

"No more hiding," said Issy. "How about that?"

"Your granddad was right about you," said the old man.

• • • •

"*Eek!*" screamed Issy suddenly, as she realized what had just happened. She ran into the café. "Pearl! We're safe! We're safe!"

Pearl's eyes widened. "What do you mean?"

Issy brandished the contracts. "We've got an extension! Graeme didn't get his loan."

Pearl stopped what she was doing, her mouth hanging open in disbelief.

"You are joking."

Issy shook her head. "Eighteen months. We've got eighteen months."

Pearl had worked so hard to keep from Issy how much this job had meant to her. How hard it would be to find something else; how loath she was to pull Louis out of that nursery where he was so happy—and even, she reluctantly admitted, popular. The worry and the expectation of disaster had built up in her for so long that she simply sat down on the stool behind the counter and burst into tears.

"And," said Issy, "we're going to expand! We're going to take on the ironmonger's! You're going to head up the other part of the Cupcake

Café, where we make special gifts and do catering and all that. Bit of a promotion."

Pearl wiped her eyes with one of the candy-striped tea towels.

"I can't believe I've got so attached to a stupid job," she said, shaking her head. Issy looked around at the slightly confused-looking customers. Caroline stepped forward.

"I knew you'd do it," she said. "And I can stay! I can stay! Thank *God*, I don't know how I'd have coped with only three bathrooms. Thank *Christ*."

The three women hugged. Issy finally looked up.

"Sorry, everyone," she said. "We thought we were going to have to close. But I've just found out we don't."

There were smiles of pleasure up and down the queue.

"So, I think this means...I've always wanted to say this..." said Issy, taking a deep breath, with Pearl and Caroline's arms around her—

"Cupcakes on the house!!"

• • • •

It was almost worth it, Austin thought, for the admiration on Janet's face alone. Almost.

"I've seen him off for now," he said. "Won't last of course. He'll just regroup elsewhere and come back stronger than ever. That's how cockroaches work."

"You did a good thing," said Janet. She frowned. "Give me the paperwork. I'll try and smooth it with the bosses. And now go and make five hundred really amazing investments to distract their attention."

"Not right now," said Austin. "I am full of adrenalin and manliness. I'm going to get Darny out from school for lunch and we are going to the park to do roaring."

"I'll tell that to your twelve o'clock, shall I?" said Janet affectionately.

"Yes please," said Austin.

● ● ● ●

He'd been surprised Issy hadn't rung him back, but then, well, maybe not really. She was just out of a relationship and had had a narrow escape with her business, and was probably celebrating in the café or figuring things out or…well, she'd made it quite clear she wanted nothing to do with him. So. Well. Never mind. He bought sandwiches and crisps from the corner shop and popped his head into the school to pick up his boy.

Sometimes, he thought, all the aggro, all the yelling, the persuading, the restrictions to his social life and his sex life; the ongoing ruination of his plans…sometimes, all of it was vindicated by the delighted face of a ten-year-old boy when he sees his big brother surprising him with lunch in the park. Darny's smile reached his sticky-out ears.

"*Auuustiiin!*"

"Come on then, you mucker. Your big brother, by the way, is a total hero."

"Are you a goodie?"

"Yes."

"Mr. Tyler, can I have a word?" said the head teacher as he was leaving.

"Not quite at the moment," said Austin. "Soon?"

Kirsty watched him as he left the school. She had decided, when she'd seen him, to take her courage in both hands, ask him out once and for all. But he seemed so edgy and distracted and she reckoned it had better wait until afterward.

"After lunch?" she said.

"Sure," said Austin, noticing that as well as being a teacher, she was actually rather attractive. Maybe it was time to look for a nice woman who liked him, and didn't go out with dickwads. Maybe, if he was never going to get the woman he really wanted, he could start dating again. One day. Maybe.

"*But now* we have some lions to kill. By stabbing them in the heart, then we'll take out the heart, then we'll burn the heart on a fire, then we'll eat the—"

"Out, Darny. Out." Kirsty watched him cross the playground.

• • • •

Austin took off his jacket and loosened his already badly knotted tie in the hot sunshine. It was a glorious day. Clissold Park had ice cream vans stationed like sentries at the gates and chattering families, sunbathing office workers and happy old people getting some heat in their bones. Darny and Austin followed the stream through the gates. Just as they reached them, however, Austin heard someone calling his name.

"Austin! Austin!"

He turned around. It was Issy, pink in the face, carrying a large box.

• • • •

"You look very red," said Austin.

Issy closed her eyes. This was such a stupid idea. And of course she was blushing again. She was probably covered in sweat too. This was really daft. She followed them into the park. Darny had come straight up to her and taken her hand. She squeezed it, needing the reassurance.

"I like it," said Austin. "Red suits you."

He wanted to kick himself for saying something so stupid. They stared at one another for a bit. Nervous, Austin turned his attention to the box. "Are those for me? Because you know I can't take—"

"Shut up," said Issy. "I just wanted to say thank you. Thank you. Thank you. I can't…anyway, they're not for you to eat; they're for Darny. And they didn't come out right anyway, they're a mess, and…"

Without even thinking about it, without even looking at them, Austin took the box in his hands and hurled it with all his might. It flew from his long fingers straight into a copse of nearby trees. The pink of the ribbon streamed against the bright blue of the sky and the green of the trees, but the box did not burst.

"Darny," said Austin, "that was a huge box of cakes. Go find it and they're all yours."

Darny shot off like a bullet from a gun.

Issy looked after him in consternation. "Those were my cakes! With a message on them!"

Austin took her hands suddenly, urgently, feeling that he didn't have much time.

"You can make more cakes. But Issy, if you want to send me a message…please, please, just tell me what it is."

Issy felt the warm, firm pressure of his hands on hers, found herself staring up into his strong, handsome face. And suddenly, suddenly, for almost the first time in her life, she felt the nerves desert her. She felt calm, and at peace. She didn't worry about what he was thinking, or how she looked, or how she was doing, or what other people thought. She was conscious of nothing other than her absolute and present desire to be held by this man. She took one deep breath and closed her eyes, as Austin tilted her face up toward his, and she gave herself up entirely to his fierce and perfect kiss, in the middle of a busy park, in the middle of a busy day, in the middle of one of the busiest cities in the world.

● ● ● ●

"Me sick?" came an angry-sounding voice from somewhere far away. "Why are you sick? Who's sick?"

Reluctantly, and both more than a little pink and sweaty, Austin and Issy jumped apart. Darny was standing there looking puzzled.

"That's what your cakes said."

He held up the battered and bruised box, with the remnants of five cakes inside, one missing. He'd arranged the letters to spell M-E S-I-K.

"Is that the message you wanted me to get?" said Austin.

"Uh, not quite," said Issy, feeling dizzy and light-headed and thinking she was about to faint.

"OK," said Austin, smiling broadly. "OK, Darny. We are going to have lunch, then five minutes of lions, and then Issy and I have some business to attend to, OK?"

"Are you coming for lunch?" asked Darny, before haring off to chase some pigeons. "Cool!"

They stood and watched him go, smiling.

Issy looked at Austin, eyes wide.

"Wow," she said.

"Well, thanks," said Austin, looking embarrassed. Then he looked at her again. "Christ," he said urgently, "come here. I feel like I've waited bloody ages for you."

He kissed her hard, then stared at her so intensely she felt like her heart might burst.

"Stay," he said fiercely. "Please stay as sweet as you are."

simnel cake

• • • •

* 12 tbsp butter
* ¾ cup soft brown sugar
* 3 eggs, beaten
* ¾ cup plain flour
* pinch salt
* 1 tsp ground mixed spice (optional)
* 1½ cups mixed raisins, currants, and sultanas
* 4 tbsp chopped mixed peel
* zest of 1 lemon
* 1–2 tbsp apricot jam
* 1 egg, beaten, for glazing

Buy almond paste from the supermarket. You can make it yourself, but we are not crazy people. Knead the paste for one minute until it is smooth and pliable. Roll it out to make a circle 7½ inches in diameter.

Preheat oven to 280°F/gas mark 1. Grease and line a 7-inch cake tin.

For the cake, cream the butter and sugar together until pale and fluffy. Gradually beat in the eggs until well incorporated and then sift in the flour, salt, and mixed spice (if using) a little at a time. Finally, add the mixed dried fruit, peel, and grated lemon zest and stir into the mixture.

> Put half the mixture into the prepared cake tin. Smooth the top and cover with the circle of almond paste. Add the rest of the cake mixture and smooth the top, leaving a slight dip in the center to allow for the cake to rise. Bake in the preheated oven for 1¾ hours. Test by inserting a skewer in the middle—if it comes out clean, it is ready. Once baked, remove from the oven and set aside to cool on a wire rack. Top the cake with another thin layer of almond paste.

He's taken a turn for the worse," whispered the nurse; but Issy had known that already—there had been no letters, no recipes. Not for weeks.

"That's OK," said Issy, even though it wasn't, dammit. It wasn't fair. Her grandfather had lived so long, was everything to her, and surely he deserved to see her happy.

The room was hushed, with one or two machines ticking in the corner. Grampa Joe had lost even more weight, if that were possible. There was so little left of him now, just a fine layer of skin on top of a pale, hairless skeleton. Austin had wanted to come, of course; over another of their long nights of wine and shared experiences and a conversation that didn't seem able to stop, he'd told her about his mother and father, and the crash that had ended his lazy, easy student lifestyle and turned him into the carer of a bumptious four-year-old, infinitely lovable, but who'd made Austin put on a shirt and tie before he'd been quite ready for it.

It was all she could do not to say it right then. The more she got to know him, Issy realized, the more she…well, she wasn't going to say the L-word just yet. It wasn't appropriate at all. But he made every other man she'd ever known seem like pretty small beer in comparison. All of them. And now she was sure, she wanted it to spill off her tongue; to shout it to the world. But not until it was time. And now she wasn't even sure she had time.

"Gramps," whispered Issy. "Gramps! It's me! It's Isabel."

Nothing.

"I've got cake!" She rustled the wrapper. For once, she'd made his favorite rather than hers; the hard, flat simnel cake his own mother had made for him, decades and decades ago when he was a small boy.

She hugged him, and talked to him, telling him all her wonderful news, but he didn't respond to her voice, or to her touch, or to her moving around. He was breathing, it seemed, but only just.

Keavie put her hand on Issy's arm. "I don't think it will be long now," she said.

"I wanted…this will sound stupid, but I so wanted him to meet my new boyfriend," said Issy. "I think he'd have liked him."

The nurse laughed.

"It's funny you should say that," she said, "but I wanted him to meet my new boyfriend too. He'd have approved."

"What's he like?" asked Issy.

"Well, he's strong…and good, and he's nobody's pushover…and he doesn't take any shit, and he's so funny, and he's like totally hot, and, wow, he's just amazing, and every time he calls and I see his name on my phone I just think I'm going to pee my pants, I'm so excited," said the nurse. "Oh, sorry. Sorry. That was totally uncalled for."

"No, it wasn't," said Issy. "Finally, finally in my life, I've met someone I feel that about too."

The two women smiled at each other.

"Worth the wait, isn't it?" said Keavie.

Issy bit her lip. "Oh yes," she said.

The nurse glanced at Grampa Joe.

"I'm sure he knows…Don't tell him mine's a butcher."

"Mine's a banking adviser!" said Issy. "Even worse."

"That is worse!" said the nurse, then hurried away as her beeper went off.

Issy tweaked the flowers she'd brought, and sat down, not knowing what to do. Suddenly the door creaked open. Issy looked up. There stood a woman both incredibly familiar and almost unknown. She had long gray hair, which might have looked strange but actually made her look like Joni Mitchell, and she wore a long cloak. Her face was serene, but Issy noticed the wrinkles settling deeply into her face, lines that spoke of sun and long, hard days. But it was a kind face too.

"Mum," she said, so softly it was almost a sigh.

• • • •

They sat together, the three of them, almost not talking at all, although her mother held her grandfather's hand and told him how much she had always loved him, and how sorry she was, and Issy said, honestly, that her mother had nothing to be sorry for, everything had worked out all right in the end, and both of them, mother and daughter, were sure they felt a press on their hands from Joe. Issy felt her throat go tight every time she had to wait agonizingly long for a breath.

"What is this?" her mother asked softly, picking up the bag with a plain-looking, flat-baked cake in it. She stuck her nose in it.

"Oh, Issy," she said, "my grandma used to bake this for me when I was little. It smelled exactly like this. Exactly! Your grandfather adored it, used to eat it by the ton. It was his very favorite thing."

Issy had known this already. She hadn't known her mother knew too.

"Oh my, this takes me back."

Her mother was sobbing now, tears running down her lined face. She went forward and sat on the bed, then opened the bag. She put the entire bag over his nose, so that he could inhale the spicy scent. Issy had heard somewhere that when all other senses had gone, smell lingered; a direct line to the heart of consciousness; to emotion, to childhood and to memory. But how much of her gramps remained?

Both of the women heard him take a deep, rattly breath. Then suddenly, giving them a start, his eyes popped open, weak and watery, a film across the pupil. He breathed in again, smelling the cake; and once again, deeper, as if he were trying to inhale its essence. Then he blinked a few times and tried, and failed, to focus. Then suddenly his eyes were focused—out front, gazing hard at something Issy couldn't see.

"She's here," he said, in a gentle, childish, wondering tone. "She's here!" And then he half smiled and closed his eyes again, and they knew that he was gone.

epilogue

FEBRUARY

I wouldn't have believed your boobs could get any bigger than they are," Pearl was saying to Helena. "When you stand next to the window, nobody can see. They're better than mine now."

The pale afternoon light was falling through the windows of the Cupcake Café—they'd put the awning away in the autumn when it turned windy and cold—and spreading in soft pools over the tables and the cake stands piled high with baby cupcakes in pink and blue, and the wrapping paper, cards, and baby gifts strewn all across the floor. Helena sat, a huge, imperious ship in full sail, her tight brown dress stretched unashamedly across her enormous bump, and her splendid bosom emerging over the top of it; Titian hair cascading down her shoulders. Ashok, dwarfed beside her, looked like he was going to burst with pride. Issy thought her friend had never looked more beautiful.

Outside, Ben was running around with Louis. One didn't, Pearl reflected, get everything. But if ever a boy loved his father…He wasn't always there. But when he was, Louis glowed and blossomed and there was nothing, nothing she would ever do to upset that. It wouldn't be her. She caught sight of Doti passing the entrance to the alleyway. They looked at each other for a long moment. Then they both cast their eyes away.

Helena patted her bump complacently.

"Darling baby, I do love you," she said. "But you can come out now. I can't get up."

"You don't have to get up," said Issy, leaping forward. "What do you need?"

"A wee," said Helena. "Again."

"Oh. OK. Maybe I can't help you with that." Issy offered her arm anyway, which Helena took with gratitude.

Pearl crossed the courtyard with more cakes. They had outfitted the new building as a shop in no time, and now Pearl did a roaring trade—helped by Felipe the violinist, who turned out to be quite nifty in the kitchen when he wasn't practicing in the forecourt. Even Marian had chipped in quite a lot on the weekends, before the call of the road had grown strong again, and she'd taken off to see Brick—although not before a lot of chatting with her daughter, and Issy teaching her to use email.

Meanwhile Issy had employed two young, cheerful antipodean girls who were doing wonderfully in the café with Caroline, and the entire enterprise seemed to be nearly running itself. Recently Issy had found herself wondering, in a roundabout way, whether there might not be room for another café somewhere…maybe some little out-of-the-way spot in Archway. It had certainly crossed her mind.

Des's wife Ems, a tight-skirted, tight-faced woman, was encouraging Jamie to stand up on his own against the sofa, and lavishing Helena with advice. Helena, who'd handled more babies than Ems had had hot dinners (by the looks of her, Ems had never had a hot dinner), was nodding noncommittally. Louis was standing in between Helena's legs, holding a whispered conversation between himself, Helena's bump and a small plastic dinosaur clutched firmly between his fingers.

"*But a frenly dinosaur,*" he was explaining. "*This dinosaur not eat babies.*"

"*I wan eat bayee!*" said the dinosaur.

"No," admonished Louis gravely. "*That naughty, dinosaur.*"

Pearl glanced at him fondly as she came into the shop. She hadn't wanted to tell Issy and she certainly couldn't bear the "I told you so" glances she was going to get from Caroline, but it would come out sooner or later, she supposed.

"So I, uh, put in a letter," she said. "Looks like we might be moving."

"Moving where?" said Issy, delighted.

Pearl shrugged. "Well, now I'm manager, it looks like I can afford a place somewhere else…and we thought…well, maybe Ben and I thought…"

"So it's official?" said Caroline gleefully.

"It is what it is," said Pearl heavily. "It is what it is."

"But what?" said Issy. "What are you doing?"

Pink as ever from another night at the very talented hands of the very talented builder—and did it ever annoy her ex to know who was shacked up in his front room, it was the gossip of the school gates—Caroline guessed immediately.

"You're moving up here." Then, "No…no," she said, putting her hand to her forehead in the manner of a soothsayer. "You're moving to Dynevor Road. Or thereabouts."

Pearl looked utterly exasperated. "Well," she said. "Well…"

"What!? What's in Dynevor Road?" asked Issy, getting desperate.

"*Only* William Patten, *the* best school in Stoke Newington," said Caroline smugly. "The mothers fight tooth and nail to get their children in there. It has a pottery barn, and an art center."

Caroline glanced at Louis, who was now making the dinosaur kiss Helena's bump lovingly.

"He'll probably pass the interview," she said.

"But that's great!" said Issy. "What? It's not betraying your roots to put your kid in a good school."

"No," said Pearl, looking unconvinced. "The problem is with Louis, you know, I think he might be gifted and need, like, special help, and that's just not always available in other schools…"

Caroline threw an arm around her shoulder.

"Listen to you!" she said, beaming with pride. "You sound like a Stoke Newington mother already."

Helena gathered everyone around.

"I can't wait for Austin," she announced. "He's always late. And thank you for all my gorgeous presents, we're completely delighted, and thank you so much for letting us hold the baby shower here, Issy."

Issy waved a tea towel modestly.

"We have something for you. It's taken forever as Zac has been *so* overwhelmed with work."

"Thanks to you," said Zac, smoothing down his currently lime-green Mohawk modestly. "But we have a little gift for you."

Issy stepped forward as Helena gave her a large flat parcel. Opening it up, she gasped. In the familiar pretty pink pear-blossom livery of the Cupcake Café was a book that simply said *Recipes*. And inside were page after page compiled from the scraps of paper, the letters and typed notes, the screwed-up envelopes; everything Gramps had ever sent her—well, all the ones that worked as recipes—typeset and printed guidelines to every single cake in the Cupcake Café repertoire, all with Zac's lovely floral designs down the margins.

"So you can stop leaving them lying around the flat," explained Helena helpfully, handing back the originals too.

"Oh," said Issy, too touched to speak. "Oh. He would have *loved* it. And I do too."

• • • •

The party continued late into the evening; Austin was late (Janet had warned her about this, when she had listed Austin's bad points to her in what she said was a PA's duty and Issy had felt much more resembled a delighted mother-in-law's little chat), and they had a lovely baby carrier for Helena that they wanted to give her together.

Issy had felt a complete fraud as they had wandered around John Lewis looking for something gorgeous, but once she'd got used to people saying, "Is that your boy climbing up there?" she had quite enjoyed that too. Anywhere she found herself arm in arm with Austin, she realized, made it enjoyable. They'd even had quite good fun taking Darny in for that tetanus booster. She missed him, she thought impatiently. She missed him at the end of every day, and the second he left every morning, and she wanted to show him her beautiful book.

As the moon rose behind the houses, she finally caught sight of his tall, scruffy silhouette, and her heart jumped with love, as it always did.

"Aus!" she shouted, rushing outside. Darny shot out from behind him, yelled a hello to Issy then charged in to see Louis.

"Darling girl," Austin said, somewhat absentmindedly, holding her close and kissing her hair.

"Where were you? I need you to see something."

"Ah, yes," he said. "I've had some news."

He held up the carrier, which he'd clearly wrapped in the dark. "Shall we hand over the gift first?"

"No!" said Issy, forgetting about her own present. "News is news!"

The timer Austin had fixed to the fairy lights came on. Chester got up to close the shop curtains and waved at them. They waved back. The stumpy little tree glowed and became beautiful.

"It's the office," said Austin. "They've...well, apparently I've done quite well recently in one thing or another..."

It was true. Sometimes it was as if his handling of Graeme and the snatching of the girl of his dreams had acted like a wake-up call to Austin; a reminder to stop sleepwalking through his days; to get on and achieve something before it was too late. That, plus some subtle and not-so-subtle rearranging of his affairs by Issy, who preferred things neat and cozy at home, and had moved in in all but name, had given him a spring in his step and a sudden huge appetite for new deals and new opportunities.

"Anyway…here's the thing. They wanted to know if I'd like to go, um, abroad. Away."

"Away?" said Issy, a cold fear clutching her guts. "Where?"

Austin shrugged. "I don't know. They just said 'overseas posting.' Somewhere near a good school for Darny."

"And an A&E," said Issy. "Oh gosh. Gosh!"

"You know," said Austin, "I haven't traveled that much." He looked at her expectantly.

Issy's pretty face was grave, her brow a little furrowed.

"Well, I suppose," said Issy, finally, "it could be time to expand the empire…internationally."

Austin's heart leaped.

"You think?" he said delightedly. "Cor!"

"Somewhere," reflected Issy, "where the bank managers are very receptive to bribes."

They smiled at one another. Issy's eyes were shining.

"God, though, Austin. I mean, it is huge. Scary, and huge."

"Would it help," said Austin, "if I told you that I love you?"

"Would you kiss me under the fairy lights while you say it?" whispered Issy. "Then I think I'd follow you anywhere. Please let it not be Yemen."

"I do love Stokey," reflected Austin, later. "Though you know what? Maybe home is just wherever you and Darny are."

And he kissed her hard, beneath the glowing branches of the little, stunted pear tree, already dreaming of spring.

baking your first cupcake
by the caked crusader

So, you've read this fab novel and, apart from thinking, gosh, I want to read all of Jenny Colgan's other novels, you're also thinking, I want to bake my own cupcakes. Congratulations! You are setting out on a journey that will result in pleasure and great cake!

Firstly, I'll let you into a little secret that no cupcake bakery would want me to share: making cupcakes is easy, quick and cheap. You will create cupcakes in your own home—even on your first attempt, I promise—that taste better and look better than commercially produced cakes.

The great thing about making cupcakes is how little equipment they require. Chances are you already have a cupcake tin (the tray with twelve cavities) knocking about in your kitchen cupboards. It's the same pan you use for making Yorkshire puds and, even if you don't have one, they can be picked up for under £5 in your supermarket's kitchenware aisle. The only other thing to buy before you can get started is a pack of paper cases, which, again, any supermarket sells in the home baking aisle. Before we delve into the workings of a vanilla cupcake recipe, it's important to absorb what I think of as the four key principles of baking (this makes them sound rather grander than they are!):

- Bring the ingredients (particularly the butter) to room temperature before you start. Not only will this create the best cupcake but also it's so much easier for you to work with the ingredients...and why wouldn't you want to make it easy on yourself?

- Preheat your oven, i.e., switch it on to the right temperature setting about 20 to 30 minutes before the cakes go into the oven. This means that the cake batter receives the correct temperature straightaway and all the chemical processes will commence, thus producing a light sponge. Thankfully, in order to bake a great cupcake, you don't need to know what all those chemical processes are!

- Weigh your ingredients on a scale and make sure you don't miss anything out. Baking isn't like any other form of cooking—you can't guess the measurements or make substitutions and expect success. If you're making a casserole that requires two carrots and you decide to put in three, chances are it will be just as lovely (although perhaps a touch more carroty); if your cake recipe requires, for example, two eggs and you put in three, what would have been an airy fluffy sponge will come out like eggy dough. This may sound restrictive but actually, it's great—all the thinking is done for you in the recipe, yet you'll get all the credit for baking a delicious cupcake.

- Use good-quality ingredients. If you put butter on your bread, why would you put margarine in a cake? If you eat nice chocolate, why would you use cooking chocolate in a cake? A cake can only be as nice as the ingredients going into it.

failsafe recipe for vanilla sponge cupcakes with vanilla buttercream

• • • •

It will make 12 cupcakes.

For the cupcakes:

* 8 tbsp unsalted butter, at room temperature
* ½ cup superfine sugar
* 2 large eggs, at room temperature
* ½ cup self-rising flour, sifted (i.e., passed through a sieve)
* 2 tsp vanilla extract (N.B. "extract," not "essence." Extract is natural whereas essence contains chemicals and is nasty)
* 2 tbsp milk (you can use whole milk or semi-skimmed but not skimmed, as it tastes horrible)

For the buttercream:

* 8 tbsp unsalted butter, at room temperature
* 1 cup icing sugar, sifted
* 1 tsp vanilla extract
* Splash of milk—by which I mean, start with a tablespoon, beat that in, see if the buttercream is the texture you want, if it isn't add a further tablespoon, etc.

Preheat the oven to 370°F/convection oven 340°F/gas mark 5.

Line a cupcake pan with paper cases. This recipe will make 12 cupcakes.

Beat the butter and sugar together until they are smooth, fluffy and pale. This will take several minutes even with soft butter. Don't skimp on this stage, as this is where you get air into the mix. How you choose to beat the ingredients is up to you. When I started baking I used a wooden spoon, then I got handheld electric beaters and now I use a stand mixer. They will all yield the same result; however, if you use the wooden spoon, you will get a rather splendid upper arm workout…who said cake was unhealthy?

Add the eggs, flour, vanilla, and milk, and beat until smooth. Some recipes require you to add all these ingredients separately, but for this recipe, you don't have to worry about that. You are looking for what's called "dropping consistency"; this means that when you take a spoonful of mixture and gently tap the spoon, the mixture will drop off. If the mixture doesn't drop off the spoon, mix it some more. If it still won't drop, add a further tablespoon of milk.

Spoon into the paper cases. There is no need to level the batter, as the heat of the oven will do this for you. Place the tray in the upper half of the oven. Do not open the oven door until the cakes have baked for twelve minutes, then check them by inserting a skewer (if you don't have one, use a wooden cocktail stick) into the center of the sponges—if it comes out clean, the cakes are ready and you can remove them from the oven. If raw batter comes out on the skewer, pop them back in the oven and give them a couple more minutes. Cupcakes, being small, can switch from underdone to overdone quickly so don't get distracted! Don't worry if your cakes take longer than a recipe states—ovens vary.

As soon as the cupcakes come out of the oven, tip them out of the tin onto a wire rack. If you leave them in the tin they will carry on cooking (the tin is very hot) and the paper case may start to pull away from the sponge, which looks ugly. Once on the wire rack they will cool quickly—about thirty minutes.

Now make the buttercream: beat the butter in a bowl on its own, until very soft. It will start to look almost like whipped cream. It is this stage in the process that makes your buttercream light and delicious.

Add the icing sugar and beat until light and fluffy. Go gently at first otherwise the icing sugar will cloud up and coat you and your kitchen with white dust! Keep mixing until the butter and sugar are combined and smooth; the best test for this is to place a small amount of the icing on your tongue and press it up against the roof of your mouth. If it feels gritty it needs more beating. If it's smooth, you can move on to the next step.

Beat in the vanilla and milk. If the buttercream isn't as soft as you would like, then add a tiny bit more milk but be careful—you don't want to make the buttercream sloppy.

Either spread or pipe over the cupcakes. Spreading is easier and requires no additional equipment. However, if you want your cupcakes to look fancy it might be worth buying an icing bag and star-shaped nozzle. You can get disposable icing bags, which cut down on washing-up.

Add any additional decoration you desire—this is where you can be creative. In the past I have used sugar flowers, sprinkles, malt balls, edible glitter, sprinkles, nuts, crumbled Flake...the options are endless.

Bask in glory at the wonderful thing you have made.

Eat.

me and the 1981 royal wedding

I was nine years old in 1981, for what I like to call the real royal wedding—the marriage of Prince Charles and Lady Diana Spencer. It really was an optimal time for frothy-dress-based princessy excitement (that was then, of course. I realize that these days, according to the tabloids, all nine-year-olds have tattoos and drink Bacardi Breezers and things, but those were more innocent times).

Me, Alison Woodall, and Judi Taylor thought that it was all absolutely fantastic, and managed to refine our dress-designing skills to the point where I could still draw that dress now—ruffly sleeves; bow in the middle; her hair, too short and flicky—with my eyes shut.

I watched the entire thing (TV in the morning was a novelty then), even that incredibly long boring bit where they all went in for the wedding breakfast, which seemed utterly tedious to me. It turned out I was right about this: unless you're sat next to people you like, wedding dinners can be incredibly dull. Can you imagine what it must have been like if you'd been sat next to, e.g., the Dowager Duchess of Chessingham?

Despite growing up in a nominally republican part of the world (the Catholic West Coast of Scotland), we still had a street party, and I have a clear memory of saying to my mother, "God would have lost a lot of believers if it hadn't been a sunny day today, wouldn't he?" (it was), to which my mother replied, "Hmmm" (I was a terribly priggish child).

In fact, a friend of mine who married very young, in her last year of college, actually managed to be part of that generation, familiar from all eighties snapshots; she was among the last to get married in a Diana-style dress, including the enormous puffed sleeves with the lace and the bows. Apart from the fact that she, like Diana, looked like a tiny child buried in a pile of lacy laundry, it was slightly gorgeous.

When we were passing through Las Vegas about four years ago, my husband and I decided to renew our vows with Elvis (as you do). He and my eldest son wore matching white tuxedos. I dealt with my pent-up royal wedding issues by wearing the hugest, widest, most enormous, flower-festooned frock I could hire. It went on for miles. It got caught in lifts. It was great. In fact, I think I secretly preferred it to my very stylish, expensive, subtle, Grace Kelly-esque wedding dress I got married in the first time around. It was brilliant.

For all the sadness and tragedy that followed—and it is almost impossible to now look at the famous pic of the laughing Diana, collapsing in that huge meringue surrounded by her little brides-maids, without feeling melancholic—it was a huge jolly occasion, and it is only the most churlish, I think, who wouldn't wish all the very best now to her son, and someone who seems like a perfectly nice girl.

If nothing else, it's lovely to have a little day of national celebra-tion and an excuse for a street party. And some cake, of course! My daughter is only one, so not quite old enough to get caught up in wed-ding dress fever alas, and chances are Kate will go for something very low-key and stylish anyway (she does seem like that kind of person), which, I think, is a bit of a shame for budding nine-year-old wed-ding dress designers everywhere. But hopefully having a slightly more mature princess, who knows what she wants, will bode very well for their years ahead.

And, to be the total opposite of that, look at the next page for some great big, indulgent, frothy cupcakes. To get a proper frou-frou icing, use a bag or an icing kit and start from the center, making a snail shape, then building the icing up as high as you can!

Jenny x x x

royal wedding street party
red, white, and blue cupcakes

• • • •

White Queen Victoria sponge base
* 12 tbsp butter
* ¾ cup superfine sugar
* 3 eggs (organic, of course)
* ¾ cup self-rising flour
* splash of milk
* 1 tsp vanilla

Cream the butter and sugar until it's light and fluffy. Add the eggs with a spoon of flour if it looks like it's curdling, then fold in the rest of the flour. Add a splash of milk until the mixture is dropping consistency. Fill twelve cupcake cases two thirds of the way, then bake at 355°F for 12–15 minutes.

Red cream cheese topping
* 1 cup cream cheese
* 5 tbsp butter
* 1 cup icing sugar (or to taste)
* add a few drops of rosewater and some food coloring

To make: whizz everything up. Decorate with blue sugar flowers. Scoff and toast the happy couple!

acknowledgments

Special thanks to Ali Gunn and Jo Dickinson. Also to Ursula Mackenzie, David Shelley, Manpreet Grewal, Tamsin Kitson, Kate Webster, Rob Manser, Frances Doyle, Adrian Foxman, Andy Coles, Fabia Ma, Sara Talbot, Robert Mackenzie, Gill Midgley, Alan Scollan, Nick Hammick, Andrew Hally, Alison Emery, Richard Barker, Nigel Andrews, and all the amazing team at Little, Brown, "2010 publisher of the year." Thanks to Deborah Adams for the copyedit.

Also: the very wonderful Caked Crusader, whose true identity must NEVER be uncovered, at thecakedcrusader.blogspot.com; Patisserie Zambetti, whose entire repertoire I have repeatedly worked through with unashamed gusto and who are never short of a friendly smile, a cup of coffee, and a vanilla slice (sorry, millefeuille) on a rainy morning. Geri and Marina; Mads for that lunch; Lise, world's best workmate; the board, as ever; and assorted Warings, Dingles, Lee-Elliotts, and McCarthys for your kindnesses and friendship. And to Mr. B and my three wee Bs: I love you to pieces and think you are all totally tremendous in every way. But no, you can't have another cake; you'll spoil your dinner. Not even you, big yin.

about the author

Jenny Colgan is the bestselling author of more than eleven novels, including *Rosie Hopkins' Sweetshop of Dreams* and *The Loveliest Chocolate Shop in Paris*. She also writes regularly for *The Guardian* and *The Times*, as well as BBC's *Doctor Who*. She is married with three children and lives in London and Cannes, where she bakes, drinks pink wine, and plays the piano to an extremely disappointing standard.

THE LOVELIEST CHOCOLATE SHOP IN PARIS

Jenny Colgan

Available from Sourcebooks Landmark

As dawn breaks over the Pont Neuf and Paris comes to life, Anna Trent is already awake and at work, mixing the finest, smoothest, richest chocolate in France. It's a huge shift from the chocolate factory she worked in at home in England. But when an accident changed everything, Anna was thrown back in touch with her French teacher, Claire, who offered her the chance of a lifetime—to work in Paris with a master chocolatier. With old wounds about to be uncovered and healed, Anna is set to discover more about real chocolate—and herself—than she ever dreamed.

Praise for international bestseller Jenny Colgan:

"The sweetest, loveliest book I've read in a long time. Gorgeous, glorious, uplifting. A very happy-making book." —*Marian Keyes*

"It's a book which should be devoured in one sitting, along with a box of chocolates." —*Sophie Kinsella*

"*The Loveliest Chocolate Shop in Paris* will make you want to pack your bags and head across the channel. An evocative, sweet treat." —*Jojo Moyes*

For more Jenny Colgan books, visit:

sourcebooks.com